CROWNED CROWS II

LOYALTY IN THE SHADOWS

CROWNED CROWS BOOK II

VERONICA EDEN

LOYALTY IN THE SHADOWS

Photography: Wander Aguiar | www.wanderbookclub.com | @wanderaguiar_photography

Model: Ben Selleck

AUTHOR'S NOTE

This is the second book in the Crowned Crows series following a gritty brotherhood of antihero bad boys and the feisty heroines that capture their hearts. Each book in the series should be read in order to understand the continuing plot. If you're not a fan of morally bankrupt book boyfriends, steer clear.

This mature new adult romance contains dubious situations, crude language, and intense sexual/violent content that some readers might find triggering or offensive. **Content warning** for themes of PTSD, kidnapping, past rape, and trafficking. Please proceed with caution.

Crowned Crows series:
#1 Crowned Crows of Thorne Point
#2 Loyalty in the Shadows
#3 A Fractured Reign
#4 The Kings of Ruin

Sign up for Veronica's newsletter to receive exclusive content and news about upcoming releases: bit.ly/veronicaedenmail

Follow Veronica on BookBub for new release alerts: bookbub.com/authors/veronica-eden

ABOUT THE BOOK

THE CROWS DON'T WANT YOUR MONEY. THEY THRIVE ON YOUR DESPERATION. WHAT WILL YOU SACRIFICE TO BUY THEIR HELP?

ISLA

Thorne Point sunk its claws in me at a young age.
I refused to let its harsh truths snuff out my light.
When an attempt to kidnap me is stopped, I know they'll never give up.
The city's seedy underbelly won't let me escape forever.
My only choice is to run into the arms of monsters for safety.
The Crows have a terrifying reputation, and Levi Astor lives up to it.
But my protective monster will never be worse than the ones who buried their ugliness deep in me.

LEVI

Levi Astor you are under arrest.

Our unchallenged rule over this city is crumbling.

We'll hunt down the ones behind this and make them pay.

Come out, come out, wherever you are.

Guarding the senator's daughter isn't on my agenda, yet I couldn't ignore her if I tried.

Sunshine might break through the shadows, but it will only illuminate what makes me a deadly monster.

Isla Vonn should run in the opposite direction instead of into my arms.

Because everyone fears the Leviathan in Thorne Point.

PLAYLIST

Chaos—Like A Storm

Animal in Me—Solence

Almost Touch Me—Maisy Kay

I'm Not Afraid—Tommee Profitt, Wondra

Acid Rain—Lorn

Inside—Chris Avantgarde, Red Rosamond

Catacombs—Like A Storm

Love the Way You Hate Me—Like A Storm

Make Me Believe—The EverLove

Liar—Like A Storm

Dance in the Dark—Au/Ra

skeletons—KINGS, Drew Ryn

Dark in My Imagination—of Verona

Enjoy The Silence—Ki:Theory

Who Are You—SVRCINA

Solitary—Like A Storm

Stockholm—Bianca

Monsters—Tommee Profitt, XEAH

Choke—Royal & the Serpent

Bullet With Butterfly Wings—Tommee Profitt, Sam Tinnesz

Silence—No name faces

The Devil Inside—Like A Storm

If These Scars Could Speak—Citizen Soldier

Painkiller—Three Days Grace

Cruel World—Tommee Profitt, Sam Tinnesz

Slower—Tate McRae

Cravin'—Stileto, Kendyle Paige

Beast—8 Graves

Play Dirty—Kevin McAllister, [SEBELL]

Never Surrender—Liv Ash

In The End—Tommee Profitt, Fleurie, Jung Youth

Royalty—Egzod, Maestro Chives, Neoni

Paint It Black—Hidden Citizens, Rånya

MIDDLE OF THE NIGHT—Elley Duhé

Ocean Eyes—American Avenue

Dancing After Death—Matt Maeson

Can't Help Falling in Love (Dark)—Tommee Profitt, brooke

"I love you as certain dark things are to be loved."

Pablo Neruda

CCOTP RECAP

PREVIOUSLY IN THE CROWNED CROWS SERIES...

WELCOME to Thorne Point, where darkness rules. In this gritty city on the coast of Maine, everyone who is anyone can be found amongst the city's elite high society, and their heirs populate the prestigious Thorne Point University.

One student is Isla Vonn, the savvy daughter of a prominent senator and a socialite. She is an energetic, fashion-minded college senior. Recently she decided to change majors to pursue her dance passion.

Not all is well in Thorne Point, especially for those less fortunate. Isla's best friend, Rowan Hannigan, a scholarship student, is at her wit's end when her brother goes missing. She can't get help from anyone to find him. Desperate, she listens to the rumors that run rampant throughout the campus about the mafia-esque Crowned Crows—four friends, the richest boys in school, and the ones who run everything on campus. Wren Thorne, the ruthless king of control. Levi Astor, the brooding shadow and lethal fighter. Colton DuPont, the cocky jokester and genius hacker. And Jude Morales, the enigmatic conman. Their control doesn't stop there, stretching across the city where it's said they own the night.

Rowan seeks them out at their abandoned hotel-turned-nightclub to ask for their help. She finds them sprawled like kings on threadbare vintage furniture amidst the hedonistic partying. They don't work for free, and they don't want money. The currency they demand is a secret, a favor...something that will hurt to give up. These wicked men enjoy the leverage they hold over people. The most arrogant of the group, Wren Thorne, takes an interest in her and allows her to owe a favor instead of stealing the secret she hides from them.

They may seem like rich boys who can't get their hands dirty, but they're no strangers to violence, running several operations throughout the city including underground fighting and acting as vigilantes for the right price. There is even rumor that brooding Levi Astor could be connected to the notorious Leviathan serial killer investigation. Rowan and Isla find how far the Crows' control stretches when Levi and Colton are tasked with stalking her every move on campus.

Their rule over the night isn't without challengers, the main one being a young detective determined to make them answer for their illegal operations. Pippa Bassett isn't only a frustrated cop, but Jude's ex-girlfriend and the Crows' ex-friend.

What begins as an extra job for this chaotic brotherhood turns into so much more when their control is challenged, making it clear something... or someone is at work against them. The deeper they dig the more the dots connect. They discover Rowan's missing brother isn't an innocent bystander, but an investigative journalist who may have gotten in over his head. In order to protect Rowan, they need to bring her into their world. Wren is done denying her allure and claims her for himself.

Entering the elite high class world of the city means extravagant galas, where she meets Wren's father having a meeting with her stalker. His parting words for the evening are a family motto Wren resents: *carpe regnum*.

Nothing is a coincidence in Thorne Point, and a random missing persons case is the tipping point to a bigger secret lurking in the darkness of this gothic city. Driven by her curiosity, Rowan discovers a crossed keys emblem is connected to her brother's disappearance. With the keys comes another mysterious Latin phrase: clavis ad regnum. Rowan's world is shaken when she and Isla follow her stalker and find a hidden passageway on campus. Every answer brings more questions.

The Crows consider Rowan part of the family they've forged amongst themselves and they'd protect her with their life. Their friendship and her relationship with Wren are the only things holding her together when one of the Crows' underlings discovers a body at the docks, the body of Ethan Hannigan, shattering Rowan's world.

Grief leads to anger, then a thirst for revenge. She acts alone to set their enemy's supply of drugs on fire at the docks. Wren's bloodthirstiness comes out because no one will take his queen from the King Crow. After an emotional rescue, they fight their way out together.

All seems well as the Crows reestablish their power, however the story is only just beginning...

Once the dust settles, the Crowned Crows host a fight night. It's Levi's turn to shine in the ring, displaying his unmatched skill. Pippa returns like clockwork, except this time the sergeant they bribe for amnesty is with her barking orders. The police raid the warehouse and chaos ensues. Levi is arrested while someone bumps into Wren. They slip a card into his pocket, and when everything seems like it's falling apart he discovers it. The card is a crisp, elegant invitation with crossed keys. On the back it says one thing... *clavis ad regnum.*

Key to the kingdom.

Something else is at work in Thorne Point and the Crowned Crows are the target.

TP

U

THORNE POINT UNIVERSITY

CHAPTER ONE

LEVI

THE bite of handcuffs around my wrists is nothing new. I've spent enough time training with them to prepare for any situation. *Never be helpless again*—that's the promise I made myself years ago.

If I wanted, I could get out of the cuffs in under thirty seconds. Bet little Pipsqueak Pippa Bassett would love that trick. It's only the sharp warning look from Wren that keeps me from going the fuck off and fighting the circus of officers Pippa brought to raid fight ring.

If they expect me to go quietly, they're dead wrong.

I jerk against the hold of the two officers restraining me, baring my teeth. It took both of their efforts to wrestle my arms behind my back to cuff me. Their grip slips on my sweaty, tattoo-covered bare skin. Chaotic energy still builds in my chest with nowhere to go since I didn't get to finish the fight in the ring. I clench my teeth, reining in the ragged pants clawing my throat willing away the demons creating turmoil in my messed up head.

"Hold him." I grit my teeth at Pippa's clipped command. She folds her arms, serving me a triumphant look full of scorn. "You're not getting out of this one, Astor."

It's hard to believe she was one of us once. One of our best friends. A girl who knows too much about me and my boys. She's so different from the wild little thing she was. That was then. She doesn't know us anymore, has no idea about the kind of terror we'll cause for this stunt she's pulled.

There are unwritten rules in Thorne Point. Our city runs on a dark status quo. But now it's broken.

All around us the warehouse is in chaos. Those who came to watch the violent show find ways to slip through the cracks, fleeing before they're recognized as members of Thorne Point's elite high society. Two-faced cowards. They'll save their own hides first and sacrifice the person next to them if it means their own survival.

It's what happened to me and my mother all those years ago.

The cops Pippa brought along seize our building. It's not her fresh-faced rookies she leads around by the nose whenever we've gone through this song and dance with her before. This time it's cops we've personally bribed, led by Sergeant Warner himself.

He handcuffs the other fighter and reads him his rights, ignoring glares from Colton and Jude for this betrayal. Wren is equally enraged. Rowan moves closer to him, her brows pinched in worry. I clench my jaw, forcing myself to remain silent.

"You don't have shit, Pip." Jude gets in Pippa's face, grabbing her arm forcefully. When it comes to her, he always slips and lets his emotions get the best of him. "You're grasping at straws if you think this will stick."

There's a brief moment where she falters and leans into him, raw pain contorting her features for the barest second before she gets it under control. I don't think he notices, too caught up in his anger.

But I do. Because I'm always on high alert. I see more than anyone, especially amidst the mayhem surrounding us.

She hardens her voice. "Step back, or I'll arrest you, too. Assaulting an officer is a felony. They'll lock you back up for it. That would break your grandmother's heart, wouldn't it?"

The words have their desired effect to cover what she doesn't want any of us to find out. Because what she aims to hide is a weakness we can exploit without mercy. And we will. Make no mistake.

Jude seethes, releasing her with a snarl. "That's too far, even for you."

I catch his eye and signal for him to calm down with a quick shake of my head. He blows out a harsh breath and scrapes his fingers through his hair.

Me, Rowan, Colt, and Jude swing our gazes to Wren for our next move. We don't consider any of us a leader of our group, each of us naturally taking point whenever our skillset and strength are best suited to seize control.

A thick envelope in his hand crinkles when he flexes his fist to the point the veins bulge, drawing his furious attention. He freezes, then tears into it, pulling out a thick black card. His eyes rove over the square card before he flips it over, then darts his gaze up to meet Rowan's.

Whatever it says, it's threatening enough to paint his sharp features in deep lines of angry disbelief. It's subtle to anyone outside of our brotherhood, but I recognize how much the message rattles him.

If it's enough to unsettle Wren...

Fuck.

The muscles in my body go rigid instinctively, ready to fend off an attack we didn't see coming.

One problem at a time is the silent message I get from the look Wren gives me, his angular jaw set. Jude and Colton understand, too. Even Rowan picks up on the meaning, quickly learning how to read him from how well she fits in with us.

"Right now the force is seizing any other suspected locations in connection to your illegal fighting ring," Pippa says.

Wren rolls his eyes, but the rest of us know him too well. His icy control has cracked from whatever was on that card. I've never seen him look like he did reading the note, even the night everything went to shit when we were in high school.

Whoever is behind this wants to cut off one of our main streams of income. Lucky for us, we have Colton's genius giant brain handling our investments. Losing control of our fight rings won't cripple us, but it's the insult to our reputation that stings.

Our mutually beneficial arrangement with Sergeant Warner's force is dead in the water. Pippa thinks she has enough to get me in a cell, and keep me long enough to form a threadbare connection to the Leviathan case. On their own, these two problems wouldn't be a shitstorm, but it's not all we're dealing with.

A sickening knot tightens in my stomach as the metal cuffs dig into my wrists. The reason I was in the ring tonight was because of what's been stuck in my mind like a scab I can't stop picking. When Colton salvaged some of Ethan Hannigan's corrupted file, I almost lost it. Rowan's brother tried to email it to her when he was caught by the people who ultimately killed him.

Astor. My name—no, my *uncle*'s name—was in the decoded contents along with the words network, elite, and key. It's fucking with my head.

We pride ourselves on collecting every secret in this city. So how could this one slip through our radar?

A shove from the officers holding me makes me grit my teeth and move.

I'm not the sentimental type. Life taught me to squash sentiment from my heart. Emotions are what lead to mistakes.

Still, I spare a parting glance at the warehouse I've given sweat and blood to before I'm hauled outside into the crisp October air. A few blocks off, the low crash of ocean waves hitting the Maine coastline filter through the city's shipping district.

Everything we've spent years building is crumbling, and Pippa is the first in line with a sledgehammer.

CHAPTER TWO

LEVI

Out of everything, it's the bars of the cold cell that get to me. The minute they slam shut to lock me away, a sense memory surfaces, luring my demons out to torment me. Clenching my fists, I sit hard on the unforgiving bench in my isolated holding cell and smooth my features.

No one knows the war my mind wages against the horrific split between reality and being trapped in a memory. Her cries and screams fill the echo chamber in my head. The pleas only make it worse.

The monsters liked it. Got off on knowing how much pain their torment brought both of us.

A sharp stinging pain breaks through the spell the gruesome old nightmare has on my psyche.

My fingers ache as I unfurl them from tightly balled fists. Bloody half moons dot my palms where my nails broke the skin from digging them in so hard. They slice into old scars from all the times this has happened.

I grip my shoulder, blood smearing over the tattoo marking the day of Mom's death with flowers.

Pain. It's the only remedy to the sickening memory. It's one reason I need to fight so often, to keep the demons at bay.

I've honed myself into a lethal monster. I'm the danger to fear now, no longer helpless, no longer unable to fight back.

My glare passes over the metal bars of the cell. I tongue the inside of my lip, the ring piercing not there to worry since I took it out for the match. The sweat has cooled on my bare inked skin in the chilly jail cell.

Keeping up the mantra that I'm not trapped, I set my jaw and close my eyes. Waiting. It's all I'm able to do until the guys do something.

Above all else, I trust my brothers. It's not something I'm capable of doing easily outside of my small circle. They've each earned it. I'd trust them with my life, same as they'd do for me.

Pippa had that trust once, too. We've held back and let her be for Jude's sake, but after what she did that night in high school, I won't make that error again. This time she's taken things too far. When I'm out of this cell, I'll make her regret moving against us.

Time moves strangely in a holding cell. It's difficult to discern if it's been hours or minutes since I was shoved in here. Every second that ticks by pricks another invisible needle into me, setting my teeth on edge. It's a challenge to calm the energy building in my muscles, begging for release. But I won't pace, because I'm sure I'm being watched.

All I can do is sit on the uncomfortable bench, prodding at the scabs forming on my wounded palms to remind myself I'm alive. To ground myself before the nightmares take hold of my mind again.

I reach for a long-buried fascination to fight back the violent torrent of energy brewing in me, picturing a pretty face with bright blue eyes I shouldn't be thinking of right now. It's a dangerous game to reawaken something I laid to rest, but she won't leave my head since waltzing her way back into my field of awareness.

At last, voices echo down the hall. Pippa appears with Jude in tow. I'm surprised she's still here on the graveyard shift. Annoyance crosses her face and Jude radiates smugness. He's in a better mood than earlier. The tight band around my chest loosens. I can get the fuck out of here.

"Warner might be done with our agreement, but he's not the only one of Thorne Point's finest on the force who accepts bribes." Jude cages her in his arms from behind as she steps up to the cell. He grips the bars and leans in to murmur. "A dirty cop is a simple stone's throw away."

I watch the complicated emotions play over her face impassively. She doesn't want to believe him, but doubt flickers for a few seconds.

"You're lying." The conviction in her voice wavers and she cuts her eyes to the side.

"What's wrong? They won't let a girl in their boys' club? Everyone in Thorne Point knows it's just a matter of finding the right price." The dark wavy hair of her ponytail moves with her head shake. He slides his hands up the bars, dipping his head to further invade her space. "You're acting high and mighty for nothing. I wish you'd see that. There's no true justice in this city, baby girl."

A faint, strangled noise escapes her at the pet name. He used to say it with affection, but now those words are his weapon. They hit her like a poison arrow, making her shoulders hunch in to protect against the past.

Pippa grits her teeth and whirls around to face him. "You can't be back here."

He pushes away from the cell and catches my eye. Worry burns in his golden hazel eyes. I offer an imperceptible nod that he returns. His expression lets me know he's got my back.

"Release him," he says.

Shoving the key in the lock, she squints at me. "The Leviathan's been quiet lately. If I kept you in here, would I be able to close my case?"

I hold back a snort and give her nothing, keeping my voice devoid of any emotion. "Maybe the bastard hasn't found any entertaining victims lately. Serial killers get bored, too."

That's how the investigation and the media circus paints me. Serial killer. Deranged. A psychopath.

Well, some of those things are accurate.

Those who cross the Crows often meet a gruesome end. It's the media that latched onto my full name as the moniker of a serial killer because of the messages we left.

Pippa purses her lips. She'll never catch me. Colton makes sure of it with his deep fake photoshopping skills to provide an alibi every time. With all the insanity of the last several weeks, we haven't taken on any jobs since the frat boy serial rapist we kidnapped from his bed. So yeah, of course the *Leviathan* has been inactive.

We've been too preoccupied with a mysterious threat lurking in the shadows hiding behind an organized crime syndicate, and discovering Rowan's missing brother washed up by the docks.

"Probably needs a therapist to work that boredom out." Jude grins over Pippa's head, unrepentant.

For a moment, it seems like Pippa has the urge to laugh, like the hands of time have turned back five years to when we were at Thorne Point Academy. As if we're all hanging out, laughing over something dumb, the pair of them tangled up as usual. Back when she was one of us. Our friend. Jude's soulmate.

Clenching my teeth, I reject the recollection. I refuse to mourn what once was between us all. She turned her back, made her choice when she pulled out of her part of the plan that fateful night. The one that bonded our brotherhood together closer than ever.

"Well?" Jude drawls. "Get him out."

The cell door clangs as Pippa opens the metal bars to grant me freedom. I stride across my own personal hell, pausing in front of her when she blocks the exit of the cell. At my full height, my six-four deadly frame towers over our old Pipsqueak.

"Don't leave town," she mutters.

Fiery anger turns over in my gut, but I keep my face blank and breathe through it. I never let emotions rule me. I won't give her the satisfaction.

"You're a shitty detective," I say. "You should think about a career change."

Jude snorts. Her lips thin and her gray eyes flash fiercely. I shoulder past her and stalk down the hall to freedom. A beat later, her steps clack after me at a rapid clip on the cheap linoleum.

Wren waits in the lobby when Pippa escorts me out, hands casually tucked in the pockets of his slacks. He gives off the impression he's relaxed and in control, even after two in the morning. At the sight of us, a cruel smirk twists his lips.

"You can't arrest the nephew of one of the most important men in the city and expect it to stick," he says.

Pippa releases a frustrated noise under her breath. "You're free to go."

The corners of Wren's mouth stretch wider in cold triumph. I accept the shirt he tosses me, tugging it on while Jude steps into Pippa's space.

"How many times do we have to teach you this lesson, baby girl?" he rasps.

The low, crooning tone is meant only for her, but I catch it, always hyper aware of my surroundings.

Her anger cracks with a sharp, pained intake of breath. "Don't," she whispers hoarsely. "You promised you wouldn't."

I angle my head to study them from the corner of my eye. They're locked in a stare full of anguished longing and heartache. The razed ground between them is bridged only by the lingering memories their entwined souls can't let go of. They never fully got the message it was over between them.

Shaking my head, I meet Wren's icy blue eyes. "Let's get the hell out of here."

"Jude." Wren's hard gaze shifts to Pippa. "Bassett. Never a pleasure."

His usual parting words for her make her eyes narrow. She flicks her gaze between the two of us, then moves it to Jude. He gives her one last intense look before joining us. She spins on her heel and disappears into the diseased belly of the station before we exit, line drawn in the sand between us and her.

Jude takes the driver's seat of my blacked out Escalade. The playful mask he put on in the police station falls away to reveal the true ire beneath. I wait until we're a block away before speaking.

"Where are Rowan and Colt?"

"I sent her back to the Nest with Colt. They're pulling up security footage to find out who the fuck bumped into me to plant this." He holds up the square black notecard between two fingers, passing it back to me. "An invitation."

Taking the thick card, I read the message. My brows jump up, then flatten in a scowl.

One side has a pair of gold crossed skeleton keys with the words *clavis ad regnum* printed beneath. It's the same symbol we've been chasing all over the city after Rowan connected it to her missing brother. The other is an address with a date and time printed in stark white.

October 10th, 9PM
Thorne Point Founders Museum
2490 Old King's Road,
Thorne Point, Maine

"The fuck is this?"

"A message from the bastards toying with us," Wren growls.

The corrupted file from Ethan Hannigan flashes before my eyes again. My family name is hidden amongst the secrets it holds.

My senses are on high alert. I have a bad feeling we're being backed to the edge of a crumbling cliff. And that what we've entangled ourselves in so far is only the beginning.

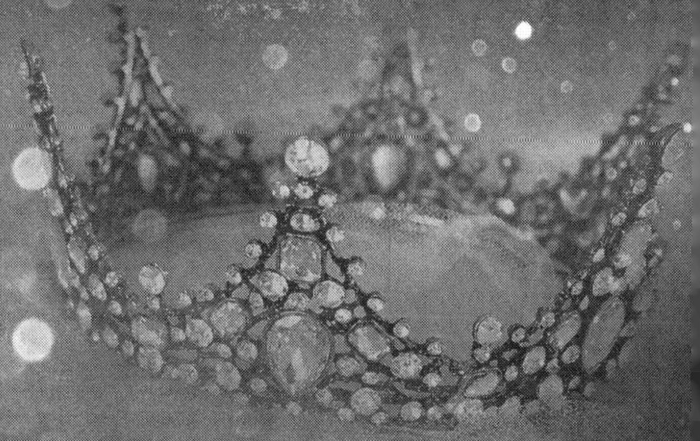

CHAPTER THREE

ISLA

THE reflection of myself in the wall of mirrors falters on the transition between a turn sequence and an aerial. I come to a stop, chest heaving, and prop my hands on my hips.

I look the part of a dancer with my dark brown hair twisted into a bun, light blue eyes gleaming, and cheeks flushed pink. The flowing, open-back shirt I'm wearing over leggings slouches off one shoulder to reveal my strappy red sports bra beneath. Yet as often as I've booked the dance studio for extra practice to catch up with my classmates who have danced their whole lives, I'm still stumbling without formal training. All I have to go on are my instincts when I move.

"One more time." I hype myself up with a bright smile.

Starting from the top, I go into the choreography we're learning for the fall showcase in November. The same turn sequence before the aerial trips me up on the third eight count. I come to a stop with a soft chuckle, stretching my thrumming limbs.

My new dance professors might believe my body has years of training because my muscles naturally adapted to the movements, however I still need to remember the steps. It comes more easily if I work for it. Even watching YouTube videos when I could sneak them in between the duties that come with being a senator's daughter, I'm not really someone who learns from watching if I don't have someone to correct my mistakes.

It's one reason I'm so happy I finally followed my heart and switched my schedule around to take dance classes instead of the political science pursuits Dad expects for me. I don't have any interest in law school after I finish my undergrad at Thorne Point University. Defying his wishes is new, something that makes me freeze in anticipation of the dark consequences, but so far my small rebellions haven't brought hell down on me. I cling to the hope that one day I'll find the courage to get out from under my parents' thumbs completely.

This is what I want to be doing. I love the feeling of freedom and rightness I get when I'm dancing. When my body hums with the energy of being alive, I'm at my happiest.

It's something I've grasped at and craved for so long. Everything I experience when I'm dancing makes my world a better place. It's easier to deal with my life, and it's my secret to finding positivity from day to day.

When I'm dancing, I'm a completely different person. The girl I'm supposed to be, the real me deep down beneath the bullshit I cover up with sarcastic jokes and a flare for drama to make the people I surround myself with smile. I don't have to think about the politically matched dates I'm forced to go on knowing someday I'll end up in a loveless marriage with one of those bland boys, or the career aspirations Dad demands I pursue.

When I'm twirling, jumping, and rolling with the music, I can be me. Just Isla.

It lets me work through and express my emotions. I do it whether I'm happy or angry. And when I'm sad? I've discovered that's the most important time for me to find a song and let go to process the things weighing me down.

Some people meditate. Others find a destructive habit to cope with their demons. This is my vice.

The first time I danced for myself at fourteen, I broke down and sobbed, unleashing everything I'd kept inside. Not an uncomfortable obligatory dance at one of Dad's campaign functions or at the country club for Mom's social calendar, but me, alone in my bedroom with a shimmery metallic purple bluetooth speaker. Something I did for myself.

When I heard the song that played on a randomized playlist, something inexplicable came over me and I needed to move. It unlocked the well of agony rooted deep within me, and my emotions overwhelmed me when the song ended. For the first time in a month since my world had shattered, I felt like me again. Dancing helped me realize what happened didn't destroy me. It helped me find a way to heal in the aftermath, to make my life better by having a tool to uplift myself when the memories become too much.

Dance grants me the freedom to decide what defines me—not the horrible experiences or the pressures and restrictive expectations put on me, but what I choose in my heart.

I have to believe my body was crafted for this purpose. It's what I've always been meant for, gifted with the ability to convey emotions through dancing. Why else would I have long legs, a lithe figure, and a deep yearning in my heart for movement if it wasn't to tell stories with my body?

If I don't believe it with every scrap of conviction I'm capable of mustering, then I'm only left with the dark thoughts that linger at the edges of my mind, waiting for me to give in. But I won't. I refuse to listen to their sinister whispers and painful disjointed nightmares.

Instead of the ballet lessons I begged my parents for at fourteen, my father taught me a very different, very difficult lesson. One that proved how cruel and ugly the world is underneath the fancy wrapping.

Power breeds greed. Greed erases morals. And without morals, both power and greed find every opportunity to shred innocence.

With a harsh exhale, I clutch at my chest. *No.* I can't go down that haunting path. It does me no good to dwell on the half-formed memories of the worst night of my life.

I have to choose positivity, pick the light every day so it doesn't drown me.

Wiping away a stray tear, I take a deep, cleansing breath, then smile at my reflection. That girl is a fighter. That girl is working to be stronger every day. That girl glows bright enough to snuff out any shadow trying to pull her under.

I set my phone up to record, start the music over, and find my starting position. This time when I run through the dance, I find the fluidity. It pulls me through the choreography, and I make it past the aerial. An elated yell slips out when I get it right.

Grinning, I work through until the music ends, then take a few giddy skipping steps over to my phone to play back the recording. My smile widens. This dance is going to look awesome in the showcase.

It's getting late and my extra time in the studio is about to end. I cast a longing look around the room, wishing I could stay, but I'm afraid my father will blow a gasket if I don't get home. The fact he didn't rip me to pieces for disobeying him by changing my schedule around, dropping classes he hand selected for me, has me on edge. He controls every other part of my life, so I don't know why he's overlooking my rebellious need to do something I love before I graduate from Thorne Point University. Still, I don't regret following Rowan's advice to do what I wanted.

Better not push my luck by going home too late.

I change out of the flowing shirt and towel off before throwing on a chic sweater dress and my favorite pair of Valentinos. Grabbing my camel-colored wool coat and my new purse, I survey myself in the mirror.

This girl is me, too. Femininity makes me feel good about myself. It instills me with confidence to take my life by its proverbial horns.

I wink at my reflection and switch off the studio lights as I head out. The campus guard on duty at night patrols the courtyard outside of the arts building. We've become good friends with all the late nights and extra time I've spent on campus in the last few weeks. I drop off coffee for him when I arrive and always wish him a good evening on my way out.

I wave. "Night, Tom."

"Goodnight, Miss Vonn. Did you get it right?"

Beaming, I do a twirl for him that makes my coat fan out. "Nailed it!"

"Good job. Keep up the practice."

A bubbly laugh full of joy escapes me while I find my phone to text my driver. With a student body flush with high profile students, I'm not the only one on campus with a chauffeur, but I wish Dad didn't insist on one. I'd rather drive myself around. To make things worse, he switched out the sweet old man who has been driving me to and from school since I was sixteen to a new guy who always stares at me.

Once I let him know I'm on my way to the garage he's waiting for me in, I switch to my message thread with Rowan. She sent a text twenty minutes ago that she's on campus with Levi tonight to meet her advisor.

A tiny thrill shoots through me at the hope of crossing paths with Levi. Tall, dark, and brooding, he always has a permanent, devilish scowl in place. It's meant to keep me at arm's length, I'm sure, but it's such a handsome look on him that I can't help finding him fascinating.

I haven't seen Rowan since I went to the Crowned Crows' run down hotel—the clubhouse they hole away in. They might have terrifying reputations that scare the pants off everyone, but I'm not afraid to stand up to them when it comes to making sure she's okay. To me, they're guys I've known forever, some since we were toddlers in the city's most prestigious pre-schools.

After I threatened to break down the door with my designer shoes while I livestreamed it, the infamous and intimidating Wren Thorne granted me access to my grieving friend.

Isla: Consider that turn sequence officially my bitch [crown emoji]
Rowan: Hell yes! [black heart]
Isla: I'm on my way to my ride, want to grab a coffee from that place you love off campus? I have maybe 30 more mins before I risk Dad's wrath.

My parents are generally absent, but when they're around I feel the tug on the collar around my neck acutely. I'm expected to obey their whims. The lesson dad gave me at fourteen is the main reason I do. Until recently, when my need to make my own path has outweighed the fear the lesson could be repeated.

A noise echoing through the garage distracts me before I read her answer. My heart thumps and I freeze, searching for the source behind me. It's just me and a few cars. Frowning, I slip my phone into my purse and continue toward the end of the row where the town car is always parked.

The closer I get, the more the hair on the back of my neck stands on end. Something is off, but I can't put my finger on it.

I don't realize what's wrong until I reach the end of the row. There's no town car.

Brows pinching, I dig my phone out of my purse to call the driver.

Another sound—this one a growled command—makes me whirl around. A man in all black melts out of the shadows. On the other side of the row, another one appears. They both stalk in my direction.

I stumble back a step, then another, nearly tripping in my heels. My eyes widen when the men exchange a look and lengthen their strides. *Shit!*

Heartbeat racing, I take off, fingers aching from gripping my phone so I don't drop it. The heavy, pounding footsteps of the men follow behind me.

"Help!" My shriek claws at my throat. "Someone help!"

CHAPTER FOUR

LEVI

THE night after the charges against me are dropped, I take Rowan to campus. Dragging her away from the Nest was a challenge, but she set up this meeting. Colton's the one who shoos her away when he says it's unlikely anything will change while she's out. He's been muttering since I got back with Jude and Wren.

The two of them watched the same few seconds of security footage on repeat, showing Wren in the warehouse the night of the raid. The security footage played frame by frame until it seamlessly finished. There was no sign of anyone bumping into Wren to slip the invitation into his pocket. Colton cursed and scrubbed through it again, swearing it wasn't possible for someone to hack his network to doctor the footage.

Some way or another, we will find out who gave Wren the card summoning him the same night our fight ring was raided.

Rowan meets with her advisor to submit paperwork for a leave of absence to grieve for her brother while I stand guard outside of the office examining the scabbed over indentations on my palms. She wears one of our comms at my insistence so I'll know if I need to protect her. Before we left, Wren met my eye and I nodded, knowing how important she is to him. Call us paranoid, but none of us are willing to let her out of our sight for long.

She's one of us.

When I gave it to her, she rolled her eyes, but accepted the earpiece with minimal grumbling. The hell we've been through in the last few weeks has taken its toll on her, too. She knows firsthand how dangerous it is to give in to the reckless urges that rule her. Until we have a better grasp on what we're up against, we need to be cautious.

The advisor offers his condolences and assures her once she's ready, he'll be there to help her finish her degree. A moment later, she emerges from the office with a tight smile, handing me the earbud.

Rowan checks her phone to read a message. When I glance at the screen and read Isla Vonn's name, my nostrils flare. I shouldn't have thought of her in the cell. I've learned once I start, I don't stop. It was difficult enough to kill off my obsession with watching her in high school, but since she's around more because of her friendship with Rowan, she haunts my dreams all over again.

Isla is a fixation I don't have time for.

The energetic senator's daughter is someone I've been forced to tolerate growing up. She's the type of person that inserts herself into your life whether you want her to or not and it irritates the hell out of me. Namely because every time she smiles or laughs, it throws me right back to the first time I saw her crying, the moment she awoke something dead in me. I hate that I can't ignore her. She even forced her way into the Nest. I hope now that Rowan is putting her degree on hold, it'll mean less time with Isla trying to talk my ear off.

"Let's go," Rowan says once she finishes texting.

We're both silent making our way through the hall with the secret door she discovered. It hides a room that dates back to the establishment of the city, marked by a bust of a founding father inscribed with the same Latin phrase on Wren's mystery card. My jaw locks. Whoever wants Wren to meet up with them, they've been operating under our noses.

As we exit the historic structure of Withermore Hall, Rowan's brow wrinkles. Her gaze roams the campus grounds on our way to the car. At night it's swallowed by shadows, the old architecture cast in darkness. It's no secret I prefer it this way rather than the pretentiousness it exudes in the light of day.

"This is the right choice," I say.

"Yeah, I'm sure Wren loves that he doesn't have to worry about setting up another bodyguard schedule to coincide with my classes." Her wry expression falls and some of the sadness weighing her down creeps into her tone. "Even without everything else going on, or if Ethan was alive, I think I would've ended up like this one way or another. I don't need to finish if my heart isn't in it. I'm not going to become a journalist."

"Do you know what else you'd want to do?" At the quick tensing of her shoulders, I add, "You don't have to do anything. Don't worry about it right now."

Rowan is quiet for a stretch, but as we reach the garage where I parked she surprises me. "You know when Wren safeguarded me in the penthouse?"

My lips twitch at her inflection on *safeguarded*. Really, my friend locked her in there and she was fucking pissed about it.

"Yes?"

"I wrote a book. When all this is over..." She shrugs. "It might be something I want to do."

"So do it."

She huffs out a soft laugh and claps a hand on my arm. "Always appreciate the stoic, straightforward support, dude."

I offer her a rare, lopsided smile. It falls when a panicked scream pierces the night and echoes off the concrete walls of the garage. Rowan goes rigid and my senses are immediately on high alert.

"Someone's in trouble." A look of horror crosses her face. "Fuck! Isla told me she was meeting her driver in the garage!"

Ice shoots into my veins and something deep inside me rears to life. My pendulum swings toward a destructive urge most of the time. The thought of Isla Vonn in danger wrenches it in the opposite direction to the need to protect, shocking me to my core.

There isn't time to analyze why. I need to act now.

I'm already moving when I bark, "Let's go."

I reach into the sleeve of my leather jacket for the blade strapped to my forearm and pause.

"What are you doing, we need to go!" Rowan collides into my back, yanking on my jacket.

"Shh." Tuning her out, I strain my ears.

This is what I train for, so that when danger comes I'm able to act. *There.* An engine rumbles and there are heavy footfalls on the level above the ground entrance.

I bend to retrieve the sharp dagger holstered in my boot. There are four more knives on me. I prefer them above any other weapon.

"Are you armed?"

"I—yeah. The gun Wren gave me."

"Be prepared. Move. When you have Isla in your sight and it's clear, you go for her and I'll handle the rest." I point her toward the stairwell. If I go up to the next level by the ramp, we'll have our best bet of ambushing. Failure isn't an option. "You get yourselves to safety, understand?"

Rowan nods in determination and flies up the steps. A burst of pride fills my chest at how quiet she manages to keep her hurried footsteps.

With a deadly swiftness I've spent a lifetime honing, I run up the incline to the second level. After a quick scan of the scattered cars, I keep to the shadows. One stocky man saunters around with a cloth rag clenched in one fist—chloroform, I'd guess. Rowan peeks around the door at the opposite end. A white van idles midway down the row of parking spaces.

"Someone, please!" Isla bursts out of her hiding place, her death trap heels scuffing when she nearly runs into the guy with the cloth.

My grip tightens on my knives, her panicked cry for help snapping something in me. I clench my teeth against the urgent need to answer her plea. *Not yet.*

"Here!" he barks. "C'mere, bitch."

As he runs her down and wraps his arms around her, covering her mouth with the rag while she struggles, a second man circles around from the other side of the cars, closer to Rowan. Gritting my teeth, I slink along the shadows.

Chloroform looks useful in the movies, but it's a bitch to work with. It helps that Isla is hyperventilating, fighting like hell against her attacker, but it still takes at least five minutes of inhaling to knock a person unconscious.

Rowan searches for me with a strained flick of her eyes, crouched at the edge of the doorway. I'm glad she's learning how to handle herself better. She would've run head first into the middle of this only a couple weeks ago.

The second attacker puts his back to me and I smirk. *Thanks for the opening.* Darting out from the shadows, I take aim, balancing the weight of the handle, then fling the smaller blade. It sinks into the forearm of the guy smothering Isla. He releases her with a garbled shout and she stumbles against the side of a car. Its alarm goes off with a droning whine.

While he groans in pain, I collide with the second man. We both crash to the floor. He lands face down, his chin crunching into the concrete with me on his back.

"Isla!" Rowan slips out of the stairwell and pulls her friend behind her, aiming her gun at the man left standing.

Good. If she has Isla, I won't be tempted to grab her myself.

"Mother—fucker!" The guy on the ground is double my weight in muscle, but his movements are sluggish, unable to reach his gun before I disarm him and toss it out of reach.

I don't waste energy on punching the guy when I have a knife in my hand. I don't need both of them to torture answers from, so that makes him expendable. Rolling him over, I pin him with a knee to his chest and fist his hair.

"Shouldn't have fucked around on Crowned Crows territory," I growl. "Now your soul belongs to the Leviathan."

Recognition crosses his face and he struggles for freedom.

I hate the name my parents gave me. It's why I go by Levi. The only thing it's good for is striking terror in my enemies.

The guy's eyes bulge as my blade pierces his neck.

CHAPTER FIVE

ISLA

Chaos feeds the adrenaline coursing through my veins. It gets me through the waves of dizziness and the nausea cramping my stomach. My best friend guards me like a vengeful angel. Her grip is firm on my wrist to keep me behind her while she aims a gun at one of my attackers. Levi Astor, one of the notorious Crowned Crows, kills the other without hesitation.

He's cold, ruthless, and unyielding driving his blade into the man's neck.

Somehow my frazzled mind snags on the contrast between Levi as the steadfast handsome guy who acted as my bodyguard at his nightclub, the shadow at the edge of society while we grew up together, and this capable killer. All three facets of the same man who's come to my rescue.

"Stay back," Rowan demands above the screech of the car alarm.

I struggle to catch my breath. My throat and nose burn. The other man who stinks of grease and cheap pomade ignores his bleeding arm and advances on us. He pays no attention to Rowan, eyes locked on me. My stomach roils and I bury my face in the back of her flannel shirt.

The harsh bang of the gunshot makes me flinch with a strangled cry when she fires.

"Damn it," she hisses. "I only grazed him."

My eyes go round and I poke my head out. "Where did you get a gun?"

She doesn't respond. Maybe my question was silly. It's the only thing I can latch on to at the moment.

The attacker she shot holds his upper arm with a furious grimace, no longer closing the distance between us. It's the opposite of the arm Levi got with his knife. Spittle flies from his lips as he takes labored breaths. His beady eyes flick from me and Rowan to his partner, weighing his options. Levi yanks his knife out of the other man's throat and he grabs his jaw in a white-knuckled grip.

"Who are you?" he demands. "Answer. You're dying here either way. What did you want with her?"

His vengeful, protective tone comes as a shock to me when he spends most of our time around each other ignoring me. It almost sounds the way I'd expect a boyfriend to sound, if I had one.

Blood oozes from the stab wound in the man's neck. He scrabbles at Levi's wrist and grunts, kicking his feet. His motions become uncoordinated until he goes still, limbs slumping to the concrete.

He's dead. I just watched a man die. A man who attempted to take me, but he was alive and now he's gone.

It takes several stuttering heartbeats to realize the rattling sound rushing in my ears is coming from me—from my ragged breathing.

"Fuck!" The remaining guy shouts before climbing into the white van he was edging toward.

"He's getting away!" I shout.

Levi glares after the tail lights while Rowan fumbles for her phone to take a video recording of the van leaving.

"Colt will be able to find it. Come on. It will be okay." She threads her fingers with mine, offering a sympathetic look before turning to Levi. "We have to take her back to the Nest."

His scowl cuts to us—to me. His eyes pass over me like he's checking for injuries, then he tears his attention away. Climbing to his feet, he nudges the dead body with the toe of his boot. "No. Somewhere else. We have safe houses."

Rowan squares her shoulders and strides up to him, towing me along. She pokes him in the chest. "Fuck you if you think I'm taking her anywhere other than the safest place I know after that. If you get in my way, I'll steal your car and leave your ass here."

Amusement flashes across his solemn features before he scrubs his face. "Fine. We need to move now, though."

Levi glances at the lifeless man on the ground. His lips twist into a severe frown. Dark blood forms a pool around the man's upper body.

When I hiccup out a distressed sound, Rowan turns around. My eyes sting, leaking from the corners. I fling my arms around her and squeeze. After a beat, she hugs me back.

"I thought I was going to die," I choke.

"If they wanted you dead, you'd be dead." Levi balls his hands into fists. "They planned to take you."

"Shut up," Rowan chides. "You're okay now."

"Actually, I feel like I might puke," I admit. "But my throat hurts. I don't want to."

"Chloroform." Without waiting for us, Levi retrieves his knives, wipes the blood on the dead body, and snaps a command over his shoulder. "Let's move."

Sniffling, I swipe beneath my eyes and hurry after Rowan to Levi's SUV.

I find my purse on the ground two spots away, the contents partially spilled from when it fell. My hands tremble as I pick it up. The car alarm still wails, the shrillness hurting my ears. Both Levi and Rowan are taking this chaotic situation in stride like it's totally normal to cut a man's throat in a parking garage, while I'm left reeling.

"Um, what about that? And the, uh, body? Clean up, aisle five." The joke I reach for falls flat, not helping me process this.

Levi shoots me a narrow-eyed look and gets behind the wheel. I don't know what I expected. He's always been broody around me, even when he lurked at my side while I did shots at the bar in the nightclub they run out of their abandoned hotel last month, not complaining when I commandeered him so I wouldn't be alone. His actions haven't left my head, painting him in a new light than the way I used to view him as growing up. I doubt he sees me as anything more than an annoyance going by the scowls he always directs my way. I sigh, rubbing my head in the hope it'll clear the lingering dizziness.

The speed he drives at doesn't help. I quickly give up on peering out the tinted windows in the backseat, staring at my hands in my lap instead. They're scraped from falling while I tried to escape the attackers who wanted to kidnap me. I swallow past a lump, my throat aching.

Who would kidnap me?

The list is unsettlingly long. With a prominent senator for a dad and a socialite for a mom, my family is familiar with being in the spotlight. There's a hashtag people use to post sightings of me on social media that started during my time in high school. To think I'm not even safe on campus where there are private security guards and every precaution offered to the affluent students of Thorne Point's most prominent families.

Then again, I haven't always been safe. The monstrous evils of this city have gotten to me before. I haven't had to worry about going through my nightmare for years. This experience shakes me from the confidence I had been building to find my freedom.

One thing is certain—those men weren't amateurs. The thought is as nauseating as the after effects of the drug running its course in my system.

And if my attackers knew what they were doing? Then I'm safest in the arms of the monster who rescued me. Levi Astor is a formidable, dangerous man.

Each of his friends has a terrifying reputation, and he's no exception. Up until tonight, I believed the worst of it was only rumor after growing up with them. Levi has always remained on the fray of every event we've crossed paths at, keeping to himself and his friends as a mysterious, wild shadow. The wildness is what's always drawn me to him.

Since getting to know them better because of Rowan, it was clear they're not the heartless bastards everyone makes them out to be. But after witnessing Levi murder a man first hand to save me, I'm not sure what to think anymore about those rumors.

I startle out of my thoughts when his arm reaches for me. "What—?"

"Clean it out." He takes my bag in his firm grip and tosses it to Rowan, then offers another knife, this one a sleek switchblade. "Completely."

Rowan gives me an apologetic look and tucks a flyaway piece of auburn hair that came loose from her braid behind her ear before she begins emptying the contents of my purse. My phone, makeup bag, a bottle of nail polish, and a wallet with keycards to access the security systems at home and the country club are placed in the cupholders of the center console. The dance clothes fall to the footwell.

While she digs through everything, Levi jabs a button on the steering wheel, speed dialing on speakerphone. His inky black tousled hair hangs over his forehead. He glances at me in the rearview mirror, a muscle in his chiseled jaw twitching. Again, he rips his attention away as if he can't look at me directly for too long.

I don't know why I piss him off so much other than inconveniencing his daily commitment to being the grumpiest person alive, but I'm grateful he saved my life.

The call connects and before the person can say hello, Levi clips out orders. "Penn. Campus. Parking garage, level two. By the blue BMW. I have the knife, but I had to leave in a hurry."

"*On it.*"

As quick as the call began, it ends. I blink. Is someone going to take care of the crime scene we left behind? My eyes widen. We should've called the police. A thousand and one questions crowd the back of my throat, but I gulp them back as Rowan slices into the lining of my new purse.

It's on the tip of my tongue to comment that cutting up a perfectly nice Dior is overkill—she's the true crime junkie that never trusts anything in this world is good—but it dies a swift death as she pulls her hand out of the lining, a small black device on a wire dangling from her fingers.

I blanche, sitting forward. "Is that what I think it is?"

Levi grabs it with deft reflexes and rolls down his window, preparing to throw it out.

"Wait!" Rowan grabs his wrist. "Don't get rid of it. Colt can check it. It could be the same as the bugs that were planted in my old apartment."

Chills break out over my skin. Shit. Rowan had to leave her apartment weeks ago when Wren Thorne and his friends found her place bugged to the tits with surveillance tech. What could they possibly want with me?

"We'll be leading whoever's tracking her to the Nest. I protect my brothers first and foremost." Levi puts his window back up and exhales heavily, examining the suspicious device. His eyes find mine again in the mirror. Holding my gaze, he snaps it in half with ease. "This is how they knew when you were approaching."

The implication hits me in the chest. If this device was planted on me, this was orchestrated. Nothing was left to chance.

"My dad gave it to me as a gift last week." My voice is hoarse. Did he know it was tampered with? Is this like the lesson he taught me before? Fear spikes uncomfortably in my stomach as another detail screams for my attention. "Oh! When I got to the garage, my driver wasn't there. He always parks in the same spot at the end of the row."

"The creeper new guy who stares at you?" Rowan clarifies.

"Yeah."

"This wasn't a chance grab for you, then." Levi's voice turns gruff and harsh, his inked knuckles tightening on the wheel. "It could be for ransom reasons."

"Or sex traffickers," Rowan adds grimly. "They're known to snatch girls right off the street."

"Jesus." My manicured nails dig into the bench seat while I struggle to breathe through the terror flooding me all over again. "What the fuck?"

My stomach clenches in revolt. First Rowan is stalked around Thorne Point University, and now I'm attacked.

Someone planned to kidnap me tonight. To take me right from school. To hurt me. The campus isn't safe for me.

If Levi and Rowan hadn't saved me, I might be reliving my nightmare in harrowing detail rather than fuzzy memories right now. Fresh tears prick my eyes and I remind myself I'm okay, I'm safe. It helps me find my way back to the light I desperately need at the moment.

"Thank you." My watery gaze lifts to Levi's profile. "Both of you."

Rowan reaches back to hold my hand. Levi remains silent for the rest of the drive. By the time he turns down the winding tree-lined road that leads to the Crow's Nest Hotel at the top of the hill, my hands have stopped shaking.

The old Georgian hotel is a building out of time. What's left of it, that is. The crumbling structure overlooks the ocean at the bottom of the jagged cliffside. Without the thumping beat of music, it gives off an eerie vibe with cracked gothic statues of angels and an overgrown hedge maze.

On the weekends, it becomes the hottest unofficial nightclub in the city for Thorne Point University students while the notorious Crowned Crows watch from a raised dais at the back of the shadowed ballroom, kings sprawled on thrones of decaying vintage settees and leather armchairs in their castle of chaotic delights. But underground is where the Crows do their real business.

I reach for my phone in the console when the car pulls into an open space amongst a row of luxury vehicles on the terrace. Levi stops me, clamping long fingers down on my wrist. The contact sends a shock of heat up my arm. It's the first time his skin has ever touched mine. His grip flexes and a shocked noise escapes him, like touching me surprises him as much as it does me.

"No." Gaining control of himself, he squints at me from the corner of his haunting eyes. As cold as attitude is, his hand is warm. "All of it needs to be checked first. You can have it back if we clear it."

Sliding my lips together, I lift my brows. "Okay, fine."

It's not like I was looking forward to calling Dad anyway. I'm not ready to face whether or not he knew about my purse, or think about him having a hand in this.

Levi holds on for another beat, thumb brushing my pulse point before he releases me like I've burned him. He gets out and opens my door.

Before I mistake it for a gentleman's gesture, I catch the closed off expression on his handsome face—thick brows flattened in a scowl, full lips turned down at the corners. He didn't like it last time I saw the inside of the Crows' secret hideout beneath the hotel, either. If he thinks his act frightens me, he's wrong. It has the opposite effect on me. My gaze lingers on his mouth and I shove away the curiosity of what it would be like to kiss him, whether it would be as rough as he is.

I tilt my head coyly and hold out my hand. "Thanks for helping a lady down."

He stares at my hand. Rowan snorts as she comes around the SUV. Our standoff stretches, neither of us giving up. His lips twitch and a challenge burns in his gaze when he falls back a step with a sardonic sweep of his arm. He wants to play it that way? Fine.

Raising my chin with all the primness and grace of my upbringing, I step out of the car. A strong wind blows in from the oceanside cliffs behind the hotel, sending my coat billowing around me. The heel of my Valentinos catches on a decaying crack in the cobblestones, and my eyes widen as I lose my balance. Before I can recover, Levi steps into me, catching me so I don't stumble. My hands land on his firm chest and a breath gusts out of both of us.

The earthy scent of leather mixed with the spicy musk of patchouli envelops me and his hands settle at the small of my back—hands that killed a man intent on hurting me tonight. Earlier, in the midst of the chaos, I couldn't fathom it. Yet now, in his strong arms, my heartbeat speeds up and an excited thrill makes my stomach dip.

Our gazes collide and the air seems to crackle with electricity. His jaw clenches. Taking me by the shoulders, he shoves me back at arm's length, eyes sliding down my body before he stiffens further and gives me his back, striding into the shadows clinging to the old hotel.

Rowan lifts a brow, eyes bouncing between us. I roll my eyes and shake my head. Whatever she sees, it's nothing. The aftereffects of adrenaline wearing off.

Levi doesn't want me like I secretly want him.

We circle around the terrace, bypassing a wide stone staircase leading to the entrance to the main part of the hotel flanked by bay windows with cracked and missing glass, going through a hidden walled in courtyard. It's connected to the hedge maze that sprawls the grounds. We come to a different door than the one I pounded on to demand access to Rowan after I heard her brother was found dead.

"You didn't get to see much before, but it's nice. We can make coffee while Colton checks for the van," Rowan says.

I pat my chest. "I don't think I need anything else to get my heart racing tonight, you caffeine addict."

She smiles. It falls when Levi halts, facing us with his arms crossed. The leather of his jacket creaks. He's guarding the door.

"Dude." Rowan tries to sidestep him.

"You can go in." His attention shifts to me. "She stays here until she meets our payment requirements." He points up to a thick vine of ivy creeping along the cracked stone above the door. Squinting, I can just make out the camera hidden there. "We're waiting."

CHAPTER SIX
ISLA

"YOU'VE gotta be kidding me!" Rowan swats at Levi's chest. "No! She doesn't have to give you anything—"

"It's fine." When Rowan opens her mouth to protest some more, I meet Levi's uncompromising gaze and shake my head. They're all able to see me from the camera he pointed out if they're paying attention to their security feeds. "A secret, right?"

He nods sharply. None of the Crowned Crows need money. They demand a different currency: secrets.

Their help doesn't come for free. He saved me from my kidnappers, and has brought me into their world for my protection. Quid pro quo—time to pay up.

"I already told Wren my juicy secrets when he let me in to see Rowan." Levi doesn't move a muscle. I smile sweetly and let more secrets spill. "I wasn't born in Thorne Point and my parents had an arranged marriage. I'm pretty sure it's some kind of weird sex cult."

"Lev," Rowan hisses when he remains statuesque. "She gave you a secret. Let's go."

"Not good enough," he says. "If you want me to care, you have to do better than that to impress me, Miss Vonn."

He must think I'm lying. It is an outlandish claim. I'm not, though. I really believe it. The weird robes I found in their closets once don't add up otherwise.

"Fine, then. What about my father's bad debts? At least I believe there's something going on financially. I've heard my parents arguing about it, how my mom's family won't help him. I know he dips into his campaign funds."

"What politician doesn't?" His expression is severe.

I huff. "Well, he's been taking all these meetings with everyone who's anyone in the city, looking for lucrative campaign donations." I blink. "Wait—do you think that's what the kidnapping was about? You mentioned ransom earlier."

Ransom is terrifying, but more settling to my mind than much worse alternatives. I latch onto it as an explanation of motive.

Nothing. Levi stares me down with shrewd eyes. My chest tightens. It's as if his perceptive gaze pierces right through me, seeking out my darkest secret. Thinking about it always hurts.

I have no choice. I don't want to tell anyone, but if I don't I have no doubt he'll leave me stranded out here. So much for saving my ass less than an hour ago.

The words stick in my throat, but I take a breath and push it all out.

"There's a men's club in Thorne Point. My father belongs to it. They buy girls' virginity." Rowan gasps, but I press on, holding Levi's gaze. If I don't, I risk breaking down. "It's set up as a dinner for a cover, but I think everyone inside knows what happens. The staff are paid off not to say anything." My heartbeat drums faster. "I...knew a girl it happened to. My maid. She told me everything about the remote estate outside of the city where the dinner happens."

Disjointed memories assault me in flashes, creeping out from the depths of my mind where I keep them buried. Rough hands. The cloying fruity scent of brandy on his breath. His face, red and grunting above me—one I've had to see for years after it happened. The deep aching pain that took days to heal from when I woke in my own bed.

My throat burns. I swallow, trying not to lose it. *You're okay,* I promise myself. I haven't let this break me for seven years, and I'm not letting it win now.

"They like them young. The girls are drugged so they're compliant." My voice is all wrong, but I continue. I don't remember a lot—to this day I still can't decide if it's a blessing or a curse that they laced my meal—but it comes to me in my nightmares. At fourteen, I was so excited to be invited to have dinner with Dad and his important business associates. Their smug smiles and veiled comments haunt me now. "After the night is over, they're returned like nothing happened."

I couldn't remember his face after that horrible night, but he came to Dad's campaign dinner a year later. It was his voice that cut through my fogged memories to awaken the dread I drowned in, submerged beneath the fog of whatever I was drugged with that night. Since then, I've known the identity of the man who paid to steal my virginity from me by force, enduring countless events where our paths crossed and his gaze sought me out.

The scar on my thigh is the only physical reminder left on my body. It's a small, circular mark the size of a ring. The harrowing event might have marked me permanently, yet I see that scar as my survivor's mark.

Levi's only reaction to the vague details I offer without giving away how I know this horrible secret is his hand dropping to one of his pockets and the sides of his mouth tightening. After another beat, he nods. Tension bleeds out of my shoulders.

"Come on," Rowan says. "Let's get inside. You've had a rough night."

She levels him with a hard look before heading through the door first. I make to follow her, but he blocks my path again. He's not as broad-shouldered or muscular as Wren, but he still cuts an imposing figure with tattoos creeping up his neck and over the back of his hands. Where Wren looks the part of a high society heir, Levi Astor has always looked dark and dangerous. I have no doubt he could easily incapacitate me.

"What, do you need to pat me down first?" I sass, eyeing him up and down. It helps burn away the memories I dredged up, packing them away in a mental box. "Unlike you, I don't go around armed to the teeth. In case you forgot, you were saving me from being kidnapped. I'm the victim, not the threat."

"I didn't forget." He holds up a length of dark fabric. "Put this on."

A blindfold. Right. I don't know where he got it from. It's not the same fabric bag Wren put over my head.

Straightening my spine, I wiggle my fingers. "How about I cover my eyes and promise not to peek this time? You can trust me."

A muscle in his jaw twitches and he rolls his eyes, muttering something under his breath. I don't wait for his approval, folding my hands over my eyes.

The gravel barely crunches beneath his boots as he moves around me. He's light on his feet. I think he could do it without making a sound if he wanted, the telltale sounds of movement allowed for my benefit.

Knowing he's circling me, my pulse jumps. Instinct tells my body he's a lethal predator, one I should be wary of. And for some reason, that thought sends a burst of heat through me, chasing away the anxiety of the kidnapping attempt and giving up my secrets. All that remains is a tingling awareness in my body of the exact distance between us. Part of me wishes he'd close it.

It's a crazy thought, but I can't take it back, not after the night he watched over me in the club.

With Levi, I'm safe because he's the most dangerous piece on the board. Nothing else could get me. Not my nightmares or anyone who wants to attack me.

"Let's go, princess." With that gruff order, his hard body brushes against mine to get me to move.

He doesn't allow me more than a step ahead of him, the sculpted lines of his chest almost plastered to me. His grip keeps me glued to him. I wish it were for different reasons, ignoring the fire flooding my veins everywhere we touch. An image of him pinning me down and ravaging me flashes across my mind, and I bite down on my cheek.

The only way I know we've moved inside is the change from uneven gravel to sturdier concrete beneath my stilettos. Each step echoes as if we're in a cramped tunnel, then the air grows cooler as he directs me down a set of steps. I only hear our movements, so Rowan must be inside already.

I almost laugh at the juxtaposition between the sound of my designer heels and his muted boots. As opposite as we are, we both come from the same world. Yet while I'm trapped in expectations, he's always escaped them to exist at the outskirts. Someday I'll be able to say the same for myself.

He tugs me to a stop. My hands begin to slip away until he squeezes my elbow.

"Not yet," he rumbles scant inches from my ear.

A shiver races down my spine. He leans into me and my brows jump up. A moment later my stomach bottoms out with the sensation of a slow, mechanical descent. An elevator in an old hotel makes no sense. When it comes to these guys, little does. Everything about them is mysterious, and that mystery lures me in, interested in knowing more.

With one of my senses out of commission, my mind wanders.

It's hard to believe I was over the moon about nailing the turn sequence before the aerial in my choreography back at the dance studio on campus barely two hours ago. With the discovery of the tracking device in my purse, hiding out here is my best bet. Knowing no one can get to me here without going through the Crowned Crows first sets me at ease.

"Penthouse. Or I suppose since we're under the hotel this would count as the creepy basement level," I joke when the elevator stops without a sound.

He grunts, nudging me forward.

The hallways in this place are a maze. Last time I was here, Wren Thorne blindfolded me and dumped me off in a random room. This time, each step I take is guided by Levi's grip on my elbow while he steers me through the hidden underground space beneath the hotel. After four more turns, we stop.

Once again his hold on me flexes, almost pulling me further into his body. Before he releases me, he rasps an order in my ear. "Clean your scraped hands."

My stomach dips again, the places he touched me going cold. "Can I open my eyes now?"

"Yeah. He left already," Rowan says.

"I didn't even hear him." Intrigue colors my words.

"That's Levi for you."

I drop my hands and peer around the room. It's simple. *Sparse.* A wide bed with dark sheets takes up the majority of the room. There are nightstands on either side, and a chair in the corner. At least it has its own bathroom.

For four boys as rich as they are—two of them from old money, older than my family's connections to the Vanderbilts—I'm surprised by the lack of creature comforts. I guess it fits. They do like to hang out in a decrepit turn of the century abandoned hotel. I always assumed they lived downtown or at their family estates, like I do. I thought that their inclinations for throwing parties in a ballroom with the chill of the night air seeping in, and the threatening vibe was part of their act. But how much is for show and how much is real?

"Cozy."

"I'm so sorry he made you tell him that stuff. I'm going to rip him a new asshole as soon as I'm done getting you settled in. God, even Wren let me get away with owing them a favor when I needed help."

"It's okay. If he needed to know I was willing to divulge my family's dirty laundry to trust me, I don't mind proving myself."

Rowan scoffs. "He doesn't trust anyone. I'm surprised he learned to trust me. You remember how he and Colton stalked me all over campus, pulling their spy crap to enter my classes so they could watch my every move when I went to them for help finding Ethan."

"Exactly," I say brightly. "He learned to recognize how awesome you are after you wore him down. I'll do the same. I even have a head start since I've known him longer."

There's a difference between knowing him because we grew up around each other, and actually knowing him. But I want to, ever since the club night in their hotel upstairs. He's guarded, but I'm determined to make him laugh at my antics one way or another. Behind the mysterious exterior, there's more to him than meets the eye. Glancing down at my scraped hands, I have to wonder again if he doesn't ignore me, like I always believed, but sees more than I'm aware of.

The bed is much plainer than the exquisite imported four-poster in my room at home, yet it calls to me all the same. My eyelids droop. After the night I've had, my usual endless well of energy feels tapped out. The only thing I want right now is sleep.

I drift to it, slipping out of my coat. Rowan follows me across the room. I perch on the edge of the mattress, kicking off my heels. A scuff on the side of the left one makes me frown. Damn, these are my favorite pair of Valentinos.

It occurs to me that I have nothing to change into other than the sweater dress over my leggings. I'm no stranger to sleeping in the nude, but typically

I like to sleep in a silk camisole. Rowan's empty handed, so I can't even wash my dance top in the sink.

"So, does this place have turndown service? Complimentary robes?" I wink. "An extra overprotective hottie to tuck me in?"

"Sarcastic deflection is a coping mechanism I recognize well." Rowan bites her lip. "Are you okay?"

My shoulder hitches. "Peachy." As long as I don't replay the last hour in my head. "How many rooms are in this place? It seemed like a maze, more so than last time."

"A lot. It's easy to get lost, so for now you should stay here." She clears her throat and winces. "Colt will have to program your handprint. The door has a hidden lock sensor. It pissed me off so much the first time Wren brought me to his room and I couldn't get out."

I smirk at the lilt in her tone and the faint pink tinge filling her cheeks. Whatever happened, she didn't hate it. "His kink really is locking you away. Are they all like that?"

Levi's handsome face fills my head. There's always been something about his brooding demeanor that has drawn me in. At society parties, around campus. Tonight, when he cut me with words, but protected me, *killed* for me without hesitation.

"Psychotic?" She jokes. "Every one of them."

"Do they cuddle?"

This is what I need right now. Teasing banter, joking about how badly I need to get laid. Laughter is the best medicine to chase away the darkness. It keeps my thoughts off everything else.

I can't picture Levi spooning in bed. It's difficult to think of him in any sort of relaxed state when he's constantly on edge, watchful of his surroundings. It makes for an amusing and enjoyable mental image, though.

"If not, that's a dealbreaker. I can handle unhinged, but I need to be held."

We both laugh. She plays with the cuff of her oversized flannel shirt, smile fading.

"It's no joke being in with them. The rumors about the things they're capable of are true. Getting caught in their web is something you can't turn back from." She rubs a hand over her face and sighs. "Things get intense. Like...burn down the docks intense."

My brows shoot up. "That was them? I thought they only dealt with matters on campus."

She shakes her head. "That was me. There's a lot going on other than a stalker and that secret passage we found."

"Babe," I whisper, reaching for her hand. She takes it, sitting beside me. "Now I need to know if *you're* okay?"

"Yeah. My brother was just mixed up in a lot of shit trying to hunt down his story and it got him killed. Without Wren and the guys having my back, I don't know what would've happened. But I trust them all with my life. They'll help you."

Her conviction is as resolute as she is stubborn. I've missed having her around.

"I believe you. Your word is good enough for me."

Rowan's lips twist in uncertainty. "You're sure you're okay? If you're not, I won't leave." Her green eyes slide to the door and she messes with a stray piece of reddish brown hair. "I don't want to, but I need to talk to Wren about what happened on campus."

"I know I'm safe here. Go on, before he decides he needs to flex his big dick energy and lock you away again."

She gives me a wry smile. "He can try. He knows the consequences if he tries to pull that again." A determined look settles on her face and she unholsters the gun she shot earlier. She places it on the bedside table. "Keep this with you. No one will bother you, but it helps knowing it's there. You'll sleep better."

"I really don't think that's necessary, I swear I'm—"

"If not for your sake, then for my own peace of mind to know you're protected." She hugs me, quick and fierce. "I don't want anyone else I love getting hurt."

I lock my arms around her, wishing I could take away the pain and grief she carries. "Go talk to your man. I'm golden, okay? I'm going to shower, meditate, then pass out."

A husky laugh huffs out of her. "You can sleep after going through that like nothing's wrong?"

"Sure."

It's how I've dealt with what I've been through.

I focus on my love for my friend, the fact I'm okay and none of us were badly injured, and the truth that I survived rather than the dark whispers at the edges of my mind. Tonight is hardly the worst thing I've ever been through. This city sunk its claws in me at a young age. I refuse to let its harsh truths snuff out my light.

I survive. It's what I do, no matter what.

At her skeptical look, I tilt my head. "I'm good at clearing my head. Tonight sucked, but we made it out. What's the point in going through it again and again when it's over? Tomorrow we can rehash it, but for now, I think I'm about ready to let it go. The adrenaline crash is a bitch and I'm really sleepy."

"Okay. Get some rest. If you're asleep when I come back, I'll see you in the morning."

I kiss her cheek affectionately and squeeze her one more time.

Rowan leaves me alone in the sparse room. I test the door, just to see. Sure enough, it won't budge, the hidden scanner not registering the foreign signature of my handprint. That level of security is overkill.

As I back away from the door, I can't help but wonder if I've become a prisoner to different monsters than the ones who crawled out of Thorne Point's seedy underbelly to capture me. Being indebted to the Crows for their protection can't be worse than living through what I did from the ones who buried their ugliness deep in me.

CHAPTER SEVEN

LEVI

Once I drop her off in one of the extra rooms as far away from my two havens in the Nest—the gym and my own room—I leave without a word. My hand flexes to forget the feeling of what it's like to touch her after fantasizing about it throughout high school every time I followed her, snapped her picture, watched her. A frustrated noise leaves me.

Rowan is pissed, but she'll need to get over it. Even if she's one of us now, even as Wren's girlfriend, she doesn't get to dictate how we've always done things. We have to do them this way—it's what keeps us safe. That comes first above all else.

On some level, Isla Vonn understands that better than her friend.

Maybe Rowan's hang ups are because she didn't grow up in the poisonous high society world like me, Wren, Colton, Jude, and Isla did. Without secrets, there's nothing to leverage. Information becomes power. We do whatever it takes to remain in power by holding all the cards.

I've learned all too well what comes of trusting anyone born in our world of wealth. Pain, betrayal, greed. Isla is from that world. It's one reason I never gave into the ways she tempted me before, shoving the dreams and the thoughts deep into my psyche once I accepted she would always be a fantasy, never a reality. The risk is too great, and I have far more riding on the line, far more to protect, far more to lose if I let her in now.

A hint of her sweet, light scent lingers around me, along with a flash of her soft curves brushing against me as I led her to a room. Fighting her temptation around campus has nothing on knowing she's here, in my space where I can easily get to her to take the things I've always wanted in my dreams.

My teeth grind all the way back to the main lounge. Colt has his feet crossed at the ankles on his desk against the wall of his computer screens. He kept quiet when we brought Isla in. I'm braced for him to run his mouth.

After all, he's the bastard who played me into watching her so closely at Thorne Point Academy for his social media game. If he hadn't run his mouth about how nice her tits were, I wouldn't have fallen further into the obsession that grew after the first time I caught her crying in an alcove, awakening something dead in my chest.

His brows jump up when he spots me and he drops his feet. "So, are you playing a new kinky game with the lovely senator's daughter with fucking delectable legs—and am I invited, or—"

I dump the broken tracker in front of him and his salacious proposition cuts off.

"Ohh, presents." Colton picks up the two pieces of the device, angling them in the light to examine it. "You shouldn't have." He turns serious, eyes cutting to me. "Was this in your car? Slipped into Rowan's bag? If someone's bold enough to pull a drop on the big guy, it wouldn't shock me for them to plant trackers, too."

"Isla's." My jaw locks and I blow out a breath. "A separate problem, I think. We stopped an attempted kidnapping attack in the garage. Found that sewn into the lining of her purse."

"Motherfuckers." His brown eyes flash with deadliness, dropping the playful act.

An odd flare of jealousy rushes through my chest. The same thing has happened lately anytime he comments on her appeal. I'm the one that saved her life. Guarded her when she was helpless. I squash the sensation, brows furrowing.

She has secrets like anyone else. I didn't need to be as observant as I am to know she's hiding something more about the secret she clearly didn't want to part with. There's more she's not saying. It should piss me off enough to want to rip the secret directly from her tongue under the threat of my knife, but the fear haunting her striking blue eyes through the brave face she put on sticks with me.

It's so much like when I saw her cry for the first time, her cheeks splotchy, silky hair hanging in her eyes. I smother the thought. That Isla only exists in my dreams.

The maid story is clearly bullshit. Sloppy for a girl like her, raised in this world, taught to wield secrets and information before we're able to walk. But then who is the girl in the story? My mind supplies Isla's radiant smile, so bright and full of life like my mother's once was before her death.

The vicious need to protect expands in my chest. Would Isla's father really...?

Knowing about how mine and my mother's kidnapping for ransom was handled, yes. I believe family members are the ones capable of the worst things against the people they're supposed to love. Blood doesn't mean shit.

Only the family you choose. They always have your back.

As soon as we're out of this shirt storm, hunting down the club Isla described will be the next top priority. I won't stand for anyone in this city making others feel helpless.

Colt grumbles under his breath while his fingers fly across his wireless keyboard. "This is definitely private security, military grade shit." The make and model of the tracking device displays on one of his screens. "What the actual fuck?"

The question is more him talking to himself than something I'm meant to answer. I scan his wall of monitors. Three screens show different angles of the security cameras in the warehouse, scrubbing through frame by frame with code running. I don't think he's slept yet, throwing himself into looking for answers for last night.

I clench my teeth at the screen showing his progress on salvaging the corrupted file from Ethan Hannigan. My uncle isn't a good man by far. Organizing the ransom to extort my dad out of his shares of their company is tame compared to the evil he's capable of. If he was willing to pay to have his own sister and young nephew kidnapped, whatever we find out when Colton decodes the encrypted file is only going to make things worse.

I shut down that line of thinking hard, refusing to give in to the shadowy corners of my mind. I can't relive my mother's pleas again after last night.

"The secret Isla paid with..." I blow out a breath and cross my arms. "There's a men's club buying the virginity of young girls. She said she knew because of her maid, but it was a flimsy cover. Think they'd be back for another taste?"

Colt's lip curls and he curses, typing faster. "Could be."

Despite Isla's secrets, it puts me on edge to have her here in our haven. I can't just give her my trust.

I glance at the door to the gym. Grunts emanate from the open door where Wren and Jude are working out. My muscles crave the burn and release, too. First I need to clean my knife. While my mind churns, I pull a switchblade from the hidden leather holster slipped inside my jeans, flicking it open and shut methodically. It helps me clear my head without hitting the bag in the gym.

Colt lifts a cocky brow, but keeps his mouth shut. Smart. He can tell that in the mood I'm in I could deck him for one wrong comment.

The four of us are brothers. We bleed for each other, give each other loyalty above all else. But we'll still fight each other to blow off steam and work out our shit.

Each metallic flick and click of the switchblade soothes me. "It's not urgent. We have other things that are more important right now. I stuck her in a back room until we have time to deal with it."

He snorts, his long brown fringe flopping across his forehead with the force of his head jerking. "Always so suspicious. Shouldn't I be the conspiracy theorist, with my access to networks people don't even want to know exist?" He waves at his kingdom of computers with a showy gesture. "Rowan's not going to like your attitude towards our friend."

"I'm right to keep my guard up and you know it." With a growl, I smack the back of his head. "She's always around us on campus. Then when our foundation is rocked, she falls in our laps with a fucking tracker on her? She could be a plant to get to us."

"Jesus, you edgelord. Listen to yourself." He swivels his gamer chair around to stare me down. "Stop being so fucking paranoid. It's Isla. Same girl we had History of Ancient Civilizations with in high school. Remember her sparkly binders and color-coded notes? She's harmless, not a goddamn sleeper agent who worked her way into the Nest to spy on us."

The rage I only let out in the ring or working out rises so fast I can't control it or contain it. I arc my arm in a swift move, jamming the tip of my knife into Colton's desk.

"Hey! Bastard." He levels me with a glare, moving his expensive equipment out of the way. "What was that?"

I pant until I stiffly yank the knife out of the wood. Drawing in a deep, even breath, I shake my head.

"You don't lose your cool. The other two? Sure. But you?" He squints, brown eyes too damn intelligent and knowing. His expression clears and he barks out a laugh. "Oh."

"Oh what? I don't know why I did that." My brows pinch.

"But I do," he says cryptically.

"Fuck you."

"Now what are you two bitching about?" Jude emerges from the gym, wiping his face with a towel. Shadows beneath his eyes and a permanent downtilt to the corners of his mouth tell me Pippa's latest betrayal still rides him hard. He can't hide it from us behind his mask of smiles. "Did you find anything new?"

Wren follows in his wake.

Colton spins back to his computer and flaps a hand at different screens. "That, no." The security feed. "This, yes. New word decoded—king. And this—" He holds up the tracker. "—is a new present Levi brought. Our favorite Vonn—the beautiful one—was slated for kidnapping. This was sewn into her purse."

"What?" Wren snarls. His vicious gaze moves around the room. "Where's Rowan?"

"Right here." Rowan strides over to our group from the hall leading to the rooms. "Relax, big guy. I wasn't leaving Isla alone, and it was nothing I couldn't handle."

"She's fine." I hold up a hand to placate his overprotective nature. "I wouldn't let anything happen to her. We heard the attack in progress when we reached the garage and stopped it." The corner of my mouth twitches. "She clipped one of them. When we have free time, she needs more target practice and training."

The tense set of Wren's shoulders relaxes from preparing to attack anything for endangering the girl he loves. With a rumble, he pulls her into his arms, cradling her face while he checks her over for himself. When he's satisfied, he draws her into a deep, possessive kiss. She winds her arms around his neck and melts into him.

"Where's Isla now?" Jude asks.

Close. Too close. Enticingly within reach.

A muscle in my jaw tics at the insistent whispers in my mind luring me to seek her out and find out how much my fantasy Isla aligns with reality. If her cries of pleasure and the bounce of her tits while my cock drives into her is the same as my imagination when I followed her around. Even with years of tight control over myself, heat rushes to my groin picturing the gorgeous woman Isla has grown into wrapping those luscious red lips around my cock.

No. Not happening. Never happening.

There are more important things that need my full attention than lust-fueled thoughts that have returned to haunt me.

"Here, where she's safest." Rowan turns a frosty glare on me. "She paid her pound of flesh. He made sure of it."

Wren and Jude look to me. I shrug, not sorry in the slightest. Jude nods, agreeing with me. Wren's icy blue eyes slide to Rowan with a complicated mix of emotions, but when he meets my gaze I know he's on the same page as me.

Loyalty above all else.

We protect our own first, and Isla hasn't earned a right to be considered part of our crew.

They would've made the same choice in my place.

"What does the new decryption tell us?" I plant a hand over the gouge mark I left in Colton's desk to cover it from the others while I scan the monitors. "This is still our priority."

"Asshole," Rowan mutters.

"The invitation," Jude says.

"Right, the address for the Founders Museum is on Old King's Road." Wren rubs his jaw. "Compile a list of anything in the city connected to or named king."

"Got it." Colton cracks his knuckles and opens a new window over the online poker games he constantly plays. As he codes a script in a language only he understands, he nods to the screen with the surveillance. "Maybe we'll luck out with an answer about who the hell tampered with my baby. No one should be good enough to hack my security protocols. No one's as good as I am."

"Then they have someone very dangerous in their pocket." Cold anger laces Wren's tone.

Rowan threads her fingers with his. "We need to figure out what to do about this summons. You're not walking into a trap blind."

"Love that you think like us, kitten," Wren murmurs.

I push away from the desk to back up, needing to take in the bigger picture. As I study the wall of screens, Jude catches my eye. He raises a brow, glancing at the stab mark in the desk. Shit. I frown, returning my attention to the computer monitors.

"At least we have time to breathe so we can figure out a plan," Jude says.

"Time is a fickle bitch," Colton snarks without taking his focus off the computer.

"Only because you can't control it," I say.

My eyes narrow in suspicion, cycling between the partial file, the security recordings of the warehouse, and the invitation blown up in Photoshop after Colton scanned it to search for anything else discerning. He deemed it just a boring ass card without microchips embedded, or hidden QR codes in the design.

"We need to figure out who sent this and what they want," Rowan says.

"It's all connected. It has to be. More than we thought it was before last night. We've hunted the crossed skeleton keys insignia all over the city looking for her brother. It matches the signet ring my uncle and Wren's father wear." My mind is stuck on elite clubs after learning Isla's secret. "Some kind of exclusive club for rich bastards, maybe."

Jude hums. "Powerful enough people to pull strings without consequences."

"But what the fuck are they doing challenging us so publicly?" Wren scowls. "We've built our own empire separate from them. We haven't been under thumb in a long time. Is this all an elaborate way to prove they can still control us?"

I swipe a hand over my mouth in thought. "At the gala, they said *carpe regnum*."

"Then my grandfather's favorite motto could be more than a family mantra." A muscle in Wren's jaw jumps. "My father might have been cryptically giving me a message then. You might be onto something. Maybe it's not just a motto."

Jude runs his fingers through his thick, shiny dark hair and purses his lips. "A creed."

"A brotherhood." Inadvertently, Isla may have given us direction in this fucked up circle we've been stuck in. "Think about it. We've been so focused on the mafia operation, but they were never in charge."

"It fits." Colton pauses typing to fold his hands behind his head. "They've been on both your backs, but only Wren got the invitation."

"I'm still in school, technically."

"And my father has been putting more pressure on me about my responsibilities to take my place now that I've graduated. I thought he meant his business, but what if it was this?" Wren sweeps an arm at the invitation sitting on Colton's desk. "Fuck, it's been in front of us this whole time."

Rowan tucks into Wren's side to comfort him. "So, like a secret society? And, what, you're like a legacy pledge, because your father is a member?"

"Status and bloodlines, two of the most valued currency amongst high society and stuffy old money fuckers," Colton says.

"Then why wouldn't you have known about it if your father and your uncle are involved?" She shakes her head in disbelief. "Wouldn't they have told you a lot sooner about belonging to a secret society?"

My lip curls. "I avoid my uncle at all costs."

"And my father and I hate each other," Wren says. "He ignored me when I showed no interest in doing as he expected, but he's realized I'm his only heir. That matters to men like him. And it's not like my mother is in any state to give him another."

He grimaces and Rowan pulls him down to her level for a kiss to steal away the pain carved in his expression.

"If we're operating under the theory of this being Wren's induction to daddy's club, I've got some ideas how we can handle it," Colton says with his signature wicked smirk. "And new toys to try out."

"Now I wish I got a summons, too." I reach for the switchblade again. "I don't like you going in alone. It leaves your back unguarded."

"I have some ideas for that, too." Colt taps his temple. "Always firing on all cylinders. Speaking of—does Isla sleep in the nude? I need to find out, for reasons. Hashtag Vonn Daily would blow the fuck up at that kind of sighting. It'll be my finest work since starting the hashtag."

I grip my knife handle so hard my skin stings, the healing nail wounds threatening to reopen as I battle the need to retaliate for the comment. Does she? Now it's all I can think about.

"Colt," Rowan hisses. "Keep your horny thoughts to yourself, and leave her alone. She's been through enough shit today."

Wren chuckles, dropping a kiss on her forehead. "So have you, brave girl." He locks his arms around her, hauling her over his shoulder. At her protest, he slaps her ass. "We'll revisit this to work out a plan."

As the pair of them disappear down the hall, his hands roaming over her body before they're full out of sight, I release my grip on the switchblade. I wouldn't have stabbed my best friend, but I couldn't say there wouldn't have been some maiming involved.

Jude watches, amusement dancing in his hazel eyes. He nods to the knife as I slip it away. "That have anything to do with stabbing the desk?" He laughs at the low growl I release. "That's what I thought. Interesting."

He whistles a song from his abuela's favorite singer on his way out of the room. I turn back to find Colton smirking at me.

"Don't start," I grumble.

He puts his hands up. "Me? Never."

I scoff. "Right."

"Unless there's something you want to tell me about why Isla's got you so tetchy? More than the usual deadly sourpuss, that is. You feeling stalker-y again?"

At the rumble of warning vibrating in my throat, Colton laughs, knowing full well I can kill a man several different ways. My threshold breaks. I need to hit something before I hit one of my friends.

"I'll be in the gym. Don't bother me."

"Enjoy organizing your knife collection, psycho," he calls after me.

"Fuck you," I toss over my shoulder. "And get some sleep. You're so damn annoying and nosy when you're not rested."

CHAPTER EIGHT

LEVI

It takes me two days to work out my demons, pausing only long enough to catch a few hours of sleep in the gym before I was back to pushing my body to its breaking point. The sleep I get is restless. It's high school all over again, my subconsciousness plagued by the first time I saw her crying, really breaking down. In my dream, it's always vivid, her blue eyes bright, glistening with tears leaking freely.

Isla Vonn was always around. It wasn't until that day when I cut class and found how broken she was behind her radiant smiles and silly personality that she ensnared me. The tears she shed were the first thing to make me feel after years of numbness following my kidnapping, then my mom's death.

When I leave the gym, Isla is in the lounge instead of locked in the room I left her in. A quick sweep of her appearance has me choking back another wave of rage. It's the most skin I've seen her show since the club night upstairs a few weeks ago, when she grabbed one of my hoodie strings and towed me after her to the bar. I kept telling myself I'd walk away once I was sure she was safe on her own. That didn't happen.

Colton's hoodie drapes off one of Isla's delicate shoulders and hits her mid-thigh. If he thinks this is funny, I'll kill him. My glare cuts to him. He's got one mischievous eye on me while Rowan sits beside him in a chair she dragged over, typing on her laptop.

"Look who's back in the land of the living." His lips twitch. "Well, as close to living as you get."

"Coffee?" Isla sidles up to me, holding up two mugs.

My attention drops to her bare legs. "Where the fuck are your clothes?"

More questions are on the tip of my tongue, each more demanding than the last. *Who let you out? Who gave you a free pass to do as you please while you're here? Why won't you get out of my head?*

"Good morning to you, too, grumpy." She shrugs, the movement revealing another inch of skin. Christ, she has nothing on underneath. "Chill, I had to borrow stuff from Rowan yesterday. In case you forgot, I came down here with the clothes off my back. I didn't exactly get to pack a weekender bag. Mine are drying in the shower after I washed them in the sink."

From Rowan? Yeah right. Colton slipped his hoodie in. I feel the itch of his attention on the back of my neck, waiting for my reaction.

A frustrated rumble works its way up my throat. "You can't wear that. Come with me."

Ignoring Colton's poorly concealed laugh, I stride from the lounge.

"Slow down."

Isla has long legs, yet they still work double time to keep up with my pace. Her bare feet slap on the cold floor. I grind my teeth and huff out a breath, tallying a mental list. We make it to my room before I realize where I've led her.

Christ. The fuck is wrong with me when it comes to this girl?

I'm rarely off my game, but with her around combined with everything else we're dealing with, I'm faltering. It's unacceptable. This is why I don't allow myself leniency. Over the years, me and my boys have closed ranks, trusting fewer and fewer people. I don't indulge, my heart hardened.

I lock my jaw, debating my options. "Wait out here." I pin her with a hard gaze. Those big blue eyes widen and her lips part, stirring a strange sensation in my chest to have her attention directly on me when I've spent so long watching her from the shadows. "Don't move."

"You never said I had to *stay* in my room. Unless I really am a prisoner here?" She lifts a brow in challenge.

The corners of my mouth turn down. My gaze sweeps over her, assessing for weak points to exploit like I've trained myself to do. A shadow catches my eye on her leg, barely visible beneath the hem of the hoodie. It's a scar. I need to know how she got it and whether I need to maim some stupid fuck for touching her, picturing one of the yuppie boys she's always on the arm of taking liberties.

My fingers twitch, the protective urge she triggers warring against my distrust. "This isn't the outside world, princess. Around here, we're in charge, and you do as we fucking say. Got it?"

She tips her chin up in another act of defiance. "You're wrong about me."

"I'm not. I never am. Now stay."

I wait another beat, just to make sure my order is obeyed before I tap my hand against the hidden scanner Colton installed in every door in the Nest and slip inside. I spare one minute in the solitude of my room to ask myself what the hell I'm doing, then dig through my clothes to give to a girl I don't even trust.

I know I'm messed up, but this is a new realm for me. Ignoring the odd burning in my chest, I pick out fitted joggers, a pair of Lycra pants I use for recon when I need to be extra stealthy, and some Henley shirts. Returning to the hall, I shove the armful at Isla.

Her stare moves from the bundle of clothes to me. She holds up the coffee cups, sipping from one.

"Those are your clothes."

"I know," I grit out. "The pants should fit. Better than traipsing around in nothing under Colton's hoodie."

Her amused snort tells me she knew. My brows flatten and I back her against the wall, planting one hand over her shoulder.

"He'll jerk off to the thought of what kind of panties you have on underneath that when you give it back to him."

The corners of her tempting, full lips curl up. "And what if I'm not wearing any? Laundry day, remember?"

A feral sound tears from me as heat pulls into my groin. I allow myself to lean into her body a fraction before I back the fuck up.

"Put the goddamn pants on, princess."

"Fine, grumpy. Hold these." She shoves the coffee mugs at me.

The clothes fall to the floor in a flutter of fabric, my deft reflexes kicking in to accept the cups. She strips out of the hoodie right in the hall without preamble, not caring that I'm standing right there. A choked noise lodges in my throat as she turns around, her wavy chestnut locks spilling down the curve of her spine, ending just above the tantalizing swell of her ass.

She does have panties on—a jewel green lace thong that has my cock hard in record time. I grind my teeth so hard my jaw aches while she slips her long legs into the stretchy workout tights. They hug every line, every soft curve. The only hint they're too big on her is the excess material bunched at her ankles and the waistband pulled almost to her tits. I catch the side view of them as she tugs on a charcoal Henley.

"Isla," I bite out. "What. The. Fuck."

Anyone could've walked down the hall to see her little show. The blood in my veins boils at the thought of my brothers watching the erotic sight of her reverse strip tease, pulling on my clothes. Fuck, *my* clothes.

"What? You wanted me to get dressed. I can't get into any of these rooms without security clearance." She wiggles her fingers pointedly, then flips her hair out from being tucked in the open neck of the shirt. "I'm not shy, it's fine."

Fine. It's fine. It's so fucking far from fine.

The urge to stab something hits me again.

I gulp down one of the coffees. The hot burn down my throat is necessary to distract myself from the forbidden thoughts swirling through my mind. She just covered up. I'm not giving in to what my dick wants—not tossing down the mugs to pin her to the wall, strip her bare for me, and shut her up with a kiss.

The desire to kiss her just to see what she tastes like always sits at the back of my mind when she's around. I've been able to keep a leash on it up to this point, but it's difficult to ignore with her presence in our space.

It occurs to me after I finish it off that the coffee was made how I like it, black with one sugar. Hers had milk in it. The insistent warmth returns in my chest, but I annihilate it.

"Ground rules," I announce. "You can't have free rein. I need to know where you are at all times if you're staying here for protection."

"Fine. Want me to move into your room, while we're at it?" She winks, adding to the way her playful sassing rakes on my frayed nerves. "I'm a great cuddler. We can rock paper scissors for little spoon."

Ignoring her, I stalk down the hall. She pads after me, feet still bare.

"You had shoes when you arrived."

"I prefer to be barefoot. It's great for your balance training, you know?"

She lunges in front of me with a graceful dance move and executes an airborne split. "See?"

I press my lips together, not willing to compliment her natural ability to move.

"Anyway, as much as I love my shoes, they're impractical prisoner fashion. I'd rather go barefoot."

"You're not a prisoner," I mutter.

I just don't trust her, and I never ignore my instincts.

Sliding a glance at her, I huff. "Are your hands okay?"

"Yes." She gives me a pretty smile, showing me the healing scrapes on her palms. "Jude cleaned them for me when he saw me trying to handle it. Talked my ear off."

It probably came off like a friendly conversation when in reality he was interrogating her under the guise of setting her at ease, like he does best. My lips press into a thin line. We stop in the kitchen area to dump the empty mugs, then she follows me to Colton and Rowan.

"Anything new?" I dart an assessing look at Isla moving around the lounge to explore it, unable to speak freely about what I want to know with her there.

"If I had anything pressing, I'd have crashed your punishing gym rat session," Colton mumbles around a mouthful of cereal. "As for the tracking device, I spliced it back together to see where it leads us—don't give me that look, yes I cut off the signal."

My teeth clack when I snap my mouth shut. Colton rolls his eyes. Rowan gets up, stretching her arms overhead.

"I'm going to call my mom." Her sorrow-filled eyes flick to Isla, who is poking her head into the gym. She lowers her voice. "I don't want to risk not being able to talk to her once the meeting goes down."

"Go." Colt jerks his chin at his many screens. "I've got this on lock."

Rowan stops by Isla to hug her before she heads for her and Wren's room. Colt gets up with his empty cereal bowl while Isla returns to my side. We both study the wall of monitors.

"I missed an important class today." Her gaze finds my stony profile. "Colton and Wren said I have to stay here since Colton can't spare the time to take me to campus."

I grunt. It's the right choice, the same one I would've made.

"You'd rather risk giving your attacker another opportunity to take you? They're not going to stop."

Isla turns back to the wall of computer screens. "I know. This is just strange. I don't enjoy feeling...caged in."

Quiet settles over us for a few seconds.

She gasps. Trepidation fills me and my gaze flies over the screens again, worrying that Colton has something up she shouldn't see. Before I register what's happening, she rushes the door. She's fucking fast. Shocked, I charge after her, biting back a curse. She got the drop on me, but I'm better trained to move than she is.

The ruthlessly tactical side of me thinks this is it, the moment I've been waiting for where she runs to spill the secrets we've given her access to, while another, deeper, primitive part of me that resurfaced with the way she fascinates me *hates* the sight of her running from me.

She should run. I'd only diminish her bright light if she spends too much time around me.

We're inches from the main stairwell when I catch her around the waist, pinning her to the wall with my front to her back.

"What do you think you're doing?" I demand.

She startles at my harsh tone, but relaxes beneath me. Another wave of shock filters through my fury. How is she completely unafraid when it should terrify her to be at my mercy?

"It's raining," she says breathlessly, excitement creeping into her tone. Raining. It was the outdoor security feed that pulled this reaction from her. When I remain silent, she elaborates. "I love the rain. Can I go outside? I want to dance in it."

The rain. An echo of grief pangs in my chest. My mom loved the rain. I've grown to hate it because I lost her twice in the rain.

Isla's excitement reminds me of Mom's.

My jaw works. It takes effort to peel myself from her.

"Come with me," I say roughly.

Instead of taking the main exit from the Nest, I lead her a different way. We climb stone steps into the hotel. They were once the steps to an old wine cellar according to the original blueprints before we renovated the sublevel. The peeling wallpaper and what's left of the warped floorboards smell musty from the moisture in the air. A misty fog clings to the grounds, visible through dusty windows, rolling in off the ocean.

I focus on Isla's bubbling excitement to keep myself from thinking of the rain splattering the car when I was a kid before it was ambushed by the men who kidnapped me and my mom.

We reach an inner courtyard with an overhang. The crumbling stone is choked with overgrowth, weeds sprouting from every crevice and ivy swallowing half of the arches. From here, she can do what she will no doubt continue hounding me about until I grant permission while I keep watch from under the overhang without getting wet.

"This is amazing," she breathes.

In the uncovered center, rainfall pours down, saturating the ground with puddles. I stiffen at the distant rumble of thunder. Storms like this are rare during fall in Maine, but when they happen they set my teeth on edge.

It was during a storm like this I was kidnapped for ransom. My shoulder tingles where one of my many tattoos honors my mother. I hate the goddamn rain.

While I'm locked in my thoughts battling sickening memories, Isla steps out with her palms and face upturned. Droplets quickly drench her skin and she grins, closing her eyes like she's in heaven.

"This is my favorite feeling in the world," she murmurs, barely loud enough to be heard over the steady rain.

We're so different. I can't imagine loving this. Not when it's brought me nothing but pain. I relive my nightmares every time it storms, unable to reconcile loving the rain.

Isla doesn't pay me much attention, stepping out into the courtyard while I stand guard. She spends a few moments holding her arms out and spinning, clearly enjoying herself. When she breaks out into a dance, my breathing grows rough.

Crossing my arms, I battle the urge to step out into the rainfall to chase her, to capture her, to kiss her like I've always dreamed of doing.

One taste.

No. I'm not built for a single taste.

I can't deny her beautiful dexterity or the emotion she evokes with each arch of her body, kick of her long legs, and the expressions on her face as she uses her entire body to tell me a story. Freedom, that's the sense I get watching her dance in the rain.

What does a spoiled, rich daughter of a corrupt senator know about freedom? She has no business dancing as if it's her only saving grace on this earth.

She's getting soaked to the bone, my shirt clinging to her skin. Her nipples are hard, but she does nothing to hide from me. A harsh exhale leaves me at her carefree laughter. She uses the space, kicking water from a puddle. If it were a fight, I'd do the same.

It's a cruel challenge to see her enjoying this so much when another boom of thunder through the hiss of rainfall has me reliving flashes of the worst day of my life in vivid detail. Screams drowned out by rain, the invasive sense of helplessness, my mother's cold fingers ripped from my small hand as the kidnappers carted her off where I couldn't see, but I could still fucking hear everything. The flashes don't stop.

Heart drumming at a rate that feels like I'll die suffering through the memories, I pivot away from the courtyard and slam a palm against the cold stone. My panting breaths come out ragged. It hasn't been this bad in years. My control is slipping, my usual methods for keeping my demons at bay no longer enough.

Another laugh from Isla is like a soothing balm to the ache in my chest. I angle my head, finding her swiping wet strands of hair back, her bright smile turned up to the sky.

I focus on her until my breathing returns to normal, the intense heartache fading. She leads me out of the shadows that chain my mind in turmoil with that unburdened smile, the natural glow of her happiness despite the dangerous reason she's here twining around me, making it impossible to look away from her.

It's the same feeling I got when I first saw her crying at fourteen. The sense that no matter how dark the world gets, there is reason to survive.

"You should come out here, this is fantastic!" Isla whoops, lifting her arms overhead. "Come on, Levi! Feel the rain with me."

"I'm good here." I push away from the wall and cross my arms, taking up my guarding stance once more. The tip of my tongue prods at my lip ring. "But I'm watching."

At the rough gravel riding my voice, she turns to meet my eyes.

"Let me give you a good show then." The corner of her mouth quirks up.

This time when she moves, I lock my attention on her. It keeps me in check, distracting me from the demons clambering for my attention.

I find myself planning out a training plan tailored to her to capitalize on her strengths. It's ridiculous. We're granting her our protection, harboring her from whoever is after her, but I only train my brothers and Rowan. I have no purpose for training her other than the satisfaction it would bring me to hone her skills and bring out her potential, to teach her how to defend herself, how to kill.

I shake my head to dispel the fantasy. That's all it is, all it can ever be between us.

Attraction is another form of weakness. I can acknowledge that she's gorgeous without acting on it. I never will.

This girl worms her way in with disarming smiles and a bubbly personality. Colton's easy, but even Wren finds her antics amusing. Isla Vonn is a distraction I don't need. A temptation that would spell my downfall. I'm closed off for a reason. I work better that way, more suited to observing everything around me, assess threats before they develop as long as I remain detached.

I've kept my distance, ignored the desire for her that simmers in my veins. If I drop my guard, she'll crash through my walls and find a monster waiting for her where my heart should be.

Monsters don't get to have the princess.

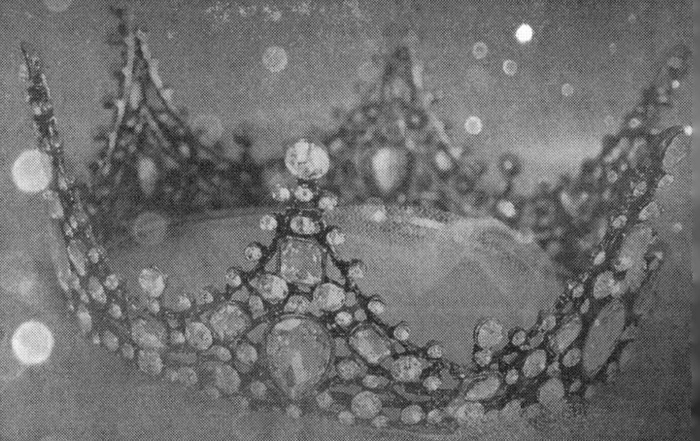

CHAPTER NINE

ISLA

When I can't move without shivering, Levi announces that it's time to go inside with a gruff order. Even his grouchy attitude doesn't dispel how invigorated I feel.

With a wide smile, I step under the covered archway, wringing out excess water from my sopping wet hair. A shudder moves through me from the chilly breeze. Without a word, he shifts to block me from the gust of wind. Warmth bubbles up in my chest. He keeps doing that—shielding me, making sure I'm okay.

"Let's go." He remains taciturn and stiff, chiseled jaw set as he strides away.

I follow through the Crow's Nest Hotel's forgotten halls, dripping water every step of the way. Nothing comforts me as much as dancing in the rain, the cool water washing away all my worries while I let go and give myself over to things I can't voice eloquently without dance. I needed this to process the lingering fears and implications from the other night.

Levi escorts me back to my room and unlocks the door for me.

"Thank you." My murmured gratitude encompasses more than the gesture, meaning letting me dance, and for saving me.

His dark gaze rips away from me, but he lingers. "You should shower. For working your muscles, and to warm up so you don't get sick." He opens and closes his mouth, glancing briefly at the wet shirt clinging to my skin. "Are your other clothes dry?"

"Probably not. I'll put the hoodie back on." A growl vibrates in his throat and I roll my lips between my teeth to hold back a smile. He never says more than he deems necessary, but he projects more than he thinks he does when he's around me. "I'll see what else Rowan lent me."

Levi nods curtly, then leaves me alone. I shake my head wryly as I strip out of the wet clothes. The rooms might be plain for boys who grew up in opulent homes, but they spared no expense on the bathrooms. I sigh in bliss as I climb beneath the dual shower head, the hot water eliciting goosebumps across my chilled damp skin. Rather than a stall or glass walls, it has an open layout with slate tile marking the area.

I'm cut off from the world in a bubble. It's odd not having my parents hovering over me. Even when they've been absent, their reach finds me. No one can get me while I'm here. The only place the kidnappers can sink their grimy claws in me are in my dreams. Sleep hasn't come as restfully as I wanted, but dancing helped.

I thought I'd be able to move on like I have from every other traumatic hardship I've faced, but when I brought up my class schedule, I was shut down. For my protection, Colton claimed.

Thank god I got to dance, or I'd go stir crazy. It's the only thing that keeps the feeling of being trapped in a cage at bay. It's not that the Nest isn't wonderful, just that I don't like standing still or feeling stuck. It's always made me feel like if I'm not moving, then the things I've worked to keep behind a wall in my mind will crash through to get to me.

My fingers sift through the silky strands of my hair as I rinse it. I'm still getting used to dancing for an audience. It was nice having Levi's brooding gaze roaming every inch of my body. He couldn't take his eyes off me. And if I go by the undeniable bulge I saw in his black sweatpants when I came closer, he liked what he saw.

I bite my lip to hold back a smile. Body talk, that's all it is between us. He was presented with a wet shirt plastered to boobs, of course he was going to react.

A small part of me allows the idea he's secretly crushing on me like I've been drawn to him and a soft laugh escapes me.

When I finish my shower, I find a stack of clothes on the bed. My gaze slides to the door left slightly ajar, no longer locking me in. I pick up a Henley that matches the one I had on twenty minutes ago, catching a hint of patchouli.

Levi.

A warm glow flickers to life in my chest. The shirt is soft between my fingers. He was so hostile toward me the first night here, yet he was somehow more centered when he emerged from the gym this morning. The shadows that haunt his alluring eyes weren't as intense. Behind his observant, brooding nature, he finds all these little ways to take care of those around him.

I get dressed in his clothes, ignoring the pleasant dip in my stomach as his spicy scent winds around me, then pad from the room with damp hair. My feminine style has always been my own form of armor, a way to hide my invisible cracks under a dazzling red smile. It's odd to go around without makeup or styling my hair, but I'm taking a page out of Rowan's comfort queen fashion book until my purse is returned to me.

Thinking of the purse brings up a fact I've been burying under everything else in the couple of days since I've been here—my dad gifting it to me. If his debts are bad enough he needs to use me in some way, I need to be careful. It won't be the first time he sold me off for his own gains. He's a ruthless politician and even as his daughter, I'm not safe from his scheming.

My stomach turns and my heart aches.

Tense voices pull my attention as I approach the main area everyone congregates in. This place is a maze. I'm impressed I found my way without Rowan to guide me.

"—need some way to cover you. They want you there alone for a reason. I still don't like it." That was Levi.

I creep along the wall and peek around the corner. The notorious Crows are all gathered, Levi leaning against Colton's desk like a hot formidable sentinel, Jude and Wren seated on the black leather couches, Rowan perched on the arm next to Wren. It's rare for me to see them like this. Their reputations built in high school like a wildfire, rapid and merciless. No one gets close to them.

Studying them from my vantage point, I can't deny how well Rowan fits in with them, her expression fierce.

My attention lingers on Levi. Heat builds in my core at the sight of him. The sleeves of his Henley shirt are pushed up to reveal his inked forearms, the veins prominent. His collar is open, giving me a peek at more tattoos painting his body, and the hint of a barbell piercing his nipple is visible through the shirt.

It's undeniable that he's imposing. It only adds to how sexy he is. Everyone is terrified of him, but I don't share their fear. I never have.

As grumpy and foreboding as he can be, he still stood guard over me in their nightclub without leaving my side, not allowing me to touch my drinks before he was satisfied they were safe to have. I've always found him interesting, but after that night, there's something about him that's taken root in my head and my fantasies.

Levi gives off the kind of vibe like he'd cut someone's eyes out for looking at his girl the wrong way, then fuck her to prove she's his to cherish. Maybe it's the horrors I've seen growing up in this city, but instead of finding the thought repulsive, it turns me on.

Cheeks prickling, I tear my gaze from checking him out.

Unlike earlier, every inch of the wall of computer monitors is covered with photos and information. Plans for a Halloween party in the far corner catch my interest until I hear more of their conversation.

"It's not just on the invite," Rowan says. "*Clavis ad regnum* is probably hidden all over the city, just like on campus."

Latin. The stuffy phrase that roughly translates to keys to the kingdom. My brows furrow. We found it together when we followed the creep stalking her around campus weeks ago.

"Their reach could extend beyond what we thought," Jude says. "If we're right about this, then it's likely every powerful player is a member. Who knows how far back their little club dates. These sort of things are passed through generations with closely guarded secrets."

"We've never met a secret we couldn't steal for ourselves," Colton says. "Not about to choke now."

What the hell is going on? I step out into the lounge, frowning at Colton's screens. What are they up to?

"Hey." Levi spots me first, coming away from bracing against the desk in a fluid movement. He scowls at me. "You shouldn't be out here. What did I say about the rules?"

Pursing my lips, I lift my chin primly. He can do his best to control me, but I'm an expert at evading those that want to cage me with orders. He'll have to do better than growling in my face every chance he gets. It won't keep me in line.

Jude strokes his chin, assessing me with an unreadable look.

"I know what that means." I point at the blown up card on the screen showing the Latin phrase. "Keys to the kingdom. It's a rough translation. It was on that ugly bust of one of the founders in Withermore Hall. I was with Rowan that day." I grimace at the memory of that man. "The guy we followed was a total sleaze."

Levi's jaw clenches.

"It's true. She's the reason I know. She told me when we were scoping out the hidden door on campus." Rowan gives me a supportive nod. "She already knows a little about it all."

"We need fresh eyes." Colton winks at me. "Let her stay."

"Bullshit." Levi looks to Wren and Jude to back him up.

I square my shoulders and stride across the room. "I want to help if it gives you answers about the sick psychos who were after Rowan."

Wren surveys me with a hint of amusement flickering in his icy blue eyes. "Is that so, Miss Vonn?"

I nod firmly.

Jude snorts, offering me a Cheshire cat type of smirk—all mystery, but no truth behind it. I'm familiar with his smoke and mirrors act. He's been perfecting it since Thorne Point Academy.

Levi and Wren exchange a look full of silent communication. A muscle in Levi's cheek twitches viciously when Wren looks to Jude, then Colt. Their bond runs deep to be able to have an entire conversation without words. It's impressive. No wonder they've grown into formidable shadows the whole city whispers about.

I relax when Wren nods at me. The decision is made whether Levi likes it or not.

Levi scoffs, returning to his post leaning against Colton's desk. I don't break under his steely gaze, meeting it with stubborn confidence. He can deal with it.

"So, what am I looking at?" I point at the screen.

"A cryptic message from a bunch of assholes," Rowan mutters.

Wren chuckles, tugging her close to kiss her temple. She ends up in his lap, leaning into him.

"My dad made me learn Latin. His aspirations for me were of the law school variety, so he deemed it one of my necessary requirements to take Latin." I fold an arm over my waist and rest my chin against my fist. "Keys to the kingdom is a prominent phrase found throughout Thorne Point's history. I used to think it was pretentious as fuck in my Latin workbooks."

"Everything since the city's founding is pretentious as fuck." Jude's handsome golden eyes almost twinkle with his acerbic humor.

"Truth." Rowan snorts.

"What does it mean?" Wren prompts.

"The obvious symbolism is Heaven." I wave a hand. "But as we've established—pretentious. The application of the phrase can cover a lot of bases. It's probably why the university puts it on plaques of unmarked founder statues. It's more like...an ideal. Your perceived Heaven."

Jude and Wren make inquisitive sounds of interest. Levi narrows his eyes, dipping his chin so his inky fringe slips into his face. He says nothing, toying with his lip ring, his tattooed forearms flexing.

"It tracks for our theory." Rowan lifts her brows at Wren pointedly. He hums in agreement. "What about the key part?"

"If kingdom is the utopia, then the key is the vehicle. The methods used to create the perfect world. The founders of the city might have picked it up because they considered themselves kings of the kingdom they were shaping."

They all nod, even Levi, brows wrinkled in thought. It feels good to help them, like the perspective I offer is a thank you for giving me a safe haven to crash after my attack. It makes me feel useful to contribute, less like I'm a helpless victim hiding away from the monsters out to get me.

"The key is power," Wren murmurs.

"Fucking keys!" Rowan and Colton say it at the same time, hands thrown up. They look at each other in surprise before breaking off in laughter.

Wren strokes his sharp jaw. "What about *carpe regnum*? What can you tell me about that?"

"Seize the kingdom. If you were to pair it with *clavis ad regnum* in conjunction, then I'd interpret it as a call to arms." My lips move to the side in consideration. I'm rusty on this stuff, but I follow my gut. "It could be a promise to the ideal."

They all share complicated looks. Whatever they're mixed up in, it's big.

"Damn, babe. Why didn't we know you had a big beautiful brain to go with those legs I dream of having wrapped around my head?" Colton dodges the pillow Rowan flings at him, only to catch Levi's swift smack to the back of his head. He holds his hands up sheepishly in surrender, winking at me. I cross my arms, popping my hip out. "Purely fantasy. But for real, this is the angle we needed. Thanks, Isles."

The nickname has an affectionate smile breaking through my stern expression. Colton's flirting is a harmless part of his disarming charm. If I've earned a nickname, I hope it means he accepts my friendship. I need someone else in my corner around here besides Rowan.

My gaze sweeps over the screens and I frown. "Anything to help you get the bastards."

Jude releases a dark laugh that sends a shiver down my spine. "I forgot how much I liked you." Again he gives me a calculating once over. "You're full of surprises."

Levi glances between us with a dangerous glint in his eyes.

"We've unleashed chaos for lesser transgressions," Wren says coldly. "Those who cross the Crows sign their death wishes in blood. Before it dries, we'll end them."

Colton's face splits in an unhinged, menacing smile and he thumps a fist on the desk. "Hear fucking hear."

In that moment, I believe all of them are capable of what the rumors say—even Rowan. The thirst for violence is evident in all of them.

Colton swivels in his orange chair, tapping a sequence of keys on the keyboard that shuffles the information around on the screens. "On that note of psychos begging for a spanking, here." He crooks his finger to call me over. When I reach him, he returns my phone and motions to my purse. "All clean."

"Thank you." Having my phone back feels like a lifeline restored. I unlock it and begin skimming missed notifications. Oddly, there aren't any messages or missed calls from my parents. Not only odd, but ominous in a way I shove down. When I register the press of eyes on me from all sides, I lift my gaze to Colton's. His expression is grim. "Is there a but?"

"There is." He blows out a sigh, nodding to the screen. It's all gibberish computer code to me. "There was malware installed in a hidden app on your phone. Ever heard of PikCell? Did you download it?"

I blink, shaking my head. "No. What do you mean a hidden app? How would it get there?"

The corner of his mouth lifts in a smile, but it's not a nice one. "Easy. I could do it in my sleep."

"I didn't even notice it was there."

"That's the intention. It's meant to look like something you would've downloaded and forgot about. This one is designed to fit in with your photography apps." His playful nature is muted with a flash of cold ire beneath. "Whoever installed it was spying on your conversations and photos. You have to be careful, babe. This is basic shit, so it's not easy to narrow down who's behind it, either. Not one of my underlings—they know their king would come for them."

Jude rolls his eyes and mutters something in Spanish that sounds like an insult. It makes Wren bark out a caustic laugh. My hands shake as I swipe through my phone. The thought of someone reading through my messages and having access to my photos makes my skin crawl. My privacy has been violated and I didn't even realize.

Swallowing, I check the texts again. The lack of messages from my parents worrying about me disappearing for two days has me stumped. They might be absent, but something about this lack of demanding to know where I am right now tugs at me. My brows pinch and I switch to the mobile browser to search for local headlines.

Nothing.

No news or police reports of me missing.

That's impossible. How could they not notice when I didn't come home the other night? Aren't they wondering where I am? I've been shirking their expectations with rebellion lately, especially with the late in the game major change to focus on dance, but I can't wrap my head around no one noticing me being gone.

Not even social media.

If they don't care...does it mean they're involved? The thought brings up bad memories from seven years ago. I can't face a repeat of that horrible night.

I look up and find Levi watching me. He's always watching. I swallow, feeling on display.

I lift the phone to my ear before Colt darts forward in a surprisingly quick move, grasping my wrist. He ends the call before it connects. Levi appears at my back, a wall of warm, firm muscle. He slips an arm around me and takes my phone, trapping me against his body.

"What—?"

"Sorry, babe. You can't call anyone." Colton's touch is gentle. He brushes my wrist with his thumb, and I swear I hear a rumble of frustration from Levi behind me. "Not yet anyway."

"Why not?" I look to Rowan for reassurance. She nods. "I should at least let someone at my house know I'm okay. Alive, healthy, and all that."

I hold up jazz hands, but it does little to make me feel better. The positive light I strive for doesn't wash away the slimy feeling clinging to my skin.

If I talk to my parents, then I'll know whether they were involved or not. My heart thumps with heavy beats. One way or another, I need to find out if my greatest fear is coming to life.

"We don't have solid answers yet." Wren draws everyone's attention. Whenever he speaks, he commands the room with ease. He's already a powerful man at twenty-three, and I imagine his power will only continue to strengthen. "We want to know who orchestrated the attack, and we're not ruling your parents out."

My heart beats harder. Not ruling out. He has the same questions I do. "It's not them."

"We'll keep you safe." Levi's rough words and the gust of hot breath coasting over the back of my neck make my heart thump and my body warm. "That's an oath I'll swear to."

CHAPTER TEN

LEVI

THE promise leaves my lips before I think about what it means. How does this keep happening? My ironclad control goes to shit when it comes to her. It's growing more difficult to keep myself in check, unfamiliar emotions surging the more time I'm forced to spend near her, in close quarters with my obsession.

I clench my teeth at Isla's demure nod. Some of the panic eases from her bright blue eyes. I don't like the way it makes a strange sensation expand and settle in my chest, like I'm personally responsible for her. I didn't sign up for this shit.

I cut a sharp look at Wren, annoyed as hell that he allowed her to stay here, to share information on our situation with her. We share our secrets with no one outside of the bond we forged to create our family.

Not only is this not Isla's goddamn business, but by bringing her in we have to worry about keeping her safe. It splits our attention from what we need to focus on to face the threat of a possible secret society going against us. We're not running a fucking babysitting service for wayward heiresses. Rowan was an exception. She carved out her space with us and earned our trust. The same can't be said for Isla Vonn.

I can't imagine her doing the things Rowan has done—the pampered princess wouldn't know the first thing about setting a warehouse on fire.

Despite the temptation of Isla's open honesty and lack of fear, I'm not ready to trust her. If I do, it will lead to me giving in to other things I've fought. The pull toward her will win, luring me to make my fantasies a reality.

Wren tips his head in my direction while absently stroking Rowan's back. He knows I'm pissed, but he won't give an inch. Bastard.

He's changed since falling for Rowan. Still deadly as any of us, but the haunted parts of our friend are less present. He's not as broken, his love for Rowan filling in the cracked spaces in his heart after his sister's suicide.

I scrub a hand over my jaw, turning away. It's getting late. My uncle will be expecting me.

"I'm due for my regular visit to see my mom," I say. "I'll find out what I can, try to get my uncle to say anything about the invitation."

"Get a photo of the signet ring, too," Wren directs. "My father will be suspicious if I go for his. Let them believe we're in the dark."

Jude pulls out a coin from his pocket, making it dance across his fingers with the practiced skill of a con man. "Let's keep it that way as long as we can. It'll be an Ace up our sleeves."

"Once you get it, we can compare it to this." Colt waves to the crossed keys printed on the card on his screen. He pushes off with his feet, riding his gamer chair to the end of his desk. "And take this. Let's kill two birds with one stone and figure out why he's in Hannigan's corrupted file."

"Is that a bug?" Rowan asks.

"Yep," Colt answers proudly. "Way more advanced than the shit they planted in your crap box apartment."

Her brows flatten. "How so?"

Colt makes a showy gesture with his hands and grins. "Because I designed and built it, babe. Duh."

A laugh huffs out of Isla. "Still full of yourself, I see."

"You have no idea, sweetheart," Jude grumbles, dragging his free hand down his face. "He's a nightmare."

"Ay, but you still love me." Colton puckers his lip and makes kissing sounds at Jude.

I plant my hand over his face and push until he nearly loses his balance. The guys chuckle. This is what I'll fight the world for, this friendship with them.

"Dick," Colton bites out affectionately. He hands over the small listening device with a gleam in his eyes. "Okay, this one's new. Watch." He uses the edge of his nail to lift an invisible catch and peels back a thin, filmy layer. "There's a frequency emitter chip embedded into the film. It'll broadcast back to me. And this part—" He indicates the round base, no bigger than the head of a thumb tack. "—is a beauty of my genius."

"Colt," I growl. "Just tell me what the fuck it does and where to plant it without whipping your dick out to stroke your pain in the ass ego."

Isla and Rowan laugh. Colton's grin stretches.

"It's a Trojan and a listening device two-in-one. Less shit to bug, perfect for when you're short on time."

"Wait—you're saying you made this? That sounds like military-grade spy equipment." Isla sounds impressed and, irrationally, it pisses me off. When the others glance at her curiously, she blushes a pretty shade of pink. "My family goes all out for security. You can never be too careful." She waves her phone. "Something I'm learning first hand."

"Damn right I made it." Colton places a hand on his chest and tugs at the collar of his graphic t-shirt. "I'm a boy genius, baby."

"Don't get him started," Wren mutters. "This will give us access to the files on his computer and record conversations?"

"Precisely, big guy."

"Good." His expression darkens. Rowan shifts closer, putting a hand over his heart. He tangles his fingers with hers. "They think they can toy with us. It's time to remind them who reigns in the goddamn dark."

My mouth curves without a trace of humor. Jude and Colton wear similar expressions.

"Does it need a certain range?" I ask.

"As long as it's in the room. Closer to the computer, the better, but if you're in a pinch it should still connect and infiltrate his firewalls from within the same room."

"Got it." I take the device and pull my walls around me like I'm going into battle. When it involves my Uncle Baron, it might as well be.

"Do you want company? Or, like, back up?" Isla peers up at me with such an open expression that my heart aches to be the protection she won't give herself. Her lips twist wryly. "Or is that not within the rules?"

"You're staying here," I grunt.

Pain in my ass or not, I'd never let her within a hundred feet of my devil of an uncle if I could help it. He takes everything I love from me. If he caught a hint of my interest toward her, he'd act without mercy to tear her away from me, too.

"Come on. I've got something better we can do." Rowan kisses Wren's cheek. He doesn't let her go without capturing her lips with a deep kiss that leaves her shivering. When she pulls out of his grasp, she takes Isla's hand. "You'll never believe the grounds here. It stopped raining. Let's explore."

"Stay out of the hedge maze. Keep to the inner areas and the cliffs."

Rowan spins around at Wren's command with a glint in her green eyes. "Why?"

Wren gets to his feet, standing tall over the girls. He gives his girlfriend a wolfish smile. "Because, kitten. If I know you're in the hedge maze, I might get the urge to hunt you down."

Color floods Rowan's cheeks and she bites her lip. Isla's gaze bounces between them and she smirks.

"You heard the man, babe." She hooks her arm in Rowan's, leading her down the hall. "And while we explore, you can regale me with erotic tales of the sexy fun time maze."

Colton snorts. "Totally calling it that from now on."

As they disappear around the corner, I ball my hands, nails digging into my callused palms to stave off the images Isla's words put in my head of *me* hunting *her* through the hedge maze.

It plays out in my head in enticing detail, how her hips would sway, the whip of her brown hair as she checked for the predator hunting her down, the moment I'd capture her, and the gasp she would make. Satisfaction and arousal ripple through me as the fantasy culminates with a feral kiss driven by the hunger she's stirred in me for years.

My brothers watch my reaction with interest, exchanging glances they think are subtle, but I miss nothing. Narrowing my eyes, I stalk away to put myself through hell.

* * *

Baron Astor's estate is much like any other Thorne Point elite family home—the historic gothic facade soaked in blood. My uncle has always said that to gain power, one must be willing to sacrifice, but to maintain it, one must become the strongest version of themself.

As a boy, before I learned the truth, I took it to heart, believing he was a strong man. Once I found out what he did to my family—his own blood—I realized what he really meant. Strength to him is really a moniker for the evil he commits to stay on top of the world.

I grimace behind the tinted shield of my motorcycle helmet as I pass through the wrought iron gates, my Ducati cutting through the fog left over from the morning's rain. He hates my bike, so I always take it when I come here.

It's not a home.

It hasn't been my home for a long time.

The earliest memories of my childhood before being kidnapped are hazy and distant. Sometimes the scent of the rose bushes Mom liked to sit by while I played trigger a memory of digging through the dirt for worms while she cheered me on for my finds. She was always smiling. What we went through tore that natural joy away from her.

The long driveway is lined with towering stone statues of gargoyles. My bike speeds past them to reach the grand entrance at the end. I pull beneath the covered structure protecting the ornate double wooden doors in its shadows. Swinging off the bike, I tug the helmet from my head.

A member of the household staff holds the door open, but I don't go inside. The young girl must be new. She doesn't know my routine.

My strides along the cobblestone path hugging the mansion are steady, but my heart thumps erratically. As much as I strive for control, this is one thing I've never managed to stamp out. I swallow when I reach the gates to the cemetery. Most of the city's families moved their old family plots, but the Astors have always been buried on their own soil.

My parents are no exception.

I push through the gate and draw a fortifying breath that burns my lungs. Their headstones are front and center, newer and better maintained than the last burial—my grandparents. I kneel before the polished granite and brush my fingers over Mom's name carved with such finality.

Isabelle Christine Astor. Loving daughter, sister, wife, and mother. In Memoriam 1976-2007.

The date she died is inked into my shoulder in Roman numerals, X IV MMVII. It's been fourteen years since I lost her. I was only eight.

"Hi mom," I rasp. "It's been a while."

I don't know why I always end up talking to the gravestone. I'm not someone that believes she's listening or watching over me. There's nothing of her left in the ground, just rotting bones.

"I miss you." My voice grows tight.

I hate that the memories of her screams while our kidnappers raped her are more vivid than the sound of her laugh from before. Remembering *before* is so hard.

Harsh breaths sear my lungs. With a jerking movement, I whip out one of my knives and drive it into the soft earth, twisting while visualizing torturing those who hurt us both. I was so helpless and small then, I couldn't fight back. Couldn't stop it.

I was excited to show her something I'd made in class. Running to the car, my green rain boots splashed in puddles. It was a good day for hunting worms. I hoped Mom would allow me outside once the rain stopped.

She met me at the car like always, her bright smile making me grin. "Hello, my clever boy. How was your day?"

We got in and the driver took her umbrella before pulling away from school.

"I made you something." Being careful, I took off my backpack and dug out the drawing. She made a delighted sound. "It's your favorites."

"It is my favorites," she agreed.

Making sure she saw it all, I pointed out what I drew, tugging on my seatbelt to reach. "See, the roses, and your book, and the worms I find you, and the necklace from Dad, and the hugs I give you before bed."

For each thing I pointed out, she hummed. "It's beautiful, Levi. Thank you."

Leaning over, she cupped my head and kissed it.

"Mom," I complained. "Kisses are for little babies. I'm a big boy now."

Secretly, I still liked them.

Her laugh cut off in a gasp when the driver slammed on the brakes, the car slipping on the wet road. My seatbelt dug into my neck and I cried out in pain. Mom reached for me. I didn't like the look in her eyes. It scared me to see her like that.

"Levi—" The door opened and men were there. They reached in and grabbed her. "No!"

"Mom!" Her screams were awful. I wrestled with my seatbelt, shrinking back when a mean-faced man grabbed me. I kicked him, but his hard grip squeezed my arms and legs. "Ow! Let go!"

The men pulled us from the car and took us away. My heart hurt it was going so fast, and Mom wouldn't stop crying. I'd never heard her like that, and it made fat tears leak from the corners of my eyes. The place the men took us was dirty and far away from home. It had big windows and a metal ceiling that the rain pounded on. They were rough with us and every time they grabbed me, I wasn't strong enough.

"It will be okay, Levi," Mom promised, hugging me so tight. Her voice was wrong. "We'll be okay. Just close your eyes, baby."

When they snatched Mom, she screamed, her whole body shaking as I clung to her leg. Terror made my stomach hurt when she was wrenched away. One of the men held me and I sobbed for Mom while they dragged her where

I couldn't see.

Her cries got worse, so bad I was sick to my stomach yelling for them to stop hurting her.

"Close your eyes, Levi!" Mom shrieked between her tormented sobs.

Gritting my teeth, I drive my fist into the soggy ground, the slap of my knuckles hitting the softened earth echoing on the chilly air.

Fucking rain. I hate it.

Isla's face filters across my mind, her gorgeous smile upturned to the droplets soaking her. I draw in ragged gasps of air. The thought of her draws me back from the brink of snapping completely, helping my pained breathing calm down.

My attention shifts to Dad's grave. He took Mom's name when he married into the family. The date is more recent. Mom died a year after we were kidnapped, but Dad died when I was in high school. We lived with Baron by then. We had to, after dad lost his company shares.

That was why Baron plotted the kidnapping, to ransom Dad for his half of the shares to their company. He gained full control of everything, including guardianship of me once Dad died in a car accident.

My dad and Baron were best friends. Dad married Baron's sister. He's stolen everything from my parents, including their heir. But I'll never be his legacy, despite the fact he sees himself as my father figure to mold me to his liking. Things between us have been strained since I learned he was behind the kidnapping, paying off a third party so it wouldn't be traced to him.

But my brothers helped me find the truth.

He thought he covered his tracks so well, switching out the usual driver who chauffeured my mother to pick me up from school. The driver was paid to wait until hours after we were boxed in by unmarked cars and taken to call for help. It wasn't meant to bring any harm to me or my mother, but the men hired to do my uncle's dirty work took liberties. Baron Astor didn't care that his machinations broke his younger sister or traumatized me. All that matters to him is his wealth and power.

It took time to track them all down, but the driver and the kidnappers met their end.

Someday my uncle will know that I know what he did. Right before he becomes another target of the Leviathan. When I whisper that the Leviathan owns his soul, I want to see the recognition dawn on his face before it's all over.

A sick smile tilts my mouth. I slide my fingers over the knives hidden on me, comforted by their presence. I never leave the safety of the Nest unarmed.

I have no room for morals or remorse. All I am now is a ruthless weapon, the helpless boy I once was burned away, replaced with a dangerous, heartless man.

This is why I can't allow Isla any closer to me, even if I gave her my trust and allowed her in. She's bright and beautiful like my mom was. A monster like me doesn't deserve to diminish her radiance. And once my uncle found out about her, he'd use her in any way he could against me to bring me under his control, then find a way to get rid of her, too.

A growl tears from me. I won't let that happen. Some part of me has accepted the need to protect her.

Heaving a breath, I come out of my crouch, scrubbing my face. Once I put away the old remorse for my parents, I head back the way I came, boots trampling the manicured damp grass. Time to work.

When I make it back to the main entrance, I have to knock. There's a short wait, then the door creaks open, the young girl wide-eyed.

"Sorry," she mumbles.

Ignoring her, I stalk through the door and head straight for my uncle's study. The gloomy atmosphere with dark, austere accents inside the house seeps into my bones like an inescapable ghostly chill. I hate this cavernous mansion.

"Should I announce you to Mr. Astor?" the girl asks.

"Don't bother," I call over my shoulder, not pausing. "He knows how this song and dance goes. He'll know where to find me. He's expecting me."

I don't stick around for her response. If she's smart, she'll learn to keep her mouth shut and her eyes down. The less she sees and hears inside these walls, the more likely she is to survive servitude under my uncle. The curious ones don't last around here.

Baron's study makes him so damn easy to read. The walls are covered in hunting trophies of big game. Endangered or not, it doesn't matter to him. A cigar and a cut crystal tumbler of Cognac sit on a squat table next to the leather wingback chair by the fireplace. Every inch of this room is a power trip fantasy.

I need to work fast. Circling the antique desk, I drop to a knee and take out a roll of lock picking tools. Only one drawer remains unlocked, so I skip down two and make quick work of the lock. Satisfaction fills me as it clicks. A man like my uncle believes his power makes him untouchable. But he's not. No one truly is.

The drawer pulls out on silent tracks. I take out the bug from Colton and peel back the film layer. Slipping it carefully into the back of the drawer until I'm satisfied it's undetectable, I lock the drawer and move underneath the desk.

His stern voice filters through the thick door. I glance up sharply.

"You didn't tell me a guest had arrived? You stupid girl," he snarls. "I don't have time for such incompetency."

My lips thin as he berates his newest staff member. Her response isn't audible through the door. I press the thumbtack-sized device to infiltrate his computer on the underside of the desk.

The handle on the door turns. I let my instincts take over, melting into the shadows with swift, near-silent movements that I've spent years perfecting.

By the time my uncle opens the door, I'm staring at the latest addition to his collection—a leopard—with detached disinterest across the room.

"Levi," he greets as he moves into the room, none the wiser to the access we now have to him.

Baron is a portly man with a thick beard. If we looked similar, I'd hate him more. Thankfully I look just like my father, something I'm sure he hates since he stole me as his own heir.

My lips twitch when he moves behind me to sink into his chair by the fire with a satisfied groan. The man is getting up there in age, and he enjoys his vices.

"Did you see your mother?" He re-lights the cigar, puffing on it.

"Yes."

He never asks about my father. Probably because he put him in the ground, too. I work my jaw, straining to stay on task. If I let my emotions rule me, I'll screw up. It's why I cut them off.

My uncle grunts in acknowledgement, eyeing my leather jacket. "You drove that infernal motorcycle here. When will you grow up? Your final year at Thorne Point University won't last forever. You need to get this insolent behavior out of your system by the time you graduate."

I almost snort. None of us needed college. Between the empire we built and Colton's savvy investments, the four of us are set for life. We don't even have to touch our trust funds. Attending school is more of a way to keep out of our parents' grip for me, Wren, and Colton. Jude doesn't have the same problem. He has a great relationship with his grandmother, but the rest of us need to evade the expectations that come with being born an heir to a family legacy.

"I haven't decided what my plans are after graduating." I know it irritates him. The throbbing vein in his temple brings me great pleasure. "Maybe I'll travel."

"You have a place. After graduation, you will take up the responsibility awaiting you."

Grumbling under his breath, he ashes his cigar. His movements are sloppy, sluggish from alcohol. He's drunk. The signet ring sits on his fat pinkie knuckle. I've rarely seen him take it off. I fake receiving a text, taking my phone out. I open the camera and put effort into the lazy steps closer to the fireplace. With the fire at my back, the lighting is the best I'll get.

"What's one more year? The company isn't hurting." I angle my phone with a bored expression. "We both know I'd be filling more of an honorary seat."

"That's not—"

He cuts off, waving his hand. When he rests it on the arm of his chair, it puts it at the perfect angle. I snap several photos, then switch to video to record a short clip for Colton to analyze.

"You are meant for greatness. Your father couldn't handle it, but you..." His eyes gleam with sinister greed. "You, my boy, are born for it. When graduation comes, then the time will be right."

That snags my interest. "Why then? What's the point of all the secrecy?"

"I'm not at liberty to say. But once you know, you'll understand why. You'll understand everything." He puffs a cloud of cigar smoke and frowns at me. "You have until then to get this ridiculousness all out."

My mind turns with what he let slip. Graduation. That's why Wren got the summons and not me or Colton.

I tap out a text without looking, letting them know it's done.

"I know you'll make me proud," he says. "You'll achieve what your father never did. He proved to be a weak man in the end, but you, Levi. You are a strong man."

My teeth grind. "I need to go."

He offers an unfriendly grin. "You never stay long anymore."

"I have a paper due," I lie, voice devoid of emotion.

"Go do the Astor name proud, son." He raises his glass in toast to me.

Sucking in a sharp breath, I get the hell out of there before one of my knives finds a new home in his carotid artery.

He doesn't know it yet, but he's dug another foot deeper in the grave waiting for him.

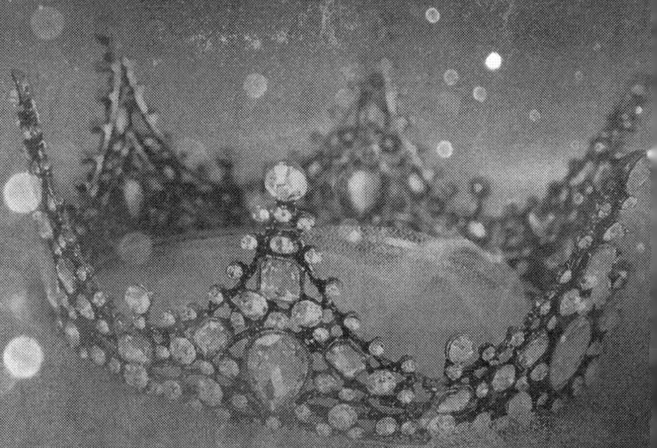

CHAPTER ELEVEN

ISLA

After I explored the extensive hotel grounds with Rowan, Levi returned late in the afternoon. Whatever he found after bugging his uncle's office, it must have been huge. Everyone became scarce for the rest of the week.

Telling time in the sublevel beneath the hotel is difficult, but with my phone back in my possession I'm able to know what day and time it is. While they're busy, I find spaces to dance. It's the only thing keeping me from going crazy surrounded by windowless walls.

Everyone believes they're keeping me safe, but without returning to my normal routine, the only thing I'm left with are my thoughts. Being alone with my thoughts without my friends to distract me has always been a dangerous cocktail for me, sending me spirality into memories. Without being able to keep moving, it forces me to relive the attack, putting the experience under a microscope without much to distract me. Dancing wherever I'm able to is my last ditch effort to center myself.

The attempted kidnapping has worked its way beneath my skin, slithered into my dreams in an inescapable cycle, just like the last nightmare I faced seven years ago at the dinner that wasn't a dinner at all. I'm not a fan of the way it makes my skin feel too tight, like I'll never be able to shake off the weight the memory leaves piled on my shoulders.

Each time I think about how terrifying it was to be grabbed in the garage, my mind amplifies it with the old, gut-wrenching horror of being drugged in a bed with no escape while I was violated.

It's never been this hard to reach for my inner light.

Maybe I need one of those UV sun lamps. The amusing thought eases the sting for a moment before everything creeps back in.

The other thing I can't stop thinking about is Wren's suspicion that my parents are behind this, painting a target on my back. It's planted a seed of unease that's only grown roots, making it something I can't ignore anymore. Dad gave me the Dior purse. I can't keep hiding from that fact, even if it slices into me, digging deep into the old wounds from the last time he used me as a pawn. That's what I've always been to him.

Every time the thought crosses my mind, my throat constricts with a searing pain. It's the same fear and disorientation I experienced in the days after I woke up in my bed after being drugged at a remote estate outside the city. Dancing is the only thing that finally helped me lay my inescapable trepidation that I'd be sent back to that awful place, and the kidnapping incident has brought it all to the forefront of my mind.

In the Nest, I'm finally free of Dad's constant control over me, but it's not as freeing as I always dreamed it would be to get away. My trust fund still chains me to my parents, otherwise I would've moved out the minute I could.

They still haven't contacted me, and dread floods my system every time I've worked up the courage to call them. I can't avoid them forever, and I can't stay here forever.

* * *

On Monday, over a week since the attack in the garage, I'm desperate to move to keep the negativity in check. It's the only way I know how to work out my problems.

Despite Levi's rules, the rest of the guys pay me little mind. They know I'm not a threat to them. I'm given the freedom to roam the halls of their hideout. Colton even programs my handprint so I don't have to rely on someone to let me inside my room.

Yesterday I found a large open room with nothing in it not far from my bedroom. It's Spartan, but it's big enough to dance in, and the acoustics are great. As long as I ignore the suspicious dark brownish-red stain in the corner, I'm golden.

My warm up playlist reverberates off the walls and the sound waves tremor in my body as I stretch to loosen up. I haven't danced seriously since that day in the rain last week, with Levi's brooding gaze tracking my every movement.

When I switch the track to the song for my Lyrical showcase routine, I find my starting position and sync my breathing to the beat of the music, allowing myself to feel everything this dance taps into. The first time I did it, it was a catharsis that touched close to home, giving me the expressive space to push my dark secret and the pain it caused me into every leap and twirl.

Since the attack, the movements feel more raw, growing sharper. I'm curious what my instructor will say when she sees the shift.

Rather than fight it, I lean into it, focusing on my rhythm and feeling the choreography.

My breathing is ragged from running through the dance until sweat beaded on my forehead when I realize I'm no longer alone. I come out of a pirouette and almost tumble off balance when I spot a shadowy figure in the corner with his arms crossed.

Levi.

He's eerily still.

It's only my natural limberness that helps me stay on my feet. Taking a breath, I fall back into the choreography after the next eight count, finishing it out. There's something about him watching me dance that tethers me, soothing the barrage of thoughts plaguing me in the last few days. The song repeats and I run through the dance twice more while he remains a silent observer.

Once he knows I'm aware of him, he takes out a short blade that he flips end over end, catching the pommel with practiced ease, then switches into an exercise that looks complicated, catching the flat side of the knife on the back of his knuckles to balance it before flicking it into the air for another skilled catch. I've noticed he seems to do it often when he's thinking. I have dance to calm myself; he has...knife flipping.

The competent display instills a different type of warmth throughout my body than the burn of exertion I've worked up from dancing, the languid heat making me slide my thighs together to stave off a coil of arousal at the sight.

I pause to gulp from the water bottle I found in the kitchen before coming down here. "Are you going to say anything, or continue to lurk?"

His eyes sweep over me, then he finally speaks. "If you don't want me to think of you as a prisoner, you probably shouldn't hang out in one of our holding rooms."

A laugh slips out of me. "You're the one who wants to keep me locked up. Do you and Wren share that kink?"

He narrows his eyes and pushes off the wall, stalking into my space. "It's not sexual. I would just rather you be out of my damn hair."

"Right." That's totally why he keeps seeking me out.

I will my attention not to drift to the corner with the mysterious stain, tracking the flick of his wrist when he falls back a step and continues throwing his knife. *Holding room.* Who the hell have these boys become, and what are they doing? Between this, the ability to kill, and the surveillance, the rumors about them only scratch the surface.

Playing with the cap to the water bottle, I tilt my head to the side. "How did it go planting the bug?"

Levi's eyes flick up to survey me, adding a neat little twist to his knife flipping so the blade twirls with as much grace as a dancer. For a moment, I'm lost in watching him perform the way he watches me.

"It must have been good. You've all been hard to pin down for days." I lick my lower lip and he follows the movement. "Even my girl."

He remains tight-lipped.

"I'd like to borrow one of those nifty things from Colton. Can you show me how to install it? Bugging someone isn't part of my skill set. I think I'd like to stick it on my Dad's phone and find out—"

"Yes, it went off without a hitch," Levi admits in a grouchy tone. He blinks, hesitating. It's almost as if he's surprised himself by answering. With a low, tetchy noise, he continues. "We've all been preparing for the meeting on the invitation. It's coming up next week."

I lift my brows. It looks like telling me cost him. His expression shutters, closing me out.

The only times I manage to push him are when I ramble. I file that nugget of information away to fit into the puzzle I'm piecing together on Levi Astor.

"Well, I appreciate that with all this stuff in your lap, you took time out of your day to save little old me." I wave a hand. My voice grows serious, throat tightening. "Truly. There was no way for me to fight against them to stop it. Who knows where they would've taken me, but they definitely would've succeeded in kidnapping me."

A low, rough sound escapes him. A beat later, he sheathes his knife, the blade disappearing before I discern where he stashed it on himself.

"Come with me."

"Where?"

He gives me his back. Sighing, I grab my phone, turning off my playlist as I hurry after him. He shrugs out of his signature leather jacket on the way through the maze of halls, revealing a fitted black t-shirt beneath. He adjusts the hem and flashes me a hint of the tattooed skin of his lower back—and some kind of flat holster hiding his weapon. My body warms at the sight.

He's dangerous with a wild, untamed air. It pulls me in with the need to know what's past his walls, what it's like to be so free.

The tattoo interested me, too. It was thick and curved around his hip, leading down to his ass under his back dimples beneath the waistband of his tight jeans. Does Levi have ink on that sculpted ass? I bite my lip around a smile, hoping the answer is yes.

He doesn't look back once to check if I'm following. While he can move around this place without making a sound, I doubt the average person is as skilled at being stealthy. He has it down to an art form.

Levi brings me to the gym. I haven't been brave enough to poke around it yet. It felt like his domain, despite the fact that everyone uses it. He drapes his jacket over a bench in the corner.

Mirrors line the back wall near the free weights and bench press. A punching bag hangs on one side of the room, and mats take up the space in the middle.

"You really do have everything you need down here. Except sunlight.

Vitamin D is important, you know—hey, okay, no need to man handle me." He has me by my shoulders, moving me to the mats. "What are we doing here? We haven't chilled together since that night at the club upstairs. You've been happy to ignore me, or grunt at me in true caveman fashion, grumpy. I didn't think you wanted to hang out with me."

He grunts in response and I laugh, bright and loud. It's the first genuinely happy laugh I've had since that night on campus. It feels good, like the attack hasn't broken me, either.

When I get control of myself, gripping the cramp in my stomach, Levi stares at me like it's the first time he's seen me, reverence bleeding into his expression.

He has one heavy boot off, the other foot lifted half off the floor, but he abandons his task in favor of roaming his gaze over me, drinking me in greedily.

"Look at that." I smile at his bare foot. "You are human after all. The jury was out for a bit there."

He clears his throat with a gravelly cough. "Debatable."

"Nah, look." I squat down, fingertips touching the mats for balance. His eyes widen, stance tensing. I poke his foot. "Big, bad, scary guy on the outside, but underneath it all you have the same blood in your veins as the rest of us mere mortals."

His throat bobs with his swallow when I peer up. Scrubbing a hand over his mouth and raking his fingers through his tousled black hair, he toes off his other boot and circles the mat.

"Try to stop me," he demands.

It's the only warning I get before he's moving, far too quick and capable for me to do much more than throw my hands up. He grabs me by my upper arms, grip flexing. The proximity warms my blood, feeling his chest brushing against mine. His jaw locks.

"Again." He releases me and stalks to a new starting point.

I blink several times in quick succession. "What's happening?"

"I want you to try to stop me." His eyes drag over me. "Block the attack, princess."

A flutter moves through my stomach at the nickname and the rough way he says it. I nod, planting my feet.

"Okay."

The corner of his mouth tilts up. "Good girl."

I bite my lip, the praise making something deep in my core twine into a delicious knot. "Like this?"

He's already started by the time I'm ready, catching me off guard again. This time his arm locks around my waist and he spins me around, crushing my back to his chest, my arm twisted behind me in a hold I struggle to break.

Levi sighs, the warm air coasting over my neck. I swear his nose brushes my hair. His body is a hard line against mine. I suck in a breath, arching into him. The arm around my waist becomes a steel band, pulling me tighter into him, wrapping me in his spicy scent. He holds me like he doesn't plan on letting go, his fingers digging into my skin.

"You really would be a good cuddler," I murmur.

Despite the point being self-defense, I'm more inclined to yield to him if it keeps his arms around me. A shaking breath hisses out of me as his arm shifts, brushing the underside of my breasts. I picture this going somewhere very different, and tingles spread over my flushed skin as I picture what would happen if he pinned me to the mat.

"Again," he mutters.

His touch lingers before he pulls away.

I swallow, my head clouded. "Yeah."

Every time he attacks from a new spot, never pulling the same move on me twice. Excitement prickles across my skin each time he captures me. His touch is everywhere—capturing my hips, my waist, my thighs. Despite being warmed up from dancing, he has me panting within minutes. It's not entirely from exertion, an ache building between my legs.

I bite back a cry when he charges me, flips me around with skill, and presses me into the wall of mirrors. His body is so close to mine, his exhales coasting over my skin.

My breath fogs the mirror and he plants a hand on either side of me, pinning me in place, drowning me in his heady scent. "Got me again."

"You're not even trying," he growls. "No one's taught you anything?"

I struggle, hoping my sweaty skin will help me wriggle free. He barely has to move to grasp my wrists, holding me in place, triggering another throb between my legs. Is he not affected by rubbing up on each other like this?

"Again?" I ask.

He steps back, swiping hair from his eyes. His jaw sets and something burns in his dark gaze that echoes within my own body, the needy ache demanding I press closer and closer until there's no space between us. I bite my lip and he zeroes in on the movement.

I move to the center of the mat and put my hands up as a shield. "Come at me. I'm ready."

He snorts, prowling around me. I get the distinct sense he's toying with me. "You're not even close to prepared."

We watch each other. Instead of rushing me, he waits. Anticipation simmers in a rush of tingles. I yelp when he darts for me. He's so damn fast.

One minute I'm on my feet, the next I'm on my back with Levi pinning me to the floor, my arms locked over my head in his firm grip. His weight feels so good holding me down, better than I imagined. He meets my gaze, then produces the short blade he flipped earlier in the holding room I turned into my dance space.

My heart pounds as he drags the tip down my throat. A new heat spreads through my body. The cool metal makes me want to shiver, but I smother the urge, aware that his knives are sharp enough to kill a man.

I have to question why my nipples tighten at the thought. He's holding me at knife point to prove how weak I am, but I'm getting more turned on. I think he's giving me a lesson in self-defense, but the exhilarating feeling of his strong body against mine is setting me on fire with want.

Eyes turning molten, he traces the blade back up, using it to tip my chin up, transfixed on my reactions. This time I do shiver. My lips part and my thighs tense with the need to rub together to help the ache building in my pussy. His knee between them prevents me from getting relief unless I rut on his thigh wantonly. The knife dragging over my body only adds to the intensity of my body's reaction.

Levi's eyes narrow. "You're dead. Five times over by now if it were me taking you out."

His deep voice washes over me, snapping me out of the haze of lust.

"I don't know if I'd stand a chance whether I knew how to handle myself against you or not," I breathe. "I've seen you kill. You're ruthless."

A growl vibrates in his chest and it makes my breasts ache. I draw in a sharp gasp, biting back the small moan lodged in my throat.

He stops moving the knife, his gaze penetrating mine. Intrigued curiosity gleams in the dark depths of his fathomless eyes, but there's something else there, too. *Desire.*

I feel it then. He shifts, just the barest movement that lets me feel how hard he is.

Licking my lips, I test his hold on my wrists above my head. "Can I try again?"

CHAPTER TWELVE

LEVI

This was a mistake. I'm playing with fucking fire.

My knife doesn't shake in my grip. The only thing keeping it from piercing the elegant, vulnerable column of the throat Isla keeps baring to me is a slight adjustment of my grip. I know at least eight ways to draw blood from this position, and four of those would end her life.

Yet she arches her tits into me, nipples pebbled beneath the thin material of the shirt she's wearing from the stash I've given her. It sends a bolt of possessiveness through me.

The lack of fear—the trust that I'm not going to hurt her even with a blade at her throat shakes me.

In all the time I've spent watching her, nothing could have prepared me for what she's actually like. It's easy to miss at first, to look at her and only see a spoiled princess. She's more than that. Intelligent. Feisty. Fucking gorgeous.

Desire stronger than I've ever known tugs from an invisible tether inside me.

The fire in her eyes is too much to resist with the lethal point of my knife hovering over her pulse point. I touch the metal to her perfect skin. She shudders, doing her level best to remain still. I drink in the flush creeping up her neck. It floods her cheeks and her lashes flutter.

A dark urge rises in me, tempting me to slice the collar of her shirt open to see how hard I can make her nipples if I tease them next. A low groan works its way up my throat. I swallow it back before it's free.

We breathe each other in. Her expression is inviting as fuck, those stunning eyes and sassy mouth luring me in. I can't stop myself from grinding my cock into her when her legs fall open for me. Her gasp is music to my ears. I've never gotten hard during training, but, shit, with her supple body plastered to mine, I'm flooded with a powerful lust I'm unable to resist.

Every fantasy I've entertained about her is nothing compared to this.

Neither of us speak, caught up in the moment.

I skim my nose up her throat, following the same path I traced with my knife. Her skin is soft and she smells intoxicating. My lips hover over hers, heart drumming in my ears.

This isn't me. I don't recognize myself. I pride myself on being the level-headed one. I'm observant, the defender always at the ready. I don't let emotions rule me, yet Isla gets under my skin, past my defenses, and fucks with my control, dismantling it with every sassy comment and smile.

Isla's lack of fear around me awakens a dangerous hunger for more—a desire I've never granted myself.

She tilts her head so I can kiss her easier, heavy-lidded eyes challenging me to do it. To take what I want, what she's offering in silent invitation. There's no denying she wants me to kiss her.

With a vicious growl, I close the scant distance between us, groaning when my lips cover hers. She opens for me without hesitation and I plunge my tongue inside her mouth. My heart thrums inside my chest at the first taste, the one I've dreamed of. A strangled cry catches in her throat at the rough kiss, like prey submitting to the predator.

The knife falls to the mat, forgotten. I sink my fingers in her hair, fisting it to angle her head back. She gives in willingly, bucking her hips against the hard length of my cock pressed against her pussy.

"Fuck," I groan into the kiss.

"More." Isla's plea comes out garbled.

Her arms strain against the hold I keep on her wrists, trying to move from where I pin them above her head. But I like her stretched out for me. My fingers dig into her delicate wrists. She gasps and I swallow it, devouring her mouth in a bruising kiss.

The sinful glide of her tongue along mine is a paradise unlike any I've ever known—better than the quick, dirty fucks I've allowed myself to take off the edge of my misery, better than balancing the weight of a knife before whipping it through the air to hit its target with perfect precision, better than the satisfaction of killing my enemies.

It's that thought that finally snaps me out of the haze of lust, sending me crashing back to reality.

I tear away with a ragged noise before I lose more control than I already have, ignoring the need to take that sweet fucking mouth again. One taste isn't close to enough.

"What lesson was that?" she murmurs.

"It wasn't," I bite out. "Forget it."

She touches her fingertips to her plush lips and her faint sigh goes straight to my straining cock. What other sounds does she make? How pliable is her lithe body?

Fuck. I shouldn't want to know. I can't be asking myself these questions. I closed this door long ago—accepted that looking was all I'd ever get. The fact she kissed me back, moaned like that when I pushed my tongue into her mouth, means nothing.

"You can try again," I say once I feel less like covering her body with mine and fucking her here on the gym mats.

No sex in the gym. It's my rule. One I'm seconds from breaking.

Isla stretches on the floor like a cat, unbothered by me pulling away or by the abrupt kiss. She seeks me out with those otherworldly blue eyes, leering at me as if she understands me. She doesn't know shit.

Still, her smile pierces my heart.

"Any pointers?" She indicates the floor with her chin. "Otherwise I have this funny hunch I'm just going to get my ass handed to me again. As much as I enjoy you holding me down..."

I clench my teeth against a wave of want, retrieving the abandoned knife. "I'm getting a sense of your weaknesses."

"Yeah, I got that." Her laughter is light and airy. "Thoroughly. I get it, you're a badass and I'm far from it. We could go back to the other thing? I liked that."

My lips twitch. I sigh. "By assessing what your body can do, then I'll know what sort of training program to design for you."

Her brows jump up at that. "Design for me?"

"You think they all got good from YouTube?" I jerk my head to the door. "I train them all. Even Rowan."

"Damn. That's impressive."

I ignore the bloom of pride in my chest, annoyed with myself that I let her affect me so much. I shouldn't have kissed her, shouldn't have come even close to it, let alone entertain thoughts of stripping her bare. I need her out of the Nest because my control is close to snapping.

Shutting everything in a box to be dealt with never, I pour my focus into what I do best, looking for my opening. I almost snort because she gives me so many. It makes it too easy, so I wait, allowing her to think she stands a chance against me.

There.

She glances down, probably aiming to watch which direction I go, but I don't project my actions. I sweep her foot out to knock her stance, catching her before she drops to the ground. I ignore the urge to drag her closer into my arms. Her eyes are luminous and the corners of her mouth curl up.

"Having fun?" I taunt.

"Yup." She pushes at my chest to let her down. "Let's go again."

My brows flatten. Fun. She's having fun in my damn gym, the one place on this earth that's as close to religion for me as I get. I come here to hone my body and train.

"Better stop treating this like a game, princess," I warn.

"Or what?" She pops a hip that draws my eye to her pert ass, twisting to smirk at me over her shoulder.

"Or I'm upping the stakes," I rumble.

Those striking blue eyes light up at the promise of consequences if she doesn't take this seriously. I'll never come into my sanctuary again without recalling the taste of her mouth. I swallow, fighting back the images swirling in my mind of her giving me every opening in invitation to own her body and soul.

Smirking, I peel out of my shirt, tossing it aside. Her eyes widen and drift over my inked, muscled body.

"Damn," she whispers.

A weird feeling expands in my chest, different from the lust keeping me in a chokehold. The girl I've watched for years watching me back with obvious want in her expression sends my mind into a new realm of possibilities.

I could take her down now, while she's distracted. Instead I wait, allowing her to look her fill. Her gaze lingers on the crow tattoo I share with my brothers, then she admires the snake twisting around my body.

She licks her lips, finding the center of the mat again, bouncing on the balls of her feet. She moves with grace, but it's a bad choice. I shake my head, but don't correct the waste of energy yet. I want to push her to the brink, see if her survival instinct kicks in. Then I'll consider training her to protect herself.

"This fighting stuff is kind of like another form of dancing," she says. "Once I get the rhythm right, your ass is toast."

My lips thin, unamused, but I can't fully argue against her point. Her hands move as she talks, her face lighting up as she continues comparing dance moves to fighting technique. The sound of her voice is nice when she talks about dance. It's brighter, more full of life.

Irritation ripples across the line of my shoulders. Blowing out a breath, I wait until Isla spins, showing me how the dance move is similar to the basic hold I put her in earlier.

Another mistake, princess. Never turn your back on monsters.

Isla gasps when she realizes she let her guard down. It's too late. I catch her mid-twirl, using her body's momentum to throw off her balance. At the same time, I slice the knife through the shirt, exposing a few inches of her cleavage from the cut. The glimpse tortures me as much as it makes a point to her.

"Take this seriously," I demand in her ear.

She stumbles away, panting and wide-eyed. My jaw works.

That's right, I want to say. *You're playing around with an animal.*

The calm, detached demeanor I maintained earlier drops, showing a hint of the Leviathan lurking beneath. She gets a taste of the monster I become, and finally her beautiful features flicker with uncertainty. There's the survival instinct I've been waiting for.

I don't allow her to regroup, charging for her again. I don't even bother going for efficiency and masking, feet pounding across the mats.

A shriek escapes Isla, but she stands her ground instead of running, foolish little thing. She struggles when I grab her. I fight to get her hands pinned behind her back, both of us gritting our teeth and panting. She keeps a brave face on and it makes me want to carve this stupid pull I feel toward her out of my fucking chest.

I want her screaming and crying, like she should be.

But I can't push further, stopped in my tracks by my own odd need to protect her. It's what drove me to bring her to the gym to figure out how she moves. What the hell is wrong with me?

She flicks hair out of her eyes with a toss of her head, tugging against the hold I have on her wrists. The position pushes her chest into mine. I stare at her and she meets it fiercely, unwavering, unflinching.

Impossible.

It should terrify her to be at my mercy.

I want to kiss her again and it pisses me off. I never struggle this much to control myself.

"Again." My voice is edged with gravel.

She shivers and nods. My grip tightens on her wrists as I ride out the irrational desire to back her against the wall of mirrors and wrap those long legs around my waist while I sink into her raw, fucking her until the imprint of my dick is permanently inside her pussy. My cock throbs at the fantasy.

Blowing out a breath through clenched teeth, I let her go and back up, opening and closing my hand to dispel the memory of her soft skin. "You haven't figured it out yet. But you will."

"What do you mean?"

"Kinesthesia. Your natural intuition and athleticism. Basically, your body is smart." I circle around her, aware of her flicking her head back and forth to track me. "You have the instinct, but you don't know *how* to move. I'm going to show you how."

"I thought that was what you were doing."

Focus. It's what I do best. I can train myself out of wanting her just like I've honed every other skill. I sweep her body with an assessing gaze, paying attention to where she carries her muscle, how her weight is balanced—ignoring everything else I want to stare at until it's burned into my brain.

"That was more like me playing with my food. But now I see how you move." I tap the side of my foot against her instep. "Shift this out a few inches. Good girl. When I come at you, push off from there to dodge my grab. You don't have the muscle density to throw around, but that doesn't mean you can't fight off anyone twice your size. You just have to be strategic about it—speed, using your opponent's momentum against them."

Recognition crosses her flushed face. "Like that thing you did when I was in the pirouette."

"Right. It's not so much about ability or knowledge, but how you utilize it all."

Backing up to the edge of the mat, I register movement in my periphery. Colton leans against the open doorway, forearm braced over his head. Goddamn it. I hope he didn't see us making out. Wren pulls him away as he passes, glancing into the gym with a smirk.

Screw them.

I square my shoulders and attack. She doesn't block me, but it's better. She pushed off too late, colliding into my side instead of dodging completely. Determination settles on her face when I correct her and offer another direction before letting her try again.

We keep going. I start giving curt pointers until she's able to successfully dodge.

Her adaptability is a nice surprise. It can be refined into a hidden strength if she needs to use this to survive.

"Boo-freaking-ya, baby!" Isla pumps her fists in the air, beaming at me. She wiggles her hips in a victory dance. "That was amazing! I feel awesome right now."

I rub at the center of my chest, wishing I could claw into my ribcage to rip out my heart for daring to swell at the sight of her excited smile.

"You have a long way to go still."

Her smile stretches. "Come on, grumpy. Positive reinforcement pairs excellently with teaching."

She flutters her lashes with the same inviting gleam in her eyes as before. *Good girl* echoes in my head. I'm not kissing her for a reward. That's a path I can't go down again.

"Training," I correct with a frown. "Self-defense technique."

She purses her lips and blows out a dismissive breath. "Same thing." Her eyes sparkle and she claps. "Can you show me how to throw a knife next? It's so cool when you do it."

Air gusts from my lungs in a startled rush. Christ, her earnest expression and eagerness are too much to handle. It makes me want to believe I can trust her. I bite the inside of my cheek.

"One thing at a time. Successfully block me before I arm you with a weapon, princess."

She smirks, getting into the correct stance. I was right, her natural ability helps her pick up the technique faster than the average person lacking innate instinct.

I tell myself I'm showing her how to defend herself so she'll never feel helpless again, but if I'm around, she never will be.

CHAPTER THIRTEEN

LEVI

LATER, past midnight, Colton crouches with his portable tablet while I stand guard. The Founders Museum stands across the street, the large brick building the location for the meeting Wren has been summoned to. We're here to scope it out.

Colton glances up at me with a smug expression for the third time. He's practically vibrating with whatever he's holding back.

I sigh. "What."

"God, I thought you'd never ask. You're such an edgelord. You're lucky she likes you." He bounces out of a crouch to connect his tablet to the large green transformer box that distributes electricity to this grid of the city. He talks with his hands as he works. "I saw that look on your face when you were in the gym. You were enjoying yourself, too. Must be way better to have her within reach instead of stalking her from afar, right?"

"Shut the fuck up." I survey our surroundings while smacking the Thorne Point Electric Company hat off his head. "There was nothing to see. I showed her how to not get her ass thrown into predatory white vans."

"And not to take candy from strangers unless the candy is your cock dipped in caramel? Hey!" He ducks the punch I throw, popping up with a shit-eating grin. Fucking troublemaker. "Ohh, you do like her back—I knew it! I'm taking the fucking pot in the bet. That's why you've always gotten that constipated look on your face when she's around, yeah? Look at you, Lev, crushing hard, no idea what to do with it other than jerk off to thoughts about her. Need me to get you an in? Your flirting game is shit. You're basically feral."

I grit my teeth, satisfied that he didn't see us kissing. He wouldn't be able to shut up about it if he did. "Stay on task. We need to have Wren's back."

"Chill." His laugh breaks off into a sober expression. "You know I'd never fuck around when any of your lives were on the line."

After a tense beat, I nod. I know it. We'd bleed for each other in a heartbeat.

"It doesn't matter." I shift to the other corner of the fenced area surrounding the transformer, stuffing my fists in the pockets of the windbreaker with the electrical company's logo across the chest. My fingers curl around my switchblade. "Let's just get this done."

"Fine, fine." He sticks his tongue out from the corner of his mouth, toying with the silver ball piercing while his fingers fly across the keyboard. "I noticed how that wasn't a denial, by the way."

A growl from me makes him snort.

"I still don't like this. Especially if we're right about all the secret society shit."

"Me either." Colt exhales. "And I'm pissed I have one dead end after another with the surveillance feed. It doesn't track. I would've known if someone tripped the firewalls to get past my security protocols."

"Feels like they're toying with us." I grit my teeth.

He darts a savage look my way. "So we play right the fuck back."

He disconnects from the transformer. We move into the shadows of an outbuilding from before this was a museum. Stripping out of the uniforms, we stash them in duffels we put beneath the bushes lining the back of the building. He hands me a black neck gaiter, then tugs his on.

At my hand signal, he nods. We split up, slipping through the dark undetected, planting bugs and signal boosters around the perimeter. The night guard won't be a problem. I've already taken care of him, knocking him out in his office with a Bruins game streaming on his phone. He'll wake up and believe he dozed off, unaware of my presence before I pinched the nerve in his neck to drop him into unconsciousness.

Security at this place is a joke, but I don't let that relax me. That means if it's easy for us to case this place, that it could be just as simple for a secret society to handle.

When I picture Wren at this meeting, I imagine robed figures with a cult vibe and old school viewpoints, the type that align with the ideals our privileged greedy community have.

With a sigh, I finish hiding the last of the tech behind a plaque dedicating the building to Hugo Thorne, Wren's ancestor and one of the founders of Thorne Point.

A sound through the door beside the plaque makes me freeze. There are no first floor windows on this side of the building. Frowning, I listen. No other sound comes. Maybe I'm being paranoid. Between dealing with this and the thoughts of Isla clouding my head, I'm not at my best. I debate breaking in to make sure.

A whistle comes from my left, drawing my attention. Colt's signal that he's done. Sighing, I head for the car.

He's tossing our supplies in the back of his Mustang when I reach it. I'd argued we should take something more nondescript, but he never listens.

"All clear?" I tug down the gaiter and glance back at the museum.

"Not a peep." He slides into the driver's seat and drums on the wheel. "So for the Halloween party at the Nest, I'm thinking—"

"We shouldn't do it. There's too much shit going on. It's a bad idea to party."

Colt slants a look at me. "That's exactly why we need it. Same with the poker party tomorrow night. Business doesn't stop. We might be dealing with all this madness, but the reputations we've crafted will suffer and rumors will spread—the kind of bad rumors we don't need—if we don't act as normal as possible."

I drop my head against the seat. He's right. We've hosted a party at the Crow's Nest every Halloween, and if it doesn't happen, people will know something is up. We can't allow anyone to think something is wrong.

The corner of his mouth kicks up when I shrug. "Atta boy. I haven't decided on my costume yet. I'm torn between Corpse Husband and a Purge-themed costume. What about you?"

"Your ability to compartmentalize is scary as hell sometimes."

His mischievous smile turns cold and he taps his temple. "Who says I stop thinking about anything?"

A beep on his phone makes him drop the act immediately. His brows furrow in concentration as he unlocks it.

"Oh fuck," he grits out.

I sit up. "What is it?"

"It's an error from the signal at your uncle's place. Someone's scrambling it so it can't transmit to us."

"How the fuck?"

His jaw locks and his grip tightens on his phone. "They have someone working for them. Someone fucking good."

Shit.

Movement registers in the corner of my eye and I snap my gaze to the museum. A figure in a dark baggy hoodie and tight pants leaves the building from the door where I thought I heard something.

"Motherfucker. Colt, company."

"What? Oh hell to the no." He starts the car and shifts into gear.

"I thought your scanner only picked up on the guard's body heat?" I should've trusted my instincts and broken in.

"It did!"

"Don't let them get away."

"Duh."

The figure looks around before jogging in the opposite direction. I swear they looked right at us before ducking around the corner.

My nostrils flare. We've never screwed up this badly. Not since the night Jude got arrested, when we were still amateurs. We're not amateurs anymore, far from it.

"Go, go, go."

Colton speeds down the road, but when we whip around the corner the street is deserted. We exchange a glance, then he pulls over. Jumping out, we don't need to speak to know what the plan is. He keeps jogging down the road while I double back toward the museum.

I go for the path I'd take if I needed to evade a tail. When I come through a row of tall hedges, I spot the person standing at the back of the museum. I keep to the shadows, moving swiftly to catch up. The low grind of stone on stone makes me falter for half a second.

I gape in fury as they throw up two fingers in a *peace out* sign and step through a hidden door, just like the secret passageway we discovered at the university.

I curse, slapping the wall as it closes before I can get through. Stepping back, I search for the trigger, but nothing jumps out in the muted moonlight.

"Goddamnit," I snarl.

Scrubbing a hand over my face, I call Colton on my way back to the car. We need to get back to tell the others.

* * *

This is the first time one of Colton's plans hasn't worked and it has all of us on edge.

Everyone keeps shouting at once until I yell, "Enough!"

Wren forces out a breath. "Take us through what you saw again."

"There was someone there." I scrub my face, pacing behind the couch in the lounge. "I should have checked when I thought I heard something inside. We missed them during perimeter check. On the way out, we spotted them and when I followed, they went into a secret passage at the museum."

"Are the signals still good?" Jude asks.

Colton double checks. "Yeah. I don't know what's up, but they'd have to be with this society, right? To know about the hidden passage. And then there's this bullshit." With angry keystrokes, he shows the dead signals on the devices I planted at my uncle's place. "No one should have been able to find this."

"I thought you kept track of people that good?" Rowan questions.

"I do." Colton drags a hand through his hair. "Somehow, this one escaped me. I don't know."

"Well, find out," Wren barks.

Rowan jumps, then elbows him. "Dude. Go spar in the gym with Lev if you're that on edge. Otherwise, keep it together."

"I'm tired of being two steps behind," he answers coldly.

"And I'm not?" Rowan snaps.

A distressed sound filters into my awareness. I still, snapping my gaze to the hall. It comes again, a panicked cry that is all too familiar in more ways than one. Ice pierces into my chest and protective instinct takes over. Without a word, I rush out of the lounge to find her.

Isla.

CHAPTER FOURTEEN

ISLA

I'M dancing in the studio on campus, but I don't remember when I got here. Might as well get the practice time in for the showcase. Pirouette after pirouette, a lunge through the air—my father watches in the corner with a disapproving glower.

"I want this," I say.

What I want doesn't matter. It never has to him.

He turns his back on me and the studio goes dark. Heart in my throat, I run through the parking garage. Wasn't I in the studio? It doesn't matter, I have to get away. This is bad—I can't be here.

If I'm here, they'll get me. They'll take me back to the estate where *he* is.

My foot catches on something and I stumble. Looking back, I scream. Rowan is on the ground, her auburn hair covering her face. A dark red pool I don't want to name surrounds her.

"No!" I yell myself raw.

Where is everyone? I race around the corner and find my attackers coming for me. They want to take me away, back to the demonic man who hunts me in my dreams. My stomach turns in protest, but I can't run fast enough. My feet are like lead blocks, hindering my escape. I choke out a desperate plea for help.

The kidnappers pick me up. One restrains my arms and the other grabs my feet. Struggling is futile. They carry me back the way I ran.

Levi kneels over Rowan's prone form. He looks up and glares. "This is your fault."

It's all wrong—the opposite of how he looked at me when he kissed me in the gym, worse than any hateful glare he's cast my way.

"You weren't here!" I hiccup, my chest collapsing when he turns away instead of saving me. "I need you!"

The attackers bring me to their van. No, no, I can't allow them to take me. Please, no!

"N-no!" Gasping, I sit upright in bed.

The room is pitch black. It takes my thundering heart a minute to register where I am. The crawling sensation from being shoved into the van doesn't dissipate. With a strangled cry, I fling the covers off and stumble barefoot to the door. Each breath I draw is hoarse and ragged.

I need—I need someone.

I nearly crash into the wall in the hallway when I burst through my door. Planting a hand on the wall for balance, I struggle for air, blindly searching the dark hall. Which way goes back to the main lounge?

Distant voices echo, so I follow them. It sounds like an argument. A broken sound escapes me and I clutch at my chest. I have no idea what time it is. Late, that's my guess.

Dizziness rushes over me and I sway with a groan of discomfort. My stomach roils. I'm either going to black out or throw up. A weak noise catches in my throat and I slide down the wall.

"Isla? Jesus, fuck." Footsteps rush in my direction. A warm hand cups my face, tilting it up. "Why are you hyperventilating?"

I open my mouth and croak.

"Goddamnit. You're having a panic attack." Levi cradles my face, thumbs sweeping tears from my cheeks. "Shh, I know. Come here."

He grunts, collapsing to the floor. He pulls me into his lap, lifting me easily. Tipping my chin up he meets my eyes in the low light.

"Hold this." He hands me a smooth, thin object. "What is it?"

I shake my head, struggling to process anything other than the terror taking root in my chest.

"Come on, princess. You can do this. Tell me what that is. Feel it."

He guides my thumb to a catch and the switchblade opens. It's the one he always has on him.

"Kn-knife," I choke.

"Right. Look at it." His deep, gruff voice grounds me, giving me a guide back to myself. "What kind of knife?"

"Switchblade." I lick my dry lips, tasting the salt of my tears.

He rubs my back. "Very good. Now you're going to count with me while we breathe. Yeah?" I nod. "Good girl. In through your nose. If you can't do it, I'll cover your mouth with my hand."

I manage another jerky nod, my chest tight.

"In. Two. Three." He squeezes the back of my neck.

"Four, five," I whisper as we inhale together.

Sweet relief blankets me. I want to gulp air into my burning lungs, but he grasps my jaw with his big hand. I focus on the handle of the knife, worried to forget it. I might accidentally drop it or cut myself.

We count and breathe until the ache in my chest eases. The whole time he murmurs to me, massaging and stroking my neck, my back, my bare legs. When I come back to myself, he has me tucked into his body, my head resting on his shoulder, nose buried in his neck. I take another deep inhale, humming at the scent of leather and spice. It brings me comfort.

When he kissed me earlier it burned me up from the inside out. With a single hot as hell kiss I learned that Levi Astor isn't the scary, emotionless shadow he wants everyone to think he is. No, underneath that angry scowl he's holding back so much. I've barely processed what that kiss meant, and how much I wanted it. How much I want him.

But this, being held in his embrace, makes me feel something different. Not lust, but something bigger that makes my chest ache. In his arms, I feel cared for. It takes me by surprise to find he's capable of being...gentle, attentive. Despite his sharp, hard edges, he holds me like I'll shatter, like if I broke again he would hold me together until I could do it on my own.

Fresh tears well up because I've never had this. I've never been held when my dreams scared me, or when my heart was heavy. I give so much of myself to those around me, but receiving it back like this is new, bringing the flickering light within me back to life. Swallowing back the tears, I wince at how tender my throat is, like I screamed my head off. I soak in his embrace and burrow deeper into it. His arms cinch tighter around me.

"I had a nightmare." My voice is wrecked and raw.

"It was only a dream." His chest expands and sags with a heavy exhale. "Whatever happened...it can't hurt you."

It sounds as if he's speaking from experience. I gulp again, nodding. It all felt so real.

His palm skims up my thigh to my hip. I realize I'm only wearing one of his shirts. They're secretly my favorite. I wear them more than what Rowan let me borrow, or my own things. Wearing his clothes feels like a hug that keeps me safe.

He continues caressing my leg. I wonder if he's unaware he's doing it until he shifts and locates the scar on the inside of my thigh. The sharp breath I draw sears my lungs as the callused pads of his fingers explore the small circular shape. No one else has touched it. My throat goes dry as disjointed memories assault me. I ignore the scar most days. It's a physical reminder I survived the unthinkable, but I don't remember the details of how it marred my skin—only what I can guess, that my legs needed to be held open.

With each brush of his fingers, the memories push back further, as if his touch tugs me back from the brink and helps wash their taint from me. My body sags into his, my free hand seeking out his tattooed skin, touching his neck lightly. He stills, closing his eyes, then tilts his head to the side to let me explore his inked skin more easily, resuming stroking my leg.

"This is a scar," he says.

My nod is shaky. A rumble builds in his chest, vibrating against my fingertips dipped into his t-shirt to follow the wings of the crow.

"Did someone mark you?" His tone is deadly. "Who hurt you?"

"It was a long time ago," I whisper. His fingers press into my thigh, covering the scar. "It reminds me I survived."

He accepts it and we return to silence, focused on the hypnotic lull of touching each other. My hand slips beneath his shirt, skating across his warm abs that contract beneath my palm. Our shared touches help calm me further.

"How did you know what to do?" I've never had a panic attack before, even after waking from nightmares of the twisted man who raped me. The inescapable anxiety was awful. "To stop it, I mean."

He grunts, gazing down the hall. After a minute, he speaks in a low, gutted rasp. "My mom used to get them when I was a kid. Before she died."

"Oh. I'm so sorry." My fingers curl in his shirt and sadness swells in my chest, wishing for a way to ease the pain of his grief.

"That's how I learned to keep a focus object handy."

A scratchy laugh leaves me. "You're saying you carry all those knives because of your mom?"

His lips brush my forehead. "Something like that."

I sit up, studying him. He's such a mystery, but emotion shines in his dark eyes. I trace down his cheek to his jaw. He gazes at me, eyes bouncing back and forth. When my thumb brushes his lower lip, his mouth tightens, the ever-present anger slipping back in place, locking away the man who coached me through a panic attack.

"Go back to bed."

"I heard raised voices." I bite my lip. "Did something happen?"

For a moment I don't think he's going to answer. Then his chin dips.

"Yes. But it's not your problem."

"Can I help?"

"What can you do? You know Latin, that's about the extent of your usefulness to us." He glares at me. No—at my mouth, as if it offends him. "You're nothing to us. To me."

I recoil at the cutting words. How can he run so hot and cold with me, rescuing me and teaching me to defend myself, helping me through a panic attack and caring who hurts me, *kissing* me like it was the answer to everything one minute, then pushing me away the next?

"I'd still like to help."

He gets up, lifting me as he gets to his feet. His hand glides over my bare thigh one more time, lingering almost like he's savoring the feel of my skin with his rough palms, then he puts me down, shooting a livid look at the leg my scar is on.

"Go back to bed, princess. This isn't like before." His voice becomes laced with shadows. "We'll handle it."

He stalks down the hall. The knife is still in my hand.

There's no way Levi, someone always aware of his surroundings, doesn't know he left me with a weapon he always has on himself. I sigh and return to my room.

* * *

In the morning, Rowan knocks on my door. I slept restlessly, but no other nightmares plagued me. The switchblade sits on the bedside table.

"I come bearing fuel." Rowan lifts two steaming mugs.

"You have a serious caffeine addiction, babe." My voice is still raspy, vocal cords tender. I accept one of the coffees and let its warmth seep into my hands.

She sits on my bed. "That's between me and my blood pressure." She hums into her mug, sipping. When I join her on the bed, leaning against the headboard, she studies me. "So...Lev told me about last night."

I lean forward. "What were they arguing about?"

She bites her lip. "Colton and Levi were doing, uh...stuff."

"Stuff?" I lift a brow. "Like his bugs? These boys are really criminally inclined."

Rowan snorts. "You have no idea."

"Do they do this *stuff* often? What would cause an argument?"

She sighs. "Well, they came across someone else who was there. That's not good because they thought they were in the clear. There was a secret door, too."

My eyes widen as I try to fill in the blank spaces she's leaving open. "What? Like the one on campus?"

She nods. "Exactly like that one. Medieval as fuck, from how Levi described it."

"Wow." I think about the holding room I danced in and frown. "Did they catch the person?"

"No. That's why they were all fighting when the guys got back. Until Levi thought he heard a scream and went all—" She wriggles her fingers. "—murder mode."

A laugh bursts out of me. It's still crackling from my sore throat. It feels really good to be able to laugh, like I've rediscovered a piece of myself that's been missing. "What is that?"

"It's what I call it when he goes all grr and stealthy. You should've seen when he caught me at the docks I snuck into to scope it out by myself. It scared the shit out of me when he grabbed me."

I splutter, choking on coffee. I set the mug down hard. "You *what*? When? Who are you, girl?"

She smirks, rubbing the back of her neck. "Stubborn." For a moment, she seems lost in a memory that puts color in her cheeks. She rakes her teeth over her lip. "Anyway. Are you okay? What happened?"

My shoulders slump. "A nightmare. I think I would've passed out if he didn't find me in the hall." This time it's my turn to blush when I recall his gravelly voice commanding me, guiding me out of my panic while his capable hands stroked my legs. My heart clenches at his tone when he touched the scar I bear on my leg. I gesture to the bedside table. "He left me with his knife to keep the nightmares at bay."

I still don't know what to make of that.

With my head clearer this morning, I replay the kiss in my head. Levi might regret it, but I don't, even if it didn't go anywhere. If it happens again, I won't regret that either. I don't have time in my life for regrets. They hold us back, weighing us down with what ifs. I promised myself long ago that I'd never let myself be burdened like that.

It's only when I'm with him that I'm able to let go and forget. I drag my teeth over my lip, recalling how it felt to be cradled safely in his lap. My mind jumps from that to picturing his strong body pinning me to the mats, stoking the flame burning in my core before his mouth descended on mine in that sensual, soul-shattering kiss. He gets my mind off my problems by owning every one of my thoughts, demanding my attention.

So why is he still so annoyed with me around? He'd have to be truly heartless to kiss me like that even if he really hates me. Someone who learned how to handle panic attacks to help his mom cope isn't a cold-hearted monster.

My gaze slides to the knife on the table. It's beautiful and sleek, with a black and brown tortoise inlay in the handle. Something custom made, perhaps. It's the knife I see in his hands most often—one that's important to him.

And he left it with me.

Chills race over my skin. Ever since high school Levi's been an enigma, a stoic shadow who lurked around Thorne Point Academy's grounds and in the corners at society parties. Despite always being aware of him, attracted to him for the edginess that speaks to the independence I crave, we never really spoke two words to each other until Rowan landed herself on the Crows' radar. I didn't need to speak to him to know he interests me. Now that I'm aware of what a fierce protector he is and the dizzying way he kisses, I want to know more about him.

"Hold up." Rowan leans over my legs to put her cup beside mine, and gapes at the knife. "He gave you that?"

"Yes."

"Levi. Levi Astor, resident knife boy, gave you one of his prized weapons?"

"I was surprised, too, but he didn't say anything. He just told me to go back to bed once he made sure I was okay." My heart twinges at what he admitted about the reason he recognized the panic attack.

"Huh." Her lips twitch with a smile that's equally relieved and surprised. She scoots closer so our knees rest against each other. "Did you dream about the attack?"

I nod. "It was..." A brittle laugh punches out of me and I shake my head. Somehow this nightmare hit me so much harder than the ones I've fought off for years. Its darkness almost shrouded me with no way out. "It sucked. I know it wasn't real, it's just..."

Rowan rests her hand on my leg. "I know. I used to have them a lot. Since I've been with Wren, I haven't dreamed of the night of the accident in a while. Talking with my mom more openly has helped, too."

I take her hand, threading our fingers together. "I'm glad."

"I have an idea." She squeezes my hand, tugging me off the bed. "You've been cooped up in here and it's getting to you. The guys don't know how much that can mess with your psyche to be trapped with your thoughts. I hated it so much when Wren shut me away in the penthouse."

"God, yes. So much." I understand more than ever what it must have been like for her. "Dancing has been the only thing keeping me sane when there's no one else around."

"Maybe if you feel more in control, it will help find some balance to deal with what happened to you. Sometimes in the mornings, Wren and I go out to this shooting range that's on the property. I haven't been doing it long, only a few weeks, but it helps me."

My brows jump up. "Seriously?"

"I know. I had the same reaction at first." She shrugs. "I didn't think I'd like it, but it helps me feel in control. Have you ever shot a gun before?"

"Once. A hunting rifle." I grimace. "Dad had a rally last year upstate at a hunting lodge. They made me do it for the photo op. I had a bruise on my shoulder for days."

Rowan gives me a wry smile. "I've only been using a handgun. The bigger ones make me feel out of my depth."

"Sounds way different than our study sessions on the quad and our lunch dates." I purse my lips to the side, mulling over the idea of shooting a gun to conquer my demons. I shake my head and offer an apologetic expression. "Sorry, babe. I totally support your hidden badass side, but I don't think that's my vibe. I enjoy the self-defense practice, but can't imagine myself following in your footsteps." A breath catches in my throat. "Not unless it's Levi showing me how he throws knives with such lethal accuracy."

Rowan snickers. "Okay, put away your thirst for a minute, girl. I've got another idea. We need to get out of the Nest one way or another."

Primly ignoring her jibe about my fantasizing, I nod eagerly. "Now you're talking. Where are we going?"

I don't question her when she gets that look in her pretty green eyes. Getting her to change her mind is impossible once it's made up. I accept the jeans she digs out from the growing stash of clothes on a chair in the corner. These are hers. They're a little short on me, since I'm taller than her. I pull them on without complaint.

I'm really going to have to see if Colton or Wren will allow me to have an online order delivered here if I continue to stay, but part of me is reluctant to give up Levi's warm clothes.

"You'll see." Her grin is secretive. She texts while I pull one of Levi's hoodies on over the shirt I slept in. "Come on. Wren even gave us permission to use one of their cars. We just can't take Levi or Jude's motorcycles, they'd cut our hands off."

I lift my brows, pausing in pulling my hair into a ponytail. "Noted."

When she gets back, her smirk is even more wicked. "Okay. Come with me."

"Should I be worried? Your first suggestion was a shooting range. What do you have in mind after I vetoed that?"

"It's a surprise." She tightens a flannel shirt knotted around her waist. "You're gonna love it."

"Is it jetsetting to the tropics with bottomless mai tais?" I giggle at the image that pops into my head of Levi on a beach, grumpy and brooding even in paradise. "If I wasn't on lockdown, I'd call my family's pilot and fly us out in a heartbeat."

"It's totally better than that and up your alley."

I follow her through the underground halls. Colton is the only one in the lounge. He waves without taking his eyes off the screen, playing online poker in one window and running some kind of computer code on another.

"You coming, Colt?" Rowan asks.

"Can't, I'm two seconds from finally beating Queen_Q, and I need to finish this." He shoots a finger gun at us. "Send photos of the options, babes. I'll see you later tonight."

They have to have a group chat for them all to know what she has planned. I squint in suspicion at him, but he gives nothing away, charming brown eyes glinting with amused excitement.

When we're outside, strolling down the row of nice cars, I lean against a sleek Maserati. "Why online poker?"

Rowan grins. "Why anything with Colt, right? He has a rivalry. The elusive Queen_Q. They're constantly playing each other. She beats him every time."

The corner of my mouth curls up. "Girl after my own heart."

"Right? Let's take his Mustang." She smooths a hand over the black muscle car.

I sway my hips as I cross to the passenger side. "Let's."

When we pull out from the hotel, I peer out the window. This is my first time leaving since the night of the foiled kidnapping. My heartbeat rabbits in my chest in relief while we pass beneath decaying leaves clinging to life on the trees lining the drive. By leaving, I feel like time is moving again, allowing me to not feel so trapped where my own haunting past can pick at my mind.

"So for real, where are we going?" I tap my nails against the buttery leather of my seat. The red lacquer is chipped and grown out, looking like a hot mess since the Nest doesn't have a hidden full service salon. I can deal without my creature comforts when there are more important things going on. "And how is your big dick energy man fine with us waltzing out of the hotel without one of them shadowing us after what's been going on?"

The corner of Rowan's mouth lifts as she navigates through Thorne Point, heading downtown. "Shopping. Kind of. And they are, but I bargained with Wren to let us ride alone. He and Jude are following."

She gestures to the mirror. Sure enough, when I check it I spot a familiar blacked out SUV on our tail, practically kissing our bumper. I smirk.

"What did you barter with?"

She lets out a husky laugh and shifts in her seat. "Something mutually beneficial."

"Clever girl." I relax back into the seat, searching my mind for a shopping experience that will lift my spirits and wash away my worries for a while. "Shopping sounds perfect. I've been trying to get you to go with me forever. Are we going to Dolce & Gabbana? Can I let my personal stylist know to expect us and have chilled champagne waiting?"

"Well, it's more like shopping second hand."

My enthusiasm rises. "Vintage?"

She shakes her head. "Closet. Wren has a thing for dressing me, but you know I'm more of a leather jacket and jeans girl. You'll appreciate the things he bought more than I will unless he's stripping them off me. Go nuts, you can have your pick of anything."

"I'm intrigued. And in desperate need of getting laid."

A sigh gusts out of me and I try not to picture the tempting shape of Levi's mouth, his hands on my body when he puts me in the correct position, or the way his gravelly voice makes me shudder with want. Maybe that's why he has me all twisted up after one kiss, because I'm going through a serious dry spell. I'm attracted to him, edges and all, but I haven't wanted to act on it until he became my own personal shadow at the nightclub, then saved my life.

"Thank you for getting me out to go shopping. I need it."

"Not only shopping." She flicks a glance at me and waggles her brows. "We're going to a party tonight."

"Really?" Excitement swells again, expanding in my chest, only to burst and deflate. I stuff my hands inside the hoodie pocket and tuck my nose into the collar. It gives me a faint hint of Levi's masculine scent. "The guys are cool with that?"

"They'll be with us. No one will let anything happen to you, and with them by our sides no one will dare touch you."

I picture the calm Levi lulled me into last night, tucked into his body, the sense memory more vivid with his hoodie drowning me in his rich scent. A flutter moves through my chest. He'll protect me from my nightmares—the ones in my head and the ones in real life that seek to hurt me. No matter what he feels for me, he swore to keep me safe.

"Let's do it."

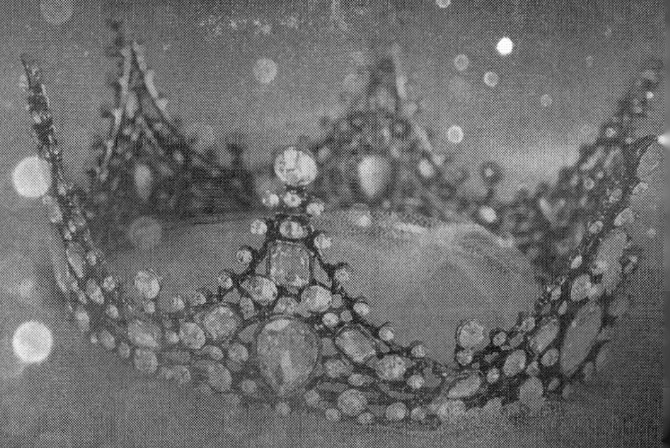

CHAPTER FIFTEEN

ISLA

It's strange being back on campus later that night after so many days locked away from the world at the Crow's Nest Hotel. My muscles seize for a moment when we get out of Levi's Escalade, then Rowan slips her hand into mine. I don't fully relax until I feel the brush of Levi's firm chest against my back.

"Move," he orders in a gruff tone that brooks no argument.

Levi puts on the grumpy facade, but he wouldn't touch me if he truly didn't care. A smile tugs at my red lips—my makeup done to perfection as my armor of choice, along with the stunning backless blouse and leather pants I plucked from Rowan's closet at Wren's penthouse earlier. The sleeves are sheer and the bodice forms a sweetheart neckline to accentuate my cleavage, creating the illusion my breasts are bigger than they are. For the first time since the attack, a sense of empowerment settles within me.

Not only do I feel gorgeous and sensual in the outfit, it was worth it for the way it drew Levi's and his friends' eyes when I strutted into the lounge with my favorite Valentinos back in action. The only one who didn't check out my ass in these killer pants was Wren, his attention transfixed on his girlfriend.

I can almost pretend the last week hasn't happened, imagining strolling around campus with Rowan as we always would, plus our two shadows. Squaring my shoulders, I lift my chin high. I won't let myself fear this place, just as I've survived living under Dad's thumb after he sold my body.

Jude and Wren stride ahead, their postures confident and commanding. Rowan hangs back with me, Levi, and Colton. All of the guys have shifted, pulling on their own armor. I didn't realize how much they'd let their guard drop around me until Wren's steely mask slid into place once we arrived. Even Colton is less languid while we navigate the cobblestone path—something I'd never realized before during all the time he spent around us flirting and smiling.

We cross campus in the opposite direction from what I expect, heading for the dorms instead of Greek row where the most prominent trust funders reside.

"Where's the party?" I ask.

"Fellstone Hall." At my raised eyebrow, Colton smirks. "You've never really partied until you've partied *with* us."

My gaze slides to Levi and I think of the night I helped Rowan dress up for Wren. I wouldn't say we were partying together, but Levi stayed by my side while I chatted his ear off. He never left me alone, his brooding gaze burning into me the entire night while I danced under his guard. That was when things shifted for me. It seems so long ago now, not less than a month ago.

"I've never been to a party at the dorms." A thrill shoots through me at the prospect of a new experience. It helps drive away the last ebbs of fear. Nothing can touch me with these four around. "This should be interesting."

"It's always interesting wherever we're at, Isles." Colton winks, then coughs when Levi elbows him with a quick jab to his ribs.

Rowan grins and knocks her shoulder into mine. "You'll see."

"As long as there's a dance floor, you know I'm down for anything." I shimmy hips, breaking off in a laugh when Colton matches my moves.

The weight of worrying about how involved my parents were in the kidnapping attempt and the plague of opening the old wound of the rape eases off my shoulders, allowing me a reprieve to breathe without as much stress. I finally feel like myself, the girl who dances around, who acts silly to make my friends laugh, who promises to live every day to its fullest experience.

The historic brownstone buildings where the dorms are loom ahead behind shadowy branches, their facades encased in ivy. During the day their brick architecture is beautiful. They're still beautiful at night, but the campus carries a foreboding air that's more prominent under the pale moonlight.

Levi doesn't stop sweeping his gaze around, his scowl more than enough to deter anyone from approaching. The few students milling around on this side of campus steer clear, whispering amongst themselves when they give us a wide berth.

"It's the Crows," one chokes out

"Don't get in their way. You'll disappear."

With an annoyed, near-silent grumble, Levi flashes a knife with a serrated edge, earning a pair of squeals from the group of students brave enough not to move when we approach. They trip over a stone bench to back away, crossing the quad to go around rather than stay on the spacious path.

Rowan snorts, hooking her arm with mine. "Sometimes I forget how scared people are of them."

"You'd think they were vengeful immortals," I joke.

"Sea snake dick, babe. Remember?" Colton winks, grabbing the crotch of his jeans while flashing his tongue piercing. "If you want to call me a god, at least let me show you what that mouth do to earn the title. It would be an honor."

"Shut the fuck up," Levi growls, elbowing Colton away from my other side with a smooth sidestep that has his friend tripping.

Unperturbed, Colton swings around to flank Rowan while Levi's warmth envelops me. Rowan lets go of my arm and the two of them fall behind while Levi's pace remains clipped with purpose. I step closer, shivering against the chilly night air. My breath hitches when his fingertips graze the small of my back automatically before falling away.

I glance at him curiously. I never know which mood I'll get with him, whether he's going to huff out a rough laugh at my sassing or the tetchy side he thinks he scares me with.

"You should've worn a coat," he mutters. "I don't get why girls ignore basic needs."

"And ruin this outfit? Not a chance." The corners of my mouth curl up and I burrow into his side. "You can keep me warm. Your temper runs hot enough for the both of us, grumpy."

He stiffens, then reluctantly wraps his arm around my waist. A beat later, he hauls me closer so our sides are plastered together, engulfing me with his spicy scent. I swear he dips his nose to my hair, inhaling. It feels right when I'm in his arms, like I fit perfectly at his side. I want this with him.

"This is impractical."

My grin widens. "Hush, grumpy."

Outside the dorms, Wren and Jude have lit cigars dangling from their fingers and ruthless expressions. They zero in on the firm arm around my waist and exchange an amused look. Levi brings us to a stop and glances back to Rowan and Colton whispering to each other trailing behind us.

"Cold, Miss Vonn?" Wren questions in a wry tone that makes Levi tense more.

"Never. This one just likes to cuddle." Wren laughs at my glib retort and Levi shakes his head. He doesn't let me step away from his side when I shift my weight. "So is it like a floor party? Do we get to drink around the world?"

"You'll see," Jude says. "You're about to enter our own wicked version of Wonderland."

Levi moves so subtly I'm barely aware of it, shifting himself in front of me. The protective move reads loud and clear to his friends. Jude's golden hazel eyes gleam under the amber glow of the old style lamps lit outside the dorms as he passes one of his unreadable looks over me. He lifts a brow, the corners of his mouth curling into that mysterious Cheshire cat grin.

"Same rules apply inside as the Nest," Wren announces. "Don't contact anyone other than one of us. And if you speak a word of what you see inside to anyone, you won't enjoy the consequences of betraying us."

The line of Levi's shoulders go rigid, but this time he doesn't put himself between me and his friends, turning on his heel to stare me down. The four of them watch me, each with varying degrees of their darkness bleeding into their demeanor—Colton's chaotic, Wren's controlling, Jude's sinister, and Levi's? His is barely concealed hostility mixed with hints of lust every time his attention locks on me. It's an alluring, heady mix that makes my heart thump faster.

I tilt my head. "There's no need to be so dramatic. I know you boys enjoy it, but it's overkill."

Wren smirks in amusement and Levi rolls his eyes. Rowan beams at me proudly.

"What if someone posts photos of me online?" I didn't notice anyone do it on our way over, too wary of the guys, but it's bound to happen. Wherever I go, people take pictures of me like I'm an exotic animal they want to document. I've been waiting for the other shoe to drop with the silence coming from my parents, but if I'm seen out and about they might contact me. "I'm not hiding out."

"We don't want that. We're counting on people posting." Colton cracks his neck side to side with a sinister smirk, holding up his phone. "I want to know who pays attention. It might get your parents to poke their heads out of la la land. You haven't popped up in over a week and there hasn't been a peep about you online outside of me emailing your professors. I want to know what happens when you do."

"So I'm really here as an experiment?"

I shouldn't be too shocked—these boys operate on their own agenda. At least my dance instructors don't think I flaked.

Colton shrugs. "Potato, po-tah-to." His eyes flick up and down my body. "A very sexy one."

With a low, fierce noise, Levi steps back into my side and I get an intoxicating inhale of leather and patchouli. He says one thing, but his actions are the complete opposite, as if his body hasn't caught up with his brain and he can't help it. The whiplash feeling returns and I frown. If he wants the right to keep doing that he needs to make me his instead of pushing me away.

"Let's ignore the part where you called me a potato," I say.

"You'll be safe," Rowan promises. "No one's letting anything happen to you. And it could lead to more answers about who attacked you."

I purse my lips, mulling that over. Answers will lead to a next step and closure. I want that more and more as the days pass.

I meet Levi's dark gaze. "Fine then. I'm all yours." I mean more than as their bait to dangle, challenging him to take what we both want more of. His attention falls to my lips at the quiet murmur stolen by the wind. "Can we go in? This is killing the mood. I want to dance."

Levi's lips quirk up sharply at the corner and he passes a swift glance over each of his friends. "Let mayhem reign."

At the smoky rasp that feels like a caress to my skin, my core tightens with a deep throb, tingles rushing across my skin. It has nothing to do with the cold.

"Come on, Isles." Colton breaks the spell by taking my hand, pulling me from Levi's side with the eagerness of a kid with a new trick to show off. "Now I can show you this sexy setup—all the result of my masterminding."

His words are a blur while I shake off the reaction to Levi's words. He explains logistics as he guides me down a set of steps, past a scary-looking guy standing guard, and into a crowded room. It takes a minute to register the tables have card games and poker chips.

Wren and Levi have a guy between them, leading him through another door into a shadowed room. Rowan follows and closes the door behind them.

I blink as a girl in a cropped purple and yellow tie-dye Hello Kitty sweater and leggings with cutouts crows about her winning hand, dragging the pot to her side of the table. "This is gambling. I thought we were going to a party?"

Colton's attention snags on the beautiful girl for a moment, taking in the glimpses of smooth dark brown skin when she stands up at the insistence of a sore loser, holding her hands up and snapping one of the cutouts in her pants to show she has no cards hidden on her.

"I'm not cheating." She props her hands on the shoulders of a taller guy seated beside her in a white Thorne Point University hoodie who looks just like her. They must be related. "You just suck at poker."

"Fuck that, you've won more than anyone else here tonight. No newcomers have as much luck as you've had." The sore loser has Thorne Point trust fund written all over him, the air of entitlement and sense of getting anything he wants seeping from his pores. That, and I recognize the gaudy gold family ring he wears when he waves his hand—he's the spoiled, greedy son of a banking family. "You're either counting or you've got concealed cards."

The girl scoffs, flipping her long braids over her shoulder like she's prepared to tackle her accuser clear across the table. It makes Colton laugh at my side. Jude steps forward without being obvious about it, circling to observe the squabble with a shrewd gaze. Colton nods to him. I get the sense that they'll let this play out, but if it gets out of hand they'll step in.

"Quinn, chill." The guy with her lifts his hand in front of her. Once he's satisfied she isn't ready to throw down, he turns to the other player. "We started this game with a fresh deck. Open another if you feel like it."

Huffing, Quinn sinks into her seat, accepting the cards dealt to her. The pile of chips in front of her is the largest at the table. Along with the majority of the chips, a gold Rolex sits in her winnings. The trust funder has a paltry amount of chips and an empty wrist.

"So you run a gambling house?" I murmur to Colton.

"*A* gambling house? Try more than that." He puffs up with pride. "If Forbes knew my bottom line, I'd be the reigning champion of their list of brilliant entrepreneurs."

"I don't think that's how the Forbes list works."

He waves me off, keeping half an eye on the game that unfolds between Quinn and the trust fund prince. "We make our own rules. Always have. Once we take care of our business here, we'll head to the party. That's where it's your time to shine." He leans in, keeping his voice low. "Only vetted players can return freely. We use the parties to fish for new blood, lure them in."

"Then suck them dry?" I guess wryly.

He winks. "Now you're getting it."

His attention returns to the game, a slight wrinkle appearing between his brow. He seeks out Jude again, and without any signals, they both move. They see something I don't.

"What's going on?"

Colton squeezes my shoulder. "Stay here. They're running a con. Jude can spot them a mile away."

Jude has already made it from his spot casually leaning against the wall to stand behind Quinn's seat. If Levi's training them all, then they've learned from the master to be stealthy fuckers. The table quiets at the bland smile he offers. It's far from his charming one.

"Problem, man?" Quinn's lookalike asks tersely.

"I think that's enough poker for you two. You're cut off."

Quinn erupts from her chair. It makes for an amusing sight, how fiercely she squares off with Jude and Colton once he closes in behind her because she's half their height, if that. Despite her short stature, she doesn't lack fire.

"You can't do that," she hisses. "We won our earnings."

"And if you leave, you can keep 'em, babe," Colton says.

She clicks her tongue, angling her head to size him up. He checks her out openly, the corner of his mouth hitching up when it reaches her ass.

"I know you didn't just do that," she snaps.

"Do what?" Colton drawls innocently. "I appreciate works of art, and you're a masterpiece, baby."

Quinn's brows lift, her eyes widening in disbelief. She opens her mouth, but the tall guy with her beats her to it, rising to his feet. Unlike her, he stands a head over Colton and Jude.

"You can take your eyes off my sister before I remove them from your head," he growls.

"Sammy, I've got it—"

"Are you insane?" The pissy trust funder gapes across the table, fear evident in his voice. "First you cheat at their tables, then you challenge them? Don't you know who you're talking to?"

Jude smirks, sticking the cigar between his teeth. He turns to him as he slips a thick fold of cash from his pocket and begins counting out bills with deft fingers. "They must be new around here, like you said. Why don't we smooth this over so your table can resume its game." He lays cash on the table for the dealer and meets the guy's eyes. "You'll kill off the energy if you keep running your mouth."

The guy shrinks back in his seat, clamming up at the clear threat lurking beneath Jude's light tone. It's impressive to see this up close, how quickly people bend to their will on reputation and rumor alone. Words have a powerful sway over people and they each wield that without remorse.

While Jude is busy placating the table, Quinn and her brother whisper to each other. Colton turns to me, grinning when he finds me watching it all unfold. Quinn uses the opportunity to shrink away from the table, dragging her brother with her. She throws up two of her fingers in the universal symbol for deuces, flashing a wily glance over her shoulder.

I point them out and Colton turns back around, but by the time he spots them they've reached the door, slipping out. They move quick, almost as fast as Levi does.

Colton narrows his eyes, but returns to my side. He doesn't seem that worried they left. Across the room, the door where the others disappeared opens and they emerge. The guy they escorted in with them is a little pale, hurrying away once Levi releases his arm.

"Now that's taken care of, we can party. After you." With a flourished hand gesture, he indicates a different door at the back of the room.

I pause on the threshold, surprise rippling through me.

CHAPTER SIXTEEN

ISLA

MUSIC hits me, reverberating through my body with a heavy bass beat. I glance over my shoulder into the gambling room, then back into the renovated area where people are partying as if this is a club downtown, not the lower level of a historic dorm building. No sound pierces the door when it's closed.

"What—?"

"Yeah." Colton laughs, nudging me through the door. "We set it up back in Wren and Jude's first year here. Lev's a genius with soundproofing."

"I know students here get away with murder, but how did you pull this off and why doesn't the whole campus know about it?"

His smirk gives away nothing. "Because I'm damn good at what I do. All of us are."

I shake my head, looking around again. Bodies grind to the beat of the music in the middle of the room. It seems like it stretches for the entire floor, rather than individual dorm rooms. There's a bar in the corner where people mix their own drinks from top shelf bottles strewn across it. High class, yet illicitly college style. I grin.

Rowan sidles up to me with Levi and Wren trailing her. "Ready for a drink?"

"Hell yes."

Levi and Jude follow us to the makeshift bar while Colton hangs back with Wren, their heads bent together. Judging by the stony scowl that Wren's face twists into, I assume Colton tells him about the pair of poker players he thought were conning them. As we reach the bar, a handsome boy gives both of us a once over.

"Ladies. Can I get you a drink?" he offers.

Levi steps around me. "No. They pour their own drinks." He grabs the guy by the front of the shirt and hauls him closer, whipping out one of his scary knives. When he twirls it, the guy's wide eyes track its movement. "And if we catch you putting shit in girls' drinks, you'll answer to us."

"Yeah. Got it."

Levi narrows his eyes, holding on for a few seconds more before shoving him away. Jude huffs out a dark laugh at the way the guy trips over his feet to move far away from us.

"Put that bottle down," Levi orders.

"But I want this," Rowan complains.

He ignores her, searching the bar until he finds an unopened bottle of the same brand. He cracks the seal, nodding in satisfaction.

"You drink from this one."

"The big guy tell you to keep an eye out?" Rowan pops out a hip. "People would piss themselves before trying to roofie anyone at your parties. Wren would put them in the ground for daring to attempt it on me."

"So would I," Levi mutters, eyes flicking to me.

A shiver races down my spine and I accept the empty cup he offers once he checks it's clean without any evidence of tampering. I take the bottle from Rowan, aware of the way he stares at me while I pour a shot. Meeting his unreadable gaze, I tip it back and swallow in a quick gulp, throat constricting around the burn of alcohol.

Levi's eyes drag down my throat, then raise to pierce into mine.

"Given the way people are keeping a close eye on us, it's best not to risk it," Jude says.

She sighs, accepting the reasoning. While she pours her own shot, I watch the dance floor.

"Okay, who's dancing with me?" I dart a bold look at Levi, smirking when he glares at me. He could be a great dancer with his dexterity and lightness on his feet, but we've established in his gym that he only moves for survival, not fun. The broody bastard wouldn't know fun if it bit him in the ass. "Rowan?"

She blows out a breath and knocks back another shot, then scans the room. When her gaze lands on Wren across the room, she narrows her eyes in satisfaction, pushing off the bar.

"Come on, sweetheart. Let's see how you move." Jude ditches his cigar and offers his hand with a flourish that has me grinning. I slip mine into his and he flashes Levi a smug grin. "Enjoy watching."

Levi makes a gruff noise, taking up a post against the wall. As we move further onto the dance floor, I find him tracking our path, the scary knife with the serrated edge back out, the tip balanced on the leg he props against the wall. Maybe something is wrong with me because the sight only makes me think of what happened in the gym. How would that one feel against my skin? A tiny gasp catches in my throat and I ignore the way my nipples tighten.

Cool it, thirsty.

Another small yelp escapes me when Jude spins me around. Muscle memory kicks in and I go with it, allowing him to lead me. I grin at him, then he does the same to Rowan. Not used to moving like that, she nearly falls. Jude catches her with a warm, rich laugh.

"Jesus, warn a girl next time," she says.

"I'll go easy on you, firecracker."

He takes turns dancing with both of us. It's not long before Wren cuts through the crowd, the dancers parting to clear his path without much effort on his part. He keeps his hands folded behind his back, his sultry gaze glued to Rowan. She bites her lip when he reaches her and his palms slide around her waist.

"Dance with me, little kitten," he rumbles.

"They don't hold back, do they?" I laugh, holding my hair up while my hips ride the highs and lows of the music. Elation builds in me. I love this feeling of freedom when I'm letting go.

"They like to play chicken with the line of decency, and half the time they're miles over it. Now that we're alone, we can really dance."

Jude moves behind me, taking my hips and controlling my movements. Levi scowls at us. A honeyed chuckle sounds in my ear.

"Something tells me he's not as fond of watching. Care to tell me how you have him so wrapped around your delicate fingers?" His grip digs in and my breath leaves me at the shift from easygoing to decidedly less so. "Because if you think you can manipulate him—"

I whip around, breaking his hold with one of the moves Levi taught me. "I'm offended you believe I'd do that to someone." My good mood vanishes. Has he been waiting to get me alone to confront me about this? What all those unreadable looks were for? Jude squints at me, mouth set in a thin line. "Why would you think that?"

"Because I've learned not to trust anyone blindly, no matter how sweet they come on. I don't want Levi to end up in knots over you." He lowers his voice. "Not anymore than he is."

This is the most open I've ever seen him and it shocks me that he's thought that way about me when I've already proven I only want to help them as a thank you for helping me.

"Fuck you," I snap. "Hell no. I've been on the wrong side of manipulation, too, Jude. I would never want to hurt someone like that, especially not any of you."

Jude blinks, head jerking back in surprise. "Is that so?"

I toss my hair and huff. "You can believe me at my word. I don't know what Levi's problem is, but my guess is because he's mad about kissing me."

At the admission, his brows hike up. "I see." He looks over my shoulder to where Levi hasn't moved from watching us since we began dancing. "That...makes a lot of sense." Nodding slowly, he sighs. "I'm just looking out for my friend, sweetheart. I'm more of a believe when I see it type when it comes to trust."

There's something haunted and bitter hanging beneath his words. It makes a pang of empathy echo through me that he harbors so much resentment behind his charming smiles.

"Then I'll just have to prove to you that I'm nothing like you thought." I lift my chin. "You shouldn't underestimate me."

"No, I won't make that mistake again." He glances in Levi's direction again. "He'll watch your back."

With that, he drifts off, his usual smile back in place. I watch him for a moment, sad that he's been burned by someone he trusts to make him wary of anyone getting close. Shaking my head, I let the music wash over me to clear away the lingering frustration from the conversation. I allow the music to consume my senses, unaware of my surroundings until someone else dances up on me. I don't stop him, too swept up in dancing.

Barely a heartbeat later, the guy is ripped away from me. Levi stands between us, his stance rigid and threatening.

"Leave," he barks.

The man glances at me, then stumbles backward when Levi brandishes his knife. I prop my hands on my hips, tonguing my cheek. Once he ensures he's scared him off, he angles his head to look at me over his shoulder.

"Was that necessary, grumpy?" I sigh. "He just wanted to dance, not ask for my hand in marriage."

"You think I'd stand by and let another man touch you?"

"If you had any claim over me, maybe. Did I dream the part where you told me to forget what happened?"

The drag of his eyes over me is a hot, possessive caress that steals my breath. It says he doesn't forget a second of the kiss we shared. He turns to face me, stepping into my body, chin tipped down to hold my gaze. I make to spin away to continue dancing, but he doesn't allow me to, pulling me against him. I can feel every firm line of his body pressed into mine, including the barbell piercing in his nipple grazing through my blouse.

"You can't let your guard down or trust random people," he rasps in my ear. "Consider this another lesson, princess."

I wind my arms around his neck. "Actually, I think it's time for me to give you a lesson."

He lifts a brow and I smile sweetly, moving slow enough for him to catch on. He groans under his breath when my body undulates against his. From one roll of my pelvis to the next, his hands find my hips like they belong there. I'd like it if they belonged there. They slide up my waist, fingers teasing the exposed skin of my back.

Our bodies move with fluid motion in time with the music. Levi's a better dancer than I thought. I knew he could move, but I didn't think he could let go enough to dance.

My mouth curves and I up the ante again, dropping down low and working my way back up slowly. His gaze burns, piercing into me. He rises to my one-upping, grabbing the back of my thighs, running his hands up them to my ass. His grip is tight and he hauls me closer. With each sensual move, we leave little doubt of what this dance is—a display of the way our bodies crave each other.

I grab the lapels of his jacket, pulsing my upper body against his chest to the heavy beat of the song. It rubs my nipples against his chest until I have to bite my lip to keep from crying out. The corner of his mouth lifts, awareness filling his smoldering gaze. He plants a hand in the middle of my back, his calloused palm a warm brand on my bare skin.

We both move together as one. I know what's next.

When our mouths collide, it's a rush of sinful heat. The dance floor melts away around us. I trace his lip ring with the tip of my tongue, moaning when he growls, sinking his fingers in my hair to hold me still while he devours my mouth. He kisses me until I'm dizzy. I grind against him, feeling his hard length against my stomach. A wild part of me has the urge to jump up to wrap my legs around him to get his cock between my legs where I'm aching for him.

Before I'm ready, he wrenches away, just like before. His eyes are a molten swirl of forbidden darkness, promising to swallow me whole. There's something feral about him that draws me in even more—I like his edgy wildness.

"That's enough," he says roughly.

"Then why do you keep kissing me like you'll die if you don't?" I challenge.

His eyes bounce back and forth between mine as he tongues at his lip ring. He buries his face in my neck, grip flexing on my hips.

If this is him barely holding himself in check, what would it be like if he snapped and took this further than making out?

"Everything about you twists me up," he mutters against my throat, mouthing at my flushed skin as if he can't help it every time he breaks to have a taste. "You make me want things I can't have."

"Who says you can't? A life of denying yourself what you want is a sad existence." I think of how I finally took that advice to stop playing my dad's game, claiming the independence I want one small rebellion at a time. "Take what you want. I make a point to after I promised myself that I would stop letting others control me. Now I only do things that make me happy, that allow me to follow my heart. If my heart wants you, grumpy, who am I to deny it?"

"If I take what I desire, there won't be any stopping." He nips my ear, catching me when I arch into him at the throb of arousal it stirs in me. "I'll keep consuming until I'm branded on every inch of you, body and soul."

My fingers curl in the material of his leather jacket. It's the first time he's admitted bluntly that he wants me. "I'm not stopping you. In fact, I'd very much like it for you to do just that, please."

"You should." He huffs, the hot breath sending tingles across my skin. "Because I want too much. Always too much. I want to slice your clothes off with my knife and take you right here. But I'd kill anyone for seeing you like that."

"Levi." I shudder, too turned on by the images he's putting in my head.

"I'm nothing but a messed up monster, princess. And you...you're not meant for the shadows. We can't. If I cross that line, there's no going back."

"I'd step into darkness to be with you," I whisper, cupping his cheek.

He allows it for a moment, eyelids lowering to half mast. Then he pulls away, shaking his head.

"No." It's final, but tortured.

Levi leaves me alone in the middle of the other dancers. But I'm never truly alone when he's around. His watchful gaze pins me in place, both a warning to anyone else and me that he won't let anyone touch me—but that he's holding himself back from doing the same. No matter how much we both want it.

CHAPTER SEVENTEEN

LEVI

The night for Wren's meeting arrives, and I still hate that we need to run ops from outside the museum. This all feels like a game we're losing. I'm tired of making the wrong moves and second-guessing everything.

At least it keeps my mind off kissing Isla. I meant what I said to her last week. I won't lose control around her again. It shouldn't have happened the first time, let alone the second. She's my own personal Siren's call, testing my survival skills against how long she's been in my head. With her in reach, knowing how goddamn sweet she tastes, it makes it that much harder to resist the pull I've always felt toward her.

She's not what I expected. I thought I knew her well from observing her, yet she's still taken me by surprise.

Between wanting her and needing to protect her, I'm going to slip up again.

I've avoided her since the party after I almost said too much, almost spilled the truth of how deep the fixation on her runs. If I'm not strong enough to withstand my own temptations, then I'll remove them from the equation, simple as that.

We prepare to leave together from our haven in the Nest, same as we would any other night for our regular jobs before shit hits the fan. Kidnapping and interrogating the slimy frat boy who was raping girls at parties on campus seems like it was a lifetime ago instead of last month.

"Wipe that look off your face." Jude hands me a bag of supplies. "We've done everything we can to prepare for this, short of posing as members ourselves. I'm good at what I do, but I'm not that good. Without studying them, like we will tonight, I would have to work on the fly."

"He's right." Wren bats Colton's hands away from his three-piece suit while ensuring his meticulously styled blond hair is in place. He's going out in full armor to face what we believe is a secret society. Colton ignores Wren's threatening expression and adjusts the button camera he designed to be undetectable with Wren's designer suit. "We'll turn this around to use to our advantage. They're inviting us in, so we'll take that and run with it."

"Don't forget to keep an eye out for the ring," Colt says. "If our hunch is right, that's their membership badge."

"I know." Wren's frown is bitter. "If it is, that means my father is one of them. And your uncle."

I lock my jaw, checking my knives are in place. The thought of my uncle having a hand in turning Sergeant Warner on us, cutting off our fight ring revenue, and getting me arrested pisses me off.

"My money has been on it from the start." Jude tugs on a black baseball cap over his thick dark brown hair. "It wouldn't surprise me that the richest men in the city are involved in a secret society. That's how this shit goes, isn't it? It's like something out of abue's telenovelas."

Colton smirks. "Ask her how the plot twist goes. We'll get ahead of the game. Better yet, I'll go over to her place and ask. Three weeks is too long without her cooking. Does she miss me as much as I miss her?"

Jude mutters about him being an asshole in Spanish and finishes packing a bag of climbing gear. We're prepared for anything tonight, armed with weapons and surveillance equipment.

Colton looks from his tablet to Wren's vest and nods. "All synced. It will start recording, but our feed will be a minute or so behind. If things get hairy, you're on your own until we get the feed, big guy."

"I'll be fine."

"You'd better be." Rowan snakes her arms around his waist from behind when she comes into the lounge. "I'll accept nothing less. If anyone tries to hurt you, I'll kill them."

Wren twines his fingers with hers, smirking. "I'm the one they should fear. Don't worry, I'll be fine, little kitten. I doubt they're going to hurt me. They've been watching close enough that they could have killed me at any point up until now."

Rowan releases a fierce growl that makes all of us snort. "No one is allowed to die. I still vote we set the place on fire once you're out."

"You and that arson habit, firecracker." Jude's golden eyes gleam. "We'll make them pay for what they did to your brother. But first we need to know our enemy. Then, when we understand what makes them tick—what they're greedy for, what they'll gladly kill for—that's when we'll know how to strike back with a devastating blow."

Wren turns in Rowan's embrace and cups her face, drawing her into a sultry kiss. They don't care that we're there, their world melting away until it's only the two of them. She gasps against his lips and he releases a deep chuckle, tugging her body against his broad frame. She's breathless when he pulls away, eyes bright with affection and desire.

I cut my gaze away with a harsh exhale. Those two are meant for each other. The inescapable pull I feel toward Isla isn't the same. I keep fighting against my longtime obsession, but maybe I should just fuck her and get it out of my system so I can go back to normal. My jaw clenches. No. I can't do that, because if I have another taste of her, I won't ever stop.

Jude watches them with a mix of envy and anguish, his thoughts likely on Pippa. They were exactly like that in high school, inseparable and devoted to each other.

We should remain just like this. The four of us, and Wren's girl. We let Rowan in because she's not like Pippa. She won't betray our trust. She understands what loyalty above all else means.

That's enough—there isn't a place for anyone else. Especially not a girl like Isla. She doesn't belong with monsters like us.

It's a treacherous game to allow anyone past the fortress I've built around my heart.

"Let's go." Wren looks at each of us with a ruthlessness glint in his eyes. "Tonight we get some fucking answers."

"Hell yeah," Colton crows.

Jude echoes the sentiment. I won't celebrate yet. We need to get through the night first.

With one last kiss, Wren leaves Rowan's side to drive in his Aston Martin ahead of us. We all pile into my Escalade. After a two minute head start, Jude pulls out from the hotel.

"Isla says good luck," Rowan murmurs from the front seat, her face illuminated by the glow of her phone. "With kissing face emojis."

Colton huffs out a laugh, tapping my shoulder with the back of his hand. My chest clenches. I expect one of them to say something, but other than sharing a smug, secretive look, they let me think in peace.

"Is the camera recording yet?" I rub my jaw, striving for my usual calm.

"Yeah, it's all good." Colt angles the screen so I can see the inside of Wren's sleek ride. "Relax, nothing exciting's happened yet."

"I'll relax when this is over. Until then, stay alert."

"That's what we've got you for." Rowan shoots me a half-smile over her shoulder that doesn't reach her eyes.

She's teasing, but she's feeling the unease as much as I am. At least she's no longer pissed off at me. Something tells me it's the fact I've been training Isla that finally assured her I wasn't going to boot her best friend out of the Nest on her tight, sexy ass to fend for herself.

"Damn it," Jude curses as we near the end of the route Colton mapped with him. "Police barrier. Looks like Pippa's pet rookies."

"They closed the road?" Rowan sits forward. "Is it a random checkpoint?"

"Nah, nothing's random in Thorne Point, Ro." Colton frowns at his tablet, scrubbing through a map app. "Plan B, Jude."

"Got it. Doubt they'd know anything if we stopped to ply them, anyway." He salutes the barricade of squad cars with his middle finger. They can't see it through the tinted windows. "I don't even think Pip realizes whose pocket she's in."

He says it more to himself, but I pick up on the tenseness in his tone. I don't know how he can still worry about her after what she did five years ago. She bailed on the plan and got him caught. If she'd been where she was supposed to be, it would have gone according to the plan Wren worked out.

"It doesn't matter if she does or doesn't." I trace the handle of the dagger hidden inside my leather jacket. "She's a traitor. She gets what she deserves for getting caught up in a dirty police force."

"I don't know her like you guys do, but I didn't get the impression she's corrupt like the rest of them. She helped with Ethan."

"Because I have something on her that would end her precious career," Jude snaps.

"She's a pain in the ass," Colton says. "Wren just arrived. His route was clear of blockades."

"Funneling him but keeping out unwanted guests," I bite out.

"Probably," he agrees. "Whoa."

"What is it?" Rowan twists around to look at Colton's tablet upside-down. Her brows jump up. "Are those candles?"

"Hundreds of them. Creep factor engaged."

I lean over to see and frown. Lit candles guide Wren's path through the museum. It's deserted, the orange light of the flames flickering off the arched ceiling.

"This is pleasant and welcoming," Wren mutters, his voice crackling over the audio feed.

We can hear him, but he can't hear us. We didn't want to risk our usual earpieces in case he was frisked. He's armed, but other than that he has the button camera and the listening devices we planted around the building.

"Why isn't it clear?" I ask.

"Feedback interference." Colton adjusts the settings on his tablet. "It's a given with older buildings. It's not a big deal."

"Better not be." Jude pulls over on a side street that connects to an alley one block over from the museum property.

All we can do now is sit and wait. I take out one of my knives, working through a routine I taught myself to learn the balance and weight, flipping and twisting the dagger from pommel to sharp tip. Faint scars remain on my fingertips from when I first picked up my weapon of choice.

Usually I use my switchblade to keep my head clear and alert, but Isla still has it. It's strange, but I couldn't bring myself to take it back. She carries it around with her in the pocket of my hoodie. I've seen it on the security cameras, watching her from afar while avoiding her. Somehow that brings me comfort to know she's taking protecting herself seriously.

Colton passes the tablet to Jude to sit on the dashboard so the four of us can watch Wren's descent down a flight of stone stairs that shouldn't be there according to the museum's blueprints. Rowan chews on the tip of her thumb.

"These are some serious vibes," Colt says.

The stairwell ends in a wine cellar. Barrels are stacked in alcoves Wren passes. Old stone arches set the gothic tone of the dungeon-like room. Rowan takes her phone out and opens Google.

"The Founders Museum was originally the residence of Hugo Thorne," she reads. "Later, he moved to his estate still occupied by descendants of his family line today, and the building became a meeting house for the city's founders until the first City Hall was built in 1781."

"Babe, none of us have been to the museum since like, the first grade." Colton waves a hand dismissively. "It's a boring field trip. Me, Lev, and Wren snuck out to play behind the building. The teacher was pissed."

"So this keys society has probably been established since then," Jude speculates.

"That would be my bet." Rowan frowns at the iron gate Wren stops at. "Doesn't look like they've updated the decor since the origination, either."

Two robed figures appear at the gate. He tilts his head and motions to the room with a cocky flourish. "This is cozy. Love what you've done with the place."

The robed figures remain silent, their faces hidden. They open the gate and frisk Wren. He weathers it, slapping a hand that goes for his belt.

"Don't forget the name I bear. I've played along with the theatrics, but my patience is a valuable commodity you don't want to extinguish." The robed figure steps back at Wren's cutthroat tone.

"No weapons are permitted, Thorne," one says in a garbled, computerized tone.

"Oh fuck." Colt throws an arm over the bench seat, dragging one of the bags over. He pulls out a pocket laptop that unfolds, muttering to himself as he boots it up. "Of fucking course they'd use voice modulators. Can't make it easy, no. Gotta go all in with the dramatics."

"Can you get around it?" Rowan asks.

"Yes, but we only have a live audio and visual feed. I can do a partial, but without isolating the specific voice in the audio extracted from the actual file like I can back at the Nest, it's as good as it'll get for now. The thing with voice modding is that there are speeds and octaves to work with, and I can only guesstimate from here."

"We'll keep our ears open," Jude says.

"Guys." I nod to the screen on the dashboard.

Wren is led through the gate into a circular room. Everyone wears a robe and those that have their hoods lowered have silver engraved masks. I narrow my eyes. Everyone in a mask has a deep purple robe, while the rest of them have black ones. I count eight in purple and twenty more in black.

"Was there a dress code I missed on the invitation?" Wren subtly turns back and forth to face the full room, giving us a good look at what he's seeing. "You'll have to forgive me, I don't do robes. Tom Ford will have to suffice."

The calculating amusement in his voice is evident to us from knowing him for so long, but it's not received well by some of the members.

"You were granted an honor, and you mock the opportunity?"

It's a woman's nasally voice. Black robe, voice unmodified. I absorb that information, reassessing the room. Colton hums beside me.

"Voice recognition will be easier to run on the ones who don't mask their voices," he says. "As long as there's an existing match, we'll nail 'em."

"Seeing as how you employed underhanded tactics to *invite* me here, I think I'll hold off on feeling honored," Wren snaps.

"Now, now, esteemed King," one of the purple robed members chides—this voice is digitized and deep. Colton makes an adjustment, but I can't place the voice. They step forward, holding out a hand to the woman who snubbed Wren. "A legacy hasn't blessed the Kings for many years. This is a time to celebrate."

The four of us exchange glances, our brows raised as we soak in the information we're getting. Kings. King was the word Colt had gotten from Ethan Hannigan's corrupted file most recently.

"Holy shit, we were right about them being a secret society. Not keys, Kings," Rowan whispers. "The keys are just their symbol."

"Legacy or not, what this one has done cannot go unpunished," the woman says. "Business has been lost after that fire at the shipyard."

"Apologies." The cutting tone isn't lost on us. "Thorne Point is a city full of pride and prestige. We don't need drugs sullying our streets. Go down to Castlebrook if that's the way you run business."

She scoffs, muttering to a robed person to her left. "He doesn't align with our ideals. He shouldn't become a King if he cannot serve the kingdom."

"That's enough," another purple-robed member orders. This one sits on the high-backed chair with towering angel statues on either side. Another person in purple robes leans down to murmur to the one who seems in charge. "Very well. He is your legacy to sponsor."

Wren inhales sharply.

"Do you think—?" Rowan bites her lip. "Is that his dad?"

"Has to be." Jude scowls. "These people like their word play too much, and that's what I'm picking up between the lines. See if he's wearing the ring."

"Left hand, pinkie finger," I say. "That's the finger he wears it on."

"There, look." Colton taps out a command to take a screen capture and zooms in. "Bingo."

"Now to look for my uncle and we'll have our smoking gun," I growl.

"Do you think Isla's parents might be members, too?" Rowan suggests. "She did tell me and Lev about these weird robes she found."

"Shit, maybe," Colton says. "It's probably a who's who of the city in there."

"Stop speaking in riddles and tell me what this is," Wren demands.

The one in charge studies him from the chair, stroking the bottom of his silver mask. "Where are we, young Thorne?"

Wren scoffs. "More riddles, wonderful. The Founders Museum."

"Correct. This has been the home of the illustrious Kings Society since our inception. Fathers of the city and their sons, and then their sons—" He waves a hand at the mouthy woman across the room. "—or their worthy daughters join together under our oath to serve Thorne Point, guiding it on the correct path to the ultimate ideal."

"*Carpe regnum*?" Wren ventures.

"Precisely. As Kings, we seize every opportunity in Thorne Point, working together to shape our kingdom. As a Thorne, your legacy has been written into our very history from one of the original founders." Wren's father straightens beside the chair, posture proud. "Should you choose to accept that you belong with us, you will know greatness. Your future is bright, young Thorne."

"Legacy, huh?" Wren puts on a show of pacing the room, giving the camera hidden in his suit a closer look at everyone.

"Good thinking," Colt says.

Wren turns toward his father standing in a position of power with a purple robe and silver mask hiding his face. "My father loves his legacy. But I—"

The audio feed crackles, then cuts out. The four of us sit forward.

Rowan shakes the tablet as if it'll bring back Wren's voice.

"What happened?" she hisses.

"Shit. More interference, this time from another frequency." Colton jerks his head as his fingers fly across his keyboard.

I pop the door, ready to sneak in to cover Wren's back. Jude moves with me, opening the back to get a gun.

"Wait!" Colt twists to hold up the tablet. "It's still recording, it's just the live feed that fucked up. Stand down."

"What if he needs us?" I clench my teeth. "We don't know what's happening."

"We do," Rowan says. "Look, he's leaving."

She points to the feed we've been watching. Wren retreats at a sedate pace, moving through the wine cellar.

I blow out a breath. "Fine. Let's get back once he's out. We'll meet him at the Nest to debrief."

Jude claps me on the shoulder. "At least now we know what we're up against."

"And who had my brother killed," Rowan says darkly. "All they care about is their bottom line, not who they eliminate to fill their pockets."

Colt leans over to hug her from his position in the seat behind hers. "Secret society or not, they're going down for it."

He returns to analyzing the signal interfering while Jude drives back. I peer at him from the corner of my eye.

"The person we ran into that got away?"

"Maybe. Probably." Colton sighs. "I don't like that they have a hacker on team Kings douchebags."

"We just confirmed Wren's father is part of a longstanding secret society pulling strings in the city, and that every man in his family has been a member, and that's what you're focusing on?" I shake my head. "You and your damn ego."

"My ego will bomb that fucker's system with a big dick Trojan that fucks them so good their computer will essentially be a gaping asshole." Colton laughs menacingly at the mental image while Rowan groans in the front seat.

"You're the worst," she says.

"That's why you all love me."

"Debatable most days," Jude says.

"I'm telling Mariela you don't love me anymore."

Out of all of our families, Jude's grandmother is the only truly loving maternal figure we all know. She took one look at us back in high school and decided we were hers, too.

"Don't." Jude chuckles. "Or I'll tell her it was you who accidentally burned down her rose trellis when you dropped your blunt without putting it out."

Colton's gasp is laced with betrayal. "You wouldn't. You swore you'd take that to the grave."

Rowan laughs at them. The fact they can relax because we're returning to our refuge settles me. I'm the only one who remains alert, watching out for tails following us. I'll always look out for the ones I love.

If the Kings Society threatens any of them, I will ensure their destruction.

I can't acknowledge it directly, but I know that now includes Isla, too. I honor my oaths, and I swore to keep her safe.

CHAPTER EIGHTEEN

ISLA

Once Rowan texts me to let me know the meeting they've been preparing for is over, I poke my head out of the holding room where I was running through my Lyrical routine to get my head off of obsessing over what happened at the party. Levi's disappearing act to avoid me makes it loud and clear he doesn't intend to kiss me again, or continue our training sessions. My dreams should catch up, because every night I dream of what would happen if he didn't hold back, if he dragged me into the shadows with him.

The halls are quiet this deep in the Nest. It's eerie by myself.

My hand finds Levi's knife in my pocket, curling around the cool tortoise shell casing. I still can't believe he parted with it for me after the panic attack, but I've been carrying it around with me for days. It might be silly, but having it instills a sense that I'm capable of anything.

Voices filter down the hall when I near the lounge. They must be back

I creep closer.

"—didn't miss much. Before they'll grant me membership, there's a test. They don't trust me outright just because of my legacy status. Something about an autumn revelry, but they kept talking in riddles." Wren loosens his tie and unbuttons the top two buttons of his suit. It's nice, tailored—this past season's Tom Ford if I had to guess. He collapses on the couch and pulls Rowan into his side. "They said it was to determine my worthiness to see if I measure up to the standards they value in a King."

My brows draw together. Wren is considered a king on campus but with the mention of membership I wonder if he's talking about an exclusive club.

Leaning around the corner, my eyes widen at Colton's screens. Video footage of a sinister looking stone basement plays. The room is filled with robes like I found in the back of my parents closet when I was a kid playing hide and seek with my nanny. I remember getting in so much trouble for being in there, and the nanny was fired. Beside the video, a signet ring is blown up. It's gold with a pair of skeleton keys crossed.

The scar on my thigh prickles with phantom sensation. The men that night all had rings. It's the only explanation I have for the shape of my scar. It's not a perfect match, but anytime I've seen someone wearing the ring, I question if they're part of the men's club.

"I recognize that," I blurt.

Levi whips around, his mouth flattening into a line. "This doesn't concern you."

"Actually, I think it might." Licking my lips, I venture into the room. Jude and the others eye me curiously, but Levi clearly doesn't want to hear what I have to say. I square my shoulders. "There's a man my father meets who wears a ring like that. And remember those sex cult robes I told you about?"

Levi's eyes widen.

"Sex cult?" Jude grins. "This is getting interesting."

"That secret wasn't interesting enough to warrant payment. When I was a little girl, I found black robes like that in my parents' things." I flap a hand at the screen. "Exactly like that. My nanny got fired over it for letting me in their closet."

Colton makes an inquisitive sound, stroking his chin. "Do you know where your parents were tonight?"

"How could I? They haven't contacted me and I haven't reached out, like you said."

"A while ago in the student union you said your driver was a dead ringer for a founding father." He crosses to his desk and pulls up a new search window. "What's his name?"

"Jeremiah Finch," I say.

Levi studies me, a crease forming between his dark brows. I never know what he's thinking, even more so since the two times we've kissed. He doesn't give anything away unless he's in a grouchy mood. Otherwise, his brooding nature is his mask.

While Colton inputs the search, he has a program running that identifies points on the blown up photo of the signet ring compared to a screenshot pulled from the video. He multitasks, opening an audio file while scrubbing through the recording.

"What's going on?" Knots form in my stomach as I try to push away the thought of the similar vibes I got from Dad's disgusting men's club. "Do you think my parents are there?"

"I think so," Rowan says.

"Given the Kings' obsession with power and shaping the city, most definitely," Wren says. "It's a secret society that likes to play puppet master. A senator would definitely match their membership requirements. It takes things one step further than paying off a senator to ensure beneficial legislation is pushed when he's a member of a secret society with matching ideals on how the city should be run."

Power. As if my father needs more of that.

"Holy shit," I whisper.

"Club's open." His grin is anything but nice. It sends a chill down my spine. "Look for your invitation after graduation."

"Fuck no." I cross my arms, needing some way to fight off the way anxiety simmers in my veins. "I don't have any shoes that go with those robes."

Jude and Colton chuckle.

"And you're missing that greedy bone that makes people bloodthirsty," Rowan adds with a proud smirk.

"Okay, Jeremiah Finch doesn't have any accounts on ancestry websites for me to hack, so that will take me a day or two." Colton jabs the enter key and shoots me a grim look. "If he's got founder blood, there's a chance your kidnapping was ordered by these douchebags."

"What, like a mob hit?" I throw my hands up. "What would they want with me? That's even more ridiculous than my working theory that my dad planned to use me to pay off his debts."

"It could be both." We turn to Rowan. She shrugs. "Who says one has to be mutually exclusive from the other? If her parents are in the club, maybe it's a test."

An unpleasant sense of dread twists my stomach. I've been avoiding accepting the truth, not wanting to believe this was happening again. But then again...my father's already done worse to me. I know the evil he's capable of when it comes to me. I close my eyes against the wave of fuzzy memories, breathing through my nose.

I can't run from it anymore.

If my father's behind this, my fear is coming true. Dad is manipulating my life again.

A bout of fire tears through me. No. No fucking way am I going to allow it to happen. I've let fear rule me for too long. My fists ball. He can't use me like this. I'm done being a pawn.

"A sacrifice before they're rewarded?" Jude grimaces. "That's sick. Fucking rich people."

"You're a rich person," Wren points out. "Self-made."

Rowan elbows him. "It's different. You're old money. The kind that eats their own babies like rabid hamsters."

"I'm sitting on a rumor from household staff that claims the Whittakers are cannibals," Colton says.

"There's no way that's true," Levi responds.

"It's the Whittakers. I wouldn't put anything past them. You've seen their horde of miniature dogs at the summer soiree." Colton shudders. "Little demons. Definitely subsisting on questionable diets."

Levi pulls a face, then tilts his head to the side like he thinks the claim has merit.

"What—and I do mean this with full awareness that you guys operate under a different code of conduct in a parallel reality to the rest of us—the *fuck*?" I gape at each of them. "What's going on in Thorne Point?"

"Madness." Jude waggles his eyebrows. "When you deal in secrets as currency, you're wealthy with the darkest skeletons in the closet."

Levi claps a hand over his mouth to stop him from continuing. "She doesn't need to know." He lowers his voice, but I'm close enough to catch his harsh tone. "You're just going to spill them to her? She's not one of us."

I flinch. I can't tell if Levi thinks he's protecting me by keeping me in the dark, or shutting me out because he still hates my presence here.

Jude lifts a brow, his intelligent and scrutinizing gaze bouncing between me and Levi. He bats the hand covering his mouth away. "Does this have to do with you sticking your tongue down her throat last week?" Levi goes rigid, scowling at his friend. "I'm taking the pot on the bet, by the way.

"Hell no!" Colton declares. "I knew about it first. That money's mine."

"Technically, I knew first." Rowan smugly tips her head toward Wren. "And I didn't crack under pressure."

Wren hums, kissing the top of her head. "That was a very pleasant interrogation."

I meet Levi's gaze across the room. "You can trust me. I'm not going to tell anyone. My closest friend is in the room."

"I think given what she's been through, she should be brought in," Colton says seriously, turning to Wren. "She's already most of the way there after we took her to the party. It's time for all-access. We missed stuff before because we kept Rowan at arm's length."

Wren rubs his jaw, nodding.

"I agree. She's already connected to this. Stop fighting it, Lev." Rowan rises from her seat beside Wren to take my hand, squeezing it in support. I smile back, glad she's got my back. "We should've had her in the loop back when we found the hidden room on campus. Especially if her parents are connected to the Kings."

"You're really okay with letting her in?" Levi glances between Jude and Wren with a hard expression, dark eyes flashing with frustration. "Once she's in, there's no going back."

"It's another angle to work." Jude shrugs.

Wren is the last to answer, studying me, fingers covering his mouth. "Miss Vonn is harmless. And if she ever deceived us? Death is only one option."

"Wren," Rowan snaps.

I put on a brave face as determination bubbles inside me. "You have nothing to worry about. I've been stowed away down here and haven't told a soul. My best friend is the only person who has my loyalty. I swear it." Tossing my hair, I stare Levi down. "If you didn't believe that, you wouldn't have saved me."

Levi's jaw clenches. After a beat, he nods. "Fine."

"Welcome to crew, Isles," Colton teases. "Want me to print you a punch card to commemorate your honorary position?"

"What would I get when it's full?" My lips twist wryly. "And what would I have to do to get it punched?"

Colton's grin is salacious and suggestive. Levi growls, stepping between us. My breath catches. It's the closest he's come since last week. I physically have to stop myself from reaching out to grasp the back of his hoodie to keep him close.

"Focus," Levi bites out. "Wren—what else happened after the audio cut out?"

"First, how did it cut out?" Wren questions. "You set up days in advance and took care of the museum's security. The person you came across that night didn't interfere then, implying no one caught you planting your equipment. They shouldn't know we were listening, even if they knew you were on the property."

The grin drops off Colton's face and he drags his tattooed fingers through dark brown hair, cracking his inked neck side to side. "They have someone on team crusty douchebag. The recording is stored on the hidden camera, but the feed crackled, then went dead from interference. Rather than taking out my stuff, their tech guru scrambled my signal boosters with their own emitter. It's like the one I use to block cell signals. They can be dialed to a specific frequency. They might not know about the planted equipment, but they definitely assumed you had a wire or line of communication to listen in."

"So they don't trust us as much as we don't trust them," Wren murmurs.

"I'll see what I can do to trace them." Colton spins to his computer.

"So..." I chew on the corner of my lip as their attention lands on me. "If my parents did this, that's why there are no reports of me being missing by the police or the news? You said you emailed my professors, but even social media hasn't been freaking out. No one took your bait to post about me at the party. Not even on the hashtag used for sightings of me."

"Hashtag Vixen Vonn Daily, right?"

My cheeks heat. I got used to life in the spotlight with Dad's political career, but sharing it with my friends makes it seem so superficial, even if I don't encourage it. "Yeah. You know it?"

Colton grins proudly. "Baby. I started it back in tenth grade when your tits came in."

"Colt." Levi's warning snarl is almost feral.

His friend's grin is completely unrepentant. "He's the one that took most of the pics for the fan account I started. He basically learned all his stalking skills practicing them on you."

"What?" I startle at the thought of Levi watching me for years without my knowledge.

A warm glow shouldn't expand in my chest at the admission, yet it does. I duck my head, hiding a small smile. Have we both always been aware of each other? Maybe more so on his part. If he's been watching for that long, he's seen my evolution from being plagued by my nightmares to fighting back against them with positivity.

Levi shifts so quickly I barely register the movement before the knife arcs through the air. Colton ducks the hurled knife. It lodges in the back of the bright orange gamer chair. Jude collapses on one of the black leather couches, covering his face with an arm as he cracks up.

Wide-eyed, Colton looks from the weapon to Levi. "Seriously? You could've maimed my perfect face, you dick."

Levi turns his back, jaw set. He glances at me, then avoids my gaze.

"Enough." Wren pinches the bridge of his nose. "To answer your question, possibly. We don't know for sure. This is our first real encounter with the Kings Society. They've been fucking with us since we started sniffing around the criminal organization that was running a multi-state drug operation until Rowan took out their supply. The fact they actually are a secret society was only a working theory until tonight."

"We'll figure it all out," Rowan promises. "They've revealed who they are, and knowing who they are means we can find more."

Answers. That's what I need now that I've accepted the likelihood of history repeating itself.

I turn to Colton. "Did you ever find anything out about the van?"

He pulls a face. "Ah, shit. I haven't. It got pushed to the back burner when the registration pulled a fake name, some guy who's been dead for the last decade."

"We should start there. Go back through what happened that night to find the connection to the Kings, her parents, or both," Jude mumbles from beneath his arm, sprawled on the couch. He lifts his arm. "This is the second time we've written off a problem that didn't seem connected. Probably shouldn't make that mistake again."

Wren hums, scrutinizing the recording on the screen. "We thought Hannigan was only mixed up with Stalenko for digging into them, but it was the tip of the iceberg. The Kings have been moving the pieces on the board the entire time."

"And considering what I keep extracting from his file, I think what he wanted to tell Ro was that he found the Kings," Colton says. "I think there has to be more member identities in there. In the meantime, we could go through every influential person and start picking apart their lives with the secrets we've collected."

Rowan's expression becomes strained, her eyes glistening with the shimmer of unshed tears. "He tried to warn me, but they got to him first."

Wren pulls her away from my side, murmuring to her in a deep, rasping tone when he tucks her into his broad frame. She nods, sniffling, burrowing deep into his chest. His arms lock around her and he drops a kiss on top of her head.

For such a cold-hearted man, the way Wren cares for her is clear for any of us to see.

My attention slides to Levi, finding him already staring back at me. I roll my lips between my teeth as hot and cold tingles of awareness rush across my body. He's always watching—maybe for longer than I ever thought. It makes my stomach dip pleasantly at the idea.

His words from the party run through my head for the millionth time, his claim that he doesn't want to tarnish me as if he's so broken he doesn't deserve love, denying himself. An aching pang echoes in my chest.

The rumors call him a monster, but it hurts my heart that he thinks of himself as one.

I draw a deep breath to stop my head spinning from information overload and touch my temple.

"You good?" Rowan murmurs.

"Yeah. This is a lot to take in." I offer a wobbly smile. "I knew you were all getting into deep stuff, but I never knew it could involve me, too."

"If I'd known, I would've told you everything sooner. The only reason I didn't was to protect you. These people are..." She swallows. "They murdered my brother. They're dangerous and they have even less morals than the guys."

I pull her into a tight hug. "They can't get away with what they've done." My tone is fierce. I'm ready for answers. "More minds are always better."

Levi meets my gaze over Rowan's shoulder, dark eyes burning with interest. It's the same way he looked at me when he first trained me to block physical attacks. His attention traps me, leaving me unable to look away. I think I've intrigued him, but I can't imagine he doesn't feel the same when his friends are in trouble.

"What's our next move?" Jude asks.

"You two spread word around campus. The Crow's Nest is on for Friday night. Now that we have a better understanding of who has had their eye on us, it's time we stand tall and make them see how little this shakes the real legacy we've built," Wren directs Levi and Colton. "Business as usual. Coming for the fighting ring doesn't put a dent in the pies we have our thumbs in, and we've already allowed the Kings to see us on our back foot. Let's show them why the Crowned Crows are a name whispered with fear and reverence."

Levi rustles his hair. Crossing the room, he yanks his knife from the gamer chair.

"So the Halloween party is on?" Colton lets out a whoop of elation at Wren's nod.

"You don't think they're going to come for either of us?" Rowan nods to me. "I'm not going back to the penthouse while the rest of you get to move around freely." She smirks. "You know what I'll do."

Wren gives her a filthy, seductive, dragging his eyes over her. She bites her lip. "I think it was their underlings who were more interested in you. And we proved they won't move in on either of you with us around last week." His gaze shifts to me. "As for you, Miss Vonn, you still shouldn't return home yet. You don't go out alone until we know more. And if your parents do contact you, we all know about it immediately. We clear?"

"Fine with me," I say.

Jude and Colton nod. Levi takes a beat longer, attention on the lethal looking dagger in his hands. His nod is barely perceptible before he stalks off, closing the door to the gym behind him.

"Is he okay?" I frown after him.

"He'll be fine." Jude waves a hand. "He gets like that. You get used to it. He just needs to hit something for a while."

Wren and Rowan slip out of the lounge together. Before they get around the first corner, Rowan's moan echoes from whatever Wren's doing to her. The corners of my mouth lifts. I'm happy she found love to guide her through such a tough time in her life.

My gaze drifts to the closed gym door again. Muted angry metal music filters through the door, interrupted by a heavy, rhythmic thumping. Something in my chest tightens at the idea of him alone with his thoughts, working his problems out with violent anger.

He believes he's a monster.

I take a step toward the gym. If he doesn't believe I'm willing to step into the dark shadows with him, I'll just have to show him that I'm not afraid. Not of him, not of what he could do to me, or of being swallowed whole by his darkness. I'll still shine bright.

A monster wouldn't save my life. A monster wouldn't teach me how to stop a panic attack. A monster wouldn't touch me the way he does, even if he's holding back.

I see the good in his heart he doesn't believe is there.

The only real monsters in this city are the ones who are truly evil.

"I wouldn't recommend whatever it is you're thinking," Jude warns. "When he's like this, it's best to leave him alone."

Alone. Unhappiness fills me.

"No one should be left alone when they're sad," I murmur.

Jude shrugs. "He likes it that way."

"Don't sweat it, babe. He'll be back to his regular emo self after a few hours in there," Colton adds.

Every instinct in me fights against leaving him alone, but I listen to his friends. The worry doesn't leave me for the rest of the night.

CHAPTER NINETEEN

LEVI

It's late, close to three in the morning. I haven't slowed down since I stepped foot in the gym, overcome with the need to hit the bag with my fists until the world makes sense again.

Light pours into the dimly lit room and I find Isla's familiar, lithe dancer's frame silhouetted in the doorway. I should send her away. If she enters, the temptation of everything I want to take from her will flare back to life with a ferocity I'm not sure I'm capable of controlling after avoiding her for days. My fists tighten at my side.

It's never been such a problem to rule myself. This thing I feel for her... it's an untamable beast, unwilling to bow to the collar I want to put on it. Especially after tasting her, knowing reality is far better than any fantasy.

"Couldn't sleep?" I resume my workout, adjusting my form to make up for the brief lapse.

She stays in the doorway. "I was worried."

A heavy breath gusts out of me. "I told you, no harm will come to you. We'll keep you safe."

I'll keep you safe goes unsaid, but it still fills my head. I throw a jab at the bag as if it'll obliterate the unnecessary responsibility I feel for her.

The fact that she might be connected to our problems doesn't explain why I still can't get my obsession with her out of my head, either. I can count on my hand the number of people I trust and protect—all of them asleep in the Nest right now. Then there's her, my anomaly. The bright beautiful beacon who has always drawn me in since the day I laid eyes on her in that alcove at Thorne Point Academy.

She wasn't as feisty back then. I'd seen her before, but something about catching her crying in the courtyard when I skipped class pierced through my chest, straight into my heart. The awareness of her never left.

Isla doesn't know I saw her crying in the alcove—I've always made sure to never get caught—but I've watched her since then, uselessly ignoring the way my heart rate picks up when she's around, mouthing off...most of all when she's laughing.

She leaves the doorway, coming closer into a dark world she needs to stay away from.

I keep waiting for Isla to break, but she surprises me by showing me the different facets of her strength. Every assumption I've harbored for her is rewritten by her refusal to cower in the face of danger.

How could I have gotten my evaluation of her so wrong? Not only do my boys and I pride ourselves on knowing people inside and out, I've been watching her for so long that somehow I never realized beneath her flair for dramatics she has a sharp mind and an admirable resilience to any challenge thrown at her. I was too blinded by her beauty and light to see it.

Now I can't fucking ignore it, no matter how hard I try.

"No, I'm not worried about being in danger. I know you'll protect me."

Her voice is soft, hard to hear over the music. I turn it off as she ventures deeper into the room, engulfed in one of my shirts. The bottom of the black Henley skims her bare thighs. Automatically, I scan her leg for the scar I touched, fighting the urge to slip into the night to hunt down everyone who's ever hurt her.

It still puts complicated thoughts in my head to see her in my clothes. The very thing I used to dream about has become a reality, an ever-present allure when she prances around in my things.

Her gaze roams my body, intrigue and hunger swirling together in those hypnotic blue irises just like the last time I was shirtless. I lost it hours ago, my skin gleaming with sweat. She takes in the tattoos covering my torso, chest, and arms, lingering on the thick snake coiling from my shoulder, around my side, and down the center of my spine. I swear I catch her mouth form the word *wow* as she stares at my abs.

"I was worried about you," she says. "Are you okay?"

"Me?" The question barrels past my lips before I can rein it in.

"Yeah, you seemed upset when you came in here. The others said to let you be, but I couldn't go to sleep without knowing if you were or not."

Fuck, her earnest, caring expression does things to me, sending my heart in a goddamn tailspin. I don't do this—feelings. I shut them off to stay efficient.

Isla comes around to stand behind the bag, placing her hands over mine where I caught it on the backswing. "It's okay if you're not."

The sharp inhale I drag in burns my lungs. "I'm fine. Just go to bed."

"I don't think you are."

Stubborn little thing. I shake my head.

"You should just—" My words trail off when she backs up with a challenge sparking in her striking eyes. "Now what are you doing?"

Instead of answering, she moves to the mat and lifts her hands. "Come on," she taunts when I remain frozen in place by the punching bag. "The only way you manage to talk anything out is by fighting your way through it. Come at me."

I prod my lip ring with the tip of my tongue, ignoring the swirl of desire those words stir. "If I fight you for real, you won't be able to handle it."

"I can handle anything you throw at me, grumpy. Come on." She angles her head and peers at me through her lashes. "Unless you're afraid if you come close to me you'll trip and your mouth will land on mine again?"

With a growl, I move, rushing her before she can get her bearings. I catch her around the waist and toss her down to the mat, kneeling over her with my hand holding the base of her throat.

"See? No contest."

The corner of her mouth lifts. "Again, you cheater."

"I didn't fucking cheat. You gave me five different openings." I keep my hold on her neck, memorizing her soft skin. I flex my grip and bite back a curse at the way her lashes flutter. "If I keep going easy on you, you'll never learn."

She pops up gracefully when I give her space. "Do I get to learn to throw knives yet?"

A grin breaks free without my permission. I scrub a hand over my mouth to hide it. "We'll see."

I picture kneeling at her feet, draping her leg over my shoulder, and strapping a thigh holster to her leg while I lap at her pussy. Fuck, the fantasy makes my head rush with want. She would look sexy as fuck armed with a knife on her thigh.

"How many knives do you own?" Her question breaks me out of my thoughts. "Do you name them?"

I scoff. "No."

"Is there a rule against it? Names have power." She turns her back on me, both a taunt for the monster and an odd comfort that she trusts me enough to show me the vulnerability. My gaze drags down to her bare thighs beneath the hem of my shirt. "I think if I had a knife I'd name it...Stevie McStabby."

"That's a ridiculous name." I slash a hand through the air. "And I don't name my weapons."

"Really? I've been calling the switchblade you gave me Teeny."

I jerk my head and pull a face. "No."

To teach her a lesson for giving me her back, I move again, this time pinning her on her belly to the mat with my feet spreading her legs wide so she can't get leverage to escape. She lets out a soft *oof* and collapses to the mat after a minute of struggling.

"Cheater," she taunts.

"Skilled and paying attention," I counter against her ear.

Her body shudders beneath mine. There's a shift in her breathing. As it grows thicker, she pushes her ass back against my cock. I squeeze her wrists, stretching them higher over her head.

"Isla," I warn.

"Why do you deny what you want? What we both do? I can feel you're hard."

She shimmies her ass again. It's fucking torturous, making me want to let go and grind against her. Instead, I shove away, pacing to the other side of the gym to get her sweet scent out of my head. The rustling of the mat tells me she's rising to her feet.

"I'm trying to understand," Isla says. "If you just wanted to fuck me, I think you're the type of guy to hit it and quit it before the sheets are cool. But you pull away every time you've kissed me, so there's something I'm missing here. Is this why you've always acted like you hate me?"

I whip around so fast the room blurs. My control unravels rapidly, until the single thread holding me back snaps. My feet close the distance between us without my permission, and I back her up until she's pinned against the mirrors on the wall. A feral noise tears from my throat as I push my chest into her body and bring a knife to her throat with a dexterous movement.

My blade against her skin should terrify her, but once again all it does is light her eyes up. I intended to scare her by dragging the knife over her skin. Her eyes only gleam brighter with arousal. I can't tear my attention away, heart thudding as she tilts her chin up to give me better access.

Why is she so drawn to my monster?

This can't happen. She's a dangerous drug for me to take a hit of because I've resisted the lure for so long. If I give in to that desire, I'll be broken, willing to raze the world to the ground for her—that's the kind of power I've never let someone else hold over me. Not even my brothers.

"I don't hate you, Isla," I grit out through clenched teeth as I trace her pulse point. "You're an obsession I can't fucking cut out."

Her blue eyes widen at the confession, lips parting. My gaze falls to them, and with another rough sound I slam my mouth against hers, taking what I've always wanted. I can't hold back anymore. One taste was never going to be enough. I'm falling for her Siren's call and there's nothing I can do to deny the way she makes me crave.

She opens for me without hesitation, sweeping her tongue against mine and arching into me with a smothered gasp. I swallow every needy sound she makes and she kisses me back fiercely. Fuck, fuck, *fuck*. She's a perfection I want to drown in.

"You're always in my head. That's the only thing I hate." I speak against her lips, barely allowing space between us. Any time not spent speaking is spent exchanging small kisses that make her shiver in my arms. "My obsession with you goes so fucking far back, princess."

"The pictures Colton mentioned?" she murmurs. "It's okay. I kind of like the idea of you watching me. I was always curious about you, too."

Her confession and acceptance of my long-buried truth pierce into my chest.

"Longer," I admit. "I saw you crying in the courtyard at Thorne Point Academy."

Her broken moment was beautiful, awakening me from the numbness I drowned in after losing my mom. The fascination with her began with intrigue and grew over the years with her radiance.

She stiffens, surprise flitting across her features. "You—When I was fourteen?" She swallows, averting her eyes. "I know what day you're talking about. That wasn't long after—"

"*Yes.*" I don't let her finish, claiming her mouth in another searing kiss because I can't wait another minute.

When we part, I stare in fascination at the path my knife takes, eyes hooding when she swipes the tip of her tongue over her lip. Growing bolder, her fingers dance over my abs, mapping my body in the same way I explore hers. My eyes close when her palm skates over my crow tattoo. I don't allow many people to touch me, but her touch is an addictive balm.

"If I could cut you out of my head, I would have done it a long time ago. But I can't. I've tried." Her pupils grow darker with each measured caress of my blade. Grasping her jaw firmly, I trace the end of my knife over her plump lips. "Open."

Isla's gaze doesn't waver as she parts them for me once more.

"Do you know what it takes to sharpen every blade I own, princess? I'm very meticulous. I keep each one sharpened to perfection." Raking my teeth over my lip, I rest the knife on hers. My cock throbs at the sight of her demurely accepting it into her mouth. "Sharp enough to slice through anything. I know how to apply pressure to draw blood, or how to carve only my initials."

Holding my gaze, she licks the blade deliberately. My grip on her jaw flexes, fixated on the heady sight. I raise it to my mouth and watch heat flare in her eyes as I swipe my tongue along the same path, licking over her saliva.

"Are you done living in denial?" Her voice is a seductive, husky drawl that makes my cock jump. "Because I'd really like you to fuck me now. Embrace obsession. Give in. Don't you dare kiss me like that and walk away again. I can't survive another night with only my fingers when I want it to be you."

Another growl rumbles in my chest, picturing her hand between her thighs while she writhes with need thinking of me like I've done so many nights wishing I had her for real instead of my hand.

She's right. Neither of us can resist this thing between us anymore.

I draw the blade back down her jaw to the loose neckline of the borrowed shirt she wears. Our eyes meet, then I grip one side of the fabric and cut from the neckline down the front until it falls open to reveal her bare tits, her nipples hardened to tight, flushed buds. Her breasts heave with her aroused gasp.

"Shit, that's hot," she whispers.

The corner of my mouth curls in satisfaction. "We're only getting started. You had your chance to run."

Leaning against the mirror, she plays with one of her nipples, smirking at me. "Does it look like I'm running? I'm not running."

Batting her hand away, I bend my head to close my lips around her nipple, enjoying the way she arches into me and cards her fingers through my hair. Her nails scrape my scalp, tearing a groan from me. The smooth metal of my piercing makes her cry out when I graze it back and forth over her sensitive skin.

"I'm taking what I've always wanted from you tonight," I rasp against her skin, tugging her into my body. I don't want any space between us. "I once thought it would make me weak, but I'm done, Isla. I don't care anymore if I'm no good for you. I've held back for too long. Tonight I'm making you mine."

"No complaints here." She mouths at my neck when I lean into her. "I want this. Want you."

I never expected the effect hearing her say those words would have on me. My body shakes and my grip on her hips flexes. My knife clatters to the floor, forgotten for the time being. I've never given up control like this, but all I'm able to focus on is her. I push the tattered shirt off her shoulders, running my hands down her body to toy with the black lace thong she's left in. She holds onto my arms, pressing on her toes to kiss me.

It turns filthy fast. I grip her hair, tugging to angle her head back while I force my tongue into her mouth. She scrabbles at my shoulders, rubbing her thighs together. I can smell how turned on she is. If I cup her pussy, I know I'll find her dripping wet and we've barely done anything.

"Get on your knees," I order, tightening my hold on her hair. "I've wanted to fuck your sassy little mouth for too long."

Isla grins at me. "If you think stuffing my mouth is going to make me stop, you're wr—ah!"

I was right. She's wet as fuck. I lift a brow while I rub her clit through the lace. "You sure about that? Pretty sure I know a lot of ways to shut people up. Some are nice, some are not so nice. So what'll it be, Isla?" I swipe my thumb along her swollen lips. "My cock, or do I need to give you a gag to keep you from running your mouth?"

She wraps her fingers around my wrist to hold me where she wants me, rocking against my hand with a gasp. "You can do whatever you want to me as long as you make me come."

I nip at the corner of her mouth, my words a gruff promise. "Have no doubt, we're not stopping until I wring every orgasm I want out of you to make up for all the times I've denied myself. You're going to be a dripping fucking mess for me, baby."

The obscene sound she makes is music to my ears. I smirk, circling her clit faster until her nails dig into my arm and a stuttered breath escapes her. She goes still, then melts back against the mirror.

"That's one," I say. "Now get on your knees."

The sight of Isla Vonn on her knees, undoing the button on my jeans, is the hottest thing I've ever seen. I chew on the inside of my cheek to stave off the heat pulling into my groin. She takes me out, pumping my shaft while she teases the tip with her tongue. A rumble from me makes her smirk and bat her lashes at me.

"How do you like it?"

"Sloppy. Deep."

When she parts her lips, I thrust into her mouth shallowly, adjusting so I have her pinned to the mirror again, my fist holding her in place by her hair. She lets me, tilting her head back for a better angle. Her eyes blaze with desire, taunting me to take anything I want.

"Fuck," I bite out, picking up the pace until I'm fucking her face against the mirrors. Her mouth is a sinful heaven. "How far can you take me down that pretty throat, princess? Swallow my cock down. Take it all."

Her eyes roll back in her head and her nails dig into my thighs as she obeys. I only last a few more thrusts before it's too much. I'm not ready to come yet, not until I've felt what it's like to be buried in her pussy. My cock falls from her mouth with a wet sound. She wipes her mouth with the back of her hand while I turn her around to put her on hands and knees on the mat, guiding her lush ass where I want it. Her spine curves beautifully with her natural flexibility.

"Please don't stop," Isla begs. "I need more."

"I'll die before I stop touching you right now." Kneeling behind her, I reach for the abandoned knife and smooth a hand over her ass. I draw the blunt side of the blade down her ass. "Do you want me to take these off and fuck this pussy until you scream for me?"

"Yes, shit, *yes*," she pushes out.

"Ass up."

She complies, pressing her tits to the mat. Jesus. I squeeze the base of my dick as I tease her through her panties until she wriggles.

Growing impatient, I hook a finger in the lace and pull the thong to give myself enough room to catch the material on the knife, drawing it back further until we hear the first tear in her delicate panties. Our heavy breaths are the only other sound in the gym.

The small round scar on her thigh catches my eye. It almost could be a brand. My lip curls and a vicious anger overtakes me.

No one will ever touch her again. Only me.

I cut the thong and leave the scraps hanging around her waist.

"Why does that feel so good?" she rasps. "Whenever you have your knives out, I always think it's hot, but this..." She cries out again when I flip the knife and press the blunt hilt against her pussy, rolling her hips. "Yes, like that. It feels amazing. I could come just like this."

"Then do it, baby." I cover her back with my body, kissing between her shoulder blades. "Come on my knife. Is it the danger that gets you off?"

"Ah! Yeah."

My teeth graze her skin each time she shudders, panting as she chases her next orgasm grinding her clit against my knife. When she stills, biting her lip to muffle the sound of pleasure, I toss the knife aside and grasp her neck, guiding her head back to kiss her.

"Don't hide another sound. When you come for me, you scream it." Eyes hazy from pleasure, she nods while I massage her throat in a loose grip. "Hands on the mirror. Good girl, keep them there."

Shoving my pants down, I line up behind her, muttering a curse as the tip of my cock glides through her slick folds. She tilts her hips, pressing her ass back into me.

"You better be on birth control, because I'm not stopping." I slide a hand around her waist, hauling her back while I enter her with a sharp thrust that makes us both go rigid and release relieved noises. "And I'm not putting anything between us."

She tips her head back and a moan slips out. "We're good. Come on. You've made me wait so long already."

My arm shifts to band around her chest and I hold onto one of her tits as I grind my cock deep inside her before pulling out to snap my hips again.

"Oh god." Her head falls on my shoulder and she clenches on my cock.

With a primal noise vibrating in my chest, I set a brutal pace. Her body grips me like it doesn't want me to leave, but welcomes me with each thrust that drives my cock into her pussy. Our breaths fog the mirror and sweat beads on our bodies. Needy sounds catch in her throat and I bury my face into it, biting her flesh to leave a mark that claims her as mine. It's the only mark I want to see on her body—ones I've put there myself because she wants them.

"Fuck," I rasp. "You feel so good, princess."

One of her hands leaves the mirror to twine around behind my neck to keep me in place plastered against her back, not an inch of space between us. I drop a hand to rub her clit, mouth curving when I feel her convulse with another orgasm.

"Good girl. That's it."

"Your turn," she murmurs.

Isla flashes a saucy look over her shoulder and moves in time with my thrusts, her pussy clamping down on my cock. Even like this she pushes me, taunts me to see how far she can go before I break. It makes me want to change positions to have her bouncing on my cock. I grit my teeth and smack a hand against the mirror, using the other buried between her legs to pull her against me.

My orgasm makes a breath punch out of me as I slam deep one last time, spilling inside her with intense pulses, my vision swimming.

We collapse on the mats with ragged breaths. She curls into my side as if she belongs there. It stirs warmth in my chest and I tug her thigh across my torso, reaching back to squeeze her ass.

"Damn, that was better than I ever pictured." Sighing, she snuggles closer, humming when my touch delves between her thighs. "It's always the quiet ones that know how to fuck like animals."

"You better not be talking about anyone but me," I say gruffly.

"Of course," she replies sweetly, dropping a kiss on my pec right above my pierced nipple. "Only you, grumpy."

My fingers move through her folds, pushing my come back into her pussy, driven by a possessive urge to keep marking her in every way imaginable. She arches, mouth dropping open.

"You think you're done?" A smoky laugh leaves me and I press my erection against her. "I'm not finished with you yet. You're mine now, princess. I told you, once I got a taste there was no stopping until I consume every part of you."

Isla's eyes hood and she cups my face, bringing me in for a kiss. "So consume me. I'm all yours."

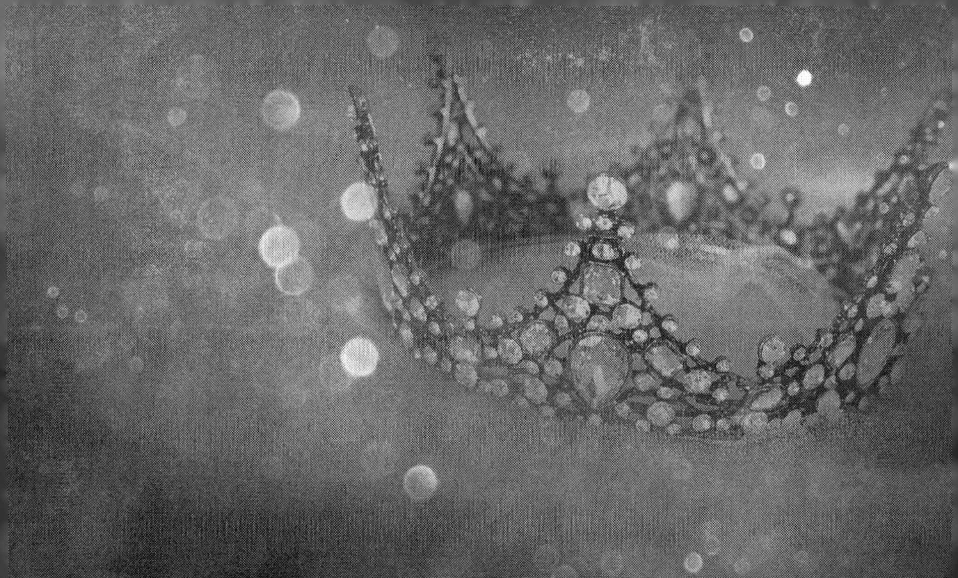

CHAPTER TWENTY

ISLA

AFTER Levi finally let go and crossed the invisible line between us, we've been entwined in each other. He took me to my room after we went another round in his gym, but he didn't leave me alone, climbing into bed with me after a sexy shower spent running our soapy hands all over each other. I'm addicted to the face he makes when I run my hands over his tattoos, like he's high on the feeling of someone touching him. My morning alarm to get up and dance around went off before we finished round...I don't know, I lost count, too delirious from pleasure to care about anything other than his head buried between my shaking legs.

Today is the first time he's stepped away to leave me on my own, citing the need to secure the perimeter around the Crow's Nest Hotel before the guys allow the university's students to descend on their gothic hideout for a night of Halloween-themed debauchery. While the guys are busy running final checks, me and Rowan finish getting ready together.

I lean closer to the mirror in my room to inspect my signature red lipstick, winking at myself when I find it's the perfect shade with the Medusa vibe I've gone with for my costume.

I feel unstoppable dressed as the goddess of female power, freedom, and transformation. Those are all strengths I need to fight back my demons. This is more than a costume. As I wing my eyeliner, a sense of determination settles within me. By surrounding myself with strong people, it's given me strength, too.

It's time I fought back for myself. I've only begun getting out from under my parents' thumb recently, but I never want to be under it again. To move forward, I need to face them. I'll embody Medusa to do it.

My skin is decorated with a pattern of black and gold scales that goes all the way down the plunging neckline of the black leather bodysuit I'm wearing with thigh high boots. Snake jewelry wraps around my legs and the motif continues in body paint anywhere I'm showing skin. I was inspired by Levi's snake tattoo. It seemed fitting since I've finally charmed his dick.

"You look hot as hell." Rowan shoots me a sly look and waggles her eyebrows. "You've been even happier than usual the last couple of days. Didn't think you could shine any brighter, but there you are blinding us all."

She was the least surprised out of everyone when it was impossible to hide what happened. Levi might be quiet, but when he stops holding back he's more tactile than Wren is with Rowan, almost as if he's starved for touch because he restricts himself to being an observer.

"Back at you, babe." I blow her a kiss, then smirk. "And I know you know how good getting dicked down is for clearing your head. Wait, no, don't touch that."

I fuss over her hair before she ruins the fabulous curls I styled her red hair with to go with her skeleton queen costume. It's a sheer mesh romper with a skeletal design over a lace bodysuit beneath. Wren's matches hers, one of his sharp suits completing their royal skull face paint looks. I adjust her black crystal diadem and nod.

"Perfectly badass."

She smiles. "I know dressing up isn't really my thing, but when I get to feel like this, I can't complain."

"See." I turn back to the mirror to adjust my own headpiece—a fabulous golden starburst crown that ends with gilded snakes. "That's what it's all about. Looking and feeling confident. You're a stunner either way."

A knock sounds at the door. "Are you decent? I hope not."

Rowan rolls her eyes affectionately. "Better not let Lev hear that. He'll cut out your tongue and pin it to the wall in the lounge."

Colton leans in the door, a sinister grinning neon light up mask from The Purge the only thing he's added to his usual hoodie. "We're ready to make our grand entrance."

I clap my hands. "I hope it's dramatic. Will there be smoke?"

"You know it, babe. I pulled out all the stops."

He offers us each an arm to escort us to the lounge. The rest of the guys wait for us there. A flutter moves through my stomach when I lock eyes with Levi. He rakes his gaze over me, approval flaring in his dark eyes.

He's dressed in a long trench coat, balancing the tip of a large dagger against his thigh. His brooding eyes are lined with liner he must have stolen from my makeup bag. It's a damn good look on him and I have to bite my lip to keep myself under control. The urge to beg him to take me to a shadowy corner to ease the edge off before we party is strong. I've never really been this girl, but with him I can't get enough.

I wasn't a virgin before Levi—my nightmare made sure of that a long time ago. But I'm not so broken from being raped that I've never had sex. I wouldn't let that hold me back from experiencing my life to its fullest. I'm capable of enjoying myself without being trapped in the warped memories. It's just never been so addictively mind-blowing like it is with him.

I move from Colton's side to Levi's, smoothing my hands up the lapels of the open coat. Rising on my toes, I whisper seductively in his ear. "What are you supposed to be, other than so hot you're making me wet just looking at you? You're like a sexy horror villain come to life."

He huffs out a laugh, slipping an arm around my waist. He uses the knife to tip my chin up, his eyes narrowing in satisfaction when I bite my lip against the reaction it causes.

"I'm the Leviathan."

Colton snorts behind me. "Lazy."

"A serial killer?" I purse my lips to the side. "Okay, I can see that with the knife thing going on. Be honest—did you pick your costume based on which one let you carry the biggest knife around?"

"I'd be armed either way. I don't ever go out without protection."

I check him out again. "Well, you make serial killer look good."

His mouth curves handsomely as if he's laughing at a joke I've made. His friends don't blink at the sight of me in his arms, fully aware of the shift between us. Colton slipped a reminder to come up for air and rehydrate under my door the morning after, and when we finally emerged from the room he was smugly counting cash for winning a bet.

"Are we ready to spread chaos?" Jude prompts with a smirk.

He's dressed as a devilish ringmaster with a top hat and a deep maroon velvet coat that has fine gold embroidery details. He shoots me a wink, rolling a coin between his fingers.

"Hell yeah." Colton's fist surges into the air. "Let's fucking party. It's theme night, bitches."

"Show no mercy out there." Wren passes a wicked smirk around our group, including me. He looks the part of a ruler tonight with the crown adorning his slicked back blond hair. "You're Crows. You don't bend or bow for anyone. Remind them all why they whisper our names with fear and respect. Remind them what we've built on our own."

I shiver, a strange sense of camaraderie taking hold of me. These ruthless boys have kept me safe, and now they've accepted me as one of their own. Rowan's mouth curves into a slow grin and she winds her arms around Wren's neck to kiss him. He's handsy with her, large palms massaging her ass possessively as they kiss. When they part he has eyes only for her.

"Let mayhem reign," Levi murmurs before brushing a swift kiss over my lips.

He's not shy about doing it in front of his friends, like I assumed he might be. He isn't hiding anything from them, taking my hand to lead me up the stairs that lead to the main interior hall of the old hotel. Muffled music echoes in the empty hall outside the ballroom, drifting through the decayed pieces of deteriorating wall.

Colton wasn't joking about the entrance. He has us climb onto a platform he rigged, messing around on his phone. Smoke billows from the base, covering our feet as it pulls us from the shadows into the main room behind their usual dais. The music swells and the partying students raise their hands in the air, screaming and hollering as the Crows appear.

Wren steps off the platform first, offering a hand to Rowan. She slips her fingers into his and yelps when he catches her around the waist to pull her down, setting her on the ground with a wolfish grin. They bend their heads close. Whatever he says to her is too quiet to be heard over the music. It makes her sway against him.

"They're definitely going to sneak off to fuck in the hedge maze later,"

Colton says.

"Not if we beat them to it," I sass, keeping my voice pitched low so only Levi hears me. His grip on my hand flexes and I rest my chin on his shoulder. "You can chase me like we're in a scary movie. It'll be sexy."

"Don't put any ideas in my head or you won't last long at the party."

A laugh shakes my shoulders as I take in the decrepit ballroom. It's more packed than usual, people coming out of the woodwork to see the Crows in the flesh.

On normal club nights at the hottest party spot in the city, the hotel's frayed vintage wallpaper and crumbling walls provide the forbidden atmosphere, but tonight things are scaled up to suit the theme. White marble busts on pedestals line the room lit by ornate candelabras with real candles dripping wax. Instead of the usual bar, drinks are at the center of the room being served out of a Victorian era hearse with black flower garlands.

"Wow." I whistle. "Is this how all the theme nights are?"

"You think frats have all the fun, but nah. We kill it." Colton's attention snags on a pair of girls filming him on their phones and goes still, tilting his head in an eerie manner. They shriek when he takes a staggering step toward them.

Jude chuckles beside us. "The parties thrown on campus are child's play compared to the resources we have access to." He tips his top hat and steps off the platform in a smooth move. "Remember, three can keep a secret if two are dead."

With that, he melts into the crowd. The only way to track him is the shrill ripples of screams as he makes his way through the revelry to sit atop the hearse at the center of it all like a true ringmaster.

"Shall we?" I swivel my hips to the music. "They're playing my song."

"Every song is your song." Levi steps off the platform like a vengeful dark angel and reaches up for me, grasping my waist. "So either you have a song or you just say you do so you can dance to all of them."

I shrug. "The music calls when it calls. I am merely its bitch. To the dance floor."

He doesn't drop me to my feet, carrying me like his prized queen. Colton, Wren, and Rowan follow, Wren's arm around Rowan's shoulders. They're the stars of the party but none of them are part of it. They're more like boogiemen. The crowd parts for us, almost as if they're afraid of getting close enough to be noticed. If the Crowned Crows notice you, then you're in for it.

Only one person doesn't move out of the way. She's dressed in a killer goddess costume with an ethereal glittering black crown and crystal gems on her forehead accentuating the look. Rather than a gown like most girls, she wears a belted jumpsuit with a lace bralette partially displayed at the deep v. Her braids are twisted into a thick bun and constellation earrings hang from her ears. Her cheeks are dusted with a silvery metallic shimmer of makeup that makes her dark brown skin look like a beautiful night sky speckled with starlight. A flute of champagne dangles from her fingers as she studies one of the busts.

Levi sets me down, subtly adjusting his grip on his knife.

She turns to us. "The fuck are these?" She nods to Colton, picking him out of our group easily. "And let me guess, they were your idea?"

Her caustic voice stirs recognition. Quinn, the fiery girl from the poker tables on campus.

"You again," Colton says. "The card counting queen."

"You were the one cheating in one of our games?" Wren's voice is hard and demanding.

Quinn lifts a brow and sips from her champagne. "Wasn't counting."

Colton pushes his mask up on his head and thumbs his lip, his gaze sweeping over her. "Sure. Maybe not then, but I did a search for you, Miss Walker. Castlebrook, Whittier, Sutton Cliff. You've been making the rounds anywhere we're running a game. Busy little bee, hmm?" He holds out a hand.

"Easy, big guy, I've got this. Rowan?"

"Yeah. We're going to get a drink." She takes Wren's hand and tugs him until he follows her. The sea of people swallows them until they're lost to the shadows of chaos.

"So what's the goddess of the night doing here?" At Quinn's flash of surprise, Colton gives her a cocky grin. "Nyx. Greek deity of the night, daughter of chaos, and..." His attention dips to follow the open neckline of her costume. "One of my favorite myths."

"You're the only one to get it right." Quinn slides her lips together, casting a sweeping glance around. "The rest of these uncultured yuppies think I'm supposed to be a dark fae or some fantasy shit."

"You look badass," I say.

She eyes me, then jerks her chin in a nod of acceptance. "Thanks. You too. Medusa's a dope choice."

Levi remains silent during the entire exchange, poised to strike at any moment. I always thought he was quiet, but standing close to him I can feel the tightly bound energy of his muscles ready to move the second he's needed to keep us all safe. He doesn't believe Quinn isn't a threat. Not yet.

"Are you here alone?" I remember her brother was with her before.

"Yup," she replies shortly. "Sampson ditched me for a hookup back in Castlebrook."

"Is that where you're enrolled?" Colton drifts closer to her with a swagger in his step and a seductive lilt in his tone.

Levi might be ready to attack her, but Colton has different ideas about this girl.

"For now." She meets his smirk over the rim of her glass, offering him a sassy toast before downing it.

"You appear to need a refill. Allow me." Colton offers his arm.

"What, you think if you're a gentleman, I might suck your dick?" Quinn scoffs in dismissal and turns away. "No dice."

Colton snags her elbow, stepping into her back, a wide grin plastered on his face. "Actually, I'm thinking you're a party crasher, so if you don't want me to throw you out, you'll stick with me, little night queen."

His tone remains light and teasing, but his grip tightens on her arm and a sinister edge lurks beneath the joking. Quinn stiffens and nods after a beat.

"Should we let her go with him?" I ask Levi.

He searches the room, still on alert. "Colt can handle himself."

"I meant is she safe with him?"

Levi smirks. "Without a doubt. The rest of us would kick her out, but Colton wants to play with his food first. Better for her to stay with him so he can find out why she needs money bad enough to hit all of our poker games before he boots her."

"You got all that from one conversation?" My brows jump up. "All I could focus on was her studded shoes. I'm pretty sure they were Louboutins, but it's dark in here."

"This is why you can't beat me, princess. I'm always paying attention to everything." Roughness edges into his voice and he teases the tip of his dagger between my cleavage, the cool metal making me shiver. "Always watching."

Biting my lip, I peer at him through my lashes. "Dance with me?"

When I back up, he follows, stalking me until we reach the dancing mass of bodies. They give us space as soon as they see him on the floor. His leer remains trained on me. I let the music flow through me and close my eyes as my hips begin to sway slowly. His touch comes from everywhere, fingertips tracing down the exposed skin of my plunging neckline, around my hip, across the back of my shoulders until he takes me by the hips and pulls me back into the hard lines of his body.

"Every time you dance, I want to gouge everyone's eyes out for looking at you," he rasps against my ear.

A shudder moves through me. "That's violent of you."

"That's who I am, princess. A violent, possessive man who wants to be the only one to ever look at you because you're mine. You've always been mine, since that day I saw you and you snuck into my head permanently."

My teeth sink into my lip. I shouldn't find Levi's smoky words hot, but they ignite a fire in my core that leaves me tingling. Coming from any other guy, I'd slap him, but from him they feel like another layer of his protectiveness. It's heady knowledge to realize he's felt this way about me for so long when all this time I believed he hated me.

Heat builds to an inferno between us from song to song. My skin tingles everywhere he touches me and my core pulses with a needy ache every time he grinds against my backside.

When I need air, I push through the crowd, Levi at my back brandishing his dagger to get drunk dancers to move. It's too warm in the room, I need to cool off. I head for the door usually used as the public entrance, the only one I used to know. A guy broodier than Levi, if that's possible, stands as still as the statues by the door. He's dressed as a grim reaper, his dark hair curling over his forehead and his shrewd light gray eyes flicking to us assessingly.

"Penn," Levi greets.

Penn. This is the guy he called the night of my attack. The one who cleaned up the dead body. I searched once I had my phone back and I couldn't find anything about a stabbing victim.

He grunts at us, jerking his chin in greeting. A beautiful girl with blue and purple streaked hair dressed in white and covered in tiny fake butterflies joins us, offering one of the drinks she's carrying to him as she leans into his side. His hard expression softens slightly at the sight of her.

"Thank you, butterfly."

We leave them, opening the door to the courtyard outside. Thick ivy creates a small overhang above us and the raucous sounds of the party spill into the damp, foggy night.

"It's raining." I hold a hand out to allow the cool drops to splash on my palm. It's a steady, light rainfall. "Feels good."

"I hate the rain," Levi mutters. "Let's go back inside."

"I love the rain." He eyes me sharply, searching my face. When I step through the door, he grumbles, glancing at the dark sky before following. "It won't hurt you. Come on, it feels nice."

"You really like the rain?" His tone is tinged with something sad.

"Yeah. It makes me feel free."

He nods slowly, watching droplets splatter my skin. "My mom loved the rain."

My breath hitches. He hasn't told me a lot about her, only that she died. The sadness fades from his eyes as he stares at me.

"Your costume will get messed up."

I smirk. "Guess I'll just have to take it off then."

"You're trouble," he mutters with a resigned shake of his head.

A laugh escapes me. "Yeah, and you love it."

His intense gaze pierces into me. My heart skips a beat.

Despite the chill in the seaside air, the heat from inside returns the longer he looks at me standing in the rain. Levi scrubs a hand over his mouth, eyeing me up and down like he's looking for his opening. It's the same way he looks at me in the gym—the way I now know is meant only for me.

"Come get me." I take off running, picking my way through the slippery, weed-choked gravel on towering emerald platform heels.

Rain pelts me and the foggy mist gives the hotel grounds a spooky atmosphere. My heart rate picks up, but it's not in fear. It's with adrenaline-fueled anticipation of our game of prey and predator.

I veer for the hedge maze, only to skid to a halt when a familiar voice moans, "*Wren*. Shit, right there."

A grin crosses my face as I hurry around the maze to the terrace, ducking behind a cracked statue of an angel covering her eyes. I give Rowan a mental cheer for living her best life before focusing on a place to evade Levi. I strain my ears to hear him, but all I pick up around me is the bass of the music and the crash of waves at the base of the cliff.

Peeking out, I find the coast clear on the terrace. I have an open shot to the wide stone steps at the hotel's front entrance.

A shriek tears from me when an arm snakes around my waist from behind. The only other sound other than our ragged breaths is the rain drops pelting the dead leaves on the tree above us. I lean into him and his arm tightens.

"You got me," I whisper.

"It was a nice try, but your mistake was doubling back." His lips skim the damp column of my throat and his hardness presses into my ass. He licks the drops of water beaded on my skin. "That doesn't always work, so don't rely on it."

Even while messing around, he's intent on teaching me how to protect myself.

Turning in his arms, I map his face, skimming over the wet sharp planes until he leans down to capture my lips in a scalding kiss that steals my breath. He grabs me by the ass and hauls me into his arms without breaking from claiming my mouth. My moan is swallowed and I wrap my legs around his waist as he navigates the grounds with expert awareness without having to do more than peer from the corner of his eye to check where he's taking me.

The rain disappears when he ducks beneath an overhang and sets me on a wide chilly stone railing. His palm skims over my thigh high boots.

"I like these." His finger dips into the leather, teasing my leg. "There's room for a knife in here."

I tug him closer by his belt until he's between my legs. "There's room for something else right here."

A wicked sound of amusement puffs out of him, eliciting a rush of hot and cold tingles spreading over my skin. He pulls out the dagger he's carried around all night and frames my waist in his hands.

"I can't wait for you another second."

The gruffness in his tone makes my breath hitch and my legs fall open wider for him. His mouth curves in a rare grin. Flicking damp tendrils of inky hair out of his eyes, he makes the first cut in my leather bodysuit.

"R.I.P. Saint Laurent. You were good to me, but this is for a better cause." My words come out husky, thick with arousal as the cold blade traces lightly along each inch of skin he exposes by cutting the outfit off me.

"What's this?" He cocks his head and narrows his eyes in interest, admiring the snake I painted on my body.

"I wanted to match yours."

His eyes flick up to peer at me through dark lashes. Keeping me trapped in his gaze he bends to lick a stripe up the body paint. I arch into him, grasping the back of his head. For each cut of the fabric that reveals more skin, he nips or kisses me as he strips me bare for him. When he gets me down to my underwear, he fists the thin scrap of lace covering me, pulling it back to slice through the delicate fabric with a quick slash. I shiver at the cool air hitting my naked body.

"Those were La Perla." I pout. "My favorite pair."

Planting his hands on either side of my hips, he scrapes his teeth over my jaw. "I'll buy you new ones, just so I can cut those off your body too before I devour you," he says in a smoky rasp. "Nothing will ever stand between us."

He shifts again, covering my pussy with his mouth. My nails scrape across his scalp, both in shock and pleasure.

Levi obliterates all thoughts with his tongue, circling my clit until I'm shuddering for him. He makes a rumbling noise of approval, gliding his lip ring over my folds, teasing my clit with it. The smooth metal is the perfect amount of pressure. He brings me right to the brink before sending me over the edge by sinking two fingers into me.

By the time I catch my breath, his cock is out. He hoists me up like I weigh nothing, switches positions with me, and settles me on his lap, straddling him. I reach between us to line him up.

When I sink down, we both groan. He pries one of my hands from gripping his shoulder and puts the knife in it, meeting my questioning look with hooded eyes. It's not the first time he's armed me, but it feels more important than when he gave me his switchblade. We've played this game with him in control, but he's handing it over to me. Licking my lips, I feel the weight of his blade in my palm and bring it to his throat. He bares it for me, meeting my eyes.

It's heady and powerful.

"Good girl. Ride me," he commands.

The first roll of my hips makes his grip flex on my hips. Our panting breaths fog the air and each time our bodies join it's a pleasure unlike any I've ever known.

"Levi," I murmur.

He slips his fingers between us to encourage me over the edge, his observant skills now including knowing exactly how to play my body to have an orgasm rippling through me. I go faster, careful to keep the knife steady so I don't hurt him. His cock swells deep inside me and his arm bands around my waist to hold me close.

A curse slips past his lips as he comes, and he looks at me like I'm a goddess—*his* goddess.

CHAPTER TWENTY-ONE
ISLA

It feels like a lifetime, yet it's only been two weeks since the attempted kidnapping on campus. A calendar notification that November's dance showcase is only three weeks away pops up on my phone while I'm hanging out in the lounge with Levi after he dragged me out of bed early to show me their shooting range. Making me run there and back in the early dawn fog was worth it to watch him throw knives at the targets with sexy, skilled precision. He rewarded me for a good workout session in the shower when we got back.

The notification reminds me that the world outside the Nest has kept turning while I'm stuck standing still.

It almost seems like another life separate from mine where I was studying dance and practicing to show the world who I am through it. By hiding out, I've missed more than classes and practice. My lips press into a disappointed line. I'm missing living to the fullest, failing the promise I made myself whe

I first found the courage to test the waters of rebellion against Dad's wishes, tired of being so afraid to stand up to his control. I hate that his actions always make me afraid to live, and I'm done with it.

The theme night over the weekend succeeded in the guys' goal to reestablish themselves as the ones in power. The Kings Society didn't cause an interference or make an appearance. I still don't know if that's a good or bad thing. They haven't made any moves for me while I've been deep in the heart of the Crows' territory—not that one of their locations has stopped them before. Rowan and Levi told me about the police raid on their fight ring right before my attack.

If the secret society's goal is to lure Wren and the others into joining, it doesn't make sense to me why they would put pressure on them to cut them off at the knees. The only explanation I've worked out is that they're trying to flex their own reach to prove that they're more powerful than the Crows.

The waiting game is getting to me.

I'm still riding the empowering high my Medusa costume gave me. The need for answers has been on my mind and today it's like a buzz beneath my skin. It's the same feeling I get when I need to move to release energy. The morning workout and the lingering pleasant ache from what Levi did to me after took off the edge, yet I still need more. As much as the Nest has provided a safe haven, I can't remain here forever. I'd rather find a way to move rather than hide, even if it could be dangerous.

Maybe I can convince Levi to take me to campus to go back to my classes. I grin at the thought of him sitting in on dance practice.

The push that solidifies my resolve comes in the form of my phone vibrating again, pulling me from my thoughts.

Life always changes when it's least expected. My heart drops into my stomach and a pulse of adrenaline spreads through my body. It's a message from Dad that says *return home TODAY*. Not a request, a demand.

Years of dreading talking back to him bubbles to the surface, my body still, frozen in place, trapped in the moment. Then I narrow my eyes and push it down. I'm done living in fear.

Levi picks up on the tensing of my muscles, always on alert. "What's wrong?"

I've gone so many days without contact from Dad that it helps me separate how I used to react, steeling myself for what my next move is. I can't continue to exist in this bubble at the Nest. I want answers for all of us, especially for myself. I show him the demand on my phone. "The post-kidnapping honeymoon period is over. My dad texted me."

"What?" His eyes flash with hatred when he reads it. "No. You're not going within a hundred feet of him."

Licking my lips, I straighten my spine. "Okay, so hear me out. What if I did?"

Levi's brows flatten and his mouth sets in a stony line. "No."

"This is what we've been waiting for. Wren said I had to let you guys know if my parents finally contacted me." I need to make him understand. "I wouldn't be going because he's demanding it, I'd be going as a way to get closer. We can use me to find out what they're up to, and find out if my parents really are Kings Society members. Just like you snuck around bugging your uncle."

"You're safer here. With us. With me." He speaks in a logical tone, but his eyes flare with a more seductive meaning. "You should stay here, out of reach from any asshole who wants to kidnap you."

"And I love being here, but enough is enough. I can't sit here idly." I throw my hands up. "What, am I going to be decking the halls of the Nest with Christmas decor?" Levi pulls a face and I smile at his grumpy reaction. "Exactly. I need to know."

"There are other ways that don't involve you putting yourself in the path of danger."

To him, the kidnapping attempt is the worst danger I've faced. He doesn't know the full truth, believing my lie about the maid in place of me. Dad sold my body before. It was unimaginable, but I still survived under his roof, crossing paths with the man who violated me for seven years. I can survive facing my parents with the threat of kidnapping over my head if it gets us more answers. The more we know, the more we can fight back to stop this.

"You put yourself in danger all the time," I challenge. "Would you really want me to stand back and do nothing? Would you do the same if someone wronged you?"

"No." The refusal is fierce. "You shouldn't have to go back to him."

Bursting from my seat next to him, I get up to pace, unable to sit still. "It's not like I'm going back to still be his perfect little daughter. I'm sick and tired of playing pawn for him, Levi. I could run and hide forever, but that's not me. I might not be a total badass like you, but I won't ignore this and stress about what would happen if I pushed back. If I do, then I'll never face my parents and prove to them I'm not their pawn."

He works his jaw, respect gleaming in his eyes. It wars with the unhappy downturn of his mouth. I think I'm getting through to him, making him understand that I won't give up.

Conviction fills me when I think of all the times in the last seven years I've wished for ways to stop the men's club that my father took me to outside of the city. "Most of all, I don't want my dad or the Kings to have any more power than they already do." I stop pacing the lounge to sink to the couch beside him, taking his hand. "We can't let them use their daughters to pay off their debts or any other horrible things."

"She has a point," Jude calls from the kitchen where he's cooking a mouthwatering breakfast with eggs and chorizo. He leans his head into the lounge, his hair messy from sleep, sweatpants slung low on his hips, and a towel draped over his bare bronze shoulder while he gestures with a wooden spoon in one hand over the frying pan he has in the other. "It's our next best play. They want something with her, so let her be our pretty little mole."

I scrunch my nose at the cheeky wink he sends me. "Moles are practically blind, they're better with their noses than anything they can see."

"But small and good at burrowing for secrets," Jude counters. "Better a mole than a rat."

"Rats are probably way more intelligent than moles," I say.

Jude gives a deep, hearty laugh while stirring the contents of his frying pan. "Clever little thing, aren't you? So full of random knowledge."

I shrug. "I like watching nature documentaries."

"If you're going, it won't be alone," Levi cuts in, rubbing his brow. "I don't like this."

"You don't have to. But I don't enjoy being treated like a delicate bird kept in a cage."

Levi surveys me with his lips pressed together. He sighs, tightening his hold on my hand to pull me closer.

"You're not delicate," he murmurs, keeping his voice lowered so Jude doesn't overhear while he cooks. "You're stronger than any of us realized, princess. But the reality is that you've only just started training. You're improving, but you're nowhere near ready to protect yourself alone if someone tries to attack you again."

The corner of my mouth lifts and I plant a peck on his jaw. "That's why I keep you around."

A dry laugh huffs out of him and he draws my hair aside to trail lazy kisses along my neck. I bite my lip, glancing toward the kitchen to gauge how much making out we could get away with before it becomes indecent and a little kinky with an audience. It takes nothing to turn my head and kiss him. He inhales and smooths a hand down my side, gripping the material of his hoodie I'm bundled in. Our tongues glide together and I need to hold back the noise threatening to escape me when he teases his lip ring over my mouth with a wicked smirk.

Someone wolf whistles and I break the kiss. Rowan and Colton exchange amused looks while they carry bags to his desk.

"Don't stop on our account. I was enjoying the show. Hey!" Colton's grin falls and he ducks the pillow Levi lobs at him. "Look at you, edgelord. You didn't try to stab me this time. Growth, my friend. It's good for the soul."

"I'll show you what's good," Levi grumbles.

I stop him from reaching for whatever knife he has hidden on him. "Where did you two go?"

Rowan holds up one of the bags. "Supplies. I don't know what for, I'm just the pack mule because I was up before everyone else and he hadn't gone to sleep yet."

"Couldn't sleep?" Jude leaves the kitchen with his food, offering a plate to Levi before he sits down on my other side.

Rowan hitches a shoulder. "Bad nightmare about Ethan."

My heart climbs into my throat in sympathy for her. Her pretty green eyes have smudged shadows from a restless night beneath them and her hair is pulled into a haphazard bun. I make to get up to comfort her, but she holds up a hand to head me off.

"I'll be okay. Some days are just harder than others." She sighs. "I'd rather keep my mind busy, so it worked out that I was up early."

Colton bumps her shoulder affectionately and pulls her into a hug, kissing her temple. "You're a way better shopping buddy than any of these animals."

She laughs. "Why, because I didn't stop you from buying half the electronics store?"

"Exactly," he says. "That's love. Now I have all these toys to build."

Jude and Levi both shake their heads at the slightly manic gleam in Colton's eyes. Levi offers me a bite of eggs and chorizo and I allow him to feed it to me, humming at the spicy flavor of the meat.

"Tasty," I say to Jude.

"It's the first thing my abue taught me to cook with her when I was a little hellion trying to eat her out of house and home. She loves feeding people, but she swore up and down I was hungry every five minutes."

His story makes me smile. That kind of familial love and support is beautiful. It's something I've never truly experienced, brought up in a family where I felt more like an object, a doll to be picked up when it was convenient and cast off to a nanny while my mother focused on climbing the social ladder and my father built his political career. Levi reads the minute shift in my mood, rubbing my back.

"You're sure you want to do this?"

"Do what?" Rowan asks as she steals a bite of food from Jude's plate.

"My dad texted." Rowan and Colton's gazes snap to me. "He's demanding I go home today."

"Damn, that's cold," Colton jokes. "Not even a hi, how are you, glad you didn't get kidnapped first?"

"Um, fuck him," Rowan says hotly.

"Agreed, but I want to do it." I hold up a hand when she opens her mouth. "It's an in that could lead to the answers we want to know. He's clearly aware the kidnapping didn't work, so what's his next move?"

"I think you should ignore it. No one gets to control you." She frowns. "Cut them out of your life."

I close my eyes for a moment, imagining how amazing that independence would feel. "Where would I go? If I cut them off, I'd lose my trust fund." I lift my chin. "But that's a road I'll cross later. I want to do this so I can face them. I've never stood on my own when it comes to them."

Colton studies me, nodding slowly when he seems to come to some decision he doesn't share with the rest of us.

"I think it's a good idea," Jude says. "You can play it like you're weak and scared, which they must believe. When people think you're weak, you rip the rug out from under them when you show your strength."

"You and your mind games," Colton mumbles, absorbed in typing something on his phone.

He shrugs. "Conning people is about confidence, not the lie you sell them. You have to believe it a little yourself." His grin finds me. "So go in there and let them believe you're easy to control. The look on their faces will be so goddamn satisfying when you prove them wrong."

I nod resolutely, bolstered by his advice.

Levi scrubs a hand over his face. "You're not going to be by yourself. I won't let you walk back into a situation that could end the same as the garage without being there to stop it."

I rake my teeth over my lip. His words twine around me as much as his rich scent has from how often I wear his clothes.

"What if you coming with me tips them off, though?" My forehead creases. "I want you there, but if we're playing the poor helpless pawn angle, won't it be more believable if I'm alone instead of with my very hot, very lethal boyfriend?"

Levi fights a smile and Colton snorts.

"Their guard needs to be down," Rowan says. "If they think they're winning, they won't be on the lookout for the rest of us."

"We have to be smart about it," Colton agrees, unpacking wires and plastic-wrapped memory cards. "That way they won't suspect and discover any tech I give her like what happened at your uncle's place."

"I can't let you go in there alone without backup," Levi says. "I'll watch the house. If this is a trap, I'll break in if I have to."

I wouldn't put it past him. Levi Astor has *go ahead and lock your door, I'll climb in through your window to get to you anyway* written all over him. Something is definitely off with me, because the thought sends a thrill down my spine when I picture him breaking into my room through the windows to slip into my bed.

"I don't think they'd do it there. Because if they wanted to, they could've done it way easier without all the hassle of hiring thugs," Colton says. "They planned it all out so perfectly to take you from campus on a night you'd be there late with less witnesses. If they did it at your house, it connects your parents to it directly if one of the maids or cooks let it slip, depending on if they're paid off or not."

My stomach clenches. He's right. Dad's already been able to get me where he wanted me more easily simply by inviting me under the guise of an important dinner. "You thought that through fast."

Jude's smile doesn't have a trace of humor to it. "Fucking rich people, sweetheart. Always remember that. Their greed always comes first."

"C'mere." Colton drops into his gamer chair, spinning to wave me over. "We won't send you off naked. I've got a new comms piece I've been working on since Wren's went dead on us during that meeting. I designed it to get around frequency interruptions. I also upped the range to pick up ambient sound better—inspired by the tracker planted on you, that thing was designed to have killer range. Easier to listen in on conversations that way." He walks his chair down the desk to point out other equipment. "Tracker—this time one of *ours* so we'll know where you are at all times. Oh, give me your phone. I'll install a panic button."

A shocked laugh bursts out of me and I reach for a humorous comeback to calm my nerves. "Will it go with my earrings?"

He smirks. "Duh, babe. I have excellent taste."

I peel away from Levi's side and give my phone to Colton.

"The second I think it's too dangerous, I'm pulling you out," Levi says.

Gratitude swells in me. With them at my back, I'll be able to stand against my parents. I won't just have an inner light, I'll be a goddamn phoenix bursting into flames.

"Thank you," I say softly.

"This is how I treat my family, and you're one of us now, Isles. Just try getting that psycho to let you go now that he's taken a bite of your cute little ass." He indicates Levi's scowl with his chin and shoots him a cocky air kiss. "He's been stalking you for years. We're proud of his dedication, really. Aww, look at him, all murderous because I called you cute."

Smirking, I meet Levi's intent gaze again, the corners of my eyes crinkling in amusement.

"And," Colton drawls. "Done. See this app next to Insta? Yup, tap that and it will sound the alarms, all systems go. We'll storm the castle to rescue the princess."

"Nerd," Jude comments around a mouthful of food.

"Elite warlord rogue, thanks very much," Colton says without missing a beat while showing me how the app he installed works.

"This is pretty genius. It doesn't look anything like a security application."

Colton smiles proudly. "I can't take full credit, as much as I totally would. I've got a business partner of sorts out in Colorado. His wife went through a situation that made him want to focus on safety and security applications in the digital sphere. Total dick, but damn good with a computer. Almost as good as me."

"Well, tell him thank you." I hand my phone to Rowan so she can examine it closer. I shift to lean against the desk and look at Levi. "So when do we leave?"

"First we need to wait for Wren to get back from meeting with his father and see if he let anything slip." He narrows his eyes. "You're not going until you run through another training session and fix your footwork."

"What!" My shoulders slump, still feeling the ache in my muscles—and between my legs—from the morning workout he put me through. "But I just washed my hair."

"That's how this goes, princess. You still abide by my rules. Take it or leave it."

Another spike of nerves moves through me. I'm ready, yet still standing on a precipice. "You'll have my back, right?"

"Always," he says fiercely. It makes my heart swell. "I'll never take my eyes off you, princess."

CHAPTER TWENTY-TWO

ISLA

Trepidation and a sense of eeriness settles in my bones when I return home later in the afternoon with Levi checking in over the earpiece Colton rigged to my earrings to let me know he's in position and ready. The estate looks the same as it has since we moved in. I can't put my finger on what feels so off—if it's me or if the trappings of my life seem superficial in the wake of everything that's happened.

Much like Levi, I'm more alert, aware that I'm potentially putting myself in harm's way to do this. I channel him, Rowan, and the others to stay strong. I'm not as helpless as I was seven years ago, or when the kidnappers attacked me. I'm like Medusa, transforming into a woman who takes charge of her life.

Everyone acts like nothing is wrong. The household staff nod politely to me and greet me with demure murmurs of, "Good day, Miss Vonn," as if I haven't been missing for two weeks.

It's fucking bizarre.

"Are my parents here?" I ask a cook in the kitchen.

"Mrs. Vonn is at the club for lunch and your father is in a meeting in his study."

"Thank you."

It was easier to be brave about this back at the Nest, but now that I'm here I'm not turning back or running. I will face everything ugly this world wants to throw at me just to stand up to them to prove I won't be knocked down easily.

"Would you like us to prepare something for you to eat?" she offers.

I almost laugh at the question and blurt out one of my own to find out what my parents told them all to act like I was on vacation. I grip my phone tighter, comforted by the knowledge that I have a panic button and my badass boyfriend staked out on the perimeter of the property.

"I'm fine, thanks." Despite my anxiousness, I muster up a genuine smile for the cook. She's always been kind to me. If she sensed what was wrong, she would worry for me, so I have to trust she really believed whatever my parents used as an excuse for my absence. "Maybe later. Have a good day."

"You too, Miss."

The heels of my Valentinos echo on the gleaming black marble flooring. I smooth down the sweater dress I wore the night of the attack. It's the first time I've put it on since Levi and Rowan brought me to the Nest. I used to love this dress and it saddens me that it's infused with a horrible memory. I pause at the base of the wide staircase to the upper floors of the estate, glancing upstairs longingly.

Isla from two weeks ago would have darted right to my room to spend an hour in my closet picking out another outfit, but I'm not quite that girl anymore. There's no returning to that life. What I've been through won't break me. I press my lips together, vowing to myself I'll be a survivor.

For now, I have to find answers. That's the only reason I'm here. Instead of taking the stairs, I veer down a hall I rarely venture willingly—the one that leads to the study Dad uses when he's not at his office or down in D.C.

The door is cracked, deep voices drifting out from within. I keep my phone in my hands, both as a precaution and a cover. Dad is a funny man. He's always seen me as a vapid girl with my head stuck in the clouds. At the same time, he also demanded I pursue the highest forms of education, following the path he planned for me to end up in a prestigious career that would make him look good to his voters. He's never cared what my actual intelligence is, only that I appear brilliant while also being an attractive choice for a demure high society wife to the boys I've been set up with for strategic connections. It's why he believed he could control me so easily.

I plan to use his own arrogance to my advantage against him. If he catches me in the hall, he'll believe I'm messing around on my phone rather than eavesdropping on his meeting.

"When this passes, it'll be one step closer to correcting the incident at the shipyard. We need the regulations and tariffs loosened to turn our profits back around."

My brows jump up at Dad's words. Jude was right. Money is the only thing that matters to people like my father.

"It's imperative we reestablish our footholds there," says another man.

I don't risk peeking in, but I crouch low and use my phone camera to see what's going on. My father is seated on the edge of his desk, toasting a nearly empty glass of amber liquid to the portly man with a beard in an expensive suit. The man plays with a ring on his pinkie finger. If I had to guess, it must be the man he meets regularly who has the crossed keys signet ring.

"For the continued success of the Castle. You know my dedication is unwavering. I will prove that to the elder." Dad throws back the last sip of alcohol. "*Carpe regnum.*"

My eyes widen. Their creed—seize the kingdom.

"*Carpe regnum,*" the man echoes, finishing off his own drink. He climbs to his feet with a groan and I back away hurriedly, leaning casually against the wall. "See that this passes, Vonn. There can't be any more mistakes. The show at our autumn celebration is the reward. The most lucrative partnerships are established thanks to the carnal entertainment provided."

The emphasis he puts on mistakes makes my heart beat faster. Does he mean my attack? It could be. Wren wasn't kidding about the riddles they speak in.

"I assure you, I won't allow any other delays or mishaps," Dad says. "The delivery will happen, as I agreed to. It's better than someone barging onto my property. I've sent the demand to summon her home from wherever she hid. Stone will get what he wants for the autumnal revelry he loves flaunting and I'll handle my loose ends."

Stone. The name makes my heart bang against my ribcage in dread. My fingers ache from gripping my phone so hard, fighting the tremors that rack my body. Paying attention becomes challenging.

Memories crash over me, dragging me back into a bed, sluggish and unable to push him off me.

"He does enjoy theatrics." The bearded man chuckles, his voice drifting closer to the hall. "I suppose you truly do have your goal in mind to let go of such a lovely thing to Silas' games. If you do it, you'll have no legacy to continue your bloodline amongst our brethren."

Dad scoffs. "Let that bastard have what he wants. If he still finds value in her after paying for her virginity, that's his own madness. I'd rather have a fertility lab start a fresh option than deal with the wild insolence she's developed."

My throat tightens with an acute ache. I pull the switchblade Levi put in my hand before he allowed me out of the car from my bra, concentrating on its shape and contours as my focus object to keep my panic from spiraling out of control.

Of course. I wanted answers and I got them. Silas Stone isn't done with me. It hurts to swallow and my vision swims. All the years I've had to endure his penetrating leers, he's been waiting for the best opportunity to get me. The nightmare of history repeating has been my greatest fear, and it clashes with my will to fight.

"Stay strong, princess." Levi's steady voice in my ear helps me anchor myself.

I'm not alone. I'm not a helpless girl anymore. This won't destroy me, no matter how much the agonizing truth hits me like a blow. I'll survive. It's my promise to myself.

All my life, my parents haven't been true parents. They're willing to throw me away and start over. Power. Greed. Their morals have been eradicated.

I'm finished letting them use me. Blinking away tears before they fall, I get myself under control, determined fire burning in my veins.

I have a new family that wants me. That keeps me safe from the real monsters in Thorne Point.

These men have hurt me, and I'm fucking done being their victim. I won't let them hurt me or anyone else again.

Everything Levi has taught me runs through my head. I picture his quiet, gruff tone telling me to block attacks and map my focus object. He sees me as a fighter. He taught me how to evade what wants to take me out.

I will fight this. Men like Dad and Silas and the Kings don't get to win. Taking a fortifying breath, I imagine myself as Medusa, waiting for the perfect moment to strike back against Silas Stone.

Whatever it takes.

By the time Dad and his associate exit the office, I'm pretending to be absorbed in my phone. They pause to look at me.

"Hey Dad." I keep my tone light, smiling with a brightness I don't truly feel. "I know our schedules haven't lined up lately, but I was thinking since you're home, we could meet Mom at the club for lunch."

His gaze falls away dismissively. He doesn't bother to acknowledge or answer me. He doesn't ask where I've been, or if I'm okay. It's further proof, driving the final wedge into my heart. He's hurt me too many times to count, but it still cuts deep to look at a man you once idolized, so long ago, before he pulled back the curtain on what a despicable person he is and know he doesn't give a shit about you. He probably never did.

The portly man doesn't share the same opinion of me, apparently. Instead of paying attention to the hand my father offers to shake, his piercing gaze is on me, giving me a once over. He's been here before and I've seen him at society events, yet it's not until this moment that something strikes me as familiar about him.

"Your daughter, correct?" he says.

"Yes," I answer.

"Lovely indeed," he says with a hint of sickening amusement. "I hope to see you at the upcoming masquerade ball. I'm sure you'll dazzle us all."

Something about this man's calculating eyes and his powerful scowl niggles at me. There's a connection I'm missing and the familiarity remains just out of reach.

My thumb hovers over the panic button the longer he stares at me. I hold out, meeting his scrutiny with my chin raised. The corner of his mouth curls up. His attention isn't pleasant. I can do this.

My father might have forgotten in all the years he's spent ignoring me when it was convenient, but I've flourished and grown by my own light into a strong woman who will take on the damn world.

"Well, I look forward to the next time we meet," Dad bites out when neither of us gives up the staring contest.

The man nods to me with a sharp smirk and they leave me alone in the hall. Licking my lips, I head for my room, needing to dance off the slimy feeling coating my skin before I use Dad's underestimation to snoop around for more answers.

CHAPTER TWENTY-THREE

LEVI

If I grip the wheel of the Maserati I drove Isla home in any harder, I'm going to rip the damn thing off. I knew I shouldn't have let her do this. The thought of her leaving scraped my nerve endings raw, my entire being revolting at the thought of a day without Isla within reach.

Once I obliterated the wall I kept between us, she wormed her way straight into my heart. The way I crave her is insane, far stronger than the obsession I harbored for years. Her kisses. The sweet sounds she makes. The way she worries her lip when she's puzzling out the best way to choreograph a move I teach her—her own eccentric way of learning self-defense. Most of all her radiant smiles.

This girl owns my damn heart. It's scary to realize how much she matters to me—that it's never been just about finding her attractive or intriguing. She's mine, that's all that fucking counts in my mind.

I let her do what she needs to because I respect that she won't give up on this. She needs answers, the same as I did to deal with my own kidnapping. It was torture to let her go after kissing her and watching the sway of her ass as she walked to the entrance of her family's estate. I'm prepared to act as I see fit, listening intently to the comms she wears. I couldn't stand the thought of not knowing every detail of what she's facing.

My courageous girl didn't have to do this at all, but she's fierce and determined, a shining light brighter than ever. Her strength hasn't failed to amaze me once since she was dragged into this mess alongside us, even when I was the one pushing back against allowing her in further.

I was a goddamn idiot blinded by my own inability to trust easily.

"The delivery will happen, as I agreed to. It's better than someone barging onto my property. I've sent the demand to summon her home from wherever she hid. Stone will get what he wants for the autumnal revelry he loves flaunting and I'll handle my loose ends." Her father's words make me fucking murderous.

At least I'm picking up that she isn't in any immediate danger. They're waiting for something. Whatever this autumn festival is, I think. Wren also pointed it out as something pivotal for the Kings when they summoned him.

I picture Isla poking around outside her father's office. She may not be able to hear the conversation clearly, but Colt's tech is top notch. I get every disparaging word crystal clear through my earpiece. When her breathing shifts into a strained pattern, I remind her to stay strong.

The next voice I hear makes my blood run ice cold. *My uncle.*

Straining my ears to grasp what's going on, my head runs through what I know without alerting her who her father is meeting with, not wanting to freak her out. Isla's mentioned a man with a ring. Goddamn it, I should have known.

I was too busy worrying about Isla to pay attention to the beginning of the conversation. Fuck. I shouldn't have missed that. She might not have walked into a trap, but they'll still strike eventually. I need to be in there with her, protecting her without tipping them off. Sweeping the street I parked on at the edge of the Vonn estate, I scope out my best access points while speed dialing Colton.

"*Yo*," he answers.

"How fast can you hack a satellite to get me a visual confirmation?"

His chuckle filters through the car's speakers. "*Ten minutes, give or take. What's up?*"

"Isla's father's meeting with my uncle."

"*Oh.*" His relaxed demeanor changes and he repeats what I told him to the others.

"Yeah, *oh*. They're saying all this fucked up shit about her." I transfer the audio to piggyback with my earpiece and slip out of the car, blending in like I belong here. Technically with the name I carry, I do. "Moving in."

"*You'll need a better excuse to insert yourself other than outing yourself as her boyfriend*," Wren cautions. "*Keep your head on.*"

A caustic laugh punches out of me. "Yeah, like you did when Rowan went to burn down the docks? Relax, I'm not going to kill anyone, though I'd love nothing more than to look her father in the eye as I ram my biggest knife down his throat and feed him his own tongue for the shit he said."

"*Just don't think with your dick and you'll be golden*," Jude says.

I force out a breath, pausing to bypass a gardener working on the meticulous grounds without being spotted. They're right and I know it. Her father mentioned a Stone guy who's obsessed with her, which adds another treacherous element to keeping her safe. I don't need the visual confirmation once I make it to an unlocked service entrance to the side of the house—my uncle's town car is in the circular drive. A plan forms in my head while I wrangle the urge to close the distance between me and Isla as fast as I can.

There'll be lower chances of putting her in more harm's way than she is if I act as her bodyguard instead of her boyfriend, especially with my uncle's involvement. He can't know what she means to me, or she could meet the same fate as my parents. Vonn is coward enough to tip off Stone to take her before we're ready to stop it. I won't paint a bigger target on her.

"Get me anything you've compiled on Vonn to use as leverage to pressure him. I'm going to blackmail him into instating me as Isla's bodyguard with round the clock access." I clench my jaw, treading carefully through an empty narrow hallway. All of these old estates are the same in their maze-like passages. Me and Wren played for hours on end exploring his estate when we were young and it's given me an understanding of exactly how to navigate any estate I enter. "We've got some time. They talked like there was something coming—an autumn event. I'll guard Isla from what they plan to do to her, and have access to find us more answers with Vonn under our thumb."

"*Rock up in there, then*," Colt says. "*I'll send it all to your phone.*"

Ending the call, I focus on moving through the house without being seen by anyone. My uncle's voice stops me in my tracks near the grand foyer.

"See you for next week's meeting, Vonn," he says.

My fists ball with the need to take a swing at him. It's an ever-present urge, but today it burns hotter and more volatile than usual for the threat he poses to my girl.

If this is what it's like having my heart in someone else's hands, I'll need to adapt quickly to return to my usual level of control and awareness.

I hang around in a side parlor off the foyer to watch my uncle leave and the senator retreat down another hall through the crack in the door. Once the coast is clear, I find my way to the closest set of service stairs to locate Isla's room. It worried me when her breathing shallowed in the telltale signs of an oncoming panic attack, but she worked through it, then texted me to say she'd check in after dancing it out. I have to find her and make sure she's okay before I do anything else.

Pausing where the landing splits in two different directions, I get my bearings, opting for the side of the house situated to get the most light. My instinct is correct and I find her in a room at the end of the hall. I hover outside the door, watching her like I have so many times over the years. I don't want to alert her to my presence, not until I've dealt with her father.

The corner of my mouth hitches up. The girly room is illuminated by the afternoon sunlight streaming in from four different large windows. She changed out of her sweater dress into leggings with crisscross patterns and a loose shirt that hangs off one shoulder. Her hair is pulled back and a pair of headphones are plugged in her ears while she dances. She'll be okay as long as she's dancing.

If she were crying, then I'd raze this whole fucking house to the ground brick by brick.

Melting back into the hall, I leave my girl to deal with the next problem.

My phone vibrates on my way downstairs with all the dirt Colt has retrieved for me on Artimus Vonn. I hide behind a grandfather clock while skimming the financial records—proof of his misuse of campaign funds and debts he owes to half of Thorne Point's elite. Shaking my head, I whip out a sleek knife from the inner pocket of my leather jacket and make my way to Vonn's study.

The trick to getting into an occupied room without being detected is to make sure the person inside is distracted. Isla said her family takes security seriously, yet I was able to enter freely from a service door the gardener likely used, so it didn't trigger any alerts. I'm betting they have it hooked up to their internet. Keeping a close eye on the study, I text Colton to get me in.

A few minutes later, he sends me a GIF of a horse sneaking into a house.

Like clockwork, a doorbell chimes, then the lights in this wing shut off.

"What the—goddamn it, I thought they fixed that after it was installed?" Vonn curses again, stalking into the hall. "Marie, get the lights on."

In his bluster, he misses me standing right there in the middle of the hall. I sidestep him silently and slip into his office to wait for him, standing as a vengeful sentry behind his antique wingback desk chair. Vonn mutters to himself as he navigates the room, yelping when he bangs his knee on the furniture.

"Get those lights on, now!" he bellows.

I send a text to signal Colt and smirk when the lights switch on.

"Thank god." Vonn groans, massaging his temple. He pours himself a generous helping of Cognac.

"Aren't you going to offer me a drink?" I almost laugh at the shocked sound he makes when I materialize from the shadows in a way that almost could pass as magic for how precisely I've honed the skill. "Guess I'll help myself."

I pick up the aged liquor and sniff from the crystal decanter. Expensive taste for a man with millions in debt.

Typically, I go for efficiency over the fanfare my brothers all prefer, but in this case I take a page from their book. It has the desired result—showing Vonn how fucking easily I can get to him. It'll lay the foundation for the threat I'm about to control him with.

"What—who—how did you get in here?" Vonn gapes at me, peering around with the realization that his security is no match for me. He takes in my leather jacket and recognition crosses his face. He knows exactly who I am and who I'm connected to. "You—you're Baron's boy."

I draw in a sharp breath and tap the tip of my knife on the desk. It gets Vonn's attention immediately. "We'll talk about my uncle later. For now, there are more pressing matters. Your daughter, Isla."

Vonn's brows furrow. "She, ah...is spoken for."

Bastard. I calm the murderous fury simmering in my veins, digging my knife into the fine grain of his polished desk. If this were only about Isla and not this whole fucking Kings Society empire, I'd make him break his deal to give her to me. It's not that simple, though. There are unanswered questions.

My sinister smirk shuts him up as I perch on the edge of his desk and flip the dagger tip to hilt. "She is," I agree, meaning she's *mine*. He doesn't need to know that yet. "Did you know where she was the last two weeks? After I saved her from a kidnapping on campus?" I'm impressed. The flash of surprise in his eyes is there and gone in a second. "Don't worry, I've been keeping her safe. Which is why you're going to instate me as her bodyguard."

"I..." Vonn shakes his head, the cogs in his head spinning too damn slow for my liking. "I don't understand. Why do you want to work as her bodyguard? You're an Astor, not muscle for hire."

True, my name and status draws attention, but I've always been good at existing on the fray. It's what I'm banking on with the bodyguard play. Patience running thin, I hurl the decanter of Cognac against the wall. It makes a satisfying crash as it shatters. Vonn startles, glaring from the mess I've made to me.

Now I have his full attention.

"That's no way to conduct yourself for an interview young m—"

His words cut off in a choking splutter when I surge off the desk with my knife aimed at him. Gripping his hair, I tip his head back to meet my hard expression. It would be so easy to slit his throat now. Satisfying. Gritting my teeth, I increase pressure. He flinches at the prick of my blade, and a line of blood runs down his neck.

"No, you don't seem to understand. This isn't an interview at all. Effective immediately, I'm your daughter's guard." My grip tightens on his hair. I stop myself from killing him now. It won't accomplish anything if I end him here. "Say you agree. For the record, I don't give a shit if I have your permission or not—I'll do what I want. But I want to hear you say it so I know you understand you have no power to stop this."

"This is assault! Breaking and entering, too, I bet!"

I slice off one of the buttons on his shirt. "I could do much worse. And I will destroy you if you don't play along." He flinches when I make another quick movement, arcing my arm to stab my knife into his desk. Grinning sadistically, I flash my phone, swiping through the financials Colton sent. "See, you're going to do whatever I want, or every media outlet gets this leak of your piss poor money management."

Vonn sneers. "You doctored those."

"Please." I scoff. "You're under the thumb of every high roller in the city. You think I can't get another well-respected member of the community to back this up?"

"I have friends who have helped me longer than you've been alive."

"Yeah, the Kings." At Vonn's widened eyes, I put my phone away and retrieve my knife, scraping the tip along the polish. "Did you forget who I am? Astor. My name carries more sway than yours ever will, Vonn. I have all of your secrets." I level the knife at him again, right between his eyes. "And I do mean all of them, including the men's club you frequent to purchase... carnal commodities."

With my snarl comes a rush of ire for Isla's father. He's hurt her and I won't allow him to get away with it. Retribution is coming for him.

"Is this a test?" Vonn grips the arms of his chair, knuckles turning white. "I'm loyal! I've proven how much!"

The skittish look in his eye tells me he's more inclined to believe my bluff than not. I push while he's on the precipice, following my instincts like Jude instructs when it comes to talking someone in circles to the point they believe everything is their idea, providing their own noose.

"You wouldn't want to fail a test, would you?" At that, Vonn pales. Right on the money. The Kings wanted to test Wren, too. "That's what I thought. Don't breathe a word of this, or you fail and I get to do what I want to you."

His neck cracks from the speed he nods his head at to fold for me. "Yes. You're right. How much do you want?"

Popping to my feet, I spit on his desk. "I don't want your money. You couldn't afford my fee." I offer another psychotic smirk, tilting my head slowly. "Your debts are big enough as it is. Your payment is not saying anything to anyone about this." I trace the tip of my blade over my lip. "If you do, you fail."

Vonn smooths a hand over his messed up hair and casts a longing look at the smashed decanter. I text Colt to kill the lights one more time without looking at my phone. As soon as the room plunges into darkness, I disappear.

On my way upstairs, I receive another text. Stopping the crooked smile that crosses my face when I see Isla's name is impossible.

Isla: Caving. I might be a strong, independent woman, but I kinda miss my grumpy shadow already. You're still watching my back, right? I have an errand I want to run.

She's in luck. As her bodyguard, I'll ensure she's never going anywhere alone.

More and more I'm sliding down the same slope Wren plummeted, because I would do anything to keep this girl happy. As long as I'm protecting her, nothing will get her. I won't stop being a monster, but maybe she was right. Her light is bright enough to penetrate the shadows I've lived in for far too long.

Isla will just have to learn to live with a monster, because there's no way in hell I'm ever letting her go.

CHAPTER TWENTY-FOUR
LEVI

THE Thorne Point Police Department is the last place I want to be, but Isla is a stubborn little thing when she wants to be. Jude is leaning against his motorcycle when we pull in. Once I relayed to the others where I was taking her, he responded that he'd meet us there.

"I'm telling you, this is a pointless waste of our time," I say.

Her lips purse in a mulish tilt I have the urge to kiss until she melts into me. Flipping her hair, she sasses me in an airy tone. "And I told you, if you're going to go rogue without giving me a heads up, you have to do what I want if you want to get head later, you grumpy asshole." There's something fierce about her ever since she finished dancing out her demons. "Now we have to sneak around, or people will label me all sorts of things for being seen making out with my bodyguard."

I sigh. I told her I did what was necessary. If I hadn't acted, we would have needed some other cover to protect her. All she did was lift a dainty eyebrow at the explanation and demanded I drive her to the station.

"We already know now that your parents and the society are connected to this." I nod to Jude as he opens the door for Isla. "Whatever, let's just get this over with."

"Exactly, we know," Isla insists, murmuring thanks to Jude for helping her out of the car. She balances on her towering heels, drawing my eyes to her legs. "And because we know, I want to put them on the police's radar so we'll be ready for anything. Let's make their lives as hard as possible. I'd rather be proactive than wait around for whatever they have planned."

"They'll just cover it up." Jude gestures to the brick building with a frown. "The cops are in the Kings' pockets. There's no doubt in my mind."

"How do you know that?" Isla's gaze bounces between us at the look we share.

"Because we know exactly how much a Thorne Point officer costs. We had one on our payroll to look the other way until the raid. We know now the Kings orchestrated the entire thing as a show to prove how easily they can get to us." I cast a hard look at the building looming over us. "So trust me when I say this isn't going to achieve what you want."

Isla frowns. "That's not right. The police are meant to serve justice."

Jude barks out a laugh. "Yeah. Sure. And they do, to the highest bidder."

"I still want to try. There has to be someone in there who isn't corrupt that can help." Isla starts across the street at a clipped pace, calling back to us. "You boys can either come with me or stay out here."

I'm already moving, falling into step behind her. "Like hell I'm letting you out of my sight in the heart of a viper's nest."

"Fine. Put your grouchy face away so I can work my magic." She leans in and stage whispers. "You might have noticed people have a hard time saying no to me."

A snort jerks my head. "I noticed."

"Don't worry, sweetheart. That's what I'm here for, to keep this one from fighting everything in sight." Jude claps me on the shoulder and squeezes. "I wouldn't let my brother go in there without backup."

The masochistic bastard also wouldn't miss a chance to square off with his ex-girlfriend, keeping the wounds in his heart alive and freshly salted. I flash him a smirk. His worry for me is misplaced. He knows last time I was arrested it messed me up, but Isla's my focus right now.

"Let's just get this over with," I say. "Then we can get back and work out our next strategy with everyone."

The station is busy when we enter. The older woman at the desk catches sight of Jude and waves us over. A large guy in cuffs openly checks Isla out and I tug her into my side, glaring at him while a uniformed cop hauls him away.

"Anything new for me today?" She moons at Jude when he leans an elbow on the counter and offers a lopsided grin.

"Afraid not, but you know you're the first one I come to when I have one of the treasures you like," he says in a smooth tone.

She flushes. Isla steps up to the counter.

"I need to report an incident from Thorne Point University to an officer."

"I'm sorry, all of our available officers are unable to take a report right now. You can file online with the form, or wait, but it will be a while."

Isla's face falls. Impatience and residual anger at Warner for his betrayal on fight night crashes over me. We don't have time for procedure or formality.

"Come on. We're going to make Warner listen to us." I take her hand, tugging her down the hall.

"Wait, he doesn't want to be disturbed, he's—"

"Always a pleasure, Rosemary," Jude says. "We know the way, it's fine."

"Are we allowed back here without, I don't know, clearance?" Isla asks.

"I don't give a damn. You want to make a report, you're going to make a report. Directly to the goddamn sergeant himself before I yank him back under our control."

Her grip tightens on my hand and I lead her through the bullpen. Rosemary wasn't kidding. It was busy out front but it's chaos back here. All of the desks have perpetrators in handcuffs. I recognize one of them as the opponent I fought the night our fight ring was raided. Warner never should've reneged on the deal we had with him.

Unlike what most people daydream about, the grass is never greener on the other side. The Kings are focused on a higher level, worried about lining their own pockets. Warner could have had our help to keep his streets under control. The Kings will never offer him the same.

"Back office," I say.

The door is open, a sandwich half eaten resting on the wrapper while Warner grumbles into his cell phone. He seems more haggard and worn down than usual. His gaze darts to us when we fill the doorway.

"No." He points at me. "Get out. I don't have time."

"Busy job when you don't have friends to scratch your back," Jude taunts. "What a shame."

Warner grits his teeth. "You punks think you're the biggest fish in the city, but you're not. You have no idea—"

"Excuse me, sir," Isla cuts in. "Sorry to interrupt, but I just want to file a police report. Can you help me with that? My friends just came to keep me company."

Warner stares at her grimly. "No."

Isla flinches at his empty tone. I put my arm around her waist, a growl working its way up my throat.

"Isla? Hey, girl! Oh my god, it's been so long. I haven't seen you since the founders gala."

All three of us whirl around at Pippa's friendly tone. It's a far cry from her usual attitude. Jude's attention slides to me, then returns to Pippa hustling across the room in dark jeans, knee-high leather boots, and a green sweater. She spares Jude a brief look. I don't understand it, but he seems to, straightening and clearing the *what the fuck* expression from his face while she pulls Isla in for a hug.

"Come with me," she murmurs. "Play along. He's watching."

"Oh my god, babe! How are you?" Isla falls right into the act, hugging Pippa like they're long lost best friends instead of high school classmates who haven't spoken more than a handful of times as far as I know.

Jude meets my eyes over the girls' heads and gives me a subtle shrug. With Warner's and half the station's scrutinizing stares on us, we can't do more than trust Pippa. It goes against the old resentful anger I harbor for her, but I'll weather it for Isla's sake.

"Let's grab coffee so we can catch up." Pippa's suggestion carries an edge I recognize in her voice. It's been years since I've heard it, but the inflection she puts on the word coffee is the same way she used to try to make us laugh with her euphemisms when she was a girl running with our boy's club. "It's a madhouse in here, come on."

Isla hooks her arm in Pippa's, beaming like this is a fortuitous reunion. She's good at putting on the dramatic chick persona. It's why I thought she was nothing more than a spoiled rich girl for a long time. Jude and I fall into step behind them. I glance back at Warner and find him speaking rapidly into his cell phone once more, eyes fastened on us as we depart.

Pippa and Isla keep up a steady stream of giggling conversation on empty topics until we're outside the station and halfway down the city block.

"Have you had a lobotomy since the last time we saw you?" Jude asks.

His hands are tucked in his pockets and his gait is casual, but tension lingers in his shoulders and around the corners of his mouth. We've had nothing but trouble for years from her, so it's no surprise her change of heart comes as a shock we're wary of.

"No." Pippa herds us into a cafe and doesn't speak again until we're seated in a booth at the back of the bustling shop. She tries to fight me for the vantage point seat—the one that puts my back to the wall and my eyes on the door—but gives it up to me at my severe glare. Her familiar, antagonistic attitude returns when she spits, "I've been thinking about what you said."

"Oh, now you decide to listen?" Jude blows out a breath. "Pip, I've been saying that shit for years. All this time you've been coming after us, like we wronged you, not the other way around. Why the change of heart?"

She can't look at him anytime he references the night she turned her back on us, some of the heartache she carries bleeding through the mask she keeps up around us. "Things have gotten...tense. Calls we should be taking are passed off and rerouted to other precincts. I've been relieved from most of my cases and shut down from more I want to take. Fucking red tape." She pauses, eyes darting to me. "The Leviathan case, too. It started with that, but I've been checking records and looking into things around the station. There are discrepancies. Big ones."

"No shit," I say.

We're probably the cause of half of those discrepancies. Warner made a lot of things disappear for us.

She sighs, leaning back against the booth. "Unless you went there to turn yourself in as the kil—" I flip her off for the joke and she smirks. "That's what I thought."

"You can help me?" Isla clarifies.

"I'll do what I can." Pippa shoots me and Jude a hard look. "I'm still a detective."

"Wow." Isla gives her a once over. "You're young for a detective."

Pippa smirks. "Yeah, I was recruited by the force right out of high school. My parents weren't thrilled. They're not on the same level as yours or Levi's families, but they didn't think I would pursue it as a career choice." She shrugs, her gaze cutting to Jude. "I wanted to make sure those at the mercy of the system—especially victimized girls—would get the justice they deserved."

Jude taps an erratic pattern on the table in the seat next to mine, fingers dancing endlessly. He narrows his eyes. "Very noble."

Her eyes bounce between his. She reaches for his hand, then halts and folds her hands in front of her. "For what it's worth...I'm sorry for what happened that night."

The admission seems to cost her, her voice tight with regret threading through the familiar stubbornness we used to tease her for.

Jude inhales forcefully and gets up. "I'll get coffee." He blocks the girls in on the opposite bench of the booth, leaning over Pippa. "Listen to her. Help her."

Pippa nods, clearing her throat. Isla waits until he's in line, peering after him with a worried crease between her brows. I reach across the table for her hand, tracing a circle on her knuckles. Pippa doesn't miss it, lifting her brows as she registers the development. Isla checks with me, launching into the story of her attack once I nod.

I don't know if we can ever fully trust Pippa again, but if she's willing to help us and has finally opened her eyes to the dirty cops she works with, it's a step in the right direction. We need every win we can get right now.

Pippa goes into cop mode. It's interesting. I've seen it countless times before, but usually when she's being a pain in our asses. She nods along while Isla tells her what happened, interjecting with questions until she has the full picture. Well, minus the secret society who wants Isla to satisfy a debt, or that her parents are the ones who orchestrated it. She also leaves out the more incriminating details, like the guy I killed and Colton's CCTV hacking, but sends the photos of the plates Rowan captured to Pippa's phone.

"I strongly suspect my parents might be behind it," Isla finishes. "Is there any way to put them on, like, a watchlist?"

"Not without more concrete proof to connect them. I believe you, and you're right to be cautious. This is just the procedure I need to follow. I don't know why this wasn't reported before you came out of the safety of where...or rather, who you bunkered down with. But I'll do what I can to keep an eye out for suspicious activity." Pippa puts a hand on Isla' shoulder compassionately. She turns to me. "I know you don't trust me."

"For good reason," I remind her, nodding toward Jude waiting to collect coffees.

She purses her lips. "I take my job seriously. And that's exactly what you have here, a case that the precinct should be handling."

"This isn't like the last girl you got wrapped up in helping." Pippa's eyes snap to Jude as he approaches the table. Knowing she's the type of person unable to let something rest, I'm sure she's haunted by the girl who came to us looking for a way to get revenge for what happened to her. If Pippa had followed the plan, maybe she'd still be alive. "I won't hold my breath, and I won't hesitate to act accordingly. You screw us over again, you shouldn't go out after dark."

The sorrowful remorse swirling in Pippa's eyes hardens. "Is that a threat?"

"You know it, baby girl," Jude croons, bracing a hand on the back of the booth behind her. "Here, I sweet talked the barista to make you a peppermint mocha."

Pippa's breath hitches, looking up at him sharply. "It's still October."

Jude winks. "I'm feeling generous today. Don't ruin the moment." His amused expression fades and he tucks a lock of curly dark hair behind her ear. She can't quite hide the flicker of longing in her eyes. His sweet gesture shifts when his fingers thread into her hair and tighten. "Don't betray us again. I don't want to cross that bridge."

He masks his meaning for Isla and the other cafe patrons, but he means that none of us will let her get away with crossing us twice. If she makes the same mistake, I'll be first in line to ensure she has nowhere to hide from our wrath.

Isla takes a sip of the coffee I pass her, eyes rounded. "And I thought I was the dramatic one in the group."

Jude laughs lightly, breaking away from Pippa. Once he sits on the bench on my side, he nods to Pippa's cup. "You should take that to go. Wouldn't want a muddy pig sniffing you out for being seen with us."

"Right." Pippa takes her cup and stands. She hesitates, studying me and Jude before pulling a card from her wallet and leaving it on the table. "My direct line. If you're in trouble, you can call me."

Jude picks it up before Isla can take it, flicking it back and forth with skilled fingers. "Later, Pipsqueak."

We all watch her go.

"I like her." Isla cradles her coffee between her fingers and grins at me. "See. Not a total waste of time. You mended a bridge!"

Jude snorts, smothering his amusement against my shoulder. I sigh, busying myself with another sweep of the cafe. No one followed us after Pippa brought us here. I can't tell if that's a good thing or a bad thing.

Instinct tells me it's bad, that it means they think it's as pointless as I did to bother with the police report. If Pippa files anything in their system, they'll just bury it. Only time will tell.

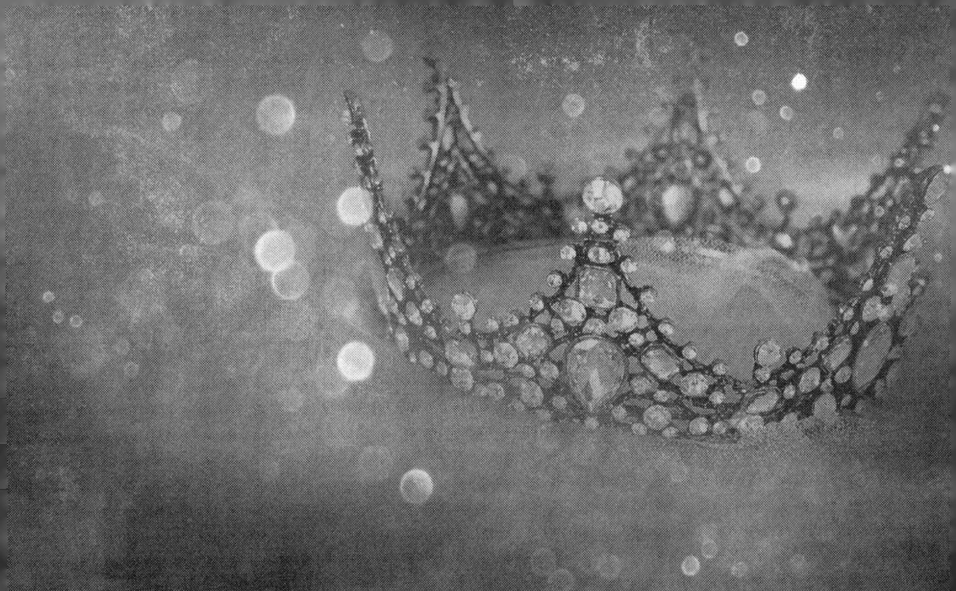

CHAPTER TWENTY-FIVE

ISLA

SLEEPING in my own bed is a strange experience. The thought of Levi watching over me is the only reason I slept at all. I'm returning to my classes. Levi was grumpy about it the entire ride back to my house after leaving the cafe, but he didn't protest, agreeing with me for once that pretending like everything is normal is the right move to keep anyone from suspecting we know more. Despite everything I faced yesterday, I already feel like I've taken a step in the right direction, no longer barred in a cage.

I face my mirror, and for the first time in weeks I recognize the strong-hearted woman looking back at me—dressed in a killer designer outfit, wearing my favorite lipstick, and ready to take whatever is thrown my way.

"Just try to get me, kidnapper jerks," I tell my reflection, holding up my fists like Levi taught me.

It helps to push away the truth lingering at the edge of my mind that

Silas Stone is the man waiting to get me.

Opening my door, I pause on the threshold, yelping. I place a hand over my heart, riding out the pulse of adrenaline that coursed through my veins at the sight of Levi leaning against the wall opposite my bedroom door.

He shifts his attention from the knife in his hands to me, offering a devious smirk. "You're cute when you're surprised."

"Lurk much?" I glance down the hall, checking we're alone. "I thought you were going to meet me downstairs?"

The corner of his mouth kicks up in a secretive smirk and he pushes off the wall in a fluid movement, stalking across the hall. He grasps my jaw and tilts my head up, sealing his mouth over mine in a hot kiss. "Always with the questions, princess."

"I have a curious and active mind," I murmur, slipping my arms around his waist.

He chuckles. "Don't I fucking know it. "Get used to staying in my sight at all times. I'm your bodyguard."

My brows lift. "You're going really hard on this. Have we discovered a little roleplay kink?"

His amusement grows and he pushes me against the wall, melding his hard body against mine. "You're all mine. Twenty-four seven." He grows serious. "No one will touch you on my watch. Only me, Isla. Only ever me."

My breath hitches and I nod. Warmth floods my body and I rest my head on his chest.

He strokes the top of my head. "Come on, Rowan's waiting for us in the car." Stepping back, he catches my hand in his and starts down the hall. "She gets annoying when she has to wait too long. Let's not trigger that hairline curiosity urge, or she'll go snooping in your house where she shouldn't without backup."

A laugh rolls out of me when I think of how we followed her stalker on campus last month and wound up finding the secret hidden passageway. "I thought she cleared a leave of absence with her advisor for the rest of the semester?"

"It's still in effect." He navigates the halls with ease, as if he already has the layout memorized. Knowing him, he probably managed it overnight with his strategic obsession. "Same rules as at the Nest, princess. You do as I say and you stay within reach at all times. You don't wander off on your own."

"And don't take candy from strangers," I finish with a teasing smirk. When he gives me a flat, unimpressed look, I widen my eyes innocently. "What? It's solid advice."

"As your bodyguard, it's fully within my right to haul your pert little ass over my shoulder for your protection if you give me lip."

Heat tingles in my core. "I hope you do."

"If I touch you right now, we're not making it to campus." Gravel rides his voice. "A quick fuck in the Maserati on a back road before we returned isn't nearly enough to be full on you."

I bite my lip around a smile. When we reach the car, he searches the front facade of the house before trapping me out of sight against the car to kiss me deeply. It goes on until I'm pushing at his chest. Rowan knocks on the window in the backseat of his SUV, her voice muffled. "Make out later, I want coffee!"

Levi gives me a smug, roguish smile and opens the passenger door for me. I twist around to face Rowan.

"What gives, you can't text your bestie to warn me?" I nod toward Levi as he rounds the front of the car. "I thought you wanted time away from campus?"

"I did, but when I heard you were going back, I wasn't about to leave you without offering support." She grins, tugging the hood of her black Thorne Point University hoodie over her red hair. "Besides, this way I can retrace our steps with the crossed keys and look for other spots around campus where the Kings may have their hideouts."

"By yourself?" While I have the threat of kidnapping hanging over my head, it's only been a short while since Rowan was stalked. I don't want her putting herself in danger.

"No, Colt's meeting me there. We'll get to have lunch together after your morning classes now that I don't have a conflicting schedule."

I grin. "Just like old times."

Levi starts the ignition and reaches across to grasp my leg, fingers tucking between my thighs. "Can they be considered old times when it was only a month ago we weren't watching our backs everywhere we went?"

"I like to think positively," I say.

"Hold onto that, babe," Rowan says. "The rest of us are a bunch of pessimistic assholes. We need you to brighten things up. You're our golden retriever friend."

My delighted laughter fills the car while we pull away from my family's estate. With their friendship, I can do this. I can face Silas Stone, my dad, and any nightmare that comes my way.

* * *

Both professors in my two morning classes welcome me back from my *retreat* and neither of them blink at Levi's presence. When I ask what retreat I went on between classes, Colton is the only explanation he offers. He keeps close, glaring at anyone as we cross campus toward the student union where we're meeting Rowan and Colton. Most people give us a wide berth based on his reputation alone.

"Aww, look, this is where you first stalked Rowan," I point out.

Levi grunts. "You had a pencil skirt on that day. Made your ass look good enough to take a bite out of."

I grin, poking his firm stomach. His lips twitch, gaze constantly moving to search our surroundings for any threat. It's lucky I don't have dance classes today. Most of my friends in my classes so far have only been brave enough to say hi from a distance with Levi as my shadow. His jealous streak could come out if we're still working in pairs.

The others have a table already when we reach the student union. Rowan waves us over, a fresh coffee in her hand.

"Babe. Real food, please," I tell her, setting my purse on an empty seat while Levi goes to get us food without me telling him what I want. "You had a huge coffee this morning when we stopped at the cafe."

Colton chuckles, shoveling a heaping bite of pasta from the Italian place into his mouth. "She gets pissy if she doesn't have a minimum of thirty-two ounces a day."

"Any luck with your stroll around campus?" I take the seat beside her, leaving the one on my other side open for Levi. "I'm surprised Wren let you come. Levi's been all over me about not being left alone."

Rowan smirks. "Wren was paid handsomely for his sacrifice of control. He's busy today, anyway. He's fielding another meeting with his dad. He says he keeps pestering him about the masquerade ball."

"We took some photos of potential spots. Penn swept campus for us before, but now that we have a better grasp of what the keys mean, I want to get a scanner here without prying eyes." Colton gestures to the students around us oblivious to the secret society operating behind the scenes. He waggles his brows. "That means new toys. I've always wanted a Batman level gadget to scan buildings."

We laugh at him while Levi returns with a full tray, glancing suspiciously at the three of us. He sets my favorite sushi roll from the Japanese restaurant in front of me wordlessly. Pleasant surprise ripples through me. He really does watch me closely.

"Do I want to know what put that look on his face?" He points at Colton with a fork.

"Do you ever?" Colton gives him a mischievous grin. "Could be anything. My new favorite porn GIF, or a sale on RFID chips in bulk."

Levi shakes his head.

"The surprise is half the fun," Colton says.

"Isn't that Quinn?" I nod over his shoulder toward the girl weaving through the tables with her brother in tow. "She looks like she's on a mission."

Colton cranes his neck to look, his mouth curving in a wicked grin when she reaches our table.

"Hey, goddess of the night. Dig the space buns. Trespassing today, or did you just miss me?"

She lifts a brow, helping herself to the seat beside him. "Psh, you wish, though."

Levi goes still, watching Quinn and Sampson with narrowed eyes. "You aren't enrolled at Thorne Point."

"We are now." Sampson settles in, slouching comfortably in his chair. He takes out a handheld gaming console and starts playing. "Transfer went through crusty ol' Barlow himself."

Rowan leans forward. "Dean Barlow at Castlebrook College?"

"Yup. Creepy old bastard," Quinn snarks.

"I know." Rowan grimaces. "I had the displeasure during a dinner hosted at his place. Why did he personally oversee your transfer?"

"And where did you get the money?" Colton tacks on, stroking his lower lip with his thumb. He hooks an arm over the back of his seat to angle toward her. "Last I looked into you, you were there on scholarship."

The corner of her mouth twitches. "Nothing gets by you. Not even private records."

"My favorite kind," he says.

Quinn purses her lips. "Inheritance finally kicked in."

"That's why you were cleaning out tables at all of our games?" Colton hums.

Her shoulders tense and she traces the neckline of her t-shirt with matte black stiletto style nails. The t-shirt looks like a ouija board with pizza slice yes and no options above the words *a slice a day keeps the demons away.*

"Keep your secrets. I'll find them out eventually."

Quinn squints at him. "Did you just quote Lord of the Rings at me?"

Colton makes a delighted sound and his eyes light up. "I was right about you. A woman of culture and taste."

Levi snorts, muttering. "God help us all. He has a crush."

"It doesn't matter how you got here, just that you're here now." I offer her a kind smile. "I'm Isla, that's Rowan, Levi, and you know Colton already."

Her laugh is husky and deep. "In his dreams."

"They're dirty and delicious, I promise." Colton winks.

"Quinn." She gestures with her thumb toward her brother. "That's Sammy."

"Sampson," he corrects without glancing up from his game. "Don't call me that unless you want to get on my bad side."

"Noted," Rowan says. "What made you transfer to TPU?"

Quinn's amused smirk falls and she lowers her voice. "Better opportunities." Her eyes bounce between Levi and Colton. "We've heard you help people. We could use somewhere to lie low."

"We're not running a B and B service," Levi says. "Who told you that?"

His hand goes to his pocket, hidden from their view on the opposite side of the table. I put a hand on his flexed arm to get him to chill out. He gives me a subtle shake of his head, always prepared for the worst.

"Anyone and everyone around here. They all talk about you like you're ghosts and royalty all at once," Quinn says. "So will you help?"

Colton drags his fingers through his hair in thought. "Do you know how we work?"

She nods. "Secrets for payment." Her gaze moves around the room and she pulls out her phone, sliding it to him. "I'm not whispering it in your ear, pretty boy."

Colton grins, skimming the note open on her phone. "You think I'm pretty?"

"I think you think you're pretty."

"Nah, I *know* I am." He blows her a kiss and slides the phone across the table to Levi, who catches it deftly. Tipping his chair back on two legs, he flips his hand back and forth. "Semantics."

While Levi reads their secret, Quinn presses her lips together.

"I can be useful in exchange for your protection," she offers.

Colton's chuckle is downright dirty. Her glare is fiery and she kicks his chair so he has to scramble to keep his balance.

"Not like that." She clicks her tongue. "I'm good with computers. I'll work for you."

"Like his recruited network?" Rowan asks.

"Yeah. I know about it." Quinn shrugs.

"Bullshit." Colton watches her closely. "Prove it."

"You'll be eating those words." Quinn holds out a hand for her phone. Levi hesitates and I take the device from him, handing it over to her. She smirks at me. "Thanks. Watch and learn, pretty boy."

"Give me a good show, babe." Colton sprawls in his chair while her fingers move faster than I thought possible across her screen. His eyes drag over her, drinking in every inch of her. "Don't forget to bypass the firewalls."

"Please, like I'm a newb," Quinn sasses. When he leans over to check what she's doing, she hides the screen against her chest. "Ah, ah. Sit back. You might learn something."

"I'm just making sure you don't choke when you come up against the encryption chain." Colton holds his hands up in surrender, an intrigued expression crossing his face.

"There are more ways than stealing the key outright and using a freezer to bypass encryption," Quinn says.

"Great, now there are two of them," Levi grumbles.

Sampson chuckles. I stroke Levi's thigh and smile at him when he covers my hand with his.

"Boom." Quinn hands her phone to Colton.

After scanning what she uncovered, he shakes his head. "Bullshit. How'd you get this?"

"Um, hello?" She blinks slowly and waves her hand around. "You just watched me extract it from an encrypted email to William Barlow."

Colton's mouth tightens and he passes the phone to Levi. This time, he allows me to peek over his shoulder to see what's on the screen. The email is mostly written in code, mentioning names of the founding fathers and an upcoming show. This means the dean of Castlebrook College is privy to Kings Society business. Levi takes a screenshot and forwards it to himself before deleting the image.

"I haven't found someone as good as you before," Colton murmurs. "How did you get past me?"

"On purpose," she assures him. "I'm not the type to take orders from others unless I have to."

Colton huffs out a laugh. "Fair."

"That's so cool you know how to do that," I say. "How'd you learn?"

Quinn shoots me a crooked smile. "Boredom, mostly. An idle mind and an insatiable hunger for knowledge."

Colton hums like he understands, studying her with a new respect. "What changed if you don't usually like to take orders? Why offer to work for us now if you avoided being recruited into my network?"

Her expression turns enigmatic.

Levi sighs. "She's your problem since it's your nerd area. Come on." He stands, taking my books. Sparing Quinn and Sampson a glance, he addresses Rowan. "Check in. We're done at two if you're not finished before then."

"Later," Rowan says.

"I hope we get to hang out again," I say to Quinn. "Let's plan a movie night."

Rowan smirks at Quinn's surprised expression. "Yeah, that's Isla for you. She loves everyone right away."

"I like making friends," I say primly.

"And we love you for it, Isles." Colton wiggles his fingers at me in a wave. "Never change, you sweet summer child."

Levi's hand brushes the small of my back and he guides me away. The crisp autumn sun is shining outside, an improvement from the dreary overcast weather we've had lately.

"What's wrong, grumpy?" I croon. "Were you jealous I wasn't paying enough attention to you?"

He smirks, halting us in the middle of the cobblestone path before herding me to a deserted arched tunnel that connects to the other side of campus. He traps me against his body and kisses me. "That answer your question? If it were up to me we wouldn't leave the gym or my bed. I'd rather spend all day with my cock buried inside you."

I shiver, nails digging into the material of his leather jacket. "Class?" My voice is dazed. "Who needs class? We should go find the library and explore this other option you've presented."

I love the sound of his dark chuckle as he drags me off in the opposite direction from my next class.

CHAPTER TWENTY-SIX

ISLA

It's unclear to me why my parents insisted on having lunch together at the club on Saturday until we arrive. Every eye in the club's upscale dining room turns to us. Appearances, how could I forget?

My parents can't outright say I haven't been around because there was an attempted kidnapping, and they can't say where I've been instead of with them. This lunch isn't for us, it's for everyone watching us.

Everything comes back to power and reputation in Thorne Point. Ridiculous.

I'd rather they be here flaunting themselves to give me time to snoop through the house for more answers.

I didn't want to come—annoyed that the first time they acknowledged my return to the estate it's in a public setting where I can't outright accuse them of their involvement in the plot to kidnap me—but Levi encouraged it, promising to raise hell. It's only because he's guarding me that I agreed to attend the most sought after reservation window at the club. It helps that he elbowed my mother out of the way to slide into the town car after me, smirking at her infuriated huff. They didn't want him to join us, but between the name he bears and the chilling glares he throws their way, they're powerless to stand up against anything he wants.

It's clear to me how much appearances and influence matters most to them by the way Mom primps, putting on her most expensive jewelry, and the smug sweep Dad gives the room.

We're guided through the dining room by a member of the waitstaff showing us to the prime table by the windows overlooking the golf course Mom had reserved for us. Dad is waylaid by someone calling his name. The man's son, Alan, is with him, eyeing me appreciatively. We've been set up on dates before, but I was never going to become the wife of a banker's son, no matter how much his father donates to Dad's campaign.

"Say hello, Isla," Mom says out of the corner of her mouth.

I avoid his gaze, plastering a serene expression on my face—my chosen mask for coming here. It's a shield I learned to wield a long time ago to deal with the cutthroat upper class always hunting for your weakness. If I pretend I'm a vapid heiress without an original thought, I blend in and I'm left alone.

"Isla. You remember the Paynes, don't you?" Mom's laugh is fabricated, her eyes flashing with a warning for my lack of social etiquette.

With a low growl, Levi steps into the guy's line of sight, blocking me from his view. While the rest of us are dressed up for the location, Levi isn't, sticking with his usual black t-shirt, ripped black jeans, and his leather jacket. He smooths a hand down my back, the move both possessive and seductive when he makes sure Alan is watching before he fits his palm to the dip in my waist, sending a signal to every man in the room staring at my ass or my tits that I'll only ever be an unobtainable fantasy to them.

Surprise filters through me. All week, he's taken care to only touch me out of sight as part of his bodyguard plan.

After shadowing me through the first half of the dining room in a protective position familiar to most high profile people here who have their own protective staff, he effectively told the room I'm sleeping with my bodyguard.

To them, it's scandalous. To me, it's a reminder he'll always have my back.

Mom pales, her knuckles turning white around her fancy clutch purse.

"Thank you," I murmur.

"You could've taken him." He shoots an unimpressed look at Alan. "Knife's in my inside pocket if he tries anything."

Mr. Payne misses the comment, too busy licking Dad's boots. Everyone in this room operates on a hierarchy of power. There are those beneath my family trying to claw their way up the rungs to the next level, and then there are those who wield more power that they hold over my parents.

Alan blanches, eyeing Levi warily. I bite my lip around a smile. Finally, some confidence in the skills he's taught me.

We share a secretive smirk as he forgoes further social etiquette by ignoring them all, guiding me the rest of the way to our waiting table. It's essentially a giant middle finger to Mr. Payne. My mother scoffs as we drift away without a goodbye, but would die before making a scene to correct me.

"Sir, your seat?" The waiter gestures to the chair he pulls out for Levi, the one he ignores to position himself behind me where he can watch everything going on in the room. I asked why he always puts his back to a wall and he called it a vantage point—a way to guard his back while looking for threats. "Sir?"

Rumbling, Levi shakes his head. "I'm good here."

"We're honored you opted to attend lunch service at the club, Mr. Astor.

I assure you we'll take excellent care of you, if you'll just take a sea—"

"I'm good. I'm working." He pats the back of my chair.

The waiter's brow furrows. "Er, I see. I'm afraid we don't allow our guests to bring any—"

At Levi's severe expression, the waiter shuts up and leaves. I feel bad for the waiter; he's only trying to do his job and follow the club's strict rules. I wouldn't typically bring an actual bodyguard with me to the prestigious country club—only Secret Service have been allowed on the grounds once when the President visited Thorne Point. He belongs here, anyway, his family's net worth is more than double my parents' money. The tables closest to us who overhear stage whisper about what the Astor heir is doing working as a bodyguard for the Vonns.

I'm sure within minutes it'll spread through the room.

"You didn't have to scare him off," I say. "What about the plan? You have to tell me when you're going rogue."

"He was annoying. And it'll be okay. I'm here with you, remember? No one will touch you."

My mouth curves as I thank a waitress who swiftly appears to fill my water glass. As I take a sip, I scan the room, relieved to find that Silas Stone isn't present. This reservation window is one he usually attends.

The meeting I overheard talking about using me as a pawn for Silas Stone's games makes it difficult to maintain my armor of positivity. He's already taken so much from me. The scar on my thigh tingles with a phantom memory. Gripping my leg over the hem of my chic wrap dress, I slam down hard on my thoughts, needing to keep my wits about me to withstand a meal with my parents.

"You okay?" Levi pulls me back to reality.

Clearing my throat, I nod. I'll be fine. I survived the first time he bought me. This time, I'll fight back like I couldn't at fourteen.

"Want to blow this off?" he asks quietly.

"Not yet. Let me remind you this was all your idea. We can use this to our advantage, like you said." I keep my voice hushed. "See if anyone else is overly interested because they're probably involved. Maybe Colton can do something with that information to uncover more members."

He nods, searching the room while my parents extract themselves to meet us at the table.

At home, neither of them have said more than two words to acknowledge me. They've ignored me, refusing to speak about my absence. It's as if they've already accepted I'm no longer in their lives, like the kidnapping was successful. Dad keeps to his study or spends time out of the house and Mom hasn't been able to look at me. In public, it's a different matter. My mother kisses my cheek before she's seated. She's never done that behind closed doors. Only when there's a chance of an audience.

Levi is a silent shadow. Whatever he has over my father's head is enough to have Dad ignoring his presence. His expression is flat. I know he'd rather be anywhere else than amongst the stuffy, stuck up people in the dining room. I don't blame him. This isn't my favorite place, either. I've only enjoyed the couple of times I've brought Rowan for lunch.

"Oh, I do hope Georgiana is here," Mom coos. "I'd love to let her know how arrangements for this year's masquerade ball are going."

Dad signals for a drink and someone leaps to acquiesce him.

"My classes are going great, thanks for asking," I say brightly.

Levi huffs out a soft laugh.

They both cut cold looks my way. I smile wider, unwilling to let them dim me. I don't know where things went so wrong. Is there some inherent gene in the wealthy that diminishes their love of their children? We're only born as pawns for them to advance themselves, but they forget we have minds of our own.

A vein throbs in Dad's temple. "Do not speak to us about your classes after you've thrown away everything you've worked on for frivolous endeavors."

I tilt my head coyly. "Dance is an art form."

"It's an embarrassment," Mom hisses. "Your early acceptance to Yale's law program, down the drain so you can be a backup dancer."

Levi rumbles, shifting his stance. A hand goes to his pocket.

"I'm doing something I love. Isn't that what's important?"

Dad scoffs. "Love? No. If you'd done as you were told, then maybe—"

"Artimus," Mom cuts in sharply, peering around the room at the attention we've drawn with the spat. "We can discuss it in private."

I draw in a sharp breath, my grip on my salad knife tightening. How did it come to this?

It strikes me how batshit insane my life is, sitting with my parents, who are secretly plotting to have me kidnapped by the nightmare of a man they've already subjected me to, pretending nothing is wrong. They might have chosen greed over their own daughter, but it's still my own existence. I'll be damned if I allow them to take it from me. Fury boils my blood.

Levi shifts, putting himself closer to me. He must pick up on thoughts running through my head because he meets my eye and tips his head, indicating the exit. If it's what I wanted, he'd get me out of here.

Sighing, I give him a barely perceptible shake of my head. I've endured my parents for twenty-one years. I can withstand this farce of a lunch. It will all be worth it when I can stop them from getting what they want and finally cut them from my life.

"Well, when is that?" I lift my chin. "Neither of you have been around *in private*. Avoiding me so you don't have to look at me?"

"Don't be so dramatic, dear, it's unbecoming," Mom drawls. "I should have fired your etiquette teacher the minute she encouraged your eccentric, excitable nature."

All my life I've bent over backwards to do as they wished—studied dead languages, achieved top grades, attended arranged dates, majored in political science—but it's never good enough. So why does some pathetic, tiny part of me still try? Even as I've fought to break their mold, rebelling against their wishes to take my freedoms, part of me still fears disappointing them. Maybe it stems from the fear of defying my father that took root in me when he took me to that dinner. An ingrained response I need to break.

Levi has the knife from his pocket out when I tune back into the conversation. I don't know what other ways they belittled me, but I can guess by the rage emanating off him in waves.

"No, I can't join you," Mom says. "I have a fitting with my stylist for the masquerade. Isla, your fitting is the same day."

"But it's a very important meeting. Rearrange your fitting," Dad demands.

"I'm not going to the masquerade ball," I say.

They both halt their discussion, studying me shrewdly. Dad grumbles under his breath, swirling his drink.

"Yes you are. You must," Mom insists. "I've already arranged your date for the evening. If you don't attend, think of how that will look."

"What sort of appearances do you need to maintain when you're already ignoring what happened to me?" It's the first chance I've had to broach the subject of what they're up to. "This whole thing is a farce. Why should I play along when you're waiting for the next opportunity to pawn me off?"

I don't know what I was expecting, given their track record, but they brush me off with dismissive non-committal hums. It underlines how different I am from them.

"This event is very important," Dad says. "You need to be there. You're going."

"No, thank you." I sip water primly.

Dad's face turns red. "You'll do as I say."

I set my glass down harder than I mean to, the liquid spilling over. I raise my voice defiantly. "No. I'm done doing as you say."

He opens his mouth, but before he launches into a tirade, Levi moves with a low, feral sound, knocking Mom's wine glass into Dad's lap threateningly. They both gasp.

"She said no," he snarls dangerously. "Isla won't be going anywhere she doesn't want to."

An acute ache pierces my chest in gratitude. For so long it's only been me in my corner standing up against them. He's on my side, always guarding me, always watching. It snuck up on me, but I'm falling for him, for this wild, hard-edged man who defends me so fiercely against any threat.

Wide-eyed, my parents splutter in outraged embarrassment. Their gazes dart around the room, assessing the damage done by Levi's undermining.

"I don't want to go," I agree, gesturing to Levi. He allows me to hold my own against them once I've found my voice again. If he can go rogue, so can I. "The only way I would is if my boyfriend was my date rather than whichever influential match of the week you've selected for me to look good with your supporters."

Mom's lips thin and she leans over to hiss at me. "You can't be seen at the ball on his arm after this public display of him playing bodyguard with you. It would be—"

"Scandalous?" I cut in. Her pinched expression says it all. Sighing, I push to my feet. "I've heard enough."

"Where do you think you're going?" Dad presses.

"Home," I mutter. "While I can still call it that."

If it ever was a home in the first place.

Levi falls into step with me, sliding his arm around my waist. I lean into him, absorbing his support to refill my own drained well.

"Next time, I'm stabbing one of them for talking to you like that," he rumbles.

My lips twitch. "Assault charges. Possible jail time, babe. Not worth it."

"So worth it." He gives me a sidelong glance. "What happened to warnings about going rogue?"

I smirk. "Not as fun on that side, is it?" I sober. "Is it safe to pull back from the whole not paint a target on my back thing?"

"I know what I said, but I decided fuck it." His hold on me tightens. "You're mine and I won't hesitate to let anyone know it. I'll keep you safe from all of them, Isla."

My heart gives an insistent thump and I press deeper against his side where I belong.

* * *

By the time we return to my family's estate, I've recentered myself with affirmations about who I am—my own independent person, not their pawn. An old ache in my chest throbs, the same one that always makes itself known whenever I've disappointed my parents or fallen short of their expectations. I smother it with positive thoughts about how much better off I am without them because I've found a real family.

"Think they'll come back?" Levi asks, dropping his jacket on my bed.

"Doubt it." I scrape my hair into a ponytail and kick off my heels. "They're going to stick it out, smooth over the scene I made by saying I didn't feel well. It gives us the time we've been waiting for to look for those robes."

Levi rifles through the pockets of his leather jacket and produces the same small device Colton gave him to plant at his uncle's mansion. "And bug your piece of shit dad's office. If he sets anything else up, we'll know. It'll be our early warning signal."

"Let's do it."

He closes the small distance between us, settling his hands on my waist. "Are you okay?"

I nod, giving him a smile. "Trust me, that was nothing. They can be much worse."

He doesn't release me, eyes bouncing between mine. Placing a soft, almost tender kiss on my forehead, he pulls me against him.

"Say the word and I'll make them disappear."

A laugh bubbles out of me. "So violent."

"They want to sell you to the highest bidder. Fuck them with an unsharpened blade up their asses."

My nose wrinkles at the gruesome image he paints. "You can take something from their closets and use it to work out your rage. It'll be therapeutic in a less murdery way."

Levi grunts, taking my hand. We leave my room, navigating to the wing my parents' rooms occupy. They share a sitting area and a massive walk-in closet, but they don't sleep in the same bed. I make a beeline for the closet, throwing open the doors with gusto.

"The last time I found them, my nanny was playing hide and seek with me. I wound up camping out in here and the robes were in a box on the floor." I scan the muted cream room separated into his and hers sides. "I wasn't allowed in here, especially not after that. I'm not sure if they're in the same place."

"They can't be far if they attended the meeting the Kings summoned Wren to," Levi mutters. "Let's split up. You take your mom's side."

We comb through the closet for twenty minutes. It's a tour of my parents by fashion and materialism, as cold and detached as they are. Levi gets my attention while I'm frowning at a conservative, bland-colored pantsuit that has no life to it. Fashion shouldn't be this sad.

"I've got something."

I put the pantsuit back and cross to Dad's side of the closet. Levi's in the back corner with an unzipped garment bag that contains two robes.

"You found them." I pull the garment bag off the rack and hang it from a hook. "Black robes."

"Look at this." He flicks the gold embroidered crossed keys. "They're members. Lower ranking, maybe. The ones in purple robes seemed to hold more sway. Wren's dad wore a purple robe, and I think my uncle must be at that level, too."

I run my fingers over my hair, wondering what they get out of giving me up, and how they're able to live with themselves. "This is crazy. I know secret societies still exist, but how has it gone on under the radar with this big of a network for so long and no one in the city noticed?"

"Because that's the point. They're all working to make sure they protect their wealth and power." Levi takes photos of the robes, texts them to the others, then shoves them away. "Let's hit the study before we run out of time."

Once we reach it, he wastes no time, palming the listening device Colton crafted and planting it in a place my father won't notice. I watch for a moment, impressed at all these hidden skills he has, then poke around Dad's desk. It's in disarray compared to its usual order. Most of the paperwork spread across the blotter are financial statements.

The rook tower logo on a letterhead snags my attention. It's Stoneworks Transport, Silas Stone's freight company. He's the CEO, the position passed to him from a long family line. I've heard him boast about it at

Dad's campaign dinners, how his company was founded right alongside the establishment of the city.

"Founding fathers," I murmur.

"What?" Levi's head pops up from beneath the desk. "Did you find something?"

"I think so. Take a look." Flipping the letterhead around, I sift through the mess on the desk to look for more. "Here's another one."

The second paper I discover is an intake receipt for expected inventory dated the same date as my attempted kidnapping. I doubt it's a coincidence, but I'm not sure how it's connected other than Dad's plan to exchange me to relieve his debts. *UNDELIVERED* is written in red across it.

"This might be what my uncle and your father were discussing last week. Why does this guy want you?"

My stomach bottoms out. I tear my gaze away, pretending to look for more paperwork. "He's the one controlling Dad's debt."

Levi surveys me silently. The truth weighs my tongue down, but I hesitate. I haven't held anything back from him except this one facet of myself.

I'm saved from him demanding a better answer by his phone going off. He checks it. "It's Colt on a video call."

"Let's take it upstairs in case my parents come back."

He answers, pressing a finger to his lips as Colton's face appears on the screen. Colton mimes zipping his lips while we hurry to my room. I check the hall, then close the door behind us and grab towels from my bathroom to stuff against the bottom of the door to muffle the conversation. Levi mutters to Colton by the window and I join him.

"What is it?" I ask.

"This corrupted file I've been working on," Colton says. "It's full of information on the Kings. Rowan's brother put it together and emailed it to her, but it never sent. We think it's when he was discovered poking around in something bigger than he realized. I recovered it from his phone after..." He clears his throat as my expression falls, realizing he's referring to Ethan's murder. "I decrypted another section. Castle."

"Castle?" Levi frowns. "Kings, castles. These pretentious dicks are driving me insane."

"I know," Colton says. "But the more we know, the better. And it was what you said they mentioned in that meeting, right? Prosperity of the castle or something."

"Maybe they have some kind of joint business?" I suggest.

"There was one other thing connected with castle—rook. I don't know the significance yet. I wanted to update everyone first."

Levi's brows pinch. I'm a step ahead of him. Colton doesn't get what rook could refer to, but I do.

"Stoneworks Transport. It's a freight company run by a man named Silas Stone." At Levi's sharp glance, I roll my lips between my teeth. "He's connected to my father's debts. There's a rook tower in his company's logo. It could be that."

Colton whistles. "Yes it could be. Good work, Isles." He pretends to bump his fist with me through the video call. "Aight, I'm out. I'm gonna go hunting for a man with a creepy alliterated name."

Levi ends the call with a grunt. Pocketing his phone, his gaze flicks to me. "You don't have to tell me yet, princess. But you will."

He doesn't have to specify what he means. I nod, looking at my hands. Silas isn't finished taking from me. Acknowledging that fact isn't something I'm ready to face yet when I've done my best to fight off the insidious memories of my nightmare for seven years. I wring my fingers together, needing some way to push the building energy out since I can't dance it off.

Levi enters my peripheral vision, barging right into my space, and presses his lips to the top of my head. I close my eyes, memorizing the feeling of what real affection feels like.

CHAPTER TWENTY-SEVEN

LEVI

Isla's dance classes have been heaven and hell in the last week. On Monday night I endure the sweet torture of watching her dance in tight leggings and a thin cropped hoodie that exposes her stomach with her cheeks flushed without being able to stalk across the room and touch her. She shoots me a wink and a little shimmy of her shoulders from her position in line just before her cue to begin the section of a group performance the class is working on.

She's always adaptable. When I decided fuck it, if my uncle found out she matters to me, I would stop at nothing to counter him, she pivoted with her own rogue move outing me as her boyfriend. We left her house for the rest of the weekend to get away from her parents as a fuck you to them. She's enjoying class tonight, her spirits higher when she's away from them.

My hungry gaze remains glued to her ethereal movements. Each arch and roll of her hips feels specifically designed to torment me. She passes the folding chair I'm seated on and gives me a sultry grin meant only for me, sinking to her knees before her upper body dives to the floor.

I grit my teeth as her dance partner for this portion of the performance grasps her waist and lifts her from the floor into the air. Her legs kick apart in a graceful split and her body bends back over his shoulders. It takes effort to keep my ass planted in the chair. Only in my head do I entertain pleasant fantasies of strangling the fucker with his hands all over my girl before I re-stake my claim on her, fucking her until she screams my name and is covered in my marks. Over his dead body, just to make sure he knows Isla doesn't belong to any other man but the deadly monster who keeps her safe.

It takes me by surprise how quickly she entrenched herself in my life, to the point I find it difficult to think of my day without her in it. Every day the intense burn in my chest grows for her. If anything happens, especially on my watch, I won't be held responsible for the havoc I'll unleash to keep her out of harm's way. Those who want to use her as a pawn in their games will meet gruesome ends at the end of my knives.

Things have been quiet enough in the days following the ridiculous farce of a lunch Isla's parents dragged us to that it puts me on edge as the end of October looms closer. Despite the things going on, Isla truly does use dance as her chosen method to cope, throwing herself into it to shut out her other problems. My uncle keeps leaving messages about the upcoming masquerade ball. I'd rather drive an ice pick into my skull than attend a masquerade ball to make him happy. I don't give a shit about appearances.

The song swells for the finale of the dance, drawing me out of my thoughts.

When Isla pulls off an impressive tumble off her partner's back, she pops up and seeks me out again, the corners of her eyes crinkling when she finds my attention trained on her. She should know by now, I only have eyes for her. I only want to watch her.

The instructor claps. "That looks great, everyone. From the top one more time, then we'll call it a night. There are two weeks left. Keep polishing and you'll have a beautiful showcase."

Isla hurries over to the instructor with a dancer's natural grace. "May I book extra studio time tonight? I'd like to work on my solo piece."

"You can have it for an hour and a half," the instructor says. "Then rest your muscles."

I smirk. I'm always telling her the same thing.

"Thank you!" Isla goes to a schedule attached to a clipboard hung on the wall and writes her time slot in before coming over to me. I hand her a water bottle and enjoy the way her throat bobs while she gulps down a few sips, tracking the beads of sweat I want to lick away. She gasps, wiping her mouth with the back of her hand. "Is it okay if we're here a little longer?"

"An hour alone where you can give me a private show?" I trace my lower lip with my tongue, flicking the ring piercing. "What's not to like?"

She turns a deeper shade of red. "Well now that's all I'm going to be thinking about while we run through this again."

"Show me your moves, princess," I taunt.

She props a hand on her hip. "Eyes on me, then."

"Always."

The performance is just as torturous to sit through as it has been every time. My jaw aches from how hard I clench my teeth by the time it finishes. The only time I take my attention off Isla is to glare daggers at her partner for the lift. He glances nervously my way when he's gathering his things and dips before the instructor is done going over feedback.

Once the room empties, I relax, spreading my legs and leaning back in the chair. Isla drifts over to me and stands between my knees.

"Careful, princess. You stand there long enough and I'm going to expect you to drop to your knees and suck me." Finally, I can touch her. I don't waste a second, skimming my palms up her legs to squeeze her hips. "The things you do to me..."

"You know exactly how to make a girl blush." She puts her hands on my shoulders when I lean into her, kissing her exposed stomach. "I really need to work on my solo piece. I haven't been able to run through it while I've been catching up on studying, reading, and the assignments I've missed."

"In a minute. You just had some other asshole's hands all over you. I need to remind your body whose it is." I stand to dispel the need to drag her down to straddle me.

"I'm yours," she murmurs. "It was just a dance."

"I know." My fingers skim the soft skin of her stomach and delve beneath the hem of her hoodie. She's wearing a sports bra, but I picture her tits bare and a rumble vibrates in my throat.

"What's that look for?"

"I never pictured you owning a hoodie." I kiss her neck and she hums. "Thought you only stole mine."

She laughs. The delicate sound curls around me, drawing me ever closer to this girl that gives me life by chasing away my darkest shadows.

I don't want to put a name to the thing I feel for her because it's too big for me to even wrap my head around.

All I know is she's the only person to make me feel like this. The only one who is capable of quelling my never ending anger.

With one last kiss, she moves to the center of the room, tossing a wink over her shoulder while shaking her ass. "We should install a stage in the nest. Then you can have a private dance show whenever you want."

My lips twitch. "You wouldn't get any dancing done. I'd be too hungry for you. Every time you move, I'd be on you."

"Well, I like that plan. As long as I get to move." Closing her eyes at the first notes of her song, she lets it sweep her away. "Just like this. I love being able to dance. This always feels amazing."

I track her with an unwavering gaze. "Have you always loved to dance? I don't remember you having recitals or anything. I would have noticed you prancing around in a tutu and tights."

"Stalker," she teases.

"Guardian," I counter.

Obsessed. Fascinated. Permanently fixated, orbiting the only sun I've found on this earth.

"I like that you've always been watching over me." She stretches her arms high overhead in a big, full-bodied movement, then reaches the quiet, somber part of the song, hunching in on herself. "Dance saved me so I didn't break. It helped me survive. The first time I did it, I was just in my room. I was probably on the verge of a panic attack. I felt like my skin was too tight and I needed to move."

Isla's fingers brush her scarred leg. She hasn't come clean about the story behind it yet, but I have a good idea it has to do with the secret she gave me. Her father won't take her from me and neither will the man who wants her. No one will get her while I'm by her side.

"When I did, I finally found my freedom." It shows in her dance when she explodes out of a crouch telling the story of a broken girl rising up from her misery. "That's why I love it so much. And the rain. And laughing, because it's the best medicine. I like making everyone around me smile. I'd rather laugh and dance to work through my problems than let them win."

My heart pangs, but it's not as heavy as it used to be when I think of the rain. Not when I know how she looks dancing in it.

"I haven't smiled in a long time. Not since you barged your way in with all your sass." I didn't have any reasons left to smile after I lost my mom. But Isla is always my exception.

Her laugh is warm and pleased. "Mission accomplished." She makes a victorious noise. "Smiling is good for the heart, grumpy. Trust me."

No longer able to sit on the sidelines and watch, I get up, prowling closer, erasing the distance between us. My palms tingle with the need to touch her. I give in, grasping her waist.

She adjusts her dance, adapting to pull me into it like she pulled me into her orbit, owning my thoughts so I could never bury her completely in my mind. Her arms twine in elegant sweeps overhead and her gorgeous smile breaks free.

"All my parents have ever done is control me. Use me." She shudders, her smile faltering. "As shiny as my life is, it's not mine. It hasn't been until you. I'm finally standing on my own, finding myself."

Something in me softens. I pull her closer while the music continues. One arm slides around her waist and the other holds her hand while we slow dance. I cradle her close. Though both of us are skilled at moving, we fumble, our movements out of sync with the melody. It doesn't matter. We're dancing to our own melody.

"Anyone who doesn't see you doesn't matter. It's been clear to me from day one, princess. When you first captivated my attention, there was no turning back. I tried to smother it, but you shine through any darkness." My voice is gruff, but I go on, exposing a part of myself to make sure she understands. "You're the most beautiful thing I've ever seen when you dance. It makes you glow so bright. Your happiness bleeds through every movement. Watching you dance is my favorite part of the day."

Her lips part in surprise, then she smiles up at me, pressing on her toes to kiss me. I rest my forehead against hers.

"You're my favorite part of every day, so we're even."

An amused sound escapes me and I twirl her away only to pull her back into my arms, continuing our slow circle in the middle of the dance studio. The music ends, but we don't stop.

"This is nice." Isla tucks her cheek against my chest and I smooth my palm up her back, beneath the cropped hoodie. "I like it when you hold me. I feel safest in your arms."

I tip her chin up and capture her lips in another languid kiss that puts fire in my veins. "You better dance, princess. Otherwise, I'm going to fuck you in every inch of this studio so I have something to remember the next time another man puts his hands on you in here. It'll keep me from cutting them off."

She giggles. "I don't know, you're kind of selling me on this idea. We already defiled the library."

A groan leaves me. "You're too tempting."

Isla has an impish glint in her gorgeous blue eyes when she slips out of my arms to drag my chair to the center of the room. "You sit. I'll dance."

"Princess..."

My warning trails off when she messes with her phone and a seductive, heavy beat starts. It's not her usual song she's practiced to so much I have the damn thing memorized. She improvises a sexy dance, twisting her body to match the beat. I draw in a deep breath as she goes down to the floor and creates a sinfully filthy display, bowing her back and twerking her ass in skintight leggings.

"Fuck, baby. That's hot." It's a challenge not to explode out of the chair and cover her body with mine. But this is her game. "I want to spread you out and make you fucking scream, beautiful."

In response, she rolls to her back in a fluid movement, draws her knees up, and spreads her legs. Her flirtatious smirk has my cock straining in my jeans.

"You love playing with fire," I rumble.

"I just like seeing that vein in your neck bulge." She rises to her feet and dances her way to me, grabbing my shoulder for support while she straddles me. She rolls her hips, grinding on the hard ridge of my cock with a breathy noise. "Someone's enjoying this."

With a growl, I grab her hips and control her speed, making her rub her pussy faster and faster until her lashes flutter. "We're both gonna enjoy it."

She grips my shoulders, tipping her head back on a moan while I get her off on my lap.

"Like that?" I demand.

"So good," she breathes. "Oh!" Her body tenses and she buries her face in my neck. "Need you right now."

"Did you come for me, pretty thing?" I kiss along her neck, dragging my lip ring back and forth. At her murmur, I chuckle. "I'm so fucking hard for you. Gonna fuck you until I'm leaking out of your pussy, then make sure every last drop is pushed back inside."

Isla moans my name, nails scraping the back of my neck. I lift her as I get up and take her to the bar that runs along the three walls of mirrors. Setting her on her feet, I tear her leggings off, pick her back up by her waist, and set her ass on the bar. Her pupils are blown and she pants as I unbutton my jeans.

"Spread." I tap her thigh and give her a savage grin when she obeys, stretching her legs wide to expose herself to me.

I drop to a knee and lick a stripe up her glistening folds and close my lips over her clit, groaning at her divine taste. She moans, tugging on my hair as I bring her to the brink again.

"Fuck, oh, fuck, Levi, please," Isla begs.

My tongue teases her clit and I plunge a finger into her soaking wet pussy. The noise my fingers make pumping into her is obscene. She clenches on them and I feel it when she comes. I lap at her like a starved man, feeling her pleasure coating my jaw.

Grabbing the bar, I haul myself to my feet. I get my cock out and run the tip through her slick folds.

"Fuck me," she whispers.

"Scream for me," I counter, slamming into her.

Isla's eyes go wide, then roll back in pleasure, her cry echoing off the walls. I grab her jaw and bring my lips to her ear.

"Good girl," I growl.

"Don't stop," Isla hisses. "Don't you ever stop."

"Never," I swear roughly.

She grabs either side of my neck and pulls me in for a kiss, swallowing my groan as my cock plunges into her tight, wet heat. Oblivion rises up fast. She has me so worked up from sitting through her class that I'm not going to last long, my control abandoned on the floor in shredded tatters. Adjusting my grip to squeeze her ass, I fuck her deep and hard until we're both panting and desperate for release.

"Oh god!" Isla's legs shake and she wraps them around my waist, her pussy fluttering with her orgasm around my dick. "Fuck, that feels so good."

It's too much. I bite down on her neck when I come.

It's on the tip of my tongue to blurt out words I've only said to one other person in my life. Shock holds them back and I crush her body to mine in a tight embrace. She's unaware of my mental dilemma, her head resting on my shoulder.

"So much for my studio time," she says wryly. "Oh well. Can't complain."

"You're too hard to resist." I help her off the bar and run my fingers over her ass. "Lets get cleaned up. We can head out, get dinner somewhere."

"Sounds like a plan."

Before she makes it further than a step away from me, I tug her back against my front, facing the mirrors. Her cheeks are tinged pink, her hair a mess, and she's naked from the waist down. I skim a hand down her stomach and dip between her legs, playing with her. She meets my gaze in the reflection and I give her a devilish smirk when I push a finger into her, making good on my promise.

Isla bites her lip, fixated on what I'm doing. Her breathing picks back up.

I kiss her temple. "Now I'll be less inclined to remove body parts when you have this class."

"And I'll be horny every time I dance in here," she shoots back.

"You're welcome," I deadpan.

We clean up before we're too tempted to go another round. I wasn't kidding about how irresistible she is. Somehow my dick is never satisfied until we've gone at least three rounds. Maybe my constant need to have her is built up from the years I've been fascinated by her, all the times she haunted my dreams, and how long I held myself back from temptation. But I'm hungry and she's spent the last four hours dancing, so I can wait to refuel and rest before I take her again.

On our way out we snark at each other, my grin breaking free at her antics. We cross campus and reach the garage. I stop when something out of place enters my peripheral vision. The pause lasts a fraction of a second, barely long enough for anyone to notice.

Isla does, though. She's learning to read every shift in me.

"Keep walking," I say. "Act normal."

She trusts me enough to follow directions when I give them. Pride unfurls in my chest when she sweeps an assessing look at our surroundings, picking up on my habits. I know it when she spots the squad car parked in a discreet spot, easily missed. A shadowed figure is seated inside, tracking our progress to the town car.

Instead of Isla's usual driver, I've had Penn following us to campus in it in case something like this happened. After the meeting my uncle had with Vonn, I'm not giving Stone any chances to snatch her. I take Isla around the other side of the car and open the door, squeezing the back of her neck so she ducks down like she's getting in.

"Trouble?" Penn asks from the driver's seat.

"Maybe. Dump this once you lose the tail if they follow you, then meet us back at the Nest." I motion for Isla to hide behind a concrete support pillar and slam the door.

Penn drives off. I stiffen when the squad car follows.

"Come on," I say.

Isla inches out of the dark and takes my hand. "They're using my attempt to file a police report against me. I'd be more likely to get into a cop's car and wary of strangers."

"Most likely." I lead her to the bike I keep parked here for emergencies and hand her a helmet while I retrieve the keys from the hiding spot in a fake piece of concrete I installed nearby. "We'll find out more back at the Nest."

Her features settle in determination and once again I'm struck by how much it would take to actually break her. She's forged herself into a survivor using her own unique way. I honed my body into a weapon to overcome my helplessness, but she's found her own strengths to guard herself against her demons.

I help her buckle the helmet and caress her cheek with my thumb. When we get on the bike, I soak in the feeling of her arms winding around me. This is the first time I've ever had someone on the back of my bike. I don't allow anyone to ride my bikes or ride with me.

But Isla is an exception to every one of my rules.

CHAPTER TWENTY-EIGHT

ISLA

My pulse races, the rush filling my ears above the growl of Levi's motorcycle on the ride to the Nest. He zips through the city streets, weaving a dizzying route as if he's worried someone could be following us, too.

Even when we reach the hotel, he remains alert. He puts his hand on the small of my back and ushers me inside.

"Do you think it could have been Pippa keeping an eye out?" I know what he's going to say, but I have to ask, clinging to the hopeful thought instead of the truth.

"No," Levi says. "Let's tell the others what happened."

He must have sent them a heads up, because everyone waits for us with grim expressions when we reach the lounge beneath the hotel. Rowan paces behind the couch Wren and Jude are seated on while Colton types at a maddening pace on a wireless keyboard.

"Thank god you're okay," Rowan says the second she spots us, hurrying across the room to crash into me with a tight hug.

"We're fine." My voice is muffled against her hair. I pat her back comfortingly. "If I was alone, I would've missed it. The police car was parked in a spot angled to watch my town car. It followed Penn."

"He says he's five minutes out," Colton says. "He lost the tail."

"They're regrouping," Wren says. "Growing antsy. They'll want to try to make their move to take you soon. If they're desperate enough, they might just say fuck it and take you from your family's estate despite the higher risks involved. You should think about coming back here permanently."

Dread sends my stomach plummeting. Maybe he's right. Maybe I never should have left, but I needed answers. It was important for me to face my parents and the fear disobeying my father instills in me.

"I didn't think they'd try the garage again," Jude says. "But baiting you with a squad car is clever."

"I probably would've fallen for it," I confess.

"You trust too easily," Levi rumbles behind me. "This is why I can't let you go anywhere alone. Did anything come across the bug we planted in Vonn's office?"

"No." Colton frowns. "This was probably organized while he was out of the house. I doubt he trusts he's safe to speak freely with you there doing your skulking creeper act."

A muscle jumps in Levi's jaw. "I was hoping he was an idiot who would take my threat against him more seriously."

"Most politicians aren't. They're paranoid by nature," I say. "We can't rely on the bug to be our early warning sign."

Muted footfalls signal Penn's arrival moments before he joins us. He lifts his chin in a nod, his sharp features twisted in a scowl nearly as fierce as Levi's.

"You lost them?" Levi asks.

Penn drags his fingers through his dark hair. "Yeah. Once it was clear I wasn't returning to the Vonn estate, the squad car sped by with the lights on. I circled back to the garage to dump the car and brought your Escalade back."

"Thanks." Levi sighs, bracing his hands on the back of the couch opposite Wren and Jude. "I thought if I was with her it would stop them."

"This Stone guy clearly believes he has more power than we do," Jude points out. "If your mere presence isn't enough to scare him off, nothing will short of putting her back in hiding."

"I can't live like that." I move to Levi's side and hold his arm. "Please. I don't want to live in fear forever. It's why I wanted to go back to stand against my parents. We have to figure out another way to stop them."

He kisses the top of my head. "We'll do anything that keeps you safe."

"Can we call Pippa? This is what she gave us her number for. Maybe she'll be able to find out who followed me and where they went after they stopped following Penn," I suggest. "Isn't there an internal system that tracks their GPS location?"

"First of all, I'm offended if you don't think I can hack that myself," Colton says. "Trackers aren't mandatory, so not all forces have them."

"I know you're skilled, but she wants to help," I say.

"I don't care if she's finally realized she fucked up, we can't trust her," Wren says coldly. "She's still one of them."

The comment makes Jude frown and scrub his jaw.

"He's right," Levi says. "Don't trust anyone but us. Assume everyone is your enemy."

"You guys are so doom and gloom." I rake my teeth over my lip. "Am I supposed to look over my shoulder for the rest of my life?"

"We're like this for good reason." Jude's eyes flash and he rakes his fingers through his hair. "This is what it takes to come out on top."

"I have a better idea." Colton spins his chair around to face us. "I've had Quinn tucked away, putting her through different tests to see if she's as good as she says—she is, by the way."

"Get to the point," Levi says.

"I am. I've had her helping me with decoding Ethan's corrupted file." Colton's mouth twists in a cocky smirk. "She doesn't know what it really is. I told her it was a puzzle I devised. For every decryption she gets, I give her a cookie. A cookie being a grand in cash—she's a greedy little thing."

"Or she thinks you're an easy mark," Jude mutters.

"You left her alone with something that sensitive?" Wren's frown is severe. "Without telling us?"

"Hey, hey." Colton holds his hands up. "I know what I'm doing, okay? I mask everything and have backups. I only let her work on it when I'm watching."

Wren narrows his eyes, but doesn't push the topic. "So what's your brilliant idea?"

"Let me take this to her and see what she can do. With the amount of shit that's come our way, I'm running on like three hours of sleep a night and surviving on energy drinks." Colton scrubs at his scalp, messing his hair up. He hides it well behind his easygoing smiles and joking around, but his exhaustion is evident. "As much as I appreciate the ego boost, I can't do it all. This is outside the scope of what my network of underlings can handle. If we're going to keep Isla safe, I need better help."

"Damn it, Colt," Jude grumbles. "How many times have I said you need to say shit if you're sliding into doing it all yourself?"

His frustration makes a pang echo in my chest. These boys are loyal to each other until the end, their bonds more important than anything in the world. They're hard-edged and can be huge jerks, but they love each other.

They're a family. One I want to be part of permanently. When I'm around them, I feel whole.

"Colton." My voice wobbles and he huffs out an exasperated laugh, holding out his arms. I cross the room to hug him. "Please don't run yourself into the ground for me."

"Babe, I would do that and more for my family. I told you, you're one of us. Can't escape now." He kisses my cheek.

My throat tightens. I wanted to put a stop to this for myself, but not at the expense of the people I care about. "If it makes your lives all easier, I can go back into hiding."

"You deserve to live in the light," Levi says.

He followed me across the room, staring at me like I'm the reason he gets up in the morning. I slip out of Colton's arms and step into Levi's. He tightens them around me.

"We'll figure this out," he says into my hair. "I'm not letting you live in a cage you don't want."

"I'm going with you," Wren says. "I want to see this girl for myself."

"Let's head out," Rowan says.

"I want this over with." I lift my head from Levi's chest and meet his eyes with unwavering determination. "Whatever it takes."

Cupping my face, he kisses me hard and fast.

I wish we could be laughing like we were on campus leaving the dance studio. But my positive thinking isn't going to save me from kidnapping, no matter how much I reach for the inner light that keeps me centered and chases away my fears. This is the real, harsh world that's out to get me.

If I'm going to evade Silas Stone, I have to start thinking like Levi and our friends.

* * *

The apartment Colton has been letting Quinn and her brother stay in is in the same building as Wren's macabre penthouse. It's clear to see Colton's touches—aside from the wall of computer equipment much like his setup at the Nest, the spacious three bedroom apartment with floor-to-ceiling windows has all kinds of movie and comic book memorabilia on every available surface. Figurines in glass display cases are backlit and framed posters hang on the walls. The bones of it are as austere as Wren's place, but Colton has brought more life to the space.

"Wow," I say as Colton leads us in, swinging his keyring around his finger.

He grins. "Yeah, I used to stream here a lot. Haven't had the chance to lately." He raises his voice. "Honey, I'm home!"

"I told you to cut it out with that shit," Quinn calls from deeper in the apartment. "If my brother doesn't kill you for it, I will."

"I do it to make sure you haven't run out on me, little queen," he taunts. "We have guests."

She makes a frustrated noise from the hall and emerges, dressed in a star-themed hoodie blanket and bright purple fishnets. Her hair is twisted into a knot on top of her head and wrapped in a pretty scarf to protect her braids. She carries a laptop with her and sets it on the island that connects the open living space to the full kitchen, an online poker game in progress.

"I'm about to sweep these bitches," she mumbles.

"Oh yeah?" Colton saunters over to stand behind her, bracketing her with his arms braced on the counter. He's a full head taller than her without the black leather platform heeled boots she favors. "Mm, nice hand. You could give this player I know a run for her money."

Quinn elbows him. "Back the fuck up before I put you on your ass again."

"I let you have that cheap shot," he says.

"Colton," Wren says in a clipped tone.

"Right." Colton snaps his fingers and picks Quinn up by her waist, carrying her to the big computer set up that takes the place of an entertainment system. She yelps, kicking her feet. "Cool it. I have another test for you."

Quinn settles, accepting the seat Colton guides her to. She tucks one knee close to her chest and frowns at the rest of us. "What is it?"

"Someone's been trying to kidnap me," I say.

Quinn's brows shoot up. "For real?"

Colton groans. "Isles, I had such a good lead in."

"Focus." Levi flicks his head.

"Alright, Jesus." As he takes a seat on a rolling stool next to her, Quinn flashes him an intrigued smirk. He wakes up the system and enters an admin password. "Don't even think about trying to crack the admin access, I have it set up to automatically change when I log out."

"So touchy with your toys." Quinn holds up her hands. Today her nails are a glossy black stiletto style with skulls on them. She looks at me curiously. "Why do they want to kidnap you?"

"The old sell a pretty girl as collateral for old men's debts," Rowan deadpans.

"A classic so foolproof they haven't stopped using it since medieval times," Colton chimes in.

"My dad," I offer up in explanation.

Fire burns in the pit of my stomach that this is happening again. He wants to hand me over to that monster Silas Stone so he can amass more power. I shudder and Levi runs a hand down my back.

"Dad of the year," Quinn murmurs. "So what am I supposed to do about it?"

Colton pulls up the security footage from the night of the attack. "Watch this. Then tell me your next move."

She folds her fingers together and leans her elbows on the desk, watching the attack unfold. I swallow past the lump in my throat as the recording shows the men running me down. Quinn's gaze shifts to Levi when he comes into the picture to rescue me.

"Obviously you aren't to repeat what you see or do in here unless you enjoy grave consequences," Wren says.

She ignores him, scrubbing through the footage to replay it. Colton watches her, stroking his fingers over his mouth. After one more replay, she taps a nail on the screen.

"Did you run the plates?" she asks.

"Duh. Falsified registration." Colton taps out a beat on the desk. "Next move?"

Quinn slides her lips together, searching the screen. "Did you ID the dead guy?"

"We were only able to get so much," Rowan says. "We left in a hurry."

She doesn't mention the tracking device found in my purse, or the other problems the Crows were already dealing with the night of my attack. Wren crosses his arms, cutting an imposing figure with his stony expression and his broad shoulders. No one brings up the Kings Society or their connection to this.

Levi's warning from earlier echoes in my head. *You trust too easily.*

Going forward I'm going to need to think W.W.L.D.—what would Levi do—to handle myself like they do.

A smile tugs at my lips when I picture his stab first, ask questions later policy.

He notices and shoots me a stern look. Growing restless, he pulls out a knife, running through his balance and dexterity drills—what he's doing when he flips his knives, he's informed me in exasperation at my cutesy term—while Quinn zooms in on different parts of the still frames from the footage and works on sharpening the clarity.

Quinn's muttering to herself cuts off and she snaps her fingers. "There."

Colton leans in, squinting at the screen. "The reflection. Shit, that's good thinking." He points out what they see—the van had a logo we missed on the other side but the reflection was captured on camera in the windshield of a car it passed when it peeled out of the garage. "Let's flip it, sharpen the image, and... Boom, baby."

Levi growls and Wren's eyes narrow dangerously at the logo they recover. It shows a rook tower with two crossed keys above the words Castle Delivery Co. Discomfort rushes through me at the uncanny similarity to the logo for the freight company Silas owns. Levi darts his gaze to me and I wonder if he's thinking the same thing.

Castle and rook, two of the words Colton recovered from the file he's been working on, are once again staring us in the face.

"First keys, now this." Rowan tugs on her thick auburn braid.

Wren bats her hand away and strokes her hair more gently. "It's definitely connected, but we knew that."

"Find the business registration," Levi says. "Make sure it's not another shell corporation like they pulled with SynCom to cover up the drugs."

Colton's fingers speed across the keyboard. Quinn clicks her tongue and steals it from him, reaching across to gain access.

"It's faster if you do it this way," she says.

His gaze drags over her and he traps the tip of his tongue between his teeth and lower lip. "By all means, show me what you've got." He leans closer. "You comfy like that? My lap is open if you don't want to stretch."

Quinn ignores him, typing at a clipped speed to hack her way into the Thorne Point business database. Colton watches her work with growing respect gleaming in his eyes.

"Here. It was registered about twenty years ago under the name Benjamin Howell," Quinn reads from the database.

"One of the founding fathers' names." I lick my lips. "Is there any way to connect a real person to it?"

"With more time," Colton answers.

"What about checking it against other similar logos? Is that too much of a stretch?" I twist my fingers together.

Colton glances at Quinn before responding. "That other company we looked at?"

At my nod, Quinn squints at us. "I already said I wouldn't say anything."

The corner of Colton's mouth lifts and he pulls up Silas Stone's company logo, overlaying it with the Castle Delivery Co. logo. The rook towers are the same. "Perfect match."

"What do they deliver?" Wren asks.

Colton opens the delivery company's website. "Product transport, working regionally. Look, it has a link to the freight company's website and says they work in close connection."

"Product," I echo. "Like people?"

"Ew, creepy," Quinn says.

"They were there to kidnap her," Wren says. "And the lengths they're willing to go to succeed."

"The meeting Vonn had with my uncle implied she was a special deal, but what if she's not a one off?" Levi's jaw works, murderous shadows clouding his eyes. "What if they're taking others?"

"You don't think it's the same as your—?" Wren scrubs at his jaw. "That was fifteen years ago, but it doesn't mean they didn't have a legitimate cover we never found. Colt."

"Two steps ahead of you." Colton's jaw is set, his relaxed nature gone.

Levi stalks away from us with his shoulders hunched as he flicks his knife faster and faster through the air, catching it with precision while he works through whatever darkness is plaguing him.

Me and Rowan exchange curious glances. She shrugs. This goes back further than either of us. Frowning, I close the distance Levi put between us. He whirls on me as I approach, his chiseled features foreboding. Unafraid, I walk right up to him and wrap my arms around him. He freezes, panting against my ear.

“Princess,” he whispers roughly before crushing my body to his, tangling his fingers in my hair.

We stay locked in the embrace until he comes back to me, stiffly untangling himself to cradle my face between his hands and rest his forehead against mine.

I don’t ask him for an explanation. It wouldn’t be fair when I haven’t given him my full truth, either. I simply provide the support and comfort he obviously needs.

“You’re not gonna like this,” Colton says a few minutes later. “Instead of searching for the fake company, I followed a hunch and found stories on missing people. College-aged girls.”

Rowan’s breath hitches and Wren tucks her into his side, murmuring to her. She nods. My heart goes out to her, wishing she didn’t have to navigate the aftermath of her brother’s terrible fate. Wren swipes her tears away and kisses her.

Sniffling, Rowan regains her composure. “Do the dates line up with the business registration?”

“Yup. And it looks like someone’s been trying to suppress the stories so they don’t make it outside of the local media cycle, if they’re reported in the first place,” Quinn says in a flat tone. She tucks her other knee into her chest and covers her legs with the oversized hoodie. "Shit, this is messed up. They've all gone missing from around the city."

"Damn it," Levi snarls.

"It's been more and more in the last month. They seem to spike around the fall." Colton cracks his knuckles and opens a new window.

The latest victim's Instagram is full of smiling selfies around Thorne Point. The last photo shows her with a gourmet donut, standing outside the grand opening of a shop downtown as she pretends to take a bite for the photo. In the background, a white van with the Castle Delivery Co. logo on the door is visible. The driver is looking at her.

"Oh shit," Quinn says in disgust.

Colton thumps a fist on the desk, making her jump. Levi peels away from my side and palms his knife.

"Don't wreck anything out here," Colton bites out, his own anger bleeding through his words. "Go stab a pillow, or something."

"Stabbing a pillow isn't going to fix anything," I say. "If they're kidnapping other girls, then there's only one thing they could be doing to them."

"Product. People. They've got a fucking sex trafficking ring," Rowan spits.

"The annual masquerade ball is this weekend," Wren says darkly. "The invitation boasted an unforgettable night. That's why they've been snatching more frequently."

My blood runs cold. The masquerade. "That's why my parents were adamant I attend. Dad and Levi's uncle mentioned an autumn revelry, but I didn't get it until now. It's the masquerade ball."

I was too busy trying not to split apart at the seams when they said Silas Stone's name to register the mention of the event.

"You think they're selling back to their own pool?" Colton presses his lips into a thin line. "If they're not transporting them out, they have to be keeping them nearby."

"Oh god," I whisper, placing a hand over my churning stomach. I hate the thought of being trapped with someone like Silas permanently and bile surges up my throat. This has gone on for too long and it has to stop. "We have to help them. We can't condemn them to that terrible nightmare."

"I agree," Rowan growls.

Levi, Colton, and Wren exchange a calculating look.

"Let's go." Wren levels Quinn with an assessing once over. "We'll need Jude on this to plan out a strategy."

Colton sends everything we've discovered to his cloud drive and shoots Quinn a crooked smile.

"Good work, little queen." She grants him a sardonic look. "Be good while I'm gone."

Her eyes narrow and she flips him off. He barks out a raspy laugh and logs out of his system, winking at her before he prepares to leave.

My mind spins on our way through the upscale apartment building. The others are lost to their own thoughts. An idea begins to form in my head. It's not what Levi would do—he's going to loathe it—but it's what I know I need to do.

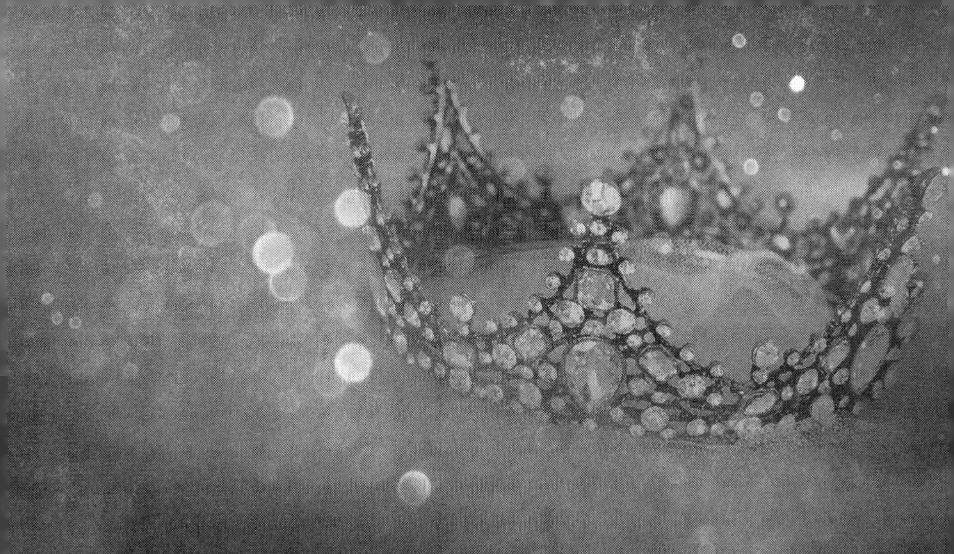

CHAPTER TWENTY-NINE
ISLA

I often wonder if anything could have been done to stop my father's sickening club if I had spoken up about what happened to me, if I wasn't too afraid he would make me go through it all over again. I might have buried the awful memories and refused to allow them to dictate how I lived my life for a long time, but in the back of my mind I knew others were facing the same nightmare I lived through. Countless others.

Silas has been behind this the whole time. I'm certain of it. Not only is he involved in the sickening men's club that awards girls' virginity to the highest bidder, he's involved in kidnapping them right off the street and selling them for the Kings Society's benefit. He's spent years feasting on the sight of me at every opportunity and my chest feels tight at the thought of him biding his time to snatch me, too.

A faint, pungent scent memory slams into me, making me choke [illegible] his cologne as if his sweaty body still pins me to a bed I don't want to be in.

My stomach sinks as we return to the Nest. Levi darts a concerned look at me and I offer a sad, trembling smile. I need to tell him the truth about my secret.

I hate that so many girls' lives have been ruined by something my father has a hand in. It can't go on.

This isn't just wrong, it's personal.

While I'm lost in my thoughts, the others catch Jude up on what we've discovered. Penn has disappeared, sometimes more elusive than the guys can be.

"So what do we plan to do about it?" Jude asks. "Find out how to locate the operation?"

"We think we know where they're going to be," Rowan says. "This fancy masquerade ball."

Jude groans. "They love to hide in plain sight."

"It's a power play," Wren mutters. "We've done the same with our fights and the gambling."

"We need juicy bait they can't resist," I blurt, lifting my chin. Every eye in the room pins me in place. I straighten my shoulders. Silas has been my nightmare for seven years. If I can do this, it will be like I'm fighting back against what I was powerless to stop before. "We already have that: me. Silas wants me."

"Fuck no," Levi barks savagely.

He crosses the room in two strides, taking hold of my shoulders. I give him a pleading look urging him to understand. Until I tell him the truth, he won't realize why this is important to me. Up to this point, I've only told him how horrible my father is, but he needs to hear the full story.

"We know they aren't going to stop. If we let them take me, we'll have our in. You can find out where they're keeping those girls."

"Or I could never see you again. I won't lose you. I can't," Levi growls.

My heart clenches and I grip his jacket. "Colton has the trackers, and—"

"Isla, this is insane," he says. "We've been trying to avoid you being taken."

"Oh, and you're all a bunch of logical, level-headed scholars?" I counter, lifting my brows. "I want to help save the girls they've stolen. And even though this idea scares me, I know you're going to get me out."

"Same," Rowan chimes in. "There's no way we can ignore this. We didn't stand for the drug ring. We have to do something about this."

Her conviction doesn't surprise me and I shoot an appreciative nod to my best friend. I knew she'd have my back for this idea.

I don't want anyone to go through what I've been through. Worse, because I at least got to go back to a pampered life—even if it was partly lived in fear if I didn't obey my parents' every wish—after that traumatic night my virginity was torn from me, but these girls are often never heard from again.

"There's no way around the fact Silas wants to add me to this menagerie, so the only option is to let me get kidnapped." When Levi opens his mouth, I cut him off, shaking him by my fierce grip on his jacket. "Think about it. They were so adamant I honor the invitation. Amidst all the excitement of the party, it would be easier to take me. If we know ahead of time, when, and where, you'll be able to follow and get us all out."

"What about the likelihood it's already too late for most of them?" Levi's brows flatten.

"I don't care." A fiery conviction threads through my words.

Levi blows out a breath. "I don't like it."

"You don't like a lot of things." I cup his face and kiss the tip of his nose.

"This is reckless," Wren says with a frown when I turn to face the others.

"It's brave," Rowan corrects. I smile at her. She hugs herself, her voice quavering. "And these girls have families wondering where they are. I know how gutting that is."

We're all quiet for a moment. Colton and Jude both study me.

"I think it's a good idea," Jude says. "Insane, but it will work."

"Trojan horse." Colton plays with the piercing in his tongue. "Yeah, I can get behind it. We'll do you up even better than the big guy when he was summoned to the Kings' creepy ass dungeon."

"You're not going alone, either." Rowan's eyes shine as she looks at Wren. "We don't do things alone."

He stills. "Rowan."

"Don't even try it." She gasps when he takes her by the arms and brings his face close to hers. She stubbornly juts her chin. "It's not like last time. We're going to plan and work together. I learned my lesson at the docks."

A growl works its way up Wren's throat. "No."

She smacks his muscular chest. "I'm not leaving my best friend to face this by herself." Her expression softens and she touches his jaw. "And you'll always come for me, right?"

"Fuck," he hisses. "Always."

He crushes his mouth to hers in a wild kiss. Levi's grip tightens on me, as if he wants to tuck my body into his where he can protect me from doing this.

"Let's vote on it," I suggest.

Levi's brittle laugh vibrates against my back. "Absolutely fucking not. That's my vote."

"It's the same for me." Wren hold's Rowan's gaze.

"Well, I see merit in the idea." Colton makes a list in one of the windows on his screens, his mind already working through what we'll need. "We'll make sure whatever trackers and comms we give them are undetectable. We'll know exactly how to find them."

"I agree." Jude holds up a hand when Wren flashes him a vicious look. "Don't give me that. You know this is a good play if you remove your emotions from it. I don't want them to get hurt, either, but I can separate that."

A chill runs down my spine at the detached way he presents his argument. Jude's always been as friendly and warm as Colton, but I can't forget that all four of them harbor darkness.

Wren clenches his jaw. "You're right."

"And with mine and Isla's votes, majority rules." Wren gives her a flat look. She smirks and pats his cheek. "Get over it, King Crow. I need you to get your head in the game to work out how to pull this off."

He sighs and pinches the bridge of his nose. "We need a plan in place before this weekend. This is going down at the masquerade ball."

Jude pulls a face. "Short timeline."

"I can work with that," Colton says. "I thrive under pressure. The chaos keeps me on my toes."

Levi snorts. "Can we access the party before Saturday night? Or do you have to tap into security remotely?"

"Let's plan for both," Colton decides after considering the question.

"I think this will work best if we remove me from the board." I slip out of Levi's grasp to stand by Colton's chair. He has one page open to elegant gowns and another with schematics for discreet camera buttons. "They'll grow frustrated and antsy if I seem like I'm hiding again after tonight with the cop. Then we'll create an opportunity where they can't resist making a move."

I picture the photos I saw of the elaborate gala event from last year while I was studying abroad. My mother was head of the planning committee and sponsored the party. Everything was over the top extravagant with an ancient Egyptian gods theme with no expense spared to create the most anticipated social event on the calendar.

"The planners try to outdo themselves every year," I continue. "With all the chaos going on, the Kings Society will believe they can get away with taking me from right under your noses."

Rowan purses her lips to the side in thought. "They'll probably be so focused on this show and getting Isla into their clutches that they won't worry about trackers. They'll think they got one over on you while you're there."

"You have a mind for strategy after all, Miss Vonn. Negotiations are another matter, but you do know how to use that head of yours," Wren praises.

I give a sarcastic bow. "Love it when men underestimate me, thank you."

He chuckles, then grows serious, his assertiveness rolling off him in waves. "And they already believe they've outwitted us for weeks, ever since we started poking around in their sandbox. I think it's why they showed their hand and summoned me to that meeting to reveal themselves." His mouth forms a ruthless curve. "Let them believe we're powerless against them. It will only be sweeter when we dismantle another of their operations."

Colton pulls up the invitation to this year's event on the screen. It announces the theme is Carnival of Decadence. Small gold script at the bottom touts *an unforgettable show to make all your dreams come true.*

"I'm thinking these dresses will work best with what I have in mind." Colton points to another browser window. "This fabric should mask the equipment. Plus, you both look great in these colors."

"Don't even think about picking out the undergarments," Rowan sasses. "Because I'll punch you myself."

Colton shoots her finger guns. "You know where to find me if you want an expert opinion."

Wren smacks the back of his head. "There's one other thing we should consider exploring for this to work." His jaw works and he sighs forcefully. "Pippa."

Jude's confident expression falls and he stiffly rises from his relaxed sprawl on the couch. "You want to trust her with this?"

"I never want to give her my trust again." Hatred drips from Wren's words. "But I think we'll need her on this."

Jude remains quiet for a long moment, rubbing his mouth.

"She did say she wanted to help." I bite my lip. "I believe her."

"She says a lot of things that sound believable," Jude mutters.

"Do it," Levi says. "If we're going through with this, I want every contingency plan in place to extract them unharmed."

A conflicted expression twists Jude's handsome features, but he nods. "I'll call her."

"Convince her," Wren instructs. "I don't want any goddamn mistakes."

"I'm always convincing," Jude says with a wide smile devoid of humor.

Rowan comes over to take my hand. We share a look that belies the nerves riding beneath our resolution.

"We're both a little crazy, aren't we?" I ask.

Rowan smirks and squeezes my hand. "I've learned to embrace it."

CHAPTER THIRTY
LEVI

A riot of emotions war within me. They haven't stopped since we learned about the kidnapping victims, only growing more tumultuous with Isla's brash idea to play bait. Everything in me revolts against the thought of letting her do it.

I finally understand how Wren felt the night Rowan ran off to set the docks on fire. The unyielding set of his jaw gives away how much he hates this plan, focusing intently on Rowan like he wants to soak up every minute he has to watch over her before she's out of his reach. Both of our girls are fearsome and strong, fitting in so well with the brotherhood we forged a long time ago. I never thought another girl could match us after Pippa turned her back on us, but Rowan and Isla have stolen their way into our circle. I thought I could fight it. The stubborn resistance was futile. This agonizing ache in my heart is all the proof I need to know how deep my feelings for Isla run.

More than bone deep, Isla Vonn has imprinted herself on my soul.

I can no longer survive without her. I need her to continue breathing, a broken monster who learned to open his heart once again.

If anything happens to her…

A gut-wrenching image of her name carved on a headstone next to my parents' and my uncle's sinister grin runs through my head.

My mind shuts down in violent rejection. *No.* I won't lose her like I lost the only other woman who mattered to me.

While the others plan, I thread my fingers with hers. She turns those big blue eyes to me. "Come with me."

"Shouldn't we help with the logistics?" She gestures to our friends gathered around Colton's desk. "It was my idea. I feel like I should contribute."

"We will. I just need to give you something." I meant to give it to her sooner after I'd selected the right one and checked its balance until I was satisfied it was her perfect match.

"Okay."

I take Isla to my room. After all the time we've spent at the Nest, it's her first time inside. Before she insisted on leaving, I wound up in her bed most nights. I'm no longer holding anything back from her—she already owns every piece of me.

She peers around with interest, making a beeline for the variety of knives lined up on a bench by the wall.

"Quite the collection," she comments.

I hum in response, sitting on the edge of the bed near the nightstand where I've tucked the gift away. My gaze tracks her as she pokes around the room, snooping in my closet. She makes an inquisitive noise at whatever she discovers in there before she emerges and stops in front of me. I hold her hips, marveling at the way every part of her fits in my palms like she was designed specifically for me by fate.

"I'm doing a shit job at being your bodyguard if I let you do this," I rasp.

The corner of her mouth lifts with sincere affection. She cups my face. "You might have it in your head that you're this messed up monster, Levi Astor." When I recoil, she forces me to continue looking at her, bringing her face close to mine. "But I see the parts of you that you hide beneath all that. You're mine. You have never failed to keep me safe."

I close my eyes and she presses her lips to mine. The kiss is sweet and soft.

"Nothing on this earth will keep me from fighting for you." I murmur my words against her lips. "I thought I would taint you with my darkness, but now I want to bask in your light every day, Isla."

She gives me a beaming smile, her eyes glistening.

The truth resonates through me and I draw in an uneven breath. This is who we are. I shield her and she rules my demons, unafraid of the darkest parts of me. Even when I pushed her away and buried my attraction to her, she fought back, fought her way past my gnarled thorns to wrap me in her light like an embrace.

Love. That's that all-consuming, terrifying thing I feel for her. My obsession was only the beginning. It's grown into this inescapable need for my heart to always be linked with hers.

My chest tightens along with my grip on her hips. I know it won't keep her secure in my arms—the arms of an unhinged beast she has run to time and again—but it doesn't stop me from trying.

A soft laugh escapes her and she brushes my stubbled cheek with her thumbs. "Can you believe I thought you hated me? Underneath it all, you're such a romantic soul, grumpy. I love that about you."

Something inside me swells. My fingers dig into her and I give her a tiny shake. "I never hated you. I was an idiot, too driven by my wariness of trusting others. I just used it as an excuse to keep myself from wanting you. It went against every safeguard I have, but I could never fucking hate you." A rough noise lodges in my throat. "You slipped right through my defenses and shattered them with your smile, no matter how hard I fought it. What I hate is how crazy I feel when you're not in my sight—not the kind of crazy I'm used to, a new, maddening fixation that tells me to keep you close instead of ever shutting you out again."

Isla's lips part in surprise at the torrent of emotional words spilling from me. Her shining eyes brim and a tear spills down her cheek. I catch it with my thumb and bring it to my lips.

"Don't cry, baby. You've shown me how strong you are with your optimistic outlook. I admire that about you, that you don't let anything break you."

She releases another laugh, this one wet with emotion. "They're happy tears because I'm in love with you, too, grumpy."

I freeze. "I didn't..."

"Not in those specific words, but you meant the same thing," she sasses.

It didn't occur to me that's what I was doing by confessing everything I was holding back from her. My lips twitch. It's been a long time since I told someone I loved them. So long, I think I've forgotten how to form the words. She understands me, though.

Tugging her down, she plants her knees on either side of me and settles on my lap. Her arms loop around my neck and I run my hands up and down her back.

"You know, before you lured me into the rain, I really hated it."

She waits patiently, not pressing me.

"I don't speak of this often," I start, voice already becoming brittle. "There's a reason I am the way I am."

"I'm listening. You can tell me."

A sigh forces its way past my lips. I hate thinking of this, but she needs to understand. "When I was seven, my mother and I were kidnapped."

Isla makes a strangled noise and collides with me as she hugs me, making me grunt at the force of her body hitting mine. I turn my nose into her throat, seeking out the calming balm her touch brings me to get through this. For so long, I turned to destruction and violence to cope with this. Isla has shown me a different way to battle the things that haunt us.

"It was storming like crazy. I remember being excited to show her this drawing I did, so I was running through puddles. I used to dig up worms for her, so all I wanted was to get home and see if I would be allowed outside when the rain stopped. The rain was our thing."

Isla squeezes me, threading her fingers into my hair to hold me closer. My words grow rougher.

"She was picking me up from school, same as always. The driver knew about what would happen when the car was blockaded. We fishtailed, then they descended on the car. My mom held me so tight, but there was no stopping it. They took us."

A tremor moves between us. I can't tell if it's from her or me. My throat convulses as I swallow, steeling myself for the worst parts. I press my face against her skin, focusing on breathing in her sweet scent to keep myself from breaking down.

"I fought, kicked at them, bit them, screamed. It didn't matter. They were stronger. I didn't find out until I was older that we were kidnapped for ransom. No one was supposed to hurt us. But—" I break off, exhaling harshly. She murmurs it's okay repeatedly. "They ripped my mom from me. Her screams while they raped her are seared into my brain. My nightmares. There wasn't anything I could do to stop them. Much later, I found out my uncle was behind it. Greedy fucking bastard wanted my dad's shares of their company. I vowed to myself I would never feel that helpless ever again. It's why I've trained so hard to become this man."

"Levi," she chokes.

"I hated the rain after that. Hated it so fucking much, but you...you made me want to love it again like you love it. Like my mom loved it."

I brush her hair aside, encouraging her to show me her face. Pink splotches color her cheeks and her eyes are red. Tears stream down her face, leaving a warm damp spot on my neck where her face was buried.

"I haven't felt helpless in fifteen years until you decided to play bait."

She sniffles. "I'm sorry. I didn't know you had lived through such a terrible thing."

"I know."

"I have to do this, Levi. It's—I'm like you. More than you know. It's not just about the kidnapping attempt or my dad using me. I've got my own nightmare to conquer." It takes Isla a minute to control the anguish in her voice. I stroke her back soothingly, hating the pain in her voice. "When you asked why Silas wanted me, I already told you. But I lied to you about it when I did."

She gives me a remorseful look. I suspect I know where this is going, but I don't push her. I've been waiting for her to come to me, needing her to trust me enough to open up on her own after we started by me wrenching the secret from her.

"When I said it was my maid who was the victim of the men's club my father belongs to...it wasn't a maid. It was me." Isla's breath hitches. "Silas Stone is the man who paid for my virginity and raped me. That dinner my father took me to, I'm pretty sure it was full of Kings Society members. They all had the ring, and for the longest time I thought when I saw anyone wearing it that they were in on it."

My hold on her tightens, needing proof that she's here in my arms right now instead of in that bastard's. He'll never fucking have her. I thought I was prepared to hear her confirm this, but hearing the truth makes me murderous.

"The secret you told me that night was about you?"

She nods. "I'm sorry I didn't tell you the truth. I've never told anyone. Rowan doesn't even know. I didn't say anything after. I was too afraid when I woke up in my own bed like nothing happened. There was so much pain. The memories were all fuzzy because of the drugs, leaving me only with the mark on my leg and flashes of his body on top of me. For years, I let my parents manipulate me into whatever they wanted because I was terrified if I didn't, I'd have to go through it again."

Isla quiets and I cradle her face to bring her back to me instead of reliving the worst night of her life. Her lips twitch into a faint smile for me and it slices into my heart. How can she find the will to smile while recounting her rape?

Taking a breath, she continues, swiping at her tears. I help her catch them. "It wasn't until a year later I found out who Silas was. He was at Dad's campaign dinner and Dad introduced me to him." I go rigid, more than ready to kill Vonn for the ways he's mistreated his daughter. She grimaces. "As if we hadn't already met. Once I heard his voice...I knew. Ever since then, he's always found one way or another to find me at events. For seven years, I've had to exist around him like he didn't violate me. That's why I have to do this. For fourteen year old me. For every girl he and the Kings have done this to."

Her strength never fails to surprise me. We've both been through so much. Cupping her cheek, I rest my forehead against hers. "He will never touch you again." My brows pinch. "Fourteen? Was it right before I found you crying in the alcove?"

"Yes. The weekend before that day. I tried to ignore it at first, but nothing I did worked. I finally broke down. It wasn't long after that I found something to help."

"Dance."

Her eyes shimmer. "It showed me how to live without suffocating from the fear and pain that followed."

Knowing the truth behind those shattered tears that first sparked my interest in her, I add more names to the list of people I need to end. It takes everything to quell the rage consuming me. "Do you want them all to pay? I'll start with your father and slit his fucking throat, then hunt down Stone."

Isla hesitates, biting her lip. "You can't kill a senator. You'd go to jail. I need you, so that can't happen."

"Baby, I know how to make it look like an accident and never get caught." My jaw works. "I'll gut every piece of shit who has ever hurt you."

Her eyes widen. She doesn't shy away from my violent promise.

"My real name is Leviathan Astor." I watch her reaction closely. "I never liked it. That's why I go by Levi. But I do have one use for the name."

Isla is a clever little thing and works it out in seconds. She licks her lips, fearlessness lighting up her eyes. "Is it only bad people?"

"Everyone I've killed has deserved worse than death," I growl. "I'm not a serial killer, that's just the media's bullshit. But the reputation comes in handy when I'm about to end someone, like the men my uncle hired to kidnap me and my mom, or the guy who tried to take you."

She nods. "Okay."

Just like that she accepts another facet of the blackest shadows I exist in. If I had any doubt left that this beautiful girl was meant for me, they'd be obliterated.

Leaning over while supporting her, I dig through the drawer and take out the bundle I want to give her. "I got you this. I want you to swear to me you'll always have it on you and always be prepared to protect yourself."

She accepts it, brows shooting up when she unwraps the leather holster from the polishing cloth I had it in. Rolling her lips between her teeth, she unsheathes the blade and examines it. The knife is a perfect match for her grip. It's sleek, lightweight. Elegant. When I selected it, I was drawn to it in the same way Isla draws me in when she dances. I wanted to teach her to use it first, but she's always been a fast learner.

"You got me a knife." She slides her attention from the blade to me, her mouth curving in a slow smile. "You should say it with flowers."

I cock my head and give her a wry look. "Let me remind you that I think flowers are pointless."

She touches my shoulder where I have a tattoo for my mother. "Not all flowers."

I cover her hand with mine. "You're right. The ones inked on my skin are the only ones I have that won't die. This one's for her."

"Maybe I'll get a flower tattoo then. You can pick it out." She winks. "It'll be just like getting me a knife to protect myself with." Examining her knife, she scrunches her face. "I'll name it...Pointy."

A chuckle shakes my shoulders as she sets the knife aside with care and pushes my jacket off my shoulders to examine the tattoo. It intersects with the crow tattoo my brothers share with me. Her fingertips map the spread wings of the bird.

"That one's for the only other family I've known."

"Do they all have a meaning?" She sneaks her hands beneath my shirt and maps the body of the snake that coils around my side. It's her favorite. "Which one did you get first?"

"The crow perched on the skull. We all got it at the same time." I chase her hands before we wind up naked. "They don't all have a meaning, some are just because they look cool."

"Does it hurt?" She purses her lips in thought. "Where should I get the flower you pick out for me?"

"I'll be there to hold your hand and distract you from any pain," I promise. "Come on, I want to show you some techniques to use this and teach you how to attach the holster to your thigh."

Her eyes spark with interest. "Do I finally get to learn how to throw one?"

"Not this one. I'd rather you keep yourself armed." I give her a deep kiss before she gets off my lap. If I could, I'd keep her in this moment forever. We part and I grasp her jaw. "I hate this. But just know one thing. I won't rest until I get you right back where you belong—here in my arms."

She presses her lips to mine again with a fierce passion. I once assumed this girl was spoiled and naive, but she's not either of those things. She's strong in her own ways, a survivor just like me.

CHAPTER THIRTY-ONE

LEVI

After showing Isla how not to stab herself by accident with her new knife, me and the guys leave the girls behind for something we never thought would happen. Pippa's apartment building is downtown, on the opposite side of the city center from Wren's penthouse.

"Are we sure about this?" Colton muses on the elevator ride. "This bitch hasn't done us any favors since she showed her true colors. She put Levi behind bars a few weeks ago."

"We don't have to trust her," Wren says. "We just need to blackmail her if she doesn't agree. We'll make her one way or another. Warner might believe he's chosen the right side of this, but Pippa knows what we're capable of."

"She did try to help Isla," I say.

It's the only reason I willingly sat in the booth at the cafe she brought us to.

"Maybe what we've been saying has finally stuck in her pretty little head," Jude mutters.

Out of all of us, he's the most on edge. The four of us are facing a girl we used to trust with the same loyalty we have for each other, but for him it's even more. He's facing the girl who was his everything—friend, first love, his damn soulmate.

Colton knocks Jude's shoulder with a friendly bump of his fist. "If you snap and break her neck, I've got your alibi ready to go. I cooked it up years ago."

Jude snorts, shaking his head. "Never change, you little psycho."

Wren smooths his fingers over his styled blond hair and straightens his suit jacket before we stride from the elevator as a group, moving down the hall like the four horsemen of the apocalypse. We come to a stop in front of Pippa's apartment and he takes charge, rapping his knuckles impatiently on the door.

After a moment, her muffled voice sounds through the door. "Who is it?"

"Let us in," Wren demands.

It takes another stretch for the lock to click. She cracks the door. My gaze snaps down to the gun she points at the ground.

"Do you really feel like filing paperwork for shooting us, baby girl?" Jude croons sardonically.

Her mouth tightens. She forces out an exhale and moves back, her gaze guarded as we file into her apartment. It's smaller than I expected. Her parents live a comfortable life. Maybe this is all she can afford on a cop's salary. The narrow hallway leads to a cramped living space.

Open folders full of case files and reports cover the available surfaces of the room in a haphazard array. A half-eaten cup of instant noodles sits on the floor next to a pillow.

"Busy bee," Colt mutters.

Wren lifts a brow at the weapon in her hand. "Put that away. We don't have time for games."

"Neither do I." Pippa's lip curls and she surveys each of us with a shadow of the ire she's always held for us. She stops on Jude. "You got me to agree to meet. What is it?"

He smirks, shuffling some of the files aside before dropping to her lumpy couch without asking permission. "That's how you say hello?" He clicks his tongue. "You used to greet me with a sweet kiss, remember?"

She huffs and puts her gun away. "Can we not?"

"Preferably," Wren bites out. "We have a problem and you're going to assist us. If you don't, the night you're desperate to bury is going to resurface—and your involvement in it."

"Jesus," Pippa grumbles. "Sometimes I forget what a giant asshole you are. I didn't think it would be any of you using the number I gave you. It was meant for Isla."

Colton hasn't stopped moving since we entered the apartment. He keeps his movements subtle enough, playing it off like he's shifting his feet as he drifts around, poking through the files she's brought home from the station. He ends up in the kitchenette.

"No tequila? What gives?" he calls from the open freezer.

Pippa scowls. "I don't talk to tequila anymore." Her gaze cuts to Jude. "It leads to stupid decisions."

Jude chuckles, the smooth sound threatening. "The only stupid decision in your future is if you refuse to lend a hand."

"You haven't even said what criminal bullshit you need me to risk my career for," she snaps.

The four of us exchange glances. We're all wondering the same thing—if we can trust Pippa Bassett not to screw us over again. The last time we put our trust in her for a plan, she bailed and Jude wound up arrested.

The old scabbed over wound from five years ago still throbs painfully for all of us. She didn't only betray us, but she turned her back on her friends.

A heavy sigh leaves me. "You know the kidnapping threat against Isla?"

"Yeah. I haven't found any leads," Pippa says.

"It doesn't matter. We know who wants her." Fucking Kings Society bastards. Silas Stone. My uncle. Wren's father. Others just like them. I shied away from Colton's work on salvaging the file Rowan's brother sent at first, but now I wish we had it cracked to know exactly who's coming for my girl. "And it's connected to the girls going missing all over the city."

Pippa stiffens. "You know about that?"

"It's been suppressed, but when's that ever stopped me?" Colton asks through a mouthful of Pringles he stole from her kitchen. She frowns at him. "If we didn't have other shit on our plates—thanks for your contribution to that—I might have found it sooner." His gaze cuts to me. "I usually keep an eye out for this stuff."

"So do I." Pippa gestures to the files. "I wanted to take every case that's been reported, but the department has been rerouting them and passing them off to other precincts. I—" She hesitates, eyeing us warily. "I don't know if I can trust Warner and the others. It's always been...a challenge to prove I'm a good detective, but they've shut me out and shut me down since your uncle bailed you out."

"We aren't the ones lining Warner's pockets anymore." Wren crosses his arms, glaring out the window at the rain streaking the glass. "But we know who holds his leash now."

"Who?" Pippa demands sharply. "Accepting bribes is grounds for more than suspension. If you have legitimate proof, they can be brought up on charges and face jail time."

Wren shoots her a cruel smirk. "This is bigger than that. But I still don't trust you, so for now this is how we'll play this. We give the orders, and you do your part without complaint. Are we clear?"

"Hell no." Pippa matches his stance, crossing her arms. She's always been stubborn and unafraid of standing up to any one of us. It was one of the reasons she became our friend. "You've barely given me anything to go on. I don't blindly follow anyone anymore, not even you."

A muscle tics in his jaw. He's barely containing himself. He turns his back on her and Jude takes over for him.

"We're going to bait the kidnappers into taking the juicy score they want—plus a bonus, because Rowan won't let Isla play bait alone." Wren growls. Jude forges on, gesturing with his hands as he explains. "We know when and where this will go down, and we know the missing girls will be there."

"Where?" Pippa digs through the mess of files to locate a small notepad, perching on the arm of the couch. Flipping the notepad open, she grabs a pen and jots down notes. "Do you have visual confirmation? Any kind of proof I can use for probable cause? I can't get a search warrant on illegally obtained information, but maybe if you doctor it—"

"Don't get ahead of yourself yet." Jude ruffles his thick dark hair, the corner of his mouth tugging up. "This is the part where it gets tricky. It's all going down at the masquerade gala."

"The ball? Oh shit." Pippa scrubs her face. "I wasn't planning on going."

"Good, because we'll need you on the outside with a team of anyone you can trust standing by without Warner and anyone up his ass knowing about it." Jude's gaze pierces into her. His voice hardens. "I know trust is a tricky concept for you, but I do mean you have to know without a doubt anyone you select will have your back."

Pippa's throat convulses with a swallow. Her gaze cuts away.

"What we need is manpower to pull this off," he continues. "It will only be us inside tracking the girls. If you're really sorry about that night, you need to bend the rules like you used to."

All of us shift at the reminder. An uncomfortable expression crosses Pippa's face. She tugs on her curly ponytail and nods.

"Got it. It's a short timeline, but I know a few good guys that will want to help find these girls."

Wren heads for the door without a word. Colton and I exchange a look and follow him. Pippa gets up and snatches my arm. I narrow my eyes and look from her hand to her determined expression.

"What?" I grit out through clenched teeth.

"I swear I won't fail Isla and these other girls the way we failed Sienna," she whispers in a tight voice.

The reminder of that night five years ago stings, images of the burning tower flashing in my head. We were such amateurs then.

I jerk my arm out of her grasp. "You'd better not. Get ready for all hell to break loose, because there is shit brewing in the city none of us saw coming."

Jude hangs back while the rest of us leave her apartment. We wait in the car with Wren growing more agitated by the second until Jude saunters out of the building. He gets in the car, ignoring all of us.

Pippa's reminder of how wrong our first job went sits heavy on my shoulders. This won't be like that night. Isla's life depends on it.

CHAPTER THIRTY-TWO
ISLA

On the night of the masquerade ball, I put on my full armor. While Levi prepares himself with all the knives he manages to hide within his tuxedo, I paint my lips like I'm going into battle. Amongst the affluent elite in Thorne Point, every social event is a clash of wills and reputation.

My hair is styled to perfection, the glossy chestnut strands shining, and my makeup is on point with winged eyeliner sharp enough to kill any man who looks at me wrong—namely, my father.

Tonight is my middle finger to him for every time he's made me fear what would happen if I stepped out of line, for what he did to me by offering up my body for his own gains, and for believing I would simply allow him to continue using me as a pawn.

I'm ready to play my part to succeed against them and Silas. The nightmare he inflicted on me has done its best to fester in my mind and poison me with pain. It can't hurt me anymore, Silas and my parents hold no power over me. Not with my champion by my side.

The six of us ride outside of the city together. The estate where the ball is held sits on a three hundred acre property surrounded by a forest. My fingertips flutter over the exquisite beading on the draped neckline of my gown as our car passes through the intricate iron gate and follows the other cars down a hedge-lined drive.

Colton catches my fingers from the back row. "Don't mess with it, remember? I don't want you to dislodge the camera or change the angle." He flashes me his phone to show what the camera hidden in the beading sees. "You'll be golden, Isles."

"I'm ready," I say.

"Me too," Rowan says from her seat beside me. She glances at Wren and Levi in the front seats. "We've got this."

Wren's eyes find hers in the rearview mirror. "Don't take any unnecessary risks, Rowan. I mean it."

"I know." She pats her lap over the small gun strapped to her thigh. She flashed it to me earlier. The skirt of her emerald gown is slitted like mine. "Last resort only."

The bodice of my gown appears more restrictive than it is. Colton is good at picking out something that looks couture but is easy and lightweight for me to move in. The black chiffon has a slit all the way up to my hip. I touch the leather sheath strapped to my thigh where my knife is hidden.

I'm no expert at using it overnight, but Levi wasn't satisfied until I memorized the fatal places on a body to stab and how to avoid having my hold broken by someone slamming my wrist.

This plan is crazy. I know it, yet Rowan and I are doing this to make sure those girls aren't condemned to a life of horror for the sick pleasures of the wealthy who play with innocent lives for their own entertainment.

More than that, this is something I have to do for myself. It's personal. For too long I've had to live with what was done to me, pretending like nothing happened while the men responsible remained a presence in my life. I'm done with it. All of it. It's time to fight tooth and nail to make my life my own.

A valet hustles for our car when we reach the entrance. Levi helps me from the car, his grip tight on my hand. I'm dreading the inevitable moment we're separated tonight.

As the others exit the vehicle, he takes my chin between his thumb and finger, tipping my face up. The kiss he gives me burns through my anxiety. I breathe him in, committing everything about him to memory to give myself the fortitude to make it out of this in one piece.

"Stay alert," he says. "And don't you dare hesitate."

He pins me with molten fire blazing in his eyes. The breath that escapes me is uneven.

"I remember every minute of the lesson you gave me," I murmur.

My skin tingles with the filthy sense memories of Levi kneeling at my feet in his sharp tuxedo, gaze flicking up to me before he drew my leg over his shoulder to buckle the holster to my thigh. He unsheathed the sharp knife and played the same erotic game we've been playing since the first time he pinned me to the mat in his gym, making me recite everything he taught me about where to strike. For each correct answer, he gave me a reward. His fingers trailed over my scar like a promise, then he hooked his fingers in my panties, tugged the material aside, and devoured my pussy until I needed to push him away. Even then, he wrenched another orgasm from me before he was satisfied.

My cheeks flood with warmth when he slips a hand into the slit in my skirt, brushing the leather sheath. A primal noise rumbles in his throat as he takes my mouth in another searing kiss. My core throbs with the endless desire he stirs in me.

"We'll never make it inside the ball at this rate." My voice is light and breathless.

"I'd prefer that," Levi says.

"Let's join the others. Wren said we had to enter together."

Sighing, he places his hand at the small of my back and guides me over to our friends. Rowan's cheeks are pink and Wren's meticulously styled suit is rumpled like she clawed at him. They both nod at us. Colton and Jude put on their masks. All the guys have matching ones, a demonic looking leather design molded into angry expressions. Rowan and I chose to use makeup to create our masks.

"Everyone ready?" Wren prompts. His cunning blue eyes pass over each of us. He smooths out the wrinkles in his tuxedo, checking the communications tech Colton loaded us all with. "Let's go stir up some chaos."

"Let mayhem reign, right?" I smirk at the heated look Levi gives me for using his little saying I picked up.

"Whoa, careful now," Colton teases. "Those are baby-making eyes. Save it for later you guys."

Jude laughs, hooking an arm around Colton's shoulders. They lead our pack to the red carpet welcoming the guests for a night of decadent delights. Other guests pause for flashing cameras from the press allowed to camp out in the hope of scoring an exclusive. Jude leans closer after he and Colton have their photo taken.

"The show's going to get exciting. I'd stick around." He passes the photographer a hundred bucks with a deft twist of his wrist and offers a debonair grin. "It'll make your career."

With a wink he moves on from the gaping paparazzi. Once they catch sight of me, they kick back into gear, shouting mine and Levi's names when they realize we're there together. The flashes burn my eyes, but I'm used to it. I find a focus point and lock my smile into place. Levi's arm tightens around my waist.

"You've been out of the public eye. Is it because a romance has developed between you and the Astor Global Holdings heir?" The woman who asks sticks a microphone toward us.

Levi grunts in displeasure at the mention of his uncle's company. I place a hand on his chest to sooth him. After what he told me, I'm ready to seek out his uncle in the crowd tonight and threaten him with Pointy for what he's done to his family.

"Yes." The cameras don't miss a second of my response or the kiss Levi presses to my cheek.

Before I can say more, the camera flashes erupt in a flurry. We turn and my stomach drops. My parents have arrived. Great.

It's the first time I've seen them since the ridiculous lunch at the country club.

They pause when they see me, then the politician and his society wife take over, working the gauntlet of cameras. The others have made it through and wait for us at the end, all of them watching my parents approach with barely concealed ire and disgust.

Levi stills at my side. The casual move to tuck his hand in his pocket is designed to set others at ease when really he's an inch from drawing one of the many knives hidden on him. I roll my shoulders back, matching his deceptively guarded stance.

"Isla." Mom speaks first when they reach us. She hooks her arm with mine and we're forced to pose with my parents. She squeezes my arm. "It's good you decided to attend after all. I'm pleased."

The photographers shout for us to look their way and ask if my parents knew of my connection to Levi. Mom's smile is serene.

"A mother always knows these things," she answers.

Levi's muscles flex, prepared to strike. I angle myself so I'm between him and my parents. It's not for their protection against him, it's for me to stand up to them on my own. It feels amazing to look them each in the eye.

I know, my steely gaze says. They're pleased because they think I don't know why they wanted me here so badly, but I do. They should never have let their greed consume them to the point it burned away their morals.

Dad's lip curls and he prepares to move on, unwilling to acknowledge me further. He pulls Mom with him.

She halts. "Isla." Regret-tinged emotion rings in her voice, her gaze roaming over my face. Dad jerks on her arm hard, snapping her name. Mom's features settle behind a mask of indifference. "Enjoy the party."

It strikes me that she could feel bad for whatever they have planned, but still chose their selfishness over their own blood.

"Don't let them snuff out your light, princess," Levi mutters in my ear when my attention tracks them. He draws me away from the red carpet. "They don't hold any power over you unless you let them. Fuck them."

"Fuck them," I echo.

He's right. Tonight they think they've won. They believe they're one step closer to more of whatever they stand to gain by using me as a pawn. But I'm not a damn pawn. I'll prove that to them when we turn the tables.

Levi smirks. "Good girl."

Rowan snags my hand when we reach them. I give her a reassuring nod.

"Let's fuck their shit up," she murmurs ferociously.

Wren's mouth curves and a menacing gleam fills his eyes. "You're beautiful when you're bloodthirsty, little kitten."

Colton checks his phone while we make our way through the extravagant halls of the estate.

"What's that look on your face for?" Jude squints at him.

He smirks and tucks his phone against his chest. "Nothing. Just a snarky comment from my protege that really means good luck. I left her with a puzzle she can't crack."

"What have I told you about getting attached to your strays?" Wren rolls his eyes. "You let her stay in your apartment. Fox wound up living with your parents."

"Chill, it's under control. Nothing's accessible from that system unless I'm there to get past the security measures. Two-factor authentication, ID scanners, multi-level encryption—it's covered by the works, big guy."

Wren doesn't bother to respond when we make it to the large ballroom. Performers on stilts blow fire and dance through the guests with rich red ribbons. The guys all fall quiet, growing more vigilant of our surroundings.

"Pay attention to anyone who has a special interest in you," Wren orders. "We have an all-new perspective on what we've been up against, but until we know what's in the file Hannigan left Rowan, we can only operate on our speculation."

"Assume everyone is an enemy," Levi mutters at my side.

"And utilize dirty tactics," Jude adds. "Fake sick to get close, then pop them in the balls." At Rowan's pointed look, he tacks on, "Or the cunt. The point is, make them believe your act, then strike."

"You're both a little crazy, but that's what we love about you." Colton grins at me and Rowan. "We've got your back. There's nowhere they can take you I won't be able to track. You're our eyes and ears, then once you use the safeword—"

"Colt," Wren cuts in when the performers pass by us.

My heart climbs into my throat. I hope they're paid dancers and not the stolen people we're here to break free.

Colton waits until we're alone by the curtained alcove we've drifted to. They don't seem to be part of the estate's architecture, perhaps an addition to add to the festival theme. If we were here under different circumstances, I might lure Levi into one for some fun.

"Anyway, once you throw up the Bat-Signal, we'll be ready," Colton finishes.

My heart swells at their version of a pep talk. I feel like I've found my place amongst them. Somewhere I can truly belong.

"Let's pair off and work the crowd," Jude suggests. "We'll pick up more if we blend in like we're not here prepared to wage war. Find out what you can and we'll meet back up before they gather the guests for the big finale."

He waggles his brows, crosses one ankle over the other, and pulls off a smooth whirl before heading for the bar. Colton follows after him, leaving the couples behind. Wren and Rowan face me and Levi.

I nudge Levi and smile. "Put your happy face on, grumpy."

He grunts. Neither of the guys have been able to wipe the wrath completely from their expressions since I first volunteered myself as bait.

"I'll be happy when this insane nightmare is over," he says.

"Come on," Rowan says. "You can't tell me you're not looking forward to the maiming you'll get to do tonight. Maybe spill some blood. Consider it payback for messing with your fight ring."

Levi rumbles a vicious agreement that makes Wren grin deviously. He offers an arm for Rowan to take. "I welcome it. Our hands will get dirty tonight."

Rowan's eyes glint with a matching savageness. Together they give off a powerful vibe. Nothing will tear them down.

Watching them slide into the fray, I get the sense things will go our way. I've seen first hand that it isn't just empty rumors spread about the Crowned

Crows—they are capable and willing to do anything to achieve their ends.

"Shall we?" I turn to Levi. "There's dancing. I bet we can pick up a lot of insight from people watching while we dance. Everyone watches the dance floor, but no one thinks the dancers are watching them back."

"I'd rather be dancing with you alone in your studio on campus." He sighs, tucking me into his side. "Let's go see what we can find out about the snakes surrounding us."

The party is in full swing and the first woman we talk to is well on her way past tipsy, enjoying a bottle of Dom Pérignon one of the masked entertainers serves her. It becomes clear immediately that he isn't only serving her champagne.

My eyes remain wide as Levi tugs me away. "Did you see?" I whisper. "They were—"

"I saw. It's not just them." Not much escapes him. He grimaces, averting his eyes from another bold display amongst four people sharing performers. "Jesus, I hate this fucking party. I didn't want to ever know what Castillo's balls look like."

"Why don't they use the alcoves? I thought that's what they were for."

"It's the masquerade. The point of this ball is hedonistic at minimum. It's why no press is allowed past the velvet ropes."

"It wasn't like this the last time I attended." Last year I was traveling for a semester abroad, but the year before I was invited to the party for the first time. "I don't think I ever made it to the main room, though. I was too busy dancing."

"I believe that." Levi's lips twitch. "You do have a habit of only seeing the best in people, so it's not like you were looking for all the flaws of everyone surrounding us."

"I only seek out the good in people because I want to believe there aren't only the evils I've known in this world."

"Miss Isla Vonn."

Our conversation is interrupted by a voice that makes my blood run cold. Silas Stone. His voice is my strongest memory of the awful night he paid my father to rape me at their men's club.

My lips purse and I prepare to face him. He's always looking his fill any time we're in the same room, but tonight I'm here to put a stop to it.

He's not a tall man, standing several inches shorter than Levi's towering height, but he's clearly a man of vanity. Botox, a nose job since I last saw him, cheek implants, and platinum hair assault me. On a despicable man like him, each attribute makes him uglier.

"Don't you look ravishing tonight." There's an uncomfortable intensity threaded through Silas' words.

Levi stills like a predator hunting a kill. His grip tightens on me. Brushing my hand over his, I step away, picturing myself as irresistible bait for the real monster amongst us.

Even knowing Levi is with me, a tremor runs through me. I swallow past the lump that lodges in my throat, reminding myself why I'm doing all of this. Facing the man who wants to put me in a cage to clear my father's debts is a small price to pay to help the girls escape and stand up for myself.

"Mr. Stone." I'm proud of myself for masking the riot of emotions clashing inside me when he steps closer as if he has a right to enter my personal space, drowning me in his too-sharp cologne. Levi remains deadly still behind me and I channel the wildness that first drew me to him to calm my racing heart. "Are you enjoying the party?"

"Much more so now," he says.

My skin crawls and the scar he left on my thigh tingles. I glance at his hand and gulp. He's wearing a gilded signet ring just like Levi's uncle wears. That confirms him as a Kings Society member, as we guessed between Dad's meeting with Levi's uncle talking about using me for his games, his shady delivery company to steal people, and my parents' insistence that I be at this ball tonight.

The only thing we're unsure of is whether he's a pawn to another player, or if he's pulling the strings.

He smirks, making no move to hide the ring. This is a man who believes he's untouchable. My teeth clench and I work to keep my breathing steady.

Silas Stone is my nightmare in the flash. My rapist who got away with murder and probably bought the chance to rape countless other girls with his money. Hatred isn't an emotion I reach for often, but for him I make an exception.

I want to take him down and stop him with every fiber of my being.

"I'm so glad I found you." Silas peers over the rim of his champagne flute.

Levi makes a low, feral noise behind me. Silas doesn't pick up on it, perhaps unthreatened because he doesn't know what Levi is capable of.

I don't feel the smile I hold in place. When Silas steps closer, making to kiss me on the cheek, I stiffen. My hand darts into my skirt, reaching for my knife on instinct.

Silas halts as Levi's arm bands around my waist possessively. He doesn't pull me against him like an object for them to fight over, allowing me to stand my ground with his support. I angle my head to peer at him over my shoulder. A gasp catches in my throat at the vicious glare he gives Silas that warns him to back the fuck off.

Silas' gaze bounces between us. He hums, mouth curving. "Enjoy the show tonight."

I don't breathe freely until Silas ambles away.

"Are you okay?" Levi demands, squeezing my back against his firm chest.

"Yes. I hate being near him." I cover his arm with mine, clutching it.

Levi's grip tightens until it's just shy of painful. "We're calling this off. Guys—"

"No!" My nails dig into his arm, urging him to calm down. "No, it's fine. Nothing's changed. We knew he wanted me. I can do this."

"Are you sure?"

Rowan's voice sounds in my ear through the new comm Colton designed to be undetectable, fitted within our ears and blending in seamlessly with the fake prop skin he grafted over the small earpiece with a technique he learned from a YouTube tutorial. The open line between us all picks up ambient conversation as well as our own voices. It's great for keeping in touch no matter what goes down, but it does make it difficult to pay attention to multiple conversations.

"Absolutely." My response is adamant. "More than ever, I want to stop what they're doing."

"Listen to that fire," Colton praises. "She could give Rowan a run for her money."

My gaze cuts across the room to him and Jude. They're with a pair of older women who are talking animatedly. Jude appears attentive with an air of smugness—something I've learned to keep an eye out for. They're interrogating those women with their silver tongues.

I return my attention to Levi, spinning in his embrace. I plant my hands on his chest and meet his gaze, willing him to understand why this is so important to me. "Let me fight my nightmare."

His jaw clenches. "You need to promise me you'll be extra careful."

"Me and Pointy have everything on lock." I grin at him. "I trust you to get me out."

"Princess," he rasps, framing my waist with his big hands. "My heart beats for you. If something happens to you, I stop living."

"Don't say that. Even if this went completely wrong, I'd want you to live an even better life for me." I cup his face. "You're being dramatic again. I see why Colton teases you about being the edgy one."

He huffs out a dry laugh. "Stab first, ask questions later."

My smile stretches. "I learned from the best."

Our moment comes to an abrupt end when the entertainers pull out matching brass horns and draw everyone's attention to the center of the room. A man in a top hat dressed as a ringmaster much like Jude's Halloween costume twirls a gold cane.

"Ladies and gentlemen, the time has come."

Excited murmurs move through the room while the ringmaster speaks. His mask is blood red and has a mouth stretched in a wide, manic grin. The guests move to form a circle around him, lured in as if the promise of the next immoral entertainment has them in a trance. Levi keeps a tight hold on my hand so we aren't separated.

"You may have heard whispers of tonight's show, but I promise you it's beyond your wildest imagination," the ringmaster says. "Are you ready to play a game of chance? The fates will lead you there."

At his gesture, three young women dressed as the Greek fates emerge, dancing with a string they share between them. While they put on a performance to dazzle the crowd, the ringmaster continues.

"They will guide you to your destinies. Some of you will lay your eyes on your greatest desires, while the rest—" He pauses for dramatic effect while the fates pull the string taut. The room descends into darkness, making several people cry out in shocked delight. A spotlight illuminates the ringmaster and the fates as they cut the thread. "—will meet your end."

Whispers pass through the room and he laughs. I glance at Levi in the muted light. His jaw is clenched.

"This is it." His deep voice is so quiet I have to strain to hear him.

"Look alive," Wren says over the comms.

"My dear friends," the ringmaster says. "Fret not. You're in good hands with our lovely fates. But whether or not you see the show... Well, you'll just have to make it through the night to see."

With another wicked laugh, he thrusts his cane into the air. Music from a hidden band fills the ballroom and the guests are divided into three groups. Wren and Rowan make their way to us. I take her hand so we aren't separated.

"The last time I went to this party, something like this happened. We were led through the gardens for a hunt in the night. There were far more people than the amount I saw at the museum meeting, though," Wren says.

"Odds on it being the same?" Rowan muses.

"Slim to none," Levi says.

Our group begins to move, the guests behind us crushing into us in their eagerness. Levi elbows someone that squawks at him until he turns around. Once they spot him, they clear their throat and comment that he should be more careful.

"Rowan—" The urgency in Wren's tone makes my chest ache.

"I know, King Crow." Her tone is sardonic, but she squeezes my hand. Her breath catches and she looks at him. "I love you, too."

"You're acting like this is a death march," I murmur. "Tits up everyone."

Colton echoes my sentiment with a whistle we all can hear in our ears. Despite my positive bolstering, my stomach clenches when we reach walls that slide open like hidden passages where the draped alcoves were. Each of my senses tingle with an instinctual knowledge that develops for survivors who have been through hell.

This is it.

Whatever's happening, it's going to be now.

CHAPTER THIRTY-THREE
ISLA

THE passage we're taken into by our fate leads down a set of stone steps to a chilly underground with arched ceilings that remind me of the churches I toured in Europe during my semester abroad. I shiver, appreciating Levi's warmth when he runs his palms down my arms.

At the end of the hall, we're faced with a wall of wooden panels that spin as people are ushered through. It's a maze, one from an old carnival, I think. The painted panels depict the ringmaster and his three fates in a garden of delights.

"Enter to find out your destiny," the girl dressed as a fate announces.

The four of us look at each other while other guests approach eagerly. The energy in the hall brims with excited anticipation. It causes the anxiety bubbling in my stomach to ratchet up another level.

"Take my hand and don't let go," Levi says.

"We'll go through together." Wren grasps Rowan's hand while Levi captures mine.

Once we join hands, we pick a panel. Before we enter the maze, we're stopped by the fate. She tilts her head and gives us a serene smile.

"One at a time. Your threads of fate may not entwine," she says.

"I think you'll find that we can do whatever the fuck we wa—"

I interrupt Wren's arrogant response and release Levi's hand. "Let's follow the rules of the game."

Rowan follows my lead, dropping her boyfriend's hand. She squeezes mine before letting go. We're here to play bait, and we can't succeed in our goal here without allowing the opportunity to be captured. As scary as it is to be separated, I'm ready to fight back in my own way. Turning to Levi, I find his jaw clenched so hard a muscle tics in his cheek. He glares at the girl.

"I'll see you on the other side of this maze," I say.

His gaze pierces through me, right into my heart. With one last fierce kiss before we're separated, he goes first through the spinning wooden panels. Wren cradles Rowan's face, pressing his forehead to hers before he follows.

Satisfied, the fate moves off to direct other guests. I square my shoulders and look at my best friend.

"Ready?"

"Hell yeah," she responds like we're going into battle.

Holding my breath, I push into the first painted panel. The maze is dimly lit with barely enough light to find the next panel. Laughter and shouts from the other guests echo off the stone walls for the first few minutes, then they fade off like half of the guests are directed in one direction.

"Still with me?" Rowan asks from somewhere behind me.

"Yeah," I call.

The whir of the wooden panels is still audible, so we're heading in the same direction as some of the filtered guests. My stomach clenches with the question of whether it's a good VIP or a bad VIP.

The answer doesn't matter when strong hands grab my arms from behind. An instinctive shriek works its way up my throat, but a cold hand covers my mouth before it tears from my lungs.

A pained grunt from the shadows makes me guess Rowan has surprise company, too.

Half of what Levi taught me flies out of my head, but I do my best. One thing that I do recall is to throw off the balance of an attacker by breaking their stance. His deep voice fills my thoughts, urging me to figure a way out. It's a lot easier to maneuver barefoot, but I'm glad Levi didn't go easy on me when it came to learning about breaking out of holds.

Struggling against the arm pinning my hands to my chest to distract my attacker, I slide my leg out of the slit in my skirt and stomp down hard, dragging the steel heel of my pumps down the inside of the man's calf. When he barks out in startled pain, I twist and duck down.

It fails when he grabs me by the hair. Shit, I didn't account for that, too proud for pulling off the move to get free.

"Fucking bitch," he spits.

In the dark I don't see him swing, but the crack of his backhand snaps my head to the side. His knuckles are hard, but it's the ring on one of his fingers that makes bile rise in my throat. I cry out as pain rockets through my face. My lip stings when I prod it with my tongue and I wince, tasting blood.

"Your cunt must be dusted in gold," he mutters as he drags me through the shadows.

I remind myself this is part of the plan when he does something that engages on the stone wall at the edge of the maze. The stone grinds as another secret passageway reveals itself.

He shoves me inside a wide tunnel. Rowan is brought in behind us by another man who grabbed her before the door slides shut, trapping us inside with the men who plucked us from the festivities. At least she'll be with me. It's comforting to know I don't have to face this alone.

The whirring of the panel maze is no longer audible, only the echo of our footsteps on concrete. My lip throbs and my face feels like it's on fire from being backhanded so hard, but I keep my eyes peeled, soaking in any information to relay to the guys once we're not being watched closely. I hope the struggle didn't dislodge the camera Colton hid in my dress.

"Is it going to matter we have an extra?" The guy restraining Rowan gives her a jerk. She glares at him.

"Take both—those were the boss' orders," says the man digging his fingers into my arms.

The plan is working. They couldn't resist the opportunity to take us.

I allow the thought to solidify my bravery, fortifying myself to face whatever awaits us at the end of the tunnel.

After several feet, we reach an intersection. The men veer down the hall to the right. The walls are lined with candelabras that have been replaced with electrical imitations, casting an eerie orange glow on the stone. We're taken through a set of double doors into another dim area. There are more mean-looking men in the room and barely dressed girls who seem despondent and out of it. My heart climbs into my throat at the sight of them. We were right.

Seeing them sends me back to the way I felt when I woke in my bed, realizing what the foggy images clouding my pounding head meant. The extent of the ways I had been violated.

I want to break away from my captor, rush over to them, and hug them all. No one hugged me after, certainly not my parents, not in the ways that matter.

The ringmaster's voice calls out from behind red velvet curtains. We're backstage in a theater. I tense when I realize what's going on.

The man holding me shoves me into the chest of a taller, bulkier guy before grabbing a girl by her elbow and wrenching her to her feet. She stumbles, her limbs not cooperating. My gaze darts around to the others. Glassy red eyes, drooping eyelids, and a sluggishness when they move—they're drugged with some kind of sedative. Probably to keep them docile.

My stomach turns. The guy who slapped me takes the girl through the curtain to a stage. I catch a glimpse of the crowd before the heavy velvet falls into place.

"Lovely, isn't she?" The ringmaster's chuckle disgusts me. "We'll start the bidding at four thousand."

"Don't fight." The girl closest to me lifts her head, her eyes less bloodshot than the others, but no less resigned. Her gaze shifts from me to Rowan and she shakes her head. Rowan forces out a breath, stopping her struggle to escape the punishing grip of the man holding her. "Fighting makes it worse for all of us. The last girl who fought was killed."

Terrified chills break out across my body. That level of intolerance has made these girls believe there's no hope for escape. To them, Rowan and I are just two more victims. I search for anything to say to these girls to reignite their will to fight, but I can't risk the guards growing suspicious.

"Do I hear eight? Eight thousand? Eight! How about ten?" The ringmaster works the stage, his voice trailing back and forth along the curtain. "Fifteen! Yes, fifteen thousand from the exquisite lady with the diamonds in the back. You'll collect your purchase at the end of the night."

My eyes sting with the prick of tears. *Stay strong. Focus on why you're here.*

A sharp tug makes my balance on my heels teeter. "Move." The order is barked in my ear. I flinch away and grimace when the bigger man I've been handed off to digs his fingers into my arms with bruising force. "You don't want to test me, little girl."

Reluctantly, I follow his orders, craning my neck to check that Rowan is also being brought with me. Her features are set in a deadly scowl, but she gives her hulking escort no trouble. The men take us back into the tunnel and we continue down a long stretch. It's too far to be part of the estate house we started in.

"Where are you taking us?" I yelp as I'm jerked like a rag doll. "Jesus, it was only a question."

"No questions," my surly captor grits out. "Shut up and do as you're told, or I'll give you a matching bruise on the other side of your face."

"Please don't do this," I whisper, aiming to appeal to his humanity. "It's wrong."

His laugh booms off the stone walls of the tunnel. "You think I give a shit? You're cattle, that's all. A piece of pussy that makes my wallet fat."

The other man laughs. I recoil, my heart pounding. These men don't care who we are or where we come from. Horror seeps into my bones and I remain quiet the rest of the way through the long tunnel, playing along as a helpless victim while counting seconds in my head to gauge how far we need to tell the guys to walk.

When the tunnel ends, we're taken up a set of steps into a different building. It's large, though not as sprawling as the estate the party's at. It may be on the estate's property as an old hunting lodge if the rustic touches are anything to go by. The tunnel connecting the two must be how they keep this operation hidden.

We're brought through the first room and deposited in a locked parlor. As soon as we're released, Rowan's hand finds mine.

"Behave," Rowan's guard grunts. "That goes for all of you. Or you'll face consequences."

His grin is sickening. The men leave us, locking the door behind them. They didn't pat us down for any concealed weapons, leaving both of us still armed with the ones we have hidden beneath our dresses. Turning around, I find we're not alone. There are double the amount of girls in the emptied out parlor with us.

"Hey, are you okay?" Rowan pulls me with her as she gets closer to the nearest girl curled up on the floor. "Did they do something to you? It's going to be okay, I'm Ro—"

"No names." We look at the girl leaning against the wall with her arms crossed. Her blonde hair hangs in her face. "We don't tell each other our names. It doesn't matter anyway. Once they come for you, half the time you don't come back."

"Jesus," I whisper hoarsely.

"Look, it's going to be fine. I know this has sucked for you all—we can't imagine what you've been through." Rowan slips a hand inside her skirt and takes out her gun. The girl against the wall pushes off it with wide eyes, a spark of fire returning to her expression. "We're getting out of this."

"How?" another girl asks. "You're not cops. You look like you came from a party."

"We did," I say. "We're the bait, but really we're more like a Trojan horse."

I pivot so Colton's camera can pick up every detail of the room. The girls exchange wary looks, as if the thought of letting hope back into their hearts is too good to be true. My chest tightens and I smile with a calm I'm struggling to maintain. For them, I'll be strong.

"We're not alone." I point to the hidden camera and tap my ear. "The cavalry's coming to make this nightmare end."

One of the girls breaks into tears. "Please."

My throat constricts and I nod, turning to Rowan. "How much time do you think we have before they move us or come for me? I doubt they're just going to leave us here."

"Not long." She swallows. "You guys better be listening."

She launches into a description of the number of guards we've encountered and a description of the room we're currently in. None of them respond. For a moment, panic surges through me, then I hear another voice filtering over the comms.

Rowan squeezes my hand. "It's okay, it probably means they're not in a position to speak freely. They can't give themselves away, either."

"Right." I force out a breath. "Sorry, this is my first heist or whatever."

She gives me a crooked smile. "I don't think this classifies as a heist, but I'm with you every step of the way."

Muffled voices sound outside the locked door, drawing our attention. "No, the ones in the gowns. The redhead and the brunette. Boss wants them both brought to his office."

Rowan curses under her breath and hands off her gun to the blonde. She seems the one with her will to fight mostly intact.

"Shoot anyone who's a dickhole grunt of this shitshow. They won't expect you to be armed, so you'll get the jump on them. If four guys our age in tuxes show up—they're the cavalry," Rowan says.

Moments after, the doors burst open and the two burly men who brought us over from the theater stalk toward us. They take us from the parlor and move through the house. As we cross through a dining room with the lights off, a strong sense of déjà vu hits me. I'm taken back seven years to a room much like this one to a night I want to erase from my memory.

Smug looks. Dad's deep laughter. The thick scent of cigar smoke. Dizziness. Hands, hands on me, touching where they shouldn't be. Rough. Pain, pain, pain tearing me in half. I don't want this. Get off, please! Stop! Get—

"What is this place?" I choke out as the familiarity claws at my mind.

The guard chuckles cruelly. "Welcome to the Castle."

"Looks like a shithole to me," Rowan says. "Ouch!"

"Shut it," her captor snarls. "If you're mouthy, I'll give you something to gag you. You're just extra. Your friend's off limits, but we're allowed a free pass to use you, girl."

Rowan keeps her mouth shut, eyes blazing. I fight against the need to break free of the harsh grip pushing me forward to comfort her against the awful things said to her.

We reach a grand staircase that makes me halt. My guard grunts and drags me up them.

I know where we are. My mind short-circuits, trapping me in more memories of that night. Of course. Of course we're here. I remember my father telling me Silas owned this hunting lodge and invited his esteemed friends to enjoy themselves.

Oh god.

Silas Stone is the boss these men refer to.

"Isla," Rowan hisses urgently.

I snap out of the horrified, catatonic daze and find we've been brought to a nicer room. Her guard finishes tightening her handcuffs, securing her to an old radiator at the side of the room. He eyes her and she glares, flipping him off.

Only one of my hands has been cuffed to the chair I'm seated in next to a large desk. My throat burns when I swallow to ease the tightness. I can't take the knife out to use as my focus object, so I trace the armrest, my chin trembling as I get my breathing under control.

We're left alone without a word by the grunts working for Silas. Rowan sends a worried look my way.

"Are you okay? You went so pale and limp I thought you passed out," she says.

"Yes. No." My throat works on another swallow. "Just fighting off a panic attack."

My limbs feel weak, all of the adrenaline that built up since we were taken from the maze bleeding out of me, leaving me lethargic.

"It'll be okay." Rowan glances at the door. "Guys, the girls are on the first floor. We've been taken upstairs."

"I'm sorry," I croak.

"Don't say that. Dude, this is crazy shit we're doing. I'm freaking out, too."

My lips twitch, but the smile doesn't quite form. It's not that.

It's that I'm in a place I never wanted to see ever again, my own personal hell on earth.

CHAPTER THIRTY-FOUR

LEVI

The maze pisses me off. I shove through each painted panel, eager to get the goddamn thing over with. My ears remain strained so I'm aware of our surroundings, but I'm guessing they set the maze up down here because sound travels off the stone walls, making it hard to place.

It's impossible to tell which way we're going until the maze spits us out. Wren straightens the lapels of his suit with an irritated rumble while we wait for the girls. Other guests spill out of the maze. One of them is a pinch-faced older woman who scoffs at us and mutters that we haven't earned the right. I stiffen when a handful of people pass and they still haven't come through.

Wren sets his jaw and shoots me a hard look. "Let's find out what this show is all about. Be ready. I think that pissed off woman was the mouthy one from the night the Kings summoned me to the museum."

I cast one last look at the maze, willing Isla and Rowan to emerge.

The panels on the left spin, dumping Colton and Jude out one after the other. Colt glares at the panel, flipping it off. Jude spots us and the four of us converge together, falling into step with the other guests without needing to communicate with each other beyond pointed glances.

"The girls?" Jude murmurs.

I shake my head, blowing out an agitated breath. Wren cracks his neck from side to side, as affected as I am wondering where they've been taken without being able to do anything about it yet.

We move through a hall lined with electric powered candelabras, following the crowd. It's a much smaller percentage of guests than the party started with. Most have been filtered out in a different direction.

"What do the others do while we see the real show?" The question comes from a pair of middle-aged women ahead of us. With their elaborate feathered masks, it's difficult to recognize either of them.

"A Cirque du Soleil type of show," the other woman answers. "They'll be none the wiser to what we're doing here."

Two shows. One for Kings Society members, I'm guessing, and one for those unaware of the secret society amongst them.

Colton peers up from the phone he snuck into the party, mouth in a flat line. He tilts the screen so I can see the tracking program, then swipes to the camera feed. "Not far. Still on site."

"Seems like they're only on the other side of this wall." Wren pauses, placing a hand to the stone with a frown.

"Another secret passage?" Jude speculates. "It would make sense."

Wren nods. "It must connect to the section the maze was set up in. The girls went in, but never came out because someone grabbed them inside it."

My hands form fists. I want to punch my way through the weathered stone to get to them.

"You'll find the more interesting aspect of this evening up ahead, boys.

Welcome to the real show."

Wren goes rigid at the sound of his father's voice echoing in the narrow hall behind us. The four of us turn as one and find him smirking proudly at our presence.

Fuck.

They wanted us here. We were specifically guided here to see what awaits us. Footsteps sound behind him and my uncle joins Thorne. The urge to let my monster loose and end him here and now is so strong I don't realize I've taken a menacing step in my uncle's direction before my brothers hold me back.

Baron chuckles. "Come on, son. Let us show you what it truly means to be a King in Thorne Point."

"This is another tradition?" Wren presses.

His father nods. "Typically you wouldn't be allowed access until you were officially through your trials. Since you bear such strong names, we pulled some strings to allow you behind the curtain for a taste."

He speaks as if he already knows the rest of us are aware, despite Wren being the only one called to meet them.

"What are you talking about?" I demand.

"Come on, my boy." Baron flashes his ring on his pudgy finger. "I know you've taken an interest in your future at last."

My muscles strain with the effort to stay in place and keep my face neutral.

"All of us?" Wren's sharp question is met with a chuckle.

"You'll all make strong legacies, even start new ones." Baron gestures to Colton and Jude. "Come. It'll begin soon. We'll discuss the rest later."

"Maybe you'll see something you'd like. You won't know unless you go into the theater," Thorne says.

Wren's sharp features remain etched in stone, giving nothing away.

With a slight twitch of his fingers, we follow his lead, joining the last two men on this earth I want to be near.

The theater has a high, intricately arched ceiling despite being on a lower level of the estate. Tall, heavy velvet curtains block the stage from view. Half of the small crowd gathered discard their masks. There's no point in hiding their identities amongst the other snakes.

Jude nudges me, discreetly gesturing to a back corner. Sergeant Warner stands away from the others with an uncomfortable expression. Colton makes an inquisitive noise and captures a sneaky photo to text to Pippa. Once the ringmaster from upstairs slips through the curtain, he keeps snapping.

While the ringmaster flits around the stage dramatically, I scan the room, picking out other familiar faces. Isla's parents are near the far side. Mrs. Vonn looks dazed, even in the ambient lighting. They're no better than my uncle for their part in this.

The one face I search for is absent—Silas motherfucking Stone.

It's no coincidence that he isn't present after Isla disappears. Coincidences don't exist in this city.

It puts me even more on edge. I want to hunt him down and rip him away from Isla. My mind floods with everything he could be doing to her. His hands on her, marking her again like that goddamn scar, violating her.

"Shall we bring out our first act?" The ringmaster winks at the tittering crowd.

The curtain parts and a half-naked girl the same age as us is brought—dragged—on stage. All four of us tense.

"Shit," Colton bites out.

"Lovely, isn't she?" The ringmaster's chuckle grates on my nerves. "We'll start the bidding at four thousand."

Hands shoot up right away and people call out their bids. The girl racks up a bill of fifteen thousand in a couple of minutes. Her head lolls, unaware of what's happening. She's drugged.

Isla told me she was drugged the night she was raped. What if they drug the girls to keep them from fighting? My nails dig half moons into my palms.

The only thing keeping me from launching into action is the ringmaster's announcement that any *purchases* will be prepared for collection at the end of the night. That means we have time. Isla has time.

It keeps me rooted in place. Barely.

I slide into the habits that keep my brothers safe by remaining alert, assessing the surroundings.

Other than the two rotating escorts bringing stolen victims to the stage, there's one other man positioned in a back corner standing guard. Each of them have a gun holstered to their hips.

Three armed guards and about forty insane assholes bidding on stolen girls to get through. Our odds could be better.

It doesn't matter. Nothing will hold us back. These people are all assholes, but me and my brothers? We're a little fucking psycho.

As Rowan's hurried voice filters over the comms to let us know they've found the girls, I get ready.

Wren signals Colton with a sharp nod. He rakes his teeth over his lower lip before he and Jude drift around the room every few minutes. They make a believable show like they're getting a better look at the stage. Jude strikes up a conversation with someone, pretending they know each other.

While he has the guy distracted, he slips a small tube in his pocket while patting his opposite shoulder. They work their way all around the room dropping the presents Colton concocted.

The small tubes are essentially homemade fireworks with a self-lighting fuse Colt rigged to an app on his phone. Once he triggers them, they'll go off once enough heat builds up to react with the gunpowder. He made enough to start a small fire to stir up pandemonium and cause a distraction.

He saunters over to me after planting the last one near the guard in the corner. "I've always wanted to make these. Can't wait to see how they work."

"They'd better work," Wren mutters dangerously.

Colton holds up his hands. "Don't you trust me, big guy? I've got it covered."

Jude stands with a woman not much older than us. He has her blushing and smiling while he offers up his signature charming grin. He throws suspicion off of himself by bidding for the current girl on stage. Whatever he does to manipulate his mark, she bids right after, doubling the offer.

Isla's voice pierces through the barrage of shit on the comms. I fight to keep my face blank while her broken voice tells someone, "It's wrong."

"Wren," I grit out. "Now."

"Now," he agrees. "No mercy."

Hearing Isla on the verge of breaking after she's held out for so long has me ready to decimate this place with my bare hands.

Colton emits a low, devious chuckle. "Boom."

A few seconds later, a scream tears through the room along with the sharp *pop pop pop* of gunpowder igniting. Bright sparks fly through the air and the crowd rushes back, only to crash into others backing away from two more fireworks erupting on the opposite side of the room.

"Fire!"

"Ow, fuck!" The man Jude spoke to earlier frantically jerks out of his smoking coat.

More panicked yells fill the room. Half of them charge for the narrow hall we entered through while others run for a door near the stage.

"Go," Wren commands.

The guard in the corner bursts forward. He's fast, I'll give him that. His attention is on the stage, on protecting their product. I come at him from behind and slam my foot into the back of his knee. He goes down hard, hand shooting for his gun. I grab his arm and wrench it behind his back, making quick work of slitting his throat.

When I climb to my feet, intent on charging for the stage, my eyes lock with my uncle's.

Someday this will be you, old man.

I don't have time for him. My grudge can wait. Isla can't.

She needs me, and I will always be what she needs.

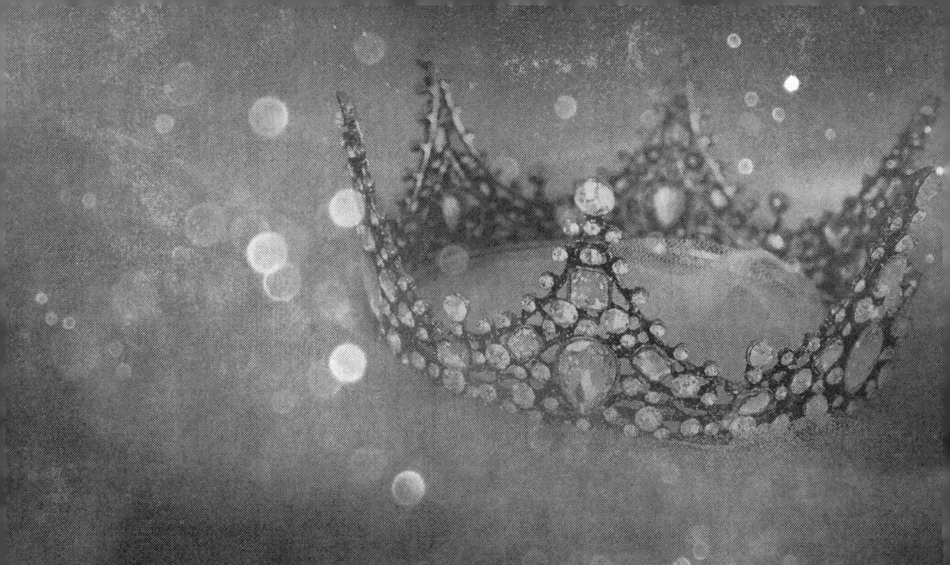

CHAPTER THIRTY-FIVE
ISLA

After recognizing the Castle for the same place where Silas Stone paid my father for my virginity, I need to fight harder than ever to center myself. Shutting out the negative emotions clanging through me seems impossible because I'm *in* my nightmare.

I never thought I'd have to face this place again.

My chest aches. More than anything, I want Levi, but he isn't here to protect me against this harrowing situation. I have to be my own champion to get through this.

It's why I chose to play bait. Not only to stop this, but because I'm done pretending nothing happened. This is as much for me as it is for the girls downstairs—for my fourteen year old self, for everyone who has been a victim. The thought fortifies me, gives me the strength to focus.

Working my thumb along the polished groves carved into the chair's armrest, I speak quickly, unsure how long we have until Silas Stone walks through the door. "I know where we are. I've...been here before." Rowan's brow furrows. "Seven years ago, my dad brought me to a dinner with his society friends. I was excited for it—except it wasn't just to show me off to his friends. My food at dinner was laced with drugs to keep me out of it and—"

"No." Rowan's voice shakes.

"Yes." I sigh, tipping my head back against the chair, my chest burning. "It wasn't a maid I knew, it was me. Other than Levi, you're the only other person I've told about this. Bestie perks."

"Isla." Her anguished voice breaks. "Oh my god, you were only fourteen. He let someone rape you. What kind of father—"

"A terrible one driven by his own greed." I shift the left with the small ring-shaped scar. It's the opposite leg my knife is strapped to. "I don't remember a lot of it. I only have hazy memories because of what they dosed me with. For a year I didn't know his face, only knew it could be anyone my parents knew. But then..." My throat closes. "He came to a campaign dinner and as soon as I heard his voice I knew."

Every time I've faced him at a society function I've weathered his smug smile.

A tear slips down Rowan's cheek. I give her a trembling smile.

"I'm sorry you went through that," she says. "I...I never would have guessed. You're so upbeat and carefree."

"I promised myself I would never let it define my life. It's work, but I never allowed it to break me." More than anything, I hated feeling like a pawn who couldn't stand on my own. My gaze drifts to the door. "And I'll be damned if I start now. It's what Silas wants and I'll never let him have that."

"The guy who's running this?"

I nod. "He made a comment earlier when he found me. He thinks he's won because we fell into his trap to get me."

"Well, fuck that. You know what he didn't learn about you?" She yanks on her handcuffs, the metal clanging against the radiator. "You're a fighter. And fighters don't ever give up."

"No we don't. We fucking survive."

Determination gleams in Rowan's eyes. "Please tell me you're armed, because otherwise the best weapon I have are these murder heels Colt picked out."

An amused huff leaves me and I examine the heels I'm wearing. "I hope it broke that dick's skin when I rammed the steel heel down his leg. My lip really hurts."

"Your jaw is all red. It'll bruise."

"We'll worry about it later. I have the knife Levi gave me. I'll use Pointy if Stone gets too close."

Rowan's brows jump up. "Pointy?"

I sit up straighter, feeling my strength return. Fighting on my own is one thing—something I've only truly begun to do against my parents more recently—but I'm stronger because I have Rowan, Levi, and the guys at my side. Thank god she's with me. Knowing I'm not facing Silas alone, and that Levi will come for me, are the only two things helping me hold it together.

"I named my knife. Names have power."

"Yeah, but Pointy?" Rowan grins. "Never change, babe."

The door opens, reminding us of our situation. Silas Stone strides in exuding power and confidence, a pleased smirk twisting his fox-like features. My muscles seize, my grip on the armrests of the chair tightening until it hurts. He glances at Rowan dismissively before folding his arms behind his back and strolling over to stand before me.

"Are you comfortable, Isla?" The pleased look in his penetrating amber eyes makes me grit my teeth as he peruses every inch of me, not bothering to hide it when he leans forward to admire my cleavage.

"Well, I am handcuffed to a chair." Pride burns in my chest when I manage to keep my voice even despite the apprehension and hatred choking me. This is it. This is the moment I face him. "So, no. Not really. There's also the shiner one of your men left on me."

This pleases him, too. His lips quirk and he reaches out to grasp my chin, angling my head to examine the split in my lip. My skin crawls and my stomach roils at his touch. I jerk my head away and he clicks his tongue.

"I couldn't risk you escaping. I told them to be gentle so they didn't mar your lovely beauty, but to do whatever was necessary to take you," he says.

"As if you had any right to kidnap me," I say incredulously. "You can't do this. People know we were at the party. They'll know we've gone missing."

"My dear pet, you think I can't make you both disappear? You have no idea the power I have at my fingertips. Besides..." He grabs my leg, clamping down on my scar. It sends a wave of revulsion careening through me, his cologne making me gag on the overpowering pungent stench. "It's not like I haven't already branded you as mine, just as we do to all the girls. It's not perfect, I imagine, since you wouldn't hold still, even doped up. No matter, I'll just have to give you another mark."

The words make my memory sharpen with his account of the events and it slices me in two with a deep, piercing sting. All these years, I've only remembered a hand forcing my leg apart. Locking my jaw to hold back a scream, I reject the truth that my scar is really a brand.

"It's wrong," I say through my teeth.

Silas laughs. "You know, it worked out that you escaped the first time I tried to bring you back to me. It gave credibility to what a precocious young woman you've become." He waves a hand, smirking. "Flighty. Known to disappear without a word for weeks on end. Storming out of the country club. Your parents will simply explain this as you running off to elope and no one will ever bother to look for you."

"Yes they will."

My parents aren't my family. But I found one that does care about me: my friends. They're what a family is supposed to be. They'll go to the ends of the earth for me, just as I would for them.

He gives me an indulgent smile with his too-white teeth. He bears all the marks of a man who loves his appearance. I strain against the cuff binding my wrist. For once, Levi's stab first, ask questions later policy sounds like a great plan. I'm not a violent person unless it comes to protecting the people I care about. This isn't only about the other girls, it's also about me fighting for myself against this despicable man.

"Why am I here? Why me?"

I can guess a thousand different answers, each of them repulsive, but I want to keep him talking. If his attention is on me, he'll leave Rowan alone and it will buy us time for the guys to track where we are.

Silas chuckles, the sound pompous and grating. I dig my nails into my palms. "I did attempt to convince your parents to arrange a marriage. I've been relentless since our first night." He pauses to rake his amber eyes over me, undressing me for his own delight. "They thought they could find a more lucrative match for you, but then your father ran up his debts. This is the more enjoyable option. Instead of divorcing my wife or dealing with you trying to run from me, you clear a debt. Rather than put you up for auction, though, I'll keep you for myself. I already have your virginity, and now I'll have you as my plaything."

Controlling my breathing becomes challenging as he spews his insane plans for me. Tears blur my vision.

The light I fill myself with flickers, its bright glow dwindling as it becomes more of a conscious effort to maintain a hopeful outlook in this dire situation. Am I strong enough to survive this?

I don't know anymore. My throat hurts when I swallow, my stomach convulsing with nausea.

"You even came with a pretty playmate for us to enjoy." Silas looks at Rowan, smirking at her glare. "She'll need some discipline. A few rounds with my men until she's obedient, I think. Then we'll bring her to our bed."

"No!" My chest heaves and I surge to my feet, almost toppling when I forget my arm is chained to the heavy chair.

Silas catches me, shushing me as he soothes a hand down my back. My vision doubles at the repulsive contact. I squirm with a strangled noise.

Everything in me calls me to plant my hands on his chest and *shove* this sickening asshole away from me. I want to reach for the knife, but not yet. It's not going to do me any good to show our hand before I can get out of the cuffs and get Rowan free. Grinding my teeth, I breathe through the disgusting feeling of his touch on my skin.

"Hush, my pet. No need to fret." Silas grasps my jaw in a controlling way. I gulp. It doesn't feel anything like it does when Levi's hands are on me. Silas' touch brings me nothing but revulsion.

"I'm the only one allowed to touch you. The Castle's knights won't know the heaven of your cunt or your sweet cries."

Mustering my strength, I meet Silas' eyes. It's strange the way my hazy memories collide with the reality of this monstrous man. In my drug-soaked recollection of the night he raped me, I pictured him so large and terrifying, unable to fight him off. He's not so large now, standing shorter than every Crow, almost even with my height in heels.

"Let her go," I spit. "You have me. That's what you've wanted. Just let her and the others go."

Rowan isn't on board with the idea, clanging her cuffs against the radiator with a hissed curse. "Robin," she mumbles just loud enough for me to catch. "Robin, Robin, Robin."

It's our code word.

Silas thankfully doesn't notice, too absorbed in his infatuation with me. "I'm afraid not, my dear. Even my wife doesn't have such pull. These are the way things are. *Carpe regnum.*" His mouth twitches into a sly smile. "Ah, but you won't know what that is now that you're mine."

Little does he fucking know, I understand exactly what seize the kingdom and the signet ring he's wearing mean to him. He buried it so deep in my skin its mark is permanently embedded in my thigh.

"I will never be yo—"

Silas clamps a hand over my mouth. "Shut the fuck up, pet. I don't want to have to punish you on your first night here."

Something fierce rises up in me, born of the pain, fear, and torment I weathered after he buried his ugliness deep within me by raping me. I bite his hand hard, grinding my teeth until the coppery tang of blood fills my mouth. Then I go for the knife, driven by an instinctive, overpowering need to face my nightmare and overcome it. I understand why Levi chooses knives over guns—the weapon makes everything more personal and visceral. As I grip it the way he showed me, fire sings in my veins with the knowledge of the pain I'm about to inflict on him.

The scream that tears from me is primal as I drive the sharp tip into Silas' body, catching low on his side close to his hip. My aim is off, but the pained sound he makes is satisfying a wild side of me.

"Augh!" Silas roars.

He shoves me until I lose my balance, crashing into the chair I'm chained to, then wrenches his hand away. I spit a mouthful of his blood out, splattering his crisp white shirt with it. Ripping the knife from his body, he tosses it aside, and it tumbles beneath the desk out of reach. Blood seeps into his shirt from the torn gash I wounded him with.

"Jesus fucking Christ." Glaring from his bloody hand, to the knife wound, to the mess I've made on his tuxedo, he snarls and rounds the desk. "You'll pay for that, you little bitch."

Panting, I slide my gaze to Rowan. Her eyes glitter with pride. I hate the vile taste in my mouth, but now I've marked him the way he believes he ruined me for anyone else.

Silas mutters to himself, blotting his wounded palm with a handkerchief and jerky movements, then plucking at his shirt and hissing as his skin pulls around the gash. He pauses to take his phone from his pocket, answering with a bark. "What?" He scowls. "What kind of disturbance? How did a fire—*what*?"

Hanging up, Silas rushes out of the room without a backwards glance. I sag against the chair, a strangled cry working its way up my throat. I'm powerless to stop it, the noise instinctive. The cry of a survivor facing down her nightmare in technicolor.

I fucking did it. Another shaky noise escapes me.

"You okay?" Rowan asks.

"I don't know what that was. It just came out of me." I swallow, tipping my head up to meet her worried gaze. "I'm sorry I freaked you out. I just thought if I kept his attention on me it would buy us time."

Rowan rests her head on the radiator. "Dude. I thought you were going all sacrificial on me. I wasn't here for it."

"Promise it won't happen again." I lick my lips, my focus blurring. "Levi?"

My voice trembles.

"I'm coming for you, princess," he says in my ear. He sounds murderous. "Swear it."

I close my eyes as wave after wave of relief crashes over me. "This is not how I wanted our first time with handcuffs to play out."

His grunt of surprise filters through the hidden device in my ear. "Only you would joke about that."

"Make sure the girls get out first," I insist.

He doesn't respond. Knowing he's coming for me gives me renewed courage. I swipe away my tears and use the flexibility and strength I've built from dance to arch out of my heavy antique chair, sinking to the floor in a twisted position to accommodate my cuffed wrist, then sweeping my leg to retrieve the knife. It takes two tries to bring Pointy close enough to reach. Success rockets through me once I close my fingers around it.

Hah! Take that, Mom. Dance skills have plenty of uses.

I spare a moment to survey Silas' blood left on the blade. Releasing a fierce little growl, I swipe the blood off on my dress like I've seen Levi do before I get up. Silas could return any minute. I turn my attention to the handcuffs, an idea forming in my head.

"Ready to stab that guy again, then cut off his dick with his blood coating the blade?" Rowan prompts.

"I was thinking more like how badass it would be if I could pick the lock on my cuffs," I say. "Don't fail me now, Pointy."

This isn't over yet. I have to keep fighting. *Fighters don't give up—we fucking survive.*

CHAPTER THIRTY-SIX

LEVI

Our plan is working, but it doesn't quell the murderous rage coursing through my veins.

Silas Stone will pay for every hurt he inflicted on my girl.

Once the four of us charged onto the stage amidst the chaos we sparked, Colton knocked the ringmaster off the edge. Someone kicked his head in their rush to escape the fireworks going off all over, knocking him out. One of the guards parted the curtain and Wren and I took him down together.

The other one isn't backstage when we barrel through the heavy curtains, ditching our masks, but one of the girls has been left behind. Jude checks her pulse and peels back her eyelids.

"Fuck. I think she overdosed on what they gave her." He digs in his pocket for his phone and tucks it between his shoulder and ear. "Pip. I need a paramedic. Yes where all the people are running from." He checks if the girl is breathing. "Don't worry about what we did, just send help, or this girl is going to die."

He allows his phone to clatter to the floor, gesturing for us to go.

"Don't get caught on the wrong side of things," Wren warns.

"Please, I can talk my way out of anything," Jude says. "Go. I'll catch up."

Colton takes out a small tablet that folds from his inside jacket pocket and plugs in a small device. "Thermal imaging will tell us if anyone's coming."

"Rowan didn't clock that many guards," Wren says as we move into a tunnel connected to the theater from backstage. "If they've been operating this long enough and haven't run into problems, they might not feel they need that much manpower."

"That's good for us," Colton says. "I like it when they're so cocky it makes them sloppy."

"Only because you're lazy and don't like to give it your all," I mutter as I put my back to the wall for cover while I check around the corner. "I keep telling you to put the effort in. It won't feel like such a chore."

"I'll stick to the tech. That speaks to me." Colton dodges the swat Wren aims at him. He waves his phone. "I'm the eyes, you're both the fists. One ahead, coming this way fast."

Heavy, purposeful footsteps fill the tunnel. Definitely a guard. I pull a sleek dagger I prefer for throwing from my ankle while Wren readies his gun. It's too risky to fire in an enclosed tunnel, but knives are perfect. We nod to each other and get into position for an ambush against the approaching guard.

Using the sound of footsteps, I judge when to throw my knife. Steadying my breathing, I feel the kinetic energy in my fingertips balancing the blade, the focus I've honed. I'll use every skill to get my girl and my friend to safety.

Now.

When I move, Wren moves in sync with me. We've trained together, fought side by side for long enough to know how we both work. He provides cover while I arc the knife without hesitation. In my eyes, all of these fuckers deserve death—not only for taking Isla and Rowan, but for all the girls they've kidnapped. I'm stronger now, no longer unable to fight back like I couldn't when me and my mom were taken for ransom. Gritting my teeth, a menacing growl tears from me as my knife sinks into the guard's shoulder.

Shit. It should have hit in the neck. There's no way he heard us, so he reacted that quickly to a threat. Flashing a look at Wren, we move as one to rush the guard before his gun is unholstered.

The man's eyes widen, then narrow. He throws an arm up to block. He's fast, but we're faster. Wren comes at him from the front, punching him with a vicious left hook while I slip around behind him, using the wall of the tunnel to propel me, increasing my force when I bring my elbow down on the junction of his neck and shoulder to inflict the most damage on the first blow.

Between the two of us, he goes down, staggering and groaning. Wren huffs, holding up a torn lapel hanging by a thread on his tux.

"This is Armani," he says coldly before kicking the man in the gut. "Unbelievable."

"Really?" I snap. "Let's move."

"Hang on." Colton produces a handful of plastic zip ties. Crouching beside the knocked out guard, he maneuvers his hands behind him and secures his wrists with the ties, chuckling to himself. "If we had more time I'd pull his pants down and stick his thumb up his ass, but c'est la vie."

"You're vicious," Wren says.

"Hey!"

Our attention snaps up to find two more men running at us. Colton ducks for cover when one fires on us while Wren and I scatter to make ourselves harder targets to hit.

"It would be great if you threw one of your death blades right about now," Wren grits out through clenched teeth, squeezing the trigger on his gun to return fire.

"Too busy dodging bullets."

Narrowing my eyes, I assess the men's stances when they halt several feet away to continue shooting at us. The one on the left favors his right leg like he has an old injury. Tapping my leg to signal Wren, we keep moving until we're close enough to engage. I grimace through the burning discomfort as a bullet grazes my arm.

Wren takes the one with the bum leg and I rush the other one, crashing into him to break his stance. He doesn't budge, using my force against me to whip me around. Goddamn it. These men are all trained. Ex-military working as private security, probably.

Adapting, I go for a different tactic I like to use in the ring to get inside his guard. I lure him into taking a swing at me and duck under his arm to jab his side and sweep out his leg at the same time. He doesn't fully go down, correcting from a stumble. He grabs me and crushes my head into the rough stone wall.

I choke back a grunt of pain as the pocked stone cuts my skin, focusing on getting a firm grasp on my switchblade. He pins me to the wall, wrenching my arm at the wrong angle. It's seconds from dislocating from my shoulder and it sends fiery agony through my muscles.

A shot rings out and the pressure disappears as the man slumps away. Panting, I shake out my arm and push away from the wall. Blood oozes from the hole in his skull, pooling on the ground. Jude lifts a brow from the intersection on the tunnel leading back to the theater with his gun lowered while Wren buries his gun in his guard's gut and fires twice to put him down.

My head swims, a dull ache forming in my temple. Blood seeps from the gash above my eye and I swipe at it in frustration, then check the superficial graze from the bullet. I've been through far worse.

"Good thing I was catching up." Jude reaches us, nudging the dead body with his foot.

"Ex-military." At my bitten off explanation, Jude whistles, studying the guards we've downed.

No more mistakes.

The look they exchange with me tells me they're on the same page. No goddamn mercy.

"Levi?" Isla's trembling voice kills me.

"I'm coming for you, princess. Swear it."

She makes a joke about handcuffs and insists we help the girls first, despite everything driving me to get to her.

We take the tunnel to a set of stairs at the end. They lead into another house. We stay alert for more guards. The muted cracks of gunfire make us freeze.

"This way," Colt directs. "Picking up lots of heat signatures. It has to be the girls."

We move swiftly until we find the right room. A guard sprawls across the thick carpet runner decorating the hall. He clutches his stomach, his face pale and clammy with sweat.

"Oof, that smarts," Colton says.

Wren opens the door and immediately ducks back when a bullet skews wide, taking a piece of wood off the door with it.

"Jesus Christ," he barks. "We're not your captors."

"Are they in tuxes?" The anxious feminine voice is muted through the door.

"Let's try this again. Ladies, we're here to help," Jude says in a calm tone. "I'm going to open the door. There aren't any other guards out here other than the one you shot."

He goes slowly, hands up to show he isn't a threat. The room is barren inside except for the women huddled together behind the one holding Rowan's gun.

"What did I arm you with a gun for, kitten?" Wren mutters to himself. "Nobleness is reckless."

"You're the guys?" The woman holding the gun furrows her brow and flicks her gaze between each of us. "We didn't think they were serious."

"As a heart attack." Colton lifts his hands in surrender. "Sorry, I can never resist that one. Yes, our girls were serious."

"Get them out." I tap Wren's shoulder. "We'll go for Isla and Rowan."

Colton checks his phone. "They're upstairs, right on top of us. Not many more heat signatures, so I think that's all the guards."

"They took them to his office," the blonde with the fighting spirit says with a grimace. "The ones who go up there... It's not good."

My nostrils flare and I'm overcome with the urge to stab something. Preferably the man responsible for this. Multiple times until I'm satisfied he's nothing more than a bad memory.

Frenzied footsteps echo through the house, lighter than the boots the guards wear. I clench my jaw and angle to face them as they approach. At my gesture, the guys go into the room, leaving me alone in the hall standing over the dying guard.

Silas Stone rounds the corner, his face red with rage. Once he spots me, he snarls, charging me.

His men might be well-trained, but this man is the type of coward who believes he's untouchable. It takes nothing to close-line him and put him on his back. He makes a satisfying strangled noise when I catch him in the throat with my arm and his head cracks against the exposed wood floor at the side of the carpet runner.

"Hello, fuckface. Welcome to your demise."

A quick survey of the bloody gash peeking through his torn shirt and the bite marks that broke the skin on his hand makes my lips twitch with pride. *Good girl, Isla.*

"You think you can come in here and take what's mine from me? I will—argh!" Silas' hands come up to his throat after I sucker punch him. It's unfortunate it didn't collapse his windpipe. He gasps, fighting to drag in air. "You—you—"

"You shouldn't have fucked with the Crows." Reaching for another knife tucked at the small of my back, I whip it out and stab Stone through the underside of his jaw into his tongue muscle. "Now shut the fuck up."

I've effectively pinned his mouth shut in a gruesome, painful way.

He makes a garbled shriek of agony, legs kicking beneath me. He scrabbles uselessly at my arm, blood from his hand smearing on me. Everything he's done to hurt Isla runs through my head. With a merciless growl, I twist the knife, enjoying every second of his agony. His eyes roll back in his head, momentarily passing out from my brutal treatment.

Silas Stone deserves this and so much more.

"Wren," I call.

My best friend appears in the doorway, glaring at the man who has our girls squirreled away in this house. His lip curls back and he ruthlessly grabs a fistful of Stone's hair, yanking him up. I help, grabbing Stone's jacket to lift him.

We bring him into the room and Wren holds him up, keeping his arms pinned behind his back. We're both taller than him, stronger because we don't have private security to stand behind.

"If you don't want to see him die, look away and cover your ears." The warning is the only one I offer to the girls before I slap Stone hard enough to startle him awake. My grin is savage, almost animalistic. I grab the pommel of the knife jammed into the underside of his jaw and jiggle it, enjoying his panicked groan. "Any last words? An apology to these girls whose lives you tried to ruin?"

As I use my most barbaric tactics to interrogate him before I end him, the memories of my own kidnapping overlay with Isla's description of what happened to her at this man and her parents' hands. It ignites my need for destruction, for retribution, for all-out mayhem.

Only a few of the girls watch, most turned away with their hands pressed to their ears. Jude and Colton observe hungrily, along with the fierce blonde who shot the guard.

Stone jerks, attempting escape. Wren's grip digs into his arms, twisting them into a more uncomfortable position that puts strain on the shoulders.

"You thought you could take my girlfriend?" Wren's voice is deadly. "Or his? That we wouldn't fucking come for you? I don't give a fuck who the Kings Society members are, or that they're related to us—we stand on our own legacy."

Stone makes a garbled noise, unable to open his jaw without excruciating pain from the knife.

I step into him, watching him with a predator's focus. Grabbing his hair, I yank his head back. "Everyone fears the Leviathan in Thorne Point, Stone. You should've, too."

His eyes bug out in shock. It's possible the Kings didn't know who I really am, or that the bodies I've left behind crossed us. If that's the case, it will stay that way.

The news and the Kings' police lapdogs thought it was a serial killer responsible, when in reality it's me taking out those who wrong the Crowned Crows and have signed their death wishes in their own blood.

Silas Stone isn't making it out of this alive to tell another soul. He's paying for his sins.

"You've taken something I love." I force him to look down. I don't bother unbuttoning his pants, using my serrated-edge dagger to tear a hole in the front of them. He struggles, causing more blood to ooze from the gash on his hip. "Yes, you know what's coming. You take from us, we take something you love from you. The more you struggle the more it will hurt, but there's no escape for you."

He goes from angry to blubbering in seconds like the pathetic worm he is. I flash him a disgusted look before grabbing his dick and making the first slice, tearing through his flesh with the most damaging blade I brought with me.

Stone wails, the choked noises trapped and unable to alert anyone to come help him. My grip on his dick is punishing as I make another cut. Blood gushes over my fist.

"For a man like you, I'd usually take my time and rip you apart piece by shitty piece," I say. "But the thing is, I need to go save my girl, and you're keeping me from her."

The soul-deep need to get to Isla is more powerful than any instinct I've ever had.

I finish severing Stone's shaft from his body with a ruthless slash, holding it in my fist while he sags against Wren. Miles past done with Stone, I flip the dagger, snatching the hilt from the air, then sink the sharp blade into his neck.

Wren drops him and he falls forward in a slump, bleeding out on the floor. A few of the girls scream.

I retrieve my knives, not bothering to wipe Stone's blood off yet, and meet Wren's hard gaze. He nods.

It's time to find our girls.

CHAPTER THIRTY-SEVEN

ISLA

PICKING the lock on handcuffs with a knife is a lot harder than it seems like it should be in theory. I release a frustrated noise when my careful maneuvering doesn't get the catch.

"Do you have a bobby pin?" Rowan suggests. "Probably would work better than a knife."

"Yes, it would. That knife is too wide for the hole, princess."

My gaze snaps up at the familiar, rough voice I love and a gasp tears from me. Levi and Wren stand in the doorway more disheveled and violent than when we left them.

"Oh. Hi." The knife falls from my grasp. My throat tightens, a wave of emotion rising up to overwhelm me. Everything I've held back floods my system. "You're here."

"Told you I would be." He rakes his gaze over me, stalking across the room. "Are you okay?"

Wren strides to Rowan's side, murmuring to her in low tones. Levi pauses in front of me, eyes trained on my split lip. My heart cracks in two and a whimper climbs my throat. I survived on my own, and I'm proud of myself, but now my supportive protector is here.

"I shouldn't have let you do this." He falls to his knees in front of the chair I'm restrained to and I fold over, cupping his face. "I'm sorry I didn't come as soon as you didn't exit that maze."

"That wasn't the plan," I whisper hoarsely. "You're hurt."

He ignores the blood trailing down the side of his face from a gash in his brow. It highlights his sharp features. His attention is on my tender jaw. He sets a bloody knife on the desk next to me and carefully angles my face.

A shuddering breath slips out of me and he gently kisses me, being mindful of my split lip. Despite the softness of the kiss, it makes me tremble, his touch erasing Silas' just as it does when he touches my scar.

I rest my forehead against his as his fingers skate down my neck, following my arm to the handcuff on my wrist. Frowning, he strokes my wrist, then touches different parts of the chair's armrest. He stands, grips the corner of the armrest, then jerks the antique wood until it splinters. It only takes two forceful tugs before he has it disconnected from the chair, sliding the other cuff off the broken piece.

"Why didn't I think of that?" My tone is light as I rub my wrist.

"Because you look at a chair and see a pretty piece of furniture. I look at it and see where the weak points are." He searches the desk, selecting a pen and discarding it before he finds a paperclip.

A bloody lump in his other hand catches my eye. "What's that?"

Levi pauses, glancing down. "I took out your demon. He won't ever hurt you again."

I gape when he shows me the severed penis. I've never seen mutilated appendages before. It's grotesquely fascinating. His words register after a moment and my attention darts back to him.

"Silas is—?"

"Dead, yes. I would've let you do it if that's what you wanted, but he really pissed me off. I'm proud of you for not hesitating. A little lower with your aim next time and he would've bled out within minutes." He tosses the bloody lump of flesh on the desk, absently wiping his hand on his pants before crouching in front of me. "Give me your wrist and I'll pick the lock."

While he makes quick work of the handcuffs with the paperclip, Wren frees Rowan from the radiator and crushes her into his body. "No more playing bait."

Rowan laughs at his muffled words, tightening her arms around him. "Did you get the girls out?"

"Colt and Jude have them," Levi says. "We need to get out. Once the chaos dies down, the Kings are going to be pissed when they realize what we've done."

"Fuck them," Wren says. "Anything on his desk to retrieve as a souvenir for Pippa?"

Levi and I sift through the paperwork. I grab an inventory list and scan it.

"The intake dates on this match up with when the girl from the donut shop went missing. I bet that the dates will line up with the others, too, and how far back the registration for the fake delivery company goes. Just like they did on the one that we found in my dad's study that said undelivered and matched up with the day they tried to kidnap me." I glare at the logo for Silas' freight company on the page. "They've been at this for decades. This is how they kept track of the money. Look at the totals."

"Estimates of value," Levi speculates. "Let's take photos for Colt of whatever we can find, then hand these to Pippa once we're out. Penn's waiting out back to burn this whole place to the ground and erase it from existence."

"What about the police? We're just going to bury what they did?" I bite my lip, flinching at the sting.

Levi sighs, kissing my forehead. "No one's going down for this. That's why I killed Stone. It's the only justice we get."

"There's no such thing as real justice." Rowan hugs herself and Wren slips his arms around her from behind. "People like this get away with murder. This is the only way."

"Pippa will make sure the victims are safe?" That's all that matters to me.

Levi nods. "And Colton will make sure they can't be traced. He has a whole network of hackers. We'll make sure the society can't do this again."

The world doesn't work in black and white, good and bad, win or lose. I have to accept this.

Wren takes photos of the paperwork, then gathers it into a stack. He folds it and tucks the wad of papers into his torn suit jacket. Rowan lifts the lapel hanging from the jacket and raises her brow.

"Don't ask," he mutters. "I should've worn the McQueen. This is my favorite tux."

"That was your fault." Rowan smirks. "Besides, you can definitely afford a replacement or five."

"It's the principle," he says.

"Come on," Levi says.

He gathers his bloody knife and Pointy, tucking both away.

I hesitate, looking at the piece of Silas Levi cut off to bring to me. My stomach clenches and I ball my hands into fists.

"What's wrong?" Levi hangs back, waving the others ahead.

"This is where it happened. The dinner, the..." I trail off, licking my lips. "What he did to me. This is the house. A man downstairs called it the Castle."

Levi's jaw clenches. "Here?"

My nod is wobbly. "I don't know where. There was a bed, so I assume a bedroom, but—"

At the catch in my voice, Levi steps into me, pressing a hard kiss to my forehead as he grips the back of my neck. "We're going to burn this motherfucker down. Penn's the best cleaner we know and he's waiting outside. Do you want to find the room and start the fire yourself?"

I shake my head, burrowing into his chest. "I just want to go and put this behind us. I'm ready to close this chapter of my life—no more nightmares. I'm cutting my parents out of my life for good. I'm not their pawn, I'm free to be myself. I'd rather help see those girls to safety than spend another minute here." I look up at him. "Then we can go home to the Nest."

It's the home that calls to me, the one I've been accepted into that they've all built for themselves.

"Home," he echoes.

Levi guides me out of the room with an arm around my shoulders. I lift my chin high as we walk out of my nightmare.

CHAPTER THIRTY-EIGHT

LEVI

We meet back up with Colton and Jude on a veranda behind the lodge. The tree line is illuminated by flashing red and blue lights on the other side of the property. Each of the girls huddle beneath curtains torn from the tall windows in the lodge to cover up. One wears Colton's suit jacket, and another brandishes a silver candlestick as a weapon.

The blonde girl with the spark of defiance in her eyes nods to Rowan and Isla.

"Penn, ready to rendezvous soon," Wren orders over comms.

"I'm ready when you are," he replies. "Let's light it up."

"Call Pippa," I say to Jude.

We move like shadows under the cover of night, crossing the lawn behind the lodge to reach the woods. The lodge sits behind the extravagant estate the masquerade was held at, blocking it from view, but it's not far from the main mansion. From here we can see squad cars filling the crowded drive in front of the estate. Camera flashes illuminate the night sporadically.

There are more people outside than there were in the theater.

"Looks like the party is over. When we went around the ballroom, we planted a few extra presents in pockets and purses," Colton says. "Is that a contortionist?"

Performers in much different costumes than the ones in the ballroom and the ringmaster's crew of miscreants are interspersed with the disarray of people rushing around. The ones who seem more sedate must be from the non-secret society guests who truly believed they were there to see an entertaining performance rather than a seedy underground auction.

Jude talks in low, crisp tones on the phone, searching the tree line. "I don't see a service road, Pip. You need to be more specific."

"There." I point over his shoulder to a space where the trees are more separated.

"You're scary sometimes," Jude says. "Yes, we're on our way."

When he waves for us to follow, we trail after him, keeping an eye out for any guards we missed. The girls are anxious, some of them crying from their overwhelming experience. Their soft cries twist something loose in my chest. I haven't felt empathy for anyone else in a long time, but I understand some of what these girls went through after they were snatched off the street.

"You're going to be okay now." Isla steps away from my side, keeping our fingers threaded together. She rubs one girl's back. "Our friends are police officers and they're going to take you somewhere safe."

Once we're closer, it's easier to see the service road behind the estate that follows the tree line and parallels the formal driveway to keep deliveries and other unsightly vehicles out of view.

Pippa has a line of SUVs waiting with the engines running.

She paces in the cloud of warm exhaust at the back of the line. When she spots us, she casts a glance toward the flashing lights at the front of the house and gestures for us to hurry.

"Oh sure, we do all the dirty work, but you're in a rush to get out of here," Wren says sardonically.

"Just make it quick. Warner came out front ready to blow a gasket, yelling about an arsonist," she says.

"Good times." Jude hums.

"I didn't put that much gunpowder in them," Colton says. "Not enough to cause more than second-degree burns, at best. Just enough to cause a chaotic distraction."

He waggles his brows. The girl he gave his jacket to blushes, tugging the lapels tighter around her.

"You trust them?" I jerk my chin at the row of SUVs. "They're not going to turn around and try to line their pockets and put these girls back where we saved them from?"

Pippa scoffs. "No. I trust them. They're good guys." Her hard gaze passes over each of us. "Guys who understand the real value of justice, not justice only served to the highest bidder."

Wren lifts his brows and reaches into his ruined jacket. He offers the wad of paperwork from Stone's office. "Check the dates the victims went missing against the intake dates. And put Castle Delivery Co. on your investigative radar for further proof." When Pippa reaches for it, he yanks it out of reach. "This doesn't make us square. Not by a long shot."

Her lips form a thin line. "Gotta start somewhere." Her attention shifts past Wren, lingering on Jude before moving to the girls. "Ladies, we're going to take you to a safe location. We have clothes, showers, hot food, and people with medical training ready for you. I know you've been through something unimaginable. It's over now. I promise."

Many of their eyes glisten with fresh tears of relief. They move to climb into the SUVs. A few of them cry out in happiness when they find the girl who was left in the theater is inside one of the vehicles. The blonde stops by Rowan's side and returns the gun.

"Thank you," she says.

"You're the one who survived. That's all you." Rowan smiles at her. It's tinged in sadness. "Your friends and family will be really happy when they get to hug you again."

A distressed noise escapes Isla. She rushes Rowan, almost knocking her over in her urgency to wrap her arms around her. Rowan's breath catches and the two girls cling to each other.

As the girls load into the SUVs, Colton prowls the row of cars. He digs in his pockets and touches the wheel wells, then snaps a photo of each plate. He makes his way back to us and at my lifted brow, he shrugs.

"Just in case." He holds up his phone, showing GPS signals for the trackers he planted. "I want to make sure they go to the addresses I gave them."

"Everyone's out, right?" Penn questions over comms.

"Yeah," I confirm. "Isla." Once I have her attention I nod to the lodge. "Watch."

Wren tugs Rowan into his arms and I tuck Isla back into my side. It's satisfying as fuck to see the first window blow out, smoke billowing into the night above the flames licking up the side of the lodge.

Isla straightens her spine, rolling her shoulders back. A shuddering, relieved breath escapes her. She lifts her head and watches intently as the site of her worst nightmare goes up in flames. Studying her reverently, I soak in the small plays of emotions on her beautiful face that pierce my heart. She'll never have to fear the things that she survived again.

We did it. We fucking won again. I stroke her back, envisioning the day

I'll be able to finally lay my own nightmare to rest.

And I will. I've allowed my uncle to get away with what he did to me and my mother for too long. He believes he got away with it, but I'm ready to come for him. It's his turn, and I won't rest until he fears the shadows every time he's in the dark because the shadows are where I live.

Colton flips the building off with both hands. It only takes a few more minutes until the whole structure is engulfed by the fires Penn lit. People at the front of the estate realize, and their distressed chatter echoes off the treetops. Someone yells to call the fire department.

Pippa thumps the last vehicle twice and casts a parting look at Jude. "I'll do what I can to keep this buried."

"You'd better, baby girl." Jude eyes her intently, swiping his thumb over his lip.

Her shoulders stiffen and her gaze cuts away. She gets into the SUV and the caravan drives along the service road with their lights off.

We keep to the shadows when Warner and other uniformed officers make their way through the darkness with flashlights.

"We should go now if we don't want to get caught," Wren says. "Penn?"

"On my way. The getaway car is at the other end of the service road."

Taking Isla's hand, I keep one eye on the officers as we move through the tree line at the edge of the forest. I freeze once we pass the burning lodge as I spot something I recognize—the crumbling, charred ruins of a tower behind the Kings Society's Castle.

"Fuck," I hiss. "Am I the only one seeing that?"

"What is—" Jude breaks off and sucks in a breath. "No."

Wren stills, glaring back at the burning building. "I've been dragged out to the estate for the masquerade and had no idea what was back here."

Rowan and Isla's gazes bounce between all of us. Isla studies my face.

"What's wrong?"

"We've been here before," I say. "Five years ago."

The night Jude was arrested. The night Pippa betrayed us. The night we ran our first job.

The one that went so wrong it ended with a girl's death.

How did the connection never occur to us? Sienna was assaulted at a remote location. It lines up so closely with Isla's story, except instead of taking her to a bedroom, Sienna said it happened in a tower. We burned it down, but we didn't know how to cover our tracks then.

Jude was arrested for arson because Pippa wasn't where she was supposed to be.

We were just kids then. We know better now.

I scrub a hand over my jaw. "It doesn't matter. Let's just get the hell out of here before history repeats itself."

Penn has the Escalade I drove here ready and idling, stolen from the valet. As the others get in, I keep Isla to myself for a second, cradling her bruised face.

"This is the last time either of us will ever have to deal with kidnapping," I promise. "And the last time I ever let you leave my side."

Isla's mouth quirks into a beautiful smile that lights up my world. I draw her into a kiss, my tongue soothing the cut on her lip. With her safe in my arms, the world realigns itself.

CHAPTER THIRTY-NINE

ISLA

THE madness of the masquerade ball is splashed across gossip sites in the following days and like fire to kindling it snowballs into trending hashtags. It's enough attention to drown out the tags on Instagram about my relationship with Levi, but we do become a related trending topic. We're the only true thing that happened that night. Every other outlandish explanation imaginable makes the rounds—a gas leak being the most popular reason behind the fire.

At least the memes about burning the rich are funny to ease the sting of the buried truth.

There's no mention of the operation we stopped, or any of the insidious things Silas Stone was behind. His remains weren't found, making me wonder if Penn had time to drag all those bodies out, or if the Kings Society are controlling the information. We know Warner is heading the investigation with a special task force that doesn't include Pippa. She sent the update to us along with a photo of the girls we freed confirming they're all safe.

I haven't heard anything from my parents after I returned to the Nest, intent on never setting foot in the Vonn estate again once Levi, Rowan, and Colton helped me rescue some of my favorite clothes that make me feel empowered and amazing. As far as I'm concerned, I bear no relation to them, cutting their toxicity from my life.

Rowan asked on our way out what I planned to do about my tuition and classes without access to my trust fund. Levi cut in that he was going to take care of everything. As much as I appreciate him taking care of me and insisting I have nothing to worry about, I'll figure it out. Maybe get a job so I can stand on my own. I don't need money as long as I have the people I care for most with me.

With each day the sun rises, I'll discover life for myself on my terms, free to make my own choices.

Levi finds me stretching in the room I claimed as my dance space when I first came to the nest. To him, it's a holding room with questionable dark stains from past interrogations, but I've come to think of it as mine. The acoustics are killer, and once I had Rowan and Jude help me bring in a roll out mat to cover the concrete, I dance barefoot to my heart's content with my music blasting.

My dance class professor emailed me yesterday to ask if I needed to pass on my performances for the showcase next weekend, offering to allow me to perform privately when I was ready. It was kind of her to offer, but screw that. I've worked hard on my assignment and I'm ready to show it off to the world.

Now that I'm out from under my parents' thumb, I can fully embrace my love of dance. I want to explore it more, unsure if I want to make a career out of it as a performer, or if I'm more drawn to learning enough to become a certified teacher to show children how moving with your body helps release and work through bad feelings. No matter which path I choose, I know I'll have support to encourage me.

"Are you planning to do the silent creeper watching act, grumpy?" I tease when he leans against the wall without a word.

"I like watching you move." Levi's lips twitch with the hint of a smile. "Give me a good show."

"I know how that mind works." I finish stretching and turn the song on, keeping the music lowered. As I move into my starting position, a grin spreads across my face. "What you really like is assessing me to plot your next torture session."

"Training," he automatically corrects.

My grin stretches and I let the music take me away, the sound lifting me up. It takes every negative feeling, worry, and stress, washing it away like the ebb and flow of the ocean's waves with each rise and fall of the song. Closing my eyes, I twirl, leap, and move my arms in graceful arcs, envisioning the story of my freedom I'm telling with this dance. Tears prick my eyes when I reach the melancholic point of the song, but they're not sad.

They're because I'm proud of myself.

Levi allows me to reach my favorite part of the dance—because I've learned all too well that nothing escapes him—before he slips his arms around me. As usual, when he wants to be stealthy, he makes it impossible to know or hear he's moving until he's already captured you. I rake my teeth over my lip and adapt my choreography, twining my arms around his neck. His skill in moving so well helps him pick up the rhythm, and he's watched me do this dance hundreds of times.

Lifting me, he balances my weight on his thigh. I run a hand down the side of his healed face, nuzzling his jaw, before I prepare to launch into the air. He reads the pressure and shift in my muscles, giving me the springboard

I need to execute a pirouette through the air, landing in a crouch. His hand grabs my forearm and guides me back into his arms.

The music goes on, but Levi claims my mouth in a deep, ravenous kiss. A joyful, relaxed laugh slips out of me.

"Come on," he says.

"What's up?" I pad to the side of my mat to get my water bottle.

"We're going out. Don't ask me where, you'll find out," he tacks on when I open my mouth.

"So secretive." I lick a stray water droplet from my lip and he tracks the movement. "Should I change? Does this require a full face of makeup, or is this an outing where I could get dirty?"

His blank face gives me nothing, even when I pout. He closes the distance between us, grasps my jaw, and kisses me until I forget what my question was.

"Or we could stay here," I murmur against his lips. "We haven't christened the dance studio yet."

"Holding room," Levi answers roughly. "As tempting as that is, you'll like this. Come on, princess."

He takes my hand and I follow him. I change out of my dance clothes into jeans and a tan blouse with hearts beneath a leather jacket I picked out shopping with Rowan once I see he's staying in his signature dark jeans and a Thorne Point University hoodie.

"This is feeling very date-like," I point out when we get on his motorcycle.

He strokes my leg, squeezing my thigh when my arms tighten around him. "Don't let go."

"Never." I press my cheek to his back, a smile breaking free at his comforting spiced earthy scent.

We weave through the streets of the city in the late afternoon light.

Everything is cast in the orange glow of autumn, signaling change. It's not the only change set in motion.

So much has changed, not all of it good. I choose to focus on the positive, though. I'm alive, healthy, and I have a family. They might not be my biological one, but they love me as fiercely as I love them.

Levi pulls up to a strip of shops on the first floor of a large, historic brick building with arched windows. The building itself seems out of use. We get off his bike and he leads me to the tattoo shop in the middle.

"What are we doing here?"

"I have an appointment." Levi nods to the girl behind the counter with full sleeves.

This must be where he goes for all of his ink because he knows everyone in the shop. It's funny to think of him as a dark and brooding loner when he does open himself up—only to people he deems worthy.

I watch in fascination as he peels off his hoodie, revealing his cut, rippling muscles covered in tattoos. I'm momentarily distracted, mapping the large snake body that coils around his side. Each of his tattoos are works of art. They're the keys to knowing him—pieces of his life, of his interests, of what matters most to him.

The artist shows Levi a design in his sketchbook and Levi's eyes gleam in approval. I lean in to peek and he covers my eyes, bringing his lips to my ears.

"Don't look yet." His tongue flicks the shell of my earlobe, his lip ring brushing it as his voice lowers. "Be a good girl for me."

A shiver races down my spine and heat throbs in my core. Biting my lip, I tilt my head, peering at him through my lashes. "Do I get to pick out something?"

He smirks. "Go ahead. I'll be back here." Before I pull away, he tugs me back into his body to steal a kiss. "Pick whatever you want."

"In that case, I'm getting a big ass princess crown on my ass," I sass.

"Only if it says this delectable little ass belongs to Levi Astor, touch it and die," he rumbles.

My laughter echoes through the shop as I dance away to hang out with the cool chick in the front. She pulls out an iPad and flicks through floral designs with me, then sketches something I describe that makes my excitement build. I won't get it today, but I can't wait to show Levi.

The tattoo we design is a crown—one encircling a knife wrapped in thorns. Some of the thorns bloom into flowers. The result is both beautiful and badass.

Too excited to contain myself, I borrow the artist's iPad and find Levi in the back to show him, bouncing on the balls of my feet."What do you think? There wasn't room for the mouthful you said, but we both know I'm yours and only yours."

He gapes at me, then his attention falls to the tattoo I'll be getting once I set up an appointment. Those handsome dark eyes burn and he swipes his tongue over his lower lip slowly.

Before he answers, my gaze locks on his chest, my breath hitching. His tattoo is almost complete. It sits over his heart and the design stuns me. It's a blue flower with a sun.

"Do you like it?" he asks.

"You got a flower."

"I did. This one won't die." He snags one of the belt loops in my jeans and tugs me closer. "It's the color of your eyes."

"Oh." My heart swells and speaking becomes difficult with the lump that forms in my throat. Leaning down I kiss the corner of his mouth. "Such a romantic, grumpy."

"Only for you, princess," he rasps. "Only ever you."

His fierce love for me is overwhelming sometimes. I give my love so freely to everyone around me, but I don't always experience it in return. With my friends, they give it back tenfold.

With Levi, it's exponentially more than that. He doesn't have to say it in words, or with flowers. He says it in his actions, in how much care he puts into protecting me, in drawing blood for me, in making sure I know proper form to defend myself, in the tattoos he inks into his skin.

Levi loves me with a soul-deep love, the same as I feel for him.

* * *

A few nights later, something pulls me from a delicious dream. I drift on the edges of sleep, my body shifting in a mimicry of the sexy dream I was having. The sensations don't stop, my body wound tight with need.

A calloused palm spreads my legs wider and fingers curl inside of me, massaging the spot that lights me up. The last vestiges of my dream slip away as reality hits—Levi. He's touching me in my sleep, his body a hard, warm line plastered against my side as his hand flexes between my thighs.

We've been insatiable, more so than we were before the ball, but this is the first time he couldn't help himself while I slept off the two rounds we had earlier. I bite my lip as a warm glow fills my chest alongside the delicious sensation of his fingers sinking into me with the same methodic precision he brings to every other aspect of his life.

"What are you doing?" The question comes out breathless as the pleasure crests.

His eyes gleam in the darkness. "Guarding your body. You know, because I'm your bodyguard."

My laugh at my stoic, grumpy man making a joke breaks off into a soft cry. "More."

"You want me to make you come, princess?" Levi rasps. "Is that what you need?"

"Yes. God, yes." I arch into his touch, pulling him closer. My nipples tighten with each firm thrust of his fingers. "Please, I want to come. Want to show you how much I'm yours. Completely yours."

He makes a feral, rumbling noise in approval. "That's it, my good girl. *Mine*."

Another flutter moves through me and I clamp my thighs around his arm. The muscles flex and his hand moves faster, making my breath catch.

"Please, please."

"Love the sweet sound of you begging me."

Ecstasy coils tight in my core, then bursts with a ripple as I fall over the edge with a soft cry. His lips brush my jaw and he mutters more possessive praise in my ear for being good for him. When the orgasm fades, his fingers brush over the circular scar on my thigh, his murderous gaze locked on the mark.

I refuse to think of it as a brand, as Silas deemed it.

The only thing the scar reminds me of is what I've been through—what I've survived. The blemish in my skin is a physical signal to myself to always choose my light to overcome. It doesn't mar me or make me any less. I was a survivor on my own, but with Levi, I've become a stronger version of myself.

Touching his jaw, I turn his attention from the scar to kiss him. His lips slide against mine and he hooks his hand around my waist, turning me into him.

"Come here, princess." He rearranges us until I'm straddling his shoulders, massaging my hips. "Take a ride. I want you to soak my face."

Our eyes meet in the darkness. I brace a hand on the headboard and don't break my gaze from his as he teases me with his tongue. My hips roll to an invisible tune only our bodies know, finding the rhythm that feels good.

"Isla." He grips my ass and tugs. "I said sit. On. My. Fucking. Face."

My teeth rake over my lip. "I was trying to be careful of your tattoo. Plus, you suffered a head injury. I really don't think the recommended activity during recovery is to have me sit—"

"I'm fine, baby. Smother me," he growls. "I want to get closer to the only god I know. If I die, then I'll go out in the best way possible with my favorite taste on my tongue."

"No dying. Period." The plea comes out with a gasp as he drags me down to stop hovering, his mouth working to set my body on fire with pleasure. "Oh my god."

Levi's hands roam over my body, playing with my breasts and holding my hips while I grip the headboard for stability as he makes me tremble. I marvel at this wild, dangerous man that knows how to kill someone, but when we're together like this I become his world. He's so good at taking care of me.

He doesn't stop until he's wrung several more orgasms out of me to the point I'm half-delirious from coming. Allowing me to collapse to the bed, he plants kisses all over my body, working his way up between my breasts as my chest heaves. When he covers his body with mine and settles his hips between the cradle of my legs, he enters me with a smooth glide. There's no resistance to our bodies joining, my pussy dripping wet and swollen from how thoroughly he worked me up to this.

My arms circle his neck and I hold on as he thrusts into me hard and slow. It's sleepy and perfect, less about finishing and more about feeling the connection we share. He's not in a hurry, content to make my lips part and my head tip back each time he drives into my body. His arms band around me and he presses his face into my throat, leaving a mark with his teeth and tongue.

It's the only brand I acknowledge—the only claim over me I agree to, and I claim Levi right back by leaving my own marks.

After he finishes, his muscles seizing as he groans into our kisses, we spend a long time covering each other in possessive marks. There's no doubt we belong to each other. No doubt that we're in love.

A tired, content smile breaks free when we finally stop, my head resting on his chest and his arms locked around me so tight I know he'll never let me go again.

No matter what happens next, Levi and I will weather it because we have our friends and each other. Nothing can break us.

CHAPTER FORTY

LEVI

It strikes me on a Friday two weeks after the masquerade ball that it should be a fight night. Our regular routines already feel like distant memories since this mess spiraled from a random missing person to something that has consumed our efforts to find answers.

We haven't held a fight since the night of the raid, but I'm not desperate to throw myself into a ring against an opponent to battle my demons. Isla settles me from the restlessness that's been my constant companion. Her bright presence isn't the distraction I once feared. She centers me, keeps me focused. In return, I'll always take care of her.

The six of us are in the lounge at the Nest. Colton called us in to show off what he's been obsessively working on since the night we took Silas Stone out.

"Any day now, Colt," I taunt.

"I know, I know, I'm interrupting quality time with your daily religion—flexing in the gym mirrors." He automatically ducks out of the way to avoid the fry I throw at him from my spot perched on the arm of the couch. His fingers don't stop their endless moving as he codes.

Jude laughs, sinking against the other arm of the couch while wheezing from the gulp of milkshake he downed. Giggling between us, Isla swats at my chest.

"Don't waste fries! That's sacrilege," she drawls.

"Agreed," Colt chimes in.

"I'll buy you more fries," I say.

"It's after midnight. They're closed now, so treat each fry with love and respect." Rowan points one of her fries at me from the couch across from us, yelping when Wren pulls her onto his lap, grabs her wrist, and steals her fry for himself, licking salt from her fingertips with a wicked, unapologetic smirk. Her cheeks turn pink. "You owe me fries, King Crow."

"You know I'll give you the world, my queen," he rumbles into her neck. "Anything your heart desires."

"Aww." Isla lays a hand over her chest. "That's so sweet."

"You're so easily moved. You got choked up at a photo of my abuela and me when I was a kid on Día de los Muertos yesterday." Jude cracks a grin at her shrug.

"I am who I am," Isla says airily. Her mouth curves with mischief. Flashing me a look over her shoulder, she nudges me with her elbow. "I need to show enough emotion for the both of us."

Jude knocks his milkshake against her cup. "Cheers."

"Does that count as my initiation into the Crows?"

I snort, nudging her over to slide into her space. Tugging her close, I mutter against her ear. "You're one of us now, princess. I'm keeping you."

Isla scoffs playfully. "What do you mean? You couldn't make me go anywhere if you tried." Smiling at me with her infinite well of glowing sunshine, she places her hand on my chest over the blue flower tattoo. "And

I'll be the one keeping you."

Warmth floods my chest. I capture her hand and kiss her. Our friends wolf whistle and whoop, stoking the content glow until it fills me. For the first time in a long time, I relax.

"Oh, I think I found a job to apply for," Isla gushes to Rowan. "The theater department is looking for more help through spring semester, so it's win-win that I'll get to spend even more time near the stage."

"Nice," Rowan says.

"It won't be much pay, but it's a start, right?" Isla beams. "For now, my next designer find will have to be cruising second-hand stores and online, but it will feel even better because I'll pay for it with my own money."

"I told you, I've got you," I say. "Anything you want, it's yours."

"I know." She leans into my side. "It's important to me to provide for myself."

A sigh gusts out of me as I battle between the drive to protect her in every way and respecting her choices. I know how much it means to have grown our own vast wealth independently from our families, but I'll still be there to give her whatever she needs.

Colton smothers a smug laugh.

"What's that about?" Jude prompts.

He cranes his neck to glance between Isla and Rowan before turning his chair. "Oh, just that this conversation is pointless. You don't need anyone but yourselves, babes."

Rowan's brow wrinkles. "What do you mean?"

Colton folds his hands behind his head and gives us all a cocky grin. "You're set. I made sure you both have as much money as the rest of us."

Isla's lips part. "Really?"

"Hell yeah."

"How? Did you hack the bank account for my trust fund and split it between us?"

"Nah, but I could do that. I told you, I'm very good at what I do. I set up investment portfolios for both of you. I was building Rowan's first, but as soon as I knew you were in with us—" He nods to me. "—I wanted you to be able to make your own choices and not be weighed down by your parents, too."

"Colton," Isla says in a watery voice. Both she and Rowan are stunned. "Thank you."

"Family, babe. We've got your back."

"I'd still give you every cent in my accounts," Wren says to Rowan.

Grinning, she gives him a playful punch. "Now who's the sugar daddy?"

Isla buries a snort of laughter into me, her grin bright and unburdened in a way that wraps my heart in warmth.

"Any closer, Colt?" Wren prods a few minutes later once he returns his attention to the computer.

"Almost." The steady clack of the keyboard continues, along with his incessant muttering to himself.

"Will you at least tell us what it is?" Isla asks.

"No. But I'll give you a hint, because it's kind of like I got us all a present and I need to see you open it early for a hit of that sweet, sweet serotonin." He downs a third energy drink and ruffles his already tousled brown hair. "It has to do with something that starts with a K and ends in asshole."

"You're cut off from energy drinks after this." Wren eyes the pile collecting on the desk with distaste.

"You say that now, until you need access only I can give you with my magic fingers. Then it's all, hack this, write a program for that. Admit it."

Wren rolls his eyes and turns his focus to carding his fingers through Rowan's hair, allowing Colton to work.

Ever since we found out the truth about the Kings Society, we've been unimpressed with their tactics. They manipulated us from the shadows, threatened us to force us into obeying. Their mistake was in thinking we'd take that shit laying down without striking back. Now we're on the offense. We won't stand for these assholes coming for anyone we consider ours and spreading poison throughout the city to gain more power and wealth.

My uncle and Wren's father expect our loyalty, but they lost it long ago and they're never getting it back. We won't join the Kings. We'll fucking dismantle their secret society.

The only legacy we recognize is the one we've forged with each other, the thrones we built up from nothing.

We're the names whispered with fear in the goddamn dark.

My uncle was already my enemy. He's become my next kill.

"Aha! Who's your daddy?" Colton pumps his fists in the air, kicking off from his desk to send his gamer chair into a victor twirl, coming to a stop grinning at us. "Well? Applause, accolades, appreciation?"

"Definitely lay off the energy drinks," Isla says. "And maybe take a nap."

"Nap? No, babe! There's no rest for the wicked, not when I've finally cracked this corrupted file and made it my bitch!"

"You did?" Rowan shoots to her feet and bolts to his side, covering her mouth as she scans the contents.

The relaxation I enjoyed moments ago fizzles away, my muscles bunching with anticipation. "Who else is in it besides my uncle?"

"Every name attached to power or influence in the city," Colton answers. "I don't know if it's all of the society members, but it's a head start Hannigan wanted Rowan to have."

"It's everything he uncovered," she says hoarsely, choked by grief.

"We'll be able to use the information to decimate them, uproot the legacy they're so proud of," Wren announces in a dangerous tone.

Colton whirls back to his computer, cracking his knuckles. "Now to—"

He cuts off when his wall of screens glitches. He types a few keys, tuning us out. At his silence, the rest of us exchange wary glances.

Sucking in a sharp breath, he hisses, "Oh, I think the fuck not. You want to dance, asshole? I fucking see you."

"Colt?" Wren barks as Colton's fingers fly over the keyboard.

The screen glitches again. Rowan makes a distressed noise. "Where did the file go?"

"No. Goddamnit, *no*!" Colton pounds a fist on his desk, shoulders rigid.

"What is it?" I demand, shooting to my feet to grip the back of his chair.

The disorder on the screen means nothing to me, but it pisses Colton off more and more by the second as his system goes nuts.

"It's a hacker," he snaps. "Fucking good one. No one should be able to touch my systems or break my security protocols—" He cuts off, eyes widening with a flash of recognition. "Only—"

A loud, bone-rattling boom from above us interrupts his answer. The girls scream while Wren and I give each other sharp, calculating looks. Moments later, an explosion rips into the ceiling.

I grab Isla, shielding her from the blaze of heat licking down from above us. She chokes on dusty debris, her body trembling. The hotel is on fire and before we catch our bearings, it spreads.

"Fuck! Go! Get out!" I yell.

"Wait, I need to—"

"Now, Colt!" Jude raises his voice above the destruction around us.

There's no time for thinking—only action. Escape. We have to get the hell out of the hotel before it collapses and buries us beneath it.

Our main emergency exit point is blocked. We backtrack through halls we know by heart to find another way. With a fierce yell, Wren shoulders his way through a splintered door to get us to the main hotel floor. Downstairs it was madness, but here it's even worse.

The flames engulf the old building, eating through the frayed wallpaper and swallowing everything in its path. Rowan and Isla choke on the smoke burning our eyes, holding their clothes up to filter it as we navigate the sweltering heat. I don't let go of Isla's hand, tugging her after me, willing her to keep moving.

A beam cracks overhead and I push Rowan to keep her from being crushed. Isla yelps behind me, releasing my hand. When I turn, my world tilts at the sight of her blocked by flames.

"Close your eyes," I order.

Yanking off my jacket, I use it to rip a chunk of wall free by a decaying hole, throwing it down to smother the fire. I take her hand again, clutching her sweaty palm in a death grip to pull her to me.

"Go! Follow Wren and Rowan."

"I'm not leaving you!" She gives me a terrified look, her cheeks smudged with soot.

"I'm right behind you. I won't ever leave you. Now move your ass!"

We have no idea if there will be another explosion and I don't believe this is a natural fire. It's burning too fast.

With her in my line of sight, we catch up with Wren and Rowan. We're almost to the ballroom—then we can get the fuck out of here. It's the only thing I focus on.

Wren kicks in the double doors to the ballroom after testing the handle for heat. It's burning, but not as badly as the central part of the hotel. We pass our dais with the vintage furniture we've used as symbols of our power for years, the worn antiques smoldering, moments from bursting into flame from the stifling heat.

It takes both of us to shoulder through the door standing between us and escape, the fire making the old wood door swell. The sharp crack when we break it is a relief.

Once we make it out, staggering several feet away from the building, the girls collapse to their hands and knees, gulping in air. I drag in a ragged lungful while Wren scrubs at his face. One by one we turn to a sight I never wanted to see.

We look on in horror at the Crow's Nest Hotel succumbing to the flames. Coldness seeps into my bones and it has nothing to do with the icy chill in the air. Our Nest has withstood time, a home we made for ourselves. It became a symbol of our status.

Now it's met its demise.

"No."

Wren's low, shocked denial cuts me. We built this place together from nothing. It means something to all of us, but to him it's so much more.

Rowan huddles into his side, tears streaming down her face. Isla squeezes my hand and sniffles.

Widening my eyes I search around us. Dread strangles me. My heartbeat drums hard against my rib cage.

Where the fuck are Colton and Jude?

This isn't happening.

No... *NO!*

I need to go back in there to make sure. Wren doesn't realize—he's on the phone with emergency services, barking demands for them to get here faster. I only make it two steps before the girls hold me back.

"What are you thinking?" Isla shouts. "You can't run back in there—it's gone, Levi!"

"I have to!" My teeth clench hard and my voice cracks. "They're still in there!"

TO BE CONTINUED...

THANK YOU + WHAT'S NEXT

Thank you for reading Loyalty in the Shadows! If you enjoyed it, please leave a review on your favorite retailer or book community! Your support means so much to me!

Need more Crowned Crows series right now? Have theories about which characters will feature next? Want exclusive previews of the next book? Join other readers in Veronica Eden's Reader Garden on Facebook!
Reader group: bit.ly/veronicafbgroup

Are you a newsletter subscriber? By subscribing, you can download a special bonus deleted scene for the Crowned Crows world.
Sign up to download it here: veronicaedenauthor.com/bonus-content

ACKNOWLEDGEMENTS

Reader, can I offer you a soft blanket? Something warm to drink? A hug? Okay, before you come for me after that very mean cliffhanger, I want to promise that this is a romance series! Things may seem dire now, but this is only the middle of the story. Trust in the madness and keep that HEA in your sights!

As always, I'm endlessly grateful for you! Thanks for reading this book. It means the world to me that you supported my work. I wouldn't be here at all without you! I love all of the comments and messages you send and live for your excitement for my characters! I hope you enjoyed your read!

Thanks to my husband for being you! He doesn't read these, but he's my biggest supporter. He keeps me fed and watered while I'm in the writer cave, and doesn't complain when I fling myself out of bed at odd hours with an idea to frantically scribble down.

Remember when I thought Rowan and Wren tried to break me? Isla and Levi said hold my drink and put me through the wringer to tell their portion of this saga. Thank you to Sarah, Becca, Ramzi, Sara, Dani, Kat, Jade, Mia, Bre, Heather, Katie, and everyone who cheered me on for keeping me arguably sane and on track until the end! With every book I write my little tribe grows and I'm so thankful to have each of you as friends to lean on and share my book creation process with!

To my lovely PA Heather, thank you for taking things off my plate and allowing me to disappear into the writing cave without having to worry. And for letting me infodump at you, because that's my love language hahaha! You rock and I'm so glad to have you on my team!

To my beta queens Jade, Katie, Mia, Bre, y'all I could never put books out there without you! Y'all are always amazing, but this book is what it is because of you! Thank you for reading my raw (really raw this time), sometimes messy words, for letting me roll into your DMs, and helping me see the forest instead of the tree. Thank you for offering your time, attention to detail, and consideration of the characters and storyline in my books!

To my street team and reader group, y'all are the best babes around! Huge thanks to my street team for being the best hype girls! To see you guys get as excited as I do seriously makes my day. I'm endlessly grateful you love my characters and words! Thank you for your help in sharing my books and for your support of my work!

Thank you to Ashlee of Ashes & Vellichor for the amazing book trailer for this series! I love the way you can look at something (or in this case, barely anything) and get it so perfectly, and I've been in awe of what you've come up with to bring my books to life!

To Shauna and Wildfire Marketing Solutions, thank you so much for all your hard work and being so awesome! I appreciate everything that you do!

To the bloggers and bookstagrammers, thank you for being the most wonderful community! Your creativity and beautiful edits are something I come back to visit again and again to brighten my day. Thank you for trying out my books. You guys are incredible and blow me away with your passion for romance!

ABOUT THE AUTHOR

ROMANCE WITH DARING EDGE

Veronica Eden is an international bestselling author of romances with spitfire heroines, irresistible heroes, and edgy twists.

She loves exploring complicated feelings, magical worlds, epic adventures, and the bond of characters that embrace us against the world. She has always been drawn to gruff bad boys, clever villains, and the twisty-turns of morally gray decisions. She is a sucker for a deliciously devilish antihero, and sometimes rolls on the dark side to let the villain get the girl. When not writing, she can be found soaking up sunshine at the beach, snuggling in a pile with her untamed pack of animals (her husband, dog and cats), and surrounding herself with as many plants as she can get her hands on.

* * *

CONTACT + FOLLOW

Email: veronicaedenauthor@gmail.com

Website: veronicaedenauthor.com

FB Reader Group: bit.ly/veronicafbgroup

Amazon: amazon.com/author/veronicaeden

ALSO BY VERONICA EDEN

Sign up for the mailing list to get first access and ARC opportunities!

Follow Veronica on BookBub for new release alerts!

DARK ROMANCE

Sinners and Saints Series

Wicked Saint

Tempting Devil

Ruthless Bishop

Savage Wilder

Crowned Crows Series

Crowned Crows of Thorne Point

Loyalty in the Shadows

A Fractured Reign

The Kings of Ruin

Standalone

Unmasked Heart

Devil on the Lake

REVERSE HAREM ROMANCE

Bound by Bounty Series

(coming soon)

Standalone

Hell Gate (coming soon)

More Than Bargained

CONTEMPORARY ROMANCE

Standalone

Jingle Wars

The Devil You Know

Printed in Great Britain
by Amazon

73265022R00262